The Golden Talisman

To T. J. —

Thank you for your support — Don't grit your teeth reading this one!!

J S Jackson

Novels by J. Stefan Jackson
Published by Mundania Press

The Golden Talisman

The Blood Star of Karachi

Cades Cove

Book One of The Talisman Chronicles

Mundania Press

Dedication

To my lovely wife, Fiona, whose steadfast support and inspiration has infused my writing with life, and whose editorial work proved to be invaluable in preparing the novel's final version.

To my sons, Christopher and Tyler, who inspired the birth of this story as a bedtime tale for their young ears long ago...

The Golden Talisman copyright © 2006 by J. Stefan Jackson

All rights reserved under the International and Pan-American Copyright Conventions. No part of this book may be reproduced or transmitted in any form or by any means, electronic or mechanical including photocopying, recording, or by any information storage and retrieval system, without permission in writing from the publisher.

This is a work of fiction. Names, characters, places and incidents either are the product of the author's imagination or are used fictitiously, and any resemblance to any actual persons, living or dead, events, or locales is entirely coincidental.

A Mundania Press Production
Mundania Press LLC
6470A Glenway Avenue, #109
Cincinnati, Ohio 45211-5222

To order additional copies of this book, contact:
books@mundania.com
www.mundania.com

Cover Art © 2006 by Trace Edward Zaber
Book Design, Production, and Layout by Daniel J. Reitz, Sr.
Marketing and Promotion by Bob Sanders

Trade Paperback ISBN-10: 1-59426-238-1
Trade PaperbackISBN-13: 978-1-59426-238-8
eBook ISBN-10: 1-59426-239-X
eBook ISBN-13: 978-1-59426-239-5

First Edition • October 2006
Library of Congress Catalog Card Number 2006927887

Production by Mundania Press LLC
Printed in the United States of America
10 9 8 7 6 5 4 3 2 1

PART I

The Murder of Dr. Mensch

"So...you're sure that's all, then?

The agent poured himself another round of coffee and carefully stirred in a measure of cream as if this simple act required complete concentration. Jack Kenney studied him from where he sat, absently drumming his fingers on top of the steel table that sat in the middle of the interrogation room. Well-defined muscles were clearly revealed beneath the tight confines of his faded black T-shirt. He seemed poised and ready to launch himself out of his chair like a hungry lion. Even his strong brow and chiseled facial features made him look predatory, with hazel eyes aglow from acute agitation. Yet, the exhaustion and weariness brought on by the endless stream of questions that began last night made him yearn painfully for sweet silence and the unlikely chance he might recoup some of the sleep he had lost since being abducted from Tuscaloosa, Alabama.

"It's just like I've been telling y'all," said Jack, tersely. "I've got nothing more to add to my statement."

The agent grimaced in irritation. Frank Reynolds never took kindly to a smart mouth, much less one belonging to a twenty-year old college kid. Agent Reynolds had been in this line of work for nearly thirty years, and could immediately tell when a suspect evaded the truth. Jack Kenney was obviously holding back. Trouble was, he had turned in an admirable performance so far. Agent Reynolds sensed the young man could go on like this indefinitely, and his patience and even-tempered nature had worn dangerously thin.

"I guess we're all just supposed to believe that Dr. Mensch's beating and subsequent death in the hospital were mere coincidences which, unfortunately, you've been linked to," said the agent. "Is that what you expect us to believe, Mr. Kenney?" He moved slowly toward Jack, the cup of coffee in one hand while he motioned with the other to his two companions, Agents Ben Casey and Steve Iverson. "You must think the three of us have shit for brains, son, and your fucking arrogant attitude is really starting to piss me off."

He stepped up to the table and leaned down into Jack's face, who remained unfazed by the advancing giant of a man glaring at him. Instead, he seemed amused and fascinated by the elder agent's behavior—perhaps intrigued by his thick southern accent or the way his face flushed with anger, in such contrast to his pale gray eyes and wavy white hair. Certainly, his large stature of nearly six and a half feet would've intimidated anyone. But Jack sat where he was, mostly unaffected by the man's direct invasion into his personal space.

Jack smiled, grinning wryly as if comparing the precarious moment to some other in his past. He studied the agent's face. Once he determined the true depth of malice he let his eyes wander over to the agent's I.D. badge dangling from the right lapel of his dark blue suit coat. The badge displayed a stoic picture of Agent Reynolds from a few years before, with the identifier 'AS419' etched in gold that glistened brightly in the glare from the long fluorescent light above the table.

"What the fuck do you find so amusing, Mr. Kenney?" Agent Reynolds hissed.

"Forgive me, sir," Jack replied unapologetically. "I guess I'm just tired...tired enough to find everything a little amusing at this point."

"Well, then, perhaps I can convince you to take Frank's words a bit more seriously." It was Steve Iverson who spoke. Standing to the left of Jack, he grasped his shoulder and began squeezing the soft area just below the collarbone. He steadily increased the pressure until the bone itself throbbed.

Jack's reflexes forced him to look down onto the steel table, where the distorted reflection of his painful grimace greeted him. The tangled mess of his thick auburn hair further obscured his rugged good looks.

Agent Iverson increased the pressure on Jack's collarbone. He nearly doubled over and was forced to clinch his teeth to keep from screaming. The agent continued to torture Jack's shoulder, forcing him out of his chair, which landed loudly on its side upon the cement floor. Jack landed just as hard on his left side, with Agent Iverson's hand still attached to his shoulder's sensitive pressure point. "Had enough, asshole?"

The agent's head hovered just above Jack's left ear. He wanted to turn and face his antagonist long enough to give him a warranted knee in his groin to even things up. Of course, in light of his present circumstances, that could be suicide.

"You know, right now may be as good a time as any to fuck this pretty boy's face up. What do you think, Frank?" Agent Iverson suddenly jerked Jack's head back by his hair. He peered into Jack's face, his ever-present smile never changing, not even slightly. Only the coldness of his steel-blue eyes seemed mutable, glowing with icy malice that thoroughly permeated his being. The man could kill someone with no more remorse than he'd have for smashing a stink beetle.

In a way, the agent's face reminded Jack of a 'down home' country singer his grandfather, Marshall Edwards, liked to listen to. For a moment, he pictured the tune "I'm Just An Old Jukebox Junkie" coming out of Steve Iverson's mouth. The image struck him as particularly funny and almost made him laugh. Unfortunately, a slight snicker escaped from his mouth anyway. It only took an instant for the agent to react.

"*You think this is funny, you sorry sack of shit??*" he screamed into Jack's ear as he pulled him onto his feet by the hair. "*Suppose I show you something that's real funny—like your dick sticking out of your ass, you stupid fuck!!*"

Jack winced from the double dose of pain administered to his eardrum and scalp. Before he could respond, Agent Iverson pushed him into the waiting arms of Ben Casey, who grabbed him and shoved his arms high behind his back. He could feel the ligaments in his joints stretch to the point of tearing. All it would take to actually separate them would be the slightest additional pressure from the meanest of the three agents.

"I'm all for giving this punk a workout," said Agent Casey, his husky voice reverberating behind Jack's back. "He sure seems to be begging for it."

Unable to move, Jack warily watched the other two men step up to him. His nostrils filled with a nauseating blend of tobacco, sweat, and a mixture of colognes—one cheap, and the other a strong musk scent. He swallowed hard, for he knew if he vomited on any of these guys, they might not let him live long enough to apologize.

Suddenly the door to the room swung open, the hinges whining loudly from the door's heavy weight. The room was well insulated, and the door reminded Jack of what a bank vault might require. Another agent stepped into the room carrying a long, black attaché case in one hand, and a small blue duffel bag in the other. Immediately, Agents Reynolds and Iverson backed away from Jack, while Agent Casey released his arms.

"Well, good afternoon, Peter," said Agent Reynolds. "Or, should I say 'evening', since it is nearing the dinner hour." He moved over to him and extended his hand in welcome. The other man sat the attaché case and duffel bag down upon the floor.

"It's good to see you, Frank," he said, returning the gesture with a hearty handshake. "I'm sorry I'm late. Traffic was worse than usual tonight. Was I interrupting anything of importance?"

"No...not really, anyway," said Agent Reynolds, casting a cautious glance toward Jack that clearly implied 'you'll keep your goddamn mouth shut if you know what's good for you'. "He's all yours, now."

The newcomer turned his attention to Jack, eyeing him as if he were a rare animal on display at a zoo or circus. Jack glared back at him until he turned away and focused his attention on Agent Iverson instead. "I don't believe we've met," Peter told him, and extended his hand for the other agent to shake.

"Forgive me, Pete," said Frank. "This is Steve Iverson, and this other fellow is Ben Casey from the New York office."

"Peter McNamee...I'm pleased to meet you both." He shook hands with Agent Casey.

"Pete's father and I go way back," said Agent Reynolds, glancing coolly toward Jack once more. "We used to work together for the bureau down in New Orleans. Isn't that right, Pete?"

"Yeah. Dad still speaks of those times quite fondly, Frank. We'll need to catch up some when our work here is through," he said, shifting his gaze back toward the haggard young man standing nearby. Once again, Jack met his gaze head on. After an awkward moment in silence, Peter returned his attention to Agent Reynolds again.

"I'm sure my dad will be interested to know what you've been up to."

"Just working, son. Same as always..."

There was a sudden thickness in the air. Peter McNamee seemed bothered by Jack's tousled appearance. Jack sensed it, and he was certain that Agent Reynolds knew it, too. He wasn't sure if the two Neanderthals with him cared one way or another.

"Well, I guess I'll get started then," Agent McNamee advised, and picked up his attaché case and duffel bag from the floor. He moved over to the table and sat both items on it with a noticeable thud.

The three other agents looked on warily, and for the moment seemed unsure of what to do next. It made Jack feel better about his own situation, for it appeared McNamee intimidated them, despite the fact he was at least fifteen years younger than any of the three. Jack was sure he was just slightly older than himself.

"If you don't mind, I'd like to interview Mr. Kenney in private," Peter told them. "As you'll be able to follow along just fine from outside the room, I hope you won't mind my request. It will be easier for me to remain focused." He pointed to the surveillance cameras barely visible in each corner of the room. The other agents nodded reluctantly, and moved over to the door.

"All right, then," said Agent Reynolds, his disappointment apparent in his voice. "Holler if you need anything, Pete. Perhaps this will give us some extra time to visit with Jeremy Kenney. Who knows, maybe he's ready to enlighten us some."

Reynolds gave Jack one last menacing look before exiting the room with the other two agents. Jack said a silent prayer for his brother's safety, although he figured Jeremy would have an easier time holding his own against this trio.

Peter McNamee smiled and moved over to Jack's side of the table and picked up his previously toppled chair for him. He extended his hand for Jack to shake, and was only slightly deterred by Jack's indifference to him.

"I guess a handshake may be a little inappropriate at this point," he chuckled. "Have a seat, Jack. We're probably going to be here for a good while."

"Actually, I need to take a piss," said Jack. "If I don't go soon, I'm sure to God I'm going to explode."

Toward the back of the room was a small closet-sized room with a toilet and sink. Jack motioned to it and the agent responded that would be fine.

"Would you like some coffee? Or, perhaps a Coke would do you better," offered Peter. "I'm sure there's one in the 'fridge over here." He moved over to a small refrigerator that sat beneath the coffee maker next to the door.

"A Coke would be great if there's one," responded Jack, quickly before closing the bathroom door.

"Yep" confirmed Peter. "There is."

The agent closed the refrigerator and brought the drinks over to the table. After finishing his other business, Jack met him there. His hair was combed back and he stood behind his chair, sizing up the agent sitting on the other side of the table.

"Please, sit down," Peter told him as he quickly unpacked his duffel bag. He placed a pair of journals in front of himself along with a small recording device in the middle of the table. Jack studied the recorder as he slowly sat down in his chair.

"Do you really need this?" he asked. "I thought the surveillance stuff already in this room would be sufficient enough." He motioned to the windowless room around them. The walls were painted in mustard yellow, which seemed to enhance the bright illumination provided by three overhead fluorescent lights that bisected the room's fifteen-foot ceiling. The middle light hung directly above the table. Along with two chairs and the refreshment cart nearby, this was the only furniture in the room.

"To be honest, the recorder is for my own personal use," Peter advised. "I'd like to review our session at a later time, if it's okay with you."

Jack shrugged his shoulders, satisfied with that explanation.

"Good, then. This thing can run for up to three and a half hours, which should be plenty of recording time to work with. Are you ready to get started?"

"Yeah, I guess so," Jack sighed. "But, nothing's changed since I started talking to your buddies two days ago. My story's the same."

Peter smiled and leaned forward. Blond, blue-eyed, and dressed in a black Armani suit and gold necktie; he looked far too pretty to be a policeman, FBI agent, or whatever he actually was. "Jack," he said. "I haven't heard what you've told anyone else. I do have the original police report from Tuscaloosa, which simply states you were the one who found Dr. Oscar Mensch unconscious and then called for an ambulance. That, and the fact you were the last person we can identify who saw him alive in the hospital after he regained consciousness."

Jack nodded his head, silently concurring the truth of this statement. "So, you're just wanting information concerning Dr. Mensch and his death? Is that all you want?" He popped open his can of Coke and took a good-sized drink before setting the can down again on the table. "It seems like a wasted use for that recorder, being it'll take just a few minutes to answer whatever questions you have on that subject."

"Perhaps...perhaps not," said Peter. "Dr. Mensch's death will be our starting point. But, to be honest again with you I've got other questions related to this whole mess in Tuscaloosa as well. Let's take it one step at a time and see where we end up."

He smiled once more and reached over to turn on the recorder. After marking the session's intro with an identifier, he picked up one of the journals sitting in front of him and leaned back in his chair. He, too, had an I.D. badge similar to the other agents. His read 'RS638' etched in gold, along with his photo in a stoic pose similar to Agent Reynolds' badge earlier. Jack presumed this must be part of the standard operating procedures for these guys, to look like someone's got a secure grip on their balls while threatening to yank them off should they crack so much as a sliver of a smile.

"Now, then. On the night of May 4th, you found Dr. Oscar Mensch, Professor of Archaeology at the University of Alabama, lying unconscious in his living room. Is that accurate?"

Accurate yes, a good description, no, Jack thought to himself. It should be Dr. Oscar Mensch, internationally renowned scholar and expert in the study of ancient civilizations. Boy, and what a bleeder he was, Agent, sir. Yes sirree, every surface in the living room was splattered with the man's corpuscles. "Pretty much so," he replied.

"What exactly did you do when you found him?" asked Peter. "Oh, and also, why were you visiting Dr. Mensch's residence?"

"Well, I needed to talk to him about an upcoming expedition to the Andes in South America," Jack explained. "Jeremy, my brother, is working on his masters' degree in ancient studies, and he wanted me to join him while he did his summer internship there. A group of graduate students had already committed themselves to go on the trip, which Dr. Mensch and Dr. Sutherland were sponsoring. But they needed a few more students to come along. Usually, this would mean other grad students. Since Dr. Mensch was like a second father to my brother, and because I'd gotten to know him pretty well myself, Jeremy suggested I approach him and see if I could go. I'll be graduating within a week, so it wasn't like I had anything in my immediate future to prevent me from going."

Peter was busy jotting down a few notes onto the back page of his journal, and Jack waited for him to finish. The agent raised his head and smiled again once he was done.

"I just wanted to reference this, in case I have other questions about this trip you mentioned," he said. "How did you get to know Dr. Mensch? He was your brother's academic advisor. Did you meet him that way?"

"Yeah, pretty much. I also took two undergraduate courses he taught, and guess I grew closer to him after being around him so much."

"Ah-huh..." Peter turned the journal back over, opening it up again to a marked page near the front. "You're graduating with a major in journalism, is that correct? Or, is it baseball?" He cracked a wry smile.

Jack couldn't help smiling a little as well. "I wish it was baseball. But I've got a knack for writing, I believe. I hope to do all right with that as a career instead."

"I see you were a two-time all-SEC selection during your sophomore and junior years—*and*, an all-American honorable selection during your junior year as well. What happened this year?"

"Tendonitis in the elbow of my throwing arm."

"Ah, I understand. That's too bad." Peter seemed genuinely disappointed for him "Well, who knows, maybe you'll become a successful reporter one day."

"That'd definitely be nice." Although unsure where this line of questions was headed, Jack appreciated Peter's approach as compared to Frank Reynolds or Steve Iverson's. At least it didn't hurt.

Peter paused to sip his coffee, and then continued. "Let's revisit the night you found Dr. Mensch, Jack," he said. "According to the report I've got here, the front door was slightly ajar, and when Dr. Mensch didn't respond to your knock or calls out to him, you went inside his house. That's when you found him lying on the floor in the middle of his living room. Correct so far?'

"Yes."

"You didn't try to move him?"

"No. But, I did check his pulse. I mean, I thought he was dead. There was blood everywhere, and his face was covered with it. I couldn't tell if he was breathing or not, and once I felt a slight pulse on his wrist, I immediately called for an ambulance."

"That's consistent so far with the evidence," said Peter. "Your shoes tracked blood from the living room to the phone in the kitchen. Other than the front door ajar, and of course the ransacked living room, did you notice anything unusual or out of place?"

With the main floor in disarray, it was hard to tell if things were where they should've been in Dr. Mensch's home. Jack did remember experiencing the creepy feeling of being watched while he stood on the professor's front porch. While he was inside the house, he was almost certain someone else was in the house with him. He figured if there was someone there, they were likely hiding upstairs. Unfortunately, by the time the police and paramedics showed up, he was so distressed about Dr. Mensch's condition that he forgot about this. He hadn't thought about it again until he visited the professor in the hospital four days later. "No...well, maybe."

Peter raised his eyebrows and motioned for him to continue.

"It's nothing I can prove, but I'm pretty sure there was somebody in the house when I arrived. I should've mentioned this to the cops that night, but I was so upset it slipped my mind."

"I see," said Peter. "Whoever it was must've made their escape before the police arrived. You're probably not aware that the upstairs rooms were in much worse shape than what you saw on the main level."

"I wasn't aware of that, no sir." *Definitely* not, Jack thought to himself, irritated that no one else had told him this fact before now.

"Okay, then. Let's move on to the eighth of May, the night Dr. Mensch died. Did you visit him in the hospital before his death?"

"I tried, on the morning following his attack. But, the nurses on duty told me I couldn't see him, that he was still unconscious. They said I could be there quite awhile before he might awaken. Dr. Sutherland was waiting there also. He told me to go on home. I guess he could tell I hadn't slept much since the incident from the previous evening. He said he'd call me when Dr. Mensch was better—when, or *if* I should say, he regained consciousness." Jack paused to take another drink from his Coke, and Peter used the opportunity to flip through a few pages in his journal while he sipped on his coffee.

"A nurse named Annette Rison stated you came to see Dr. Mensch around seven o'clock the evening of the eighth," resumed Peter. "Tell me what happened from the time you got there until the time you left."

"Since Dr. Mensch had regained consciousness, I really looked forward to seeing him that evening," said Jack. "He was pretty weak and most of his head was covered in bandages. But he was glad to see me, even if he couldn't talk much. Most of my time with him was spent sitting in a chair next to his bed. I'd say I was there for half an hour or so, and then I left."

"According to the report, Nurse Rison stated you did leave around 7:35pm. What did you discuss with the professor?"

"Nothing much. He was too weak to have any real conversation. But, he did tell me I'd be welcome to join the expedition he and Dr. Sutherland planned for this summer." Jack smiled sadly as he reminisced for a moment.

"Are you sure that was all you talked about? Nurse Rison stated she saw Dr. Mensch hand something to you as she came into his room to administer his evening medication." Peter studied Jack, as if he caught him in a lie regarding what really took place that night.

"I honestly don't recall that," said Jack, a little nervous under Peter's scrutiny, but determined to keep this fact from the agent's awareness. "If anything, it could've been a cup or something. I remember helping him take a drink at least once while I was with him. That's the last time I ever saw him—alive or dead. I couldn't bring myself to go to the visitation at the funeral home. It was just too painful."

"All right, then," said Peter. "As you know, Dr. Mensch was strangled shortly after you left the hospital. The coroner's report placed his death around eight o'clock that evening. Oh, what the hell." He closed the journal and laid it back down upon the table.

"So, are we done?" asked Jack, hopeful that this latest interrogation was over. "I told you there wasn't much to tell."

Peter smiled again, chuckling lightly under his breath. "On the contrary, we've just begun," he advised. "True enough, we're done with our questions in regard to Dr. Mensch—at least for now. Remember, I told you I've got other questions."

"Man, I've told you everything I know!" said Jack, unable to conceal his irritation. "There's really nothing more I can give you. Go ahead and check whatever recordings y'all have made since last night if you don't believe me!" He pointed to the surveillance cameras in each corner of the room, shaking his head defiantly.

"Are you sure about that?" Peter reached over and opened the attaché case. He pulled out a large envelope and a pair of tattered old books. He sat the books down on the table and opened the envelope. He then carefully removed the envelope's contents and placed them directly in front of Jack. "Recognize this?"

Jack was unable to mask his astonishment at what now sat before him. A pair of color photographs rested side by side upon the table. Both were of the same object, a footprint, which most folks would probably guess as being reptilian. Nothing extraordinary about this, unless one noticed the photo also contained a John Deere tractor, and that the tractor and the footprint were roughly the same size.

Accompanying the photographs was an item that Jack figured drew even more curiosity. A reptilian-like scale roughly the size of a standard football sat on the table beside them. It refracted light in a rainbow array of colors. Dismayed, he realized only a village idiot would fail to see that the footprint and scale were related to one another.

"*Where'd you get this??*" he demanded, his voice a mere whisper as the initial shock hadn't worn off yet.

"From you," said Peter, somewhat smugly. "Actually, this came to the FBI from Sheriff Joseph McCracken, who sent it to his nephew, Agent Marvin Depew. Apparently, you identified these items for Sheriff McCracken. That was on July 28th, 1999, nearly eight years ago."

Jack stiffened in his chair, fearful of where this interview now headed.

"This accompanied a report sent to Agent Depew by Sheriff McCracken, which was confirmed by Carl Peterson, the local Fire Chief in Carlsdale, Alabama," Peter continued. "You told them both, and I quote, 'a giant lizard that looked like a mix between a dragon and a '*tyrannosaurus rex*' chased you through the woods behind your home.' You further stated to them that this enormous creature was a 'fire breather' that you estimated to be around seventy feet in length. According to the report the creature caused a fire that engulfed the woods, but it mysteriously never spread to any surrounding areas."

He waited for Jack's confirmation, which never came. "Well, Jack?....Is this what you truly encountered, or were these two gentlemen full of shit?"

Jack remained silent. Sheriff McCracken and Carl Peterson died within a month of the incident in question, and to this day, he felt responsible for their deaths.

Carl was reported missing in early August, roughly two weeks following the July date in question. His bloated remains were recovered from an abandoned rock quarry just outside Mobile, Alabama a few weeks later. The case had been closed quickly, as it was quietly decided by the coroner's office down in Mobile that the fireman had committed suicide by swallowing the double barrel of a shotgun. There remained many unanswered questions surrounding his death, largely due to the rumored discovery of an extra shotgun casing found just a few feet from his body, lying near the splattered remnants of Carl's brain and shattered skull cap.

As for Sheriff McCracken, he along with a rookie deputy named Charlie Adams, who recently joined the Carlsdale Sheriff's Department, were found murdered in the dilapidated frame of an old barn. The unknown killer, or killers, left their nude bodies in an obscene position, with piano wire wound tightly around their necks and a pair of bullet holes through their skulls.

The sheriff's briefcase, which apparently contained some very incriminating papers along with a small vile of pure cocaine, was conveniently discovered just outside the barn. These items were enough to satisfy the ABI agents assigned to the case, who wasted little time destroying Sheriff McCracken's squeaky-clean reputation as a law enforcement officer. The 'real' Joe McCracken, they reported, was no more than a sexual deviant who preyed upon younger, vulnerable males like Deputy Adams. According to their report, the sheriff somehow lured poor Charlie to the barn and was in the process of forcing himself upon the younger man. An unidentified enemy, likely a miffed drug dealer from the evidence found at the crime scene, happened upon the two men and murdered them both execution style after torturing the pair first.

Jack never believed either report.

"Could my answer get me killed like Sheriff McCracken?"

Surprised, Peter abruptly looked up from his journal. "Why on earth are you asking me that?"

Jack eyed him evenly. "I know y'all killed them both."

"Do you mean me personally, or the agency I work for? If you mean either one, I assure you that we had nothing to do with any of this!" Peter stood up immediately and leaned over the table toward him. For a moment he simply glared at Jack, as if offended by his accusation. "I'm truly sorry that either man is gone, and partially from a selfish standpoint. I would've *loved* to talk to them about this stuff!" he said. "Do you really believe I've come here simply to hurt you?"

In disgust he turned away from Jack, moving over to the wall nearest his chair. He stood there staring at the cinderblocks in silence while he gathered his thoughts. When he was ready to continue, he returned to the table, holding Jack in his gaze as he sat down again. "There is so much that I long to learn from you—so much I believe *we* can help each other with," he said softly. "I have information that can prove useful to you, as well, Jack. I can help you tie some loose ends together of your own. But before I'll do that, you'll need to honestly answer my questions. They aren't many, but I need the truth from you in answering each one.

"I'm sorry, *truly* sorry, for the loss of people close to you, and I'd like to get to the bottom of why they were murdered and by whom—same as you. In order to do that, I need your full cooperation. You have information—key information that I really need you to share with me. *Work* with me? *Please*??....I promise I'll make this as painless as possible, and do it as quickly as possible. Then, you and Jeremy can return home later tonight. How about it, Jack?"

Jack remained quiet, silently pondering the pros and cons of co-operating or not cooperating. Potentially, there was much to lose with either option. After he reflected on the sorrow and torment he had endured over the past eight years, he relented to Peter's request. "Okay. I'll give it a try."

"You'll be glad you did. I'll make certain of it," Peter assured him as he leaned back in his chair. "Now, back to my earlier question. Is this a piece of some seventy-foot dinosaur that rampaged through the woods behind your place, and are these actual photographs of its footprint?" He picked up the scale and photographs and moved them even closer to Jack, who motioned that it wasn't necessary to do so.

"Yeah, they are."

"And this thing actually breathed fire through its mouth, like one of those mythical dragons we all read about as kids?" The agent seemed tentative, as if the question sounded absurd and preposterous once it poured forth from his mouth. Yet, the excitement written all over his face told Jack that the man was inclined to believe in the existence of such a being, if only he would confirm it.

"Yeah. It was able to shoot streams of fire through its mouth. It could fly, too." Jack was dead serious, though Peter couldn't help snicker and raise his eyebrows a little.

The agent reached over and picked up the scale, examining it like he could envision its appearance. "No shit. So it had wings, then?"

"Yes," said Jack, who could tell this information came as a surprise to the agent. "But they hardly seemed big enough to support its body. It was covered in scales just like the one you've got in your hand, and it had horns on its head and a pair of fan-like appendages on either side of its neck. If I wasn't so frightened by it, I would've thought it was the coolest damn thing on the planet."

Opening up like this seemed to put him at ease a little. He was becoming more comfortable with Peter, and increasingly unconcerned with whoever else observed them. He smiled sheepishly at the agent, searching his face for clues as to whether he was still inclined to believe in the creature.

"It must've been pretty harrowing to face something like that," said Peter. I know I would've probably pissed my pants if I'd been there. It says here in the report that Peter Aderley did in fact piss his pants after he heard the thing roar just outside of his feed lot."

"It roared something awful, that's for goddamned sure."

"It chased you to Ben Johnson's farm, from what I understand. Are we on the same page so far?"

"Well, not exactly. I actually lost track of the thing when I made it out of the woods. Sheriff McCracken was the one who told me it'd eventually made it out of the woods also, and then gone over to the Johnson's place. Apparently, it'd been tracking mine and Banjo's scent."

"The pet billy goat your grandfather, Marshall Edwards, kept?"

"Yeah," said Jack. "Actually, he was one of Grandpa's most prized possessions. He claimed he could teach Banjo more tricks than any dog he'd ever owned."

Peter nodded that he was listening while intently reading another page in the journal. "It states here that this 'dragon' or whatever it was suddenly disappeared without a trace. Don't you find that statement to be as incredibly strange and difficult to believe as the very existence of the creature in the first place?"

"Sure. But it's true. I never saw or heard from it again, and neither did anybody else from what I gather."

"Ah-huh...Well, at the very least that's an experience few people on this planet will ever share, I'd be willing to bet. We may come back to it, but for now let's move on. The next thing we've got here is the fact your home was completely destroyed by a tornado less than thirty-six hours after this event we just discussed, on July 30th. You've got to admit that's a pretty weird sequence of events. Wouldn't you agree?"

"Yeah, I figure most folks would agree on that."

"I'll bet most people would find it even more strange that for the most part, only your house was destroyed. Your neighbors, namely the Palmers, suffered only minimal damage. There wasn't a single thing left intact in your yard other than an old tool shed in the back. Just like the Palmer's place, it wasn't harmed at all, correct?"

Something in Peter's demeanor shifted ever so slightly, and Jack was certain that only the most observant eyes would've caught this. The agent was on a covert mission of some sort, and he worried that at some point he was going to call on him to define or clarify some connection in order for Peter to complete his interrogative journey.

"Correct," he finally answered.

Peter leaned back in his chair, tapping the edge of his pen against the bottom of his lip while he pondered the delivery of his next question. "You, your brother, and your grandfather fled from your home. At some point, the tornado overtook you and hurled your vehicle into a field less than a mile away. What do you remember about that experience?"

"Actually, not a whole lot," said Jack. He was now determined not to give more information than was prudent.

"Please tell me what you recall."

"Well, most of it's pretty hazy in my mind, other than jumping into Jeremy's truck and speeding away down Lelan's Road, only to be snatched up from behind by the twister before we made it to Baileys Bend Road. The last thing I remember was crashing into a ditch in the field. After that, I didn't regain consciousness for three weeks, and I didn't know if my brother and grandfather were even alive."

Peter studied him curiously for a moment, clicking his pen absently in his hand. Truly anxious to be done with the interview, Jack took this as an opportunity to try and finish things up.

"Once we recovered from our injuries enough to visit what was left of our place, we were surprised to find the old tool shed was still standing," Jack continued. "We'd already decided to stay with my Uncle Monty and Aunt Martha in Tuscaloosa for the time being. Once we saw the barren plot of land that used to be our home, all of us knew we'd never be coming back there to live.

"Almost immediately, we noticed we were being followed almost everywhere we went. Most of the time it was folks like you, agents driving nice sedans and who were hard to tell one from another. They almost always wore sunglasses and business suits, similar to what you and the others around here have on. They all made us plenty nervous, especially once we learned what had happened to Sheriff McCracken and Carl Peterson.

"Anyway, this uninvited surveillance lasted till my freshman year in college, and then it stopped almost as suddenly as it had started. Until this week."

"Anything else you want to add to that, Jack?" asked Peter, frowning as he pondered Jack's sudden change in demeanor.

"No. That pretty much sums things up."

Agent McNamee rubbed his eyes and sighed. For the moment he remained seated where he was, silently studying the young man in the faded Metallica T-shirt sitting across from him. The silence grew uncomfortable, but after spending nearly a minute like this, Peter stood up and paced slowly across the room. Jack watched him intently, praying silently that he would now be set free. But intuitively he knew it wasn't going to happen, and a moment later Peter confirmed this by resuming his interrogation.

"I realize much of what we discussed so far must be very uncomfortable for you," he told him as he returned to the table. "I cannot stress enough on how imperative it is that you share everything you know with me. Granted, it seems at first glance there's very little here that connects your past experiences with the most recent one involving Dr. Mensch—though, I think you'd be surprised." He stood next to Jack, smiling in a way that Jack could tell there was something the agent really wanted to tell him, but couldn't, either due to his vocation or that he was waiting for the right opportunity.

"You know, there were witnesses among your neighbors who saw the tornado that early morning in July, 1999," he continued. He sat on the edge of the table and leaned forward. The agent's cologne, an expensive Ralph Lauren blend, filled Jack's nostrils. "The Palmers swore they watched the twister as it blasted through your house before turning on a dime to follow your family as you raced down Lelan's Road in Jeremy's truck. They watched it turn and come back up the street after it tossed his vehicle into the field we've discussed. Now, it may have been extremely foolhardy and dangerous of them, but Joey and Linda Sue Palmer ignored the safety of their storm cellar to witness this tornado methodically obliterate everything in your yard except, of course, the tool shed. We've already agreed that your home being the sole target of the tornado was very weird. I'm not professing that either of us are experts in meteorology or to what is considered typical tornado behavior. But, doesn't the fact this particular tornado came back and took a *second* direct pass on your property seem preposterous to you?"

Jack's hands turned clammy and sweat began to form in tiny droplets above his temples and down along his spine. He never knew his next-door neighbors had witnessed those horrifying events in the early morning darkness that fateful day. According to what he had been previously told, no one living along Lelan's Road had ever come forward.

"I can see it in your face, Jack. You're holding out on me," Peter chuckled. "Well, that's fine, because I've got all night if need be." He straightened up and returned to his seat. Just before sitting down he took the two large books and stood them up so Jack could read the covers. Both were worn, although the one to his right was smaller and appeared much older than the one to his left.

"As you can see, these two volumes are fairly old. I'd be willing to bet my life that you'd love to get your hands on either one, if you knew what they were. The larger one is the detailed journal of a man named Dr. Nathaniel Stratton, originally from Murfreesboro, Tennessee, but who spent much of his life traveling throughout the world. He spent quite a bit of his time in Carlsdale, where his brother owned the farm that later belonged to the Johnson's—the same place, as you know, where that footprint was photographed."

Once again, Jack stiffened noticeably in his chair. Sure, he had seen the books sitting on the table. They both immediately looked interesting to him merely because they were old. He had been so intent on finding an opportunity to cut short the present interview that he hadn't bothered to get a closer look at the faded titles on either one. A look of recognition flashed across his face before he could stop himself.

"Well I'll be damned, Jack, we might finally be getting somewhere!" Peter enthused. "I see that you recognize the name 'Dr. Nathaniel Stratton'. He's got a lot of interesting stuff in this journal of his. Much of which, I might add, pertains to your grandfather. It spans more than fifty years, from 1896 until his disappearance under mysterious circumstances in 1949."

Peter laid the journal down and turned his attention to the other, smaller book. "This volume here is much older than Dr. Stratton's journal. It's basically a collection of local legends from Louisiana, Mississippi, and Alabama. Each one in this book is at least one hundred and fifty years old. Believe it or not, there's stuff in here about your own family's history as well. Plus, there's some pretty interesting things about the founding of the town of Carlsdale in the late 1700's."

He stopped for a moment to gauge Jack's reaction, who couldn't hide his fascination with the tattered and worn, black leather-bound book in front of him.

"You know, Jack, there's even a tale in here about your grandpa's great-great-grandfather, Sherman Edwards," advised Peter. "It may be especially interesting for you since it describes in detail the pain and effort he went through to rebuild the farmhouse you grew up in. I'll bet you never knew it was erected on the very same spot where a previous house built by your family stood. Did you?"

Speechless, Jack shook his head to indicate that he didn't. If Peter had any lingering doubts about his attention and interest in this interrogation, they were now completely erased.

"Obviously, I don't need to tell you that most folks find stories containing dragons, witches, and the like to be pure fantasy. That's why both of these books were locked up and nearly forgotten in our archives down in Richmond. We've already discussed a dragon-like creature here tonight, and there's a piece of it on the table right in front of us. So, what most folks think doesn't apply to us. Right?"

"Yes, sir," Jack replied, his respect for Peter steadily rising. He was hooked, scarcely believing his eyes and ears.

"As I was explaining to you, your house was built upon another's foundation. Can you venture a guess as to the only thing that was still standing back then from the original structure?"

"*Oh, my God!*" Jack suddenly blurted out, and felt instantly ashamed at his inability to better control his emotions and excited reaction. "The *tool shed??*"

"Yes. The tool shed."

"Would you mind if I take a quick look at that?" Jack reached for the book.

"Uh-uh-uh," Peter chided, waving his index finger. He quickly removed both books from the table, placing them back inside the attaché case.

"What'd you do that for??" Jack's eyes gleamed with fury. He hastily stood up, nearly toppling his chair again in the process. "I mean, why in the hell did you go and tell me about that shit if you weren't intending to let me read it for myself??"

Peter motioned for Jack to calm down, insisting that he return to his seat before he would explain his reasoning for doing what he did. Jack hesitated. Finally, though sullenly, he returned to his chair.

"I'd love nothing better than for you to read each volume at your leisure, Jack," Peter told him earnestly. "But, there's much I need to learn from you first. Not so much about Dr. Mensch as I do about what truly happened back in July of 1999. I know we've only scratched the surface in what we've discussed so far, and I'd give most anything to hear the rest. If you'll divulge what you've kept hidden in your heart and mind, I'll see to it that you're allowed to review both books for as long as you like."

Jack slowly sank back against his chair, eyeing the agent curiously. What did the agent really want from him? Everything sitting upon the table engendered a thousand questions on their own. Not to mention the report Peter read earlier. Still, he couldn't shake the feeling that Peter was after something specific and different than what they had discussed so far.

After pondering the proposal for another moment, he shook his head to advise he wasn't sharing any more information. Whatever the government had gathered up until now would have to suffice, regardless of whether he could see the books or not.

"Why are you so reluctant to talk about it?" Peter persisted, frustrated at Jack's stubborn refusal to even elaborate on why. "What have you got to hide? What could possibly be important enough to keep quiet about all of these years??"

Jack looked down at his distorted reflection in the table's face. He sighed and slowly shook his head from side to side. "You'd never understand. Unless you'd been there yourself, there'd be no way in hell you'd *ever* understand."

The sadness in his voice revealed the heaviness of the secret he carried within his heart. Peter stood up from his chair. He moved over to him and stooped down to his knees, so that he was now looking up into the trembling young man's face. He slowly brought his arm around as if to hug and comfort Jack, but stopped short of actually doing so, afraid how this simple act of compassion would be perceived. Instead, he tried to use his words to comfort him, and in so doing unleashed the pent-up torment and pain in his own soul.

"Jack", he began, surprised that his voice was now quivering. "I have my own reasons for wanting to know what you know. I'm about to take a huge risk here that could cost me dearly. Beyond the complete exposure of my personal demons, it could cost me my livelihood. That's how badly I need to know everything that happened to you. You'll soon see that my hell and yours are *connected*, Jack. Probably in ways you might never imagine."

Jack turned enough to face him, narrowing his eyes in a determined effort to discern the true depth of sincerity in Peter's words. It was difficult to know for certain, but he really thought Agent McNamee was on the verge of tears. A volatile mixture of bitter sorrow and anger seemed to bubble and boil within the agent's eyes, turning them into dark pools of sadness.

"Does the name Bobby Northrop mean anything to you?" Peter remained in his awkward stance, peering anxiously up into Jack's face. For the moment, Jack gave no indication he had any idea what the agent just asked him.

"I'm going to take a chance and assume that you have heard this name. Even if for some reason you haven't, I hope you'll bear with me as I tell his story. Can you do that for me?"

Jack nodded he would.

"All right." Peter paused momentarily, gathering his thoughts until he was ready to begin. "About two months after the destruction of your home in Carlsdale, on October 24th, 1999, Bobby Northrop celebrated his eighth birthday. Up until that day, he was a beautiful and happy child. His parents were affluent, having recently purchased a magnificent home in Shipley Farms, which was located near the edge of Bienville National Forest. That's just to the east of Jackson, Mississippi. Ever been there, Jack?"

"No. I can't say that I have," Jack quietly responded.

"Yeah, I guess it's most likely that you haven't," Peter sighed sadly. "I suppose you haven't been out of the state of Alabama much. Except for baseball and your recent journey here." He smiled weakly. "Well, that day promised to be special. It turned out to truly be a special day, though not for the reasons anyone had hoped for or even dreamed of. Bobby's parents, Robert Northrop the Second and his wife, Eileen, had prepared quite an event for Bobby. Perhaps this was because their little boy's birthday was the first ever to be celebrated in their fabulous brand-new home.

"It seemed like there were kids everywhere, and the main level of the home was completely decorated with expensive garlands and balloons. The place was crammed full of people as they watched Bobby blow out the candles on his cake. You may have seen the video of this event later on CNN and the major networks, as Robert Northrop was recording it with his digital camcorder. Bobby looked up and smiled at his daddy, right after blowing out the last candle. His eyes sparkled with excitement, for he hoped the wish he just made came true. Such a simple pleasure only the innocence a kid his age can know..." Peter's voice trailed off and he looked down for a moment. He shifted his weight to relieve the pressure upon his knees, and then looked back up into Jack's face again. Tears welled in his eyes.

"As soon as the cake was cut and everybody had their plates heaped with it and ice cream, Bobby's parents took him outside to open his birthday gifts. They were in a huge stack out on the back deck. Are you familiar with RavenWolff?"

"Yeah," Jack replied, thinking of the cartoon superhero of his youth. His tongue feeling thick and slow, he cleared his throat before completing his answer to the agent's question. "That was all the rage back then, I remember."

"Yes it was," Peter responded thoughtfully. "It's pretty much all little Bobby talked about. For his birthday present, his mom and dad really splurged and bought him a Tower Den Clubhouse. Are you familiar with that, also?"

"Complete with the double slides on either end of it? *That* Tower Den??" Jack remembered how much he wanted one.

"Yes, that Tower Den. Bobby's dad and uncle, Lawrence Northrop, spent the better part of two days setting it up. How they kept Bobby from finding out about it before his birthday celebration is a story in itself...perhaps for some other time. It truly was a magnificent piece of equipment."

"I would've died for one of those things when I was a kid," Jack admitted. "But, there's no way in hell my grandpa'd ever shell out two grand for something like that."

"It may have been pricey," Peter said, "but the thing was definitely worth it, you'd have to admit. It had the spiral slides you mentioned and all kinds of other fun stuff between them, and could keep up to twenty kids occupied for hours. The coolest thing about it was the clubhouse on top. It sat fifteen feet above the ground, and was large enough to hold five or six kids at once. You could only reach that part of the Tower Den by way of a rope ladder or a striped fire pole. Hell, if it wasn't for all of the outdated RavenWolff insignias plastered across the damn thing, I'm sure most any kid would still dig it now." Peter paused, giving in to a moment of nostalgia.

"As soon as Bobby discovered this 'surprise' birthday gift waiting for him in the backyard, he immediately went nuts, thrusting his fists into the air as he ran screaming and dancing over to the Tower Den," he continued. "All the other kids converged on it with him, and they remained there until each one's parents arrived later that afternoon to pick them up from the party.

"It was after four o'clock, and by that time, the temperature had started to drop. Once Bobby's aunts, uncles, and cousins had also left, he and his older sister, Jenny Northrop, went back into the house. Jenny decided to remain inside and visit with her grandparents for a while, who were in from New Orleans. Before long, she went upstairs to play Bobby's Nintendo 64 with her eighteen-year old uncle, who had also come up from New Orleans with her grandpa and grandma. Meanwhile, Bobby grabbed a jacket and ran back outside. Along the way out, he picked up the RavenWolff mask, cape, and glove-claws that his sister had given him for his birthday to go along with the Tower Den..." Unable to finish, Agent McNamee lowered his head and began to weep.

Jack was overwhelmed with compassion and alarm for the man, but didn't know how to properly respond. Why was he *so* upset? Jack was also beginning to tremble inside, wondering how this incident was connected to him. He started to say something, but Peter abruptly looked up, causing Jack to recoil. Peter's face was red with fury and his eyes were blurred by grief. Jack prepared to hear something horrible.

"That was the last time anyone ever saw him, Jack!" he nearly shouted. "At least, on record, that's the last time. But, you know what? Bobby's eighteen-year old uncle saw something! *'Goddamned right, he did!!!'*"

Peter was now openly sobbing. Deeply alarmed, Jack looked toward the door, expecting the agent's colleagues to bust into the room at any moment. For the present time, though, the door remained shut and undisturbed.

Undeterred, Peter continued to sob. "And, you know what else?? Some kid in Carlsdale, Alabama saw the exact same type of thing just two months earlier!"

Jack felt the words hit him physically, as obviously the kid he referred to was him. Peter's discerning eyes saw that he made the connection.

"Yes, Jack! I'm talking about *you*!!" he declared. "Bobby's uncle just happened to look outside into the backyard from Bobby's bedroom window the same instant the little boy jumped down off the deck. He was all dressed up in his RavenWolff outfit with his arms stretched out in front of him. But, as soon as he landed on the grass, he stopped in his tracks, Jack. Do you have any idea why?"

Jack quietly shook his head from side to side, knowing why, but wishing he didn't.

"He stopped because a goddamned golden mist started pouring out of the Tower Den's clubhouse. It headed right for him. Do you know what happened next? The fucking thing *took him!*" Peter moved closer to Jack, his rage and pain radiating heat fervent enough for Jack to clearly feel it from where he sat. "The uncle and his niece screamed through the window for Bobby to get away from the mist, but this innocent little kid walked right into it on his way to the Tower Den. All of a sudden, the mist began to shimmer and glow, steadily growing brighter until the entire backyard seemed like it was immersed in an ethereal fire. The intense energy from this became so unbearable that Jenny and her uncle were forced to turn away from it.

"They both ran downstairs crying, and raced into the sitting room, which was located at the far end of the house. They alerted the adults as to what was happening in the backyard. As it turned out, Robert had noticed the strange glow himself and passed it off as the setting sun combining its rays with the security lights just turning on. Once Jenny and her uncle explained what they had just witnessed from upstairs, he quickly recognized his error in discernment: the golden light emanated from the east—not the west, as it should have. That's when he panicked.

"Robert and Eileen sprinted for the door and threw it open. Once they stepped out onto the patio, though, the strange mist and its incredible intensity had vanished, along with any remaining trace of Bobby."

Peter looked away from Jack and sat down upon the concrete floor, for the moment relieving the painful stress on his knees and hamstrings from his crouched stance. "Jack, me carrying on like that has to look so fucking pathetic to you, I'm sure," he sniffed while looking back up into Jack's bewildered face, the tears and redness beginning to retreat. "If you can bear with me for just while longer, I'll try and tie everything together.

"I believe you can guess that Bobby was never seen or heard from again. When his mom and dad ran out onto the patio, Eileen fell to her knees and cried uncontrollably. She kept saying, 'They came to take my baby, and he's *never* coming back!'. Robert was never able to console her, though God knows how hard he tried.

"Jenny, her uncle, and her grandparents were outside with them by this point, and everyone searched for Bobby throughout the entire yard. Everyone except Eileen, who remained sprawled out upon the back deck in her debilitating grief. All efforts to find him were in vain. It was as if the little guy simply vanished into thin air! The last thing ever found of him was the RavenWolff outfit, which Jenny discovered lying on the floor of the Tower Den's clubhouse.

"The entire neighborhood soon joined in the search, and the police joined in as well. Eileen's father had recently retired from the FBI, and was able to obtain the agency's assistance by the very next morning.

"A small breakthrough came in the middle of the day, October 25th, when a police canine unit picked up Bobby's scent and followed it for nearly three miles into the forest, until it abruptly disappeared at a hot spring and rock formation. For much of the distance tracked by the dogs and their trainers, a strange set of markings lined up next to Bobby's scent. At first, the only thing determined from the markings was that they were some kind of footprint. No one could tell what kind of creature had made them, but they weren't human. Near the end of the very next day, October 26th, a prominent zoologist flown in from Memphis finally was able to identify them, though only generally so. The tracks were reptilian."

Peter's eyes danced as they intently studied Jack's reaction to this last statement, as if he fully expected some important revelation to come forth. When it didn't do so within the next few moments, he slowly looked away in disappointment. "Goddamn it, Jack! What's it going to fucking take??" he wearily implored, lowering his head in his hands in obvious frustration. "You've *got* to help me out here. I mean, you've got strange reptilian footprints in Carlsdale, Alabama. Then, there are smaller, but nearly identical ones found near Jackson, Mississippi. You've got a strange golden mist outside your home in Carlsdale, that your next-door neighbors, the Palmers, confirmed they witnessed taking place during the early hours of July 28th. Then, another one is witnessed by Bobby Northrop's sister and uncle on October 24th at the Northrop home."

Jack silently met Peter's expectant gaze head-on. The agent's unstable behavior was really starting to worry him. Still, he wasn't about to fully cooperate just yet.

"All right ...that's fine," Peter acknowledged, nodding as if he just read Jack's thoughts. "Let's move forward, then. Apparently it's not enough that I've humiliated myself before you. Is it?"

Jack remained stoic. He needed time to absorb this story before responding.

"Very well. Follow me deeper into this personal hell of mine," the agent sighed, forcing a smile onto his face that almost broke Jack's steadfast refusal to collaborate or validate the account.

"I'll bet you're wondering why this means so much to me...right? Did you know Eileen Northrop told her husband, Robert, that she felt like they were being watched by an unseen presence located somewhere in the woods, and that this had been going on ever since they moved in just two months prior?"

Jack wasn't able to resist raising an eyebrow at this latest revelation. Of course, Peter noted this reaction as well. Encouraged, he continued.

"Did you ever see a photograph of this amazingly beautiful woman,

Jack?" Peter asked. "Here, check this one out. This was taken the day before Bobby's disappearance."

Peter pulled out several photographs from the inside breast pocket of his jacket. He took one of the pictures and placed it directly in front of Jack on the table, who suddenly recognized the image of the woman standing in the middle of the photograph. It had been years since he had seen this person's likeness, as the last time had been on a tabloid cover near the end of 1999. Over time, he had forgotten their names, but back then he knew the Northrop's tragedy was connected to his own.

"I thought so," Peter whispered softly, completely void of any triumph on account of this revelation. He stood up and brushed his suit off, and then moved back to his side of the table. Jack's eyes followed his exact progress as he did so.

"Eileen never recovered from this," he resumed, his voice hollow and just barely audible. "She died the very next spring, on April 19th, leaving her grief stricken husband to care for their only remaining child. Shortly after that, in June, Eileen's mother passed away suddenly from a stroke. The doctors told her husband and Eileen's younger brother, who had just turned nineteen and was finishing his first semester at Lehigh University, that her health was most likely severely impaired by the stress and sorrow she had endured over the past eight months."

Jack sniffled, and Peter abruptly stopped. The younger man's façade was crumbling.

"This only gets worse, my friend," said Peter, sadly. "Remember I told you we share the same hell? I'm quite serious in telling you that."

He slipped back into his chair and leaned toward Jack, his shoulders trembling as if he might start bawling again at any moment. "You see...Eileen Northrop was my sister. I was the eighteen-year old uncle at Bobby's birthday celebration. I was the only one who watched him disappear into that *goddamned mist!!* I'm still the one who routinely checks up on my niece to make sure she doesn't take her life when she enters one of her many deep depressions. And I'm the only one who makes sure her grandpa, my dad, the former FBI agent Merten McNamee, doesn't do the same thing by swallowing the barrel of his service revolver!"

Peter sighed again and buried his face in his hands, the burden of sorrow far too big for him to carry any further. He broke down and sobbed, no longer caring about how he looked to anyone, either inside or outside the room. He may have remained like this for quite a while, but suddenly he felt a pair of strong hands upon his shoulders.

"Agent McNamee," said Jack, just inches above him. "I'll tell you what you want to know. I'll tell you everything."

PART II

The Lizard and the Sphere

"Are you ready?" asked Peter, finding it difficult to contain his eagerness. Since cleaning himself up in the tiny restroom at the end of the interrogation room, he seemed refreshed. Only the red rims around his piercing blue eyes suggested he had recently wept.

While waiting for Peter to return to the table, Jack spent a few minutes walking around the room. To any observer he would've appeared calm, though silently he debated whether he was doing the right thing or not. Once Peter was set to resume their interview, Jack grabbed another Coke from the tiny refrigerator and then joined the agent at the table.

"Jeremy is going to kill me for sure once he finds out about this," said Jack. "But, we still get to check out those books you've got. Right?"

"Absolutely," said Peter. "Don't worry about your brother, Jack. I'll talk with him just as soon as we're done. All I ask is that you be thorough...*very* thorough. I want to know every detail, including things you might normally view as unimportant—like your feelings, thoughts, and even your physical surroundings. Describe them *all* for me. Okay?"

"I guess I can do that," said Jack, surprised at the level of detail the agent wanted from him. "Some shit's pretty personal, though."

"Everything, Jack," Peter repeated. "I do mean *everything*."

"All right," he agreed, and leaned forward in his chair. Peter did the same, and then Jack told him his story. "It all started on the afternoon of July 27th, 1999, just four days following my thirteenth birthday. My grandfather and I'd just finished lunch, and as I placed my dirty dishes in the kitchen sink, I noticed this weird looking lizard resting on the back porch when I glanced out the kitchen window. I'd never seen this lizard, or another like it, during any of my explorations of our property

"I told Grandpa about it, but he kept reading his newspaper at the kitchen table. I believe he only half-acknowledged what I said until I told him it looked sort of exotic. At that point, he almost got up to take a look. But the phone rang and he answered it instead. I kept watching the lizard through the kitchen window, hoping it didn't move from its perch near the steps leading down into the backyard. It sat there motionless, except for an occasional head-twitch and the flicking of its forked tongue.

"As soon as Grandpa was done talking on the phone, I told him it was still sitting on the porch. 'Son, you'd be better off just leaving that thing alone, I'm warning you,' he told me. 'It could be poisonous for all we know...I wish people'd keep better track of their goddamned pets around here!'

"'It's okay, Grandpa,' I assured him. 'I doubt very seriously it'll bite. Besides, even if it does, I'll bet it won't hurt much.'

"My grandfather frowned and straightened up in his chair at the kitchen table. I remember he stared down thoughtfully into his coffee mug, absently stirring his coffee while he considered what I just said. He might've remained lost in his thoughts if it hadn't been for the sudden creak and slam of the screened door leading out to the back porch. Before he could tell me to stay away from the critter, I was already outside. Peering back through the screen, I caught him smiling at me. He warned me again to be careful.

"I remember it was really hot that day. With the heat index over a hundred degrees, only the most desperate and foolhardy folks were outdoors right then—like me, I guess. But I just had to get a closer look at the lizard. It remained in the same spot while I moved carefully over to it, eyeing me tentatively from atop the steps. It seemed somewhat fragile and vulnerable, although I could see powerful muscles flexing beneath its green leathery skin, especially along its lower legs, as if it was ready to bolt back down the steps at any moment. The lizard's back was arched high in a multi-colored fan that ran along its spine, and brilliant hues of purple, red, and orange converged down its sides.

"Its most unusual feature was a crown of golden spikes and curved horns that adorned its slender head. In fact, if it wasn't for this crown, the critter could've passed for someone's wayward pet. I'd seen similar lizards on display at Pet World up in Tuscaloosa. However, the closest living thing I'd ever seen to this one was in a picture inside one of Grandpa's National Geographics. As it was, it reminded me of the colorful dragons depicted in the video games I used to play with Jeremy.

"The lizard cocked its head warily to one side as it studied me, for I now stood just a few feet away. Its incandescent blue and gray eyes shifted slowly back and forth. I took another step and leaned down toward it, closing the gap between us to a mere foot. Suddenly, it stood up on its hind legs and took a swipe at me with its front claws.

I barely escaped the attack, which scared the holy shit out of me and made me stumble backward and land hard on my ass.

"The little fucker hissed loudly and flashed a mouth full of sharp needle-like teeth at me. I scooted away as quickly as I could while it took a menacing step forward. But then it stopped and retracted its leg. It turned its attention toward the backyard, like it was listening to something—maybe some inaudible command to call off the attack. With a low grunt-like growl, it turned on its hind legs and raced down the porch steps, leaving me staring after it in disbelief.

"'Jack!' Grandpa called to me from the kitchen. 'Are you all right?' He moved over to the back door and peered anxiously at me through the screen. For the moment I was sprawled out on the back porch.

"'Yeah, I'm fine,' I told him as I sat up. "That lizard startled me, but it's long gone now." Even though I smiled up at him, Grandpa stood quietly while he studied me, frowning again as if trying to decide for his own self what'd truly happened. He finally stepped back from the doorway, chuckling to himself in amusement. As he did so, he reminded me to be careful and not linger outside in the heat.

"I told him I'd only be outside for a little while, and that I was fixing to go over to the swing since it was in the shade. I waited until his footfalls and the switching on of another floor fan confirmed he'd turned his attention to other tasks inside our old farmhouse. I remember wishing he'd use the air conditioner more often, especially on a day like that one. Aside from the house staying cooler, the kitchen storm door would've been closed and Grandpa wouldn't have known about the recent commotion on the porch. I now had to be very discreet in my pursuit of the lizard, since he'd likely be watching.

"I stood up and quietly rummaged around the porch searching for something suitable to help me apprehend the critter. I finally settled on using a large steel bait bucket with a retractable lid that I found under some boxes in a corner. I picked it up and carried it over to the porch steps, and then set it down while I decided where to search first.

"Our backyard spanned for nearly a full acre. Grandpa'd let the lawn deteriorate over the years, and it was badly overgrown in spots—in particular, near some old worn-out appliances to the right of the back porch and near the rusted-out remains of an old pickup truck to the left. The junk seemed sorely out of place if you considered the contrasting beauty provided by the mimosa trees that dotted the yard along with the majestic oak that sat in the middle of everything back there. Then again, I suppose it wasn't quite so out of place compared to the enormous stone sphere resting near the back wall of the property."

"I've got a bunch of pictures of that thing, Jack," said Peter. "They're also in my attaché case, along with a report from 1989 detailing the sphere's composition."

"Can I see that, too?" Jack was surprised again by this latest revelation.

"Sure. Just as soon as you're done with your story. I appreciate the descriptive detail so far."

"Thanks, I'll try to continue that way" said Jack, finding it difficult to focus on that very same story in light of this latest tidbit. "I have to admit it's all so strange for me, Agent McNamee. Even though this all happened years ago, as I'm telling it to you it's as if it all just took place yesterday.

"Anyway, people often wondered about the way Grandpa had the backyard set up. When I was younger, I figured he was trying to create some bizarre work of art with the trees' beauty and that strange looking globe, along with the yard's assorted junk. As I got older, I just wished Grandpa'd let us help him clean up the place and remove all that shit once and for all. Supposedly, he'd tried to do that very thing long ago, but couldn't get it done.

"Regardless, it certainly made a great hiding place if you were a three-foot long lizard wishing to be left alone. The critter could be anywhere with so many nooks and crannies to hide in. With that in mind, I braced myself for the worst of the summer's heat and headed down the worn wooden steps into the yard.

"As soon as I moved a few feet away from the porch, I turned toward the house and scanned the walls, roofs, and gables for any sign of it, shielding my eyes from the sun's brightness. There was nothing to indicate that it'd climbed the walls or chalices up to the second floor or beyond. The light-blue painted walls and gables revealed no small footprints or claw marks—which I figured they would've done, given the heat and the fact they'd been painted less than two months before.

"I stood there, dripping sweat while trying to decide if the lizard might've jumped up on the roof. Then I remembered how it behaved on the porch when I first saw it. At the time, it seemed to enjoy *not* being out in the burning sun. If anything, I figured it'd try to find some place where it could stay cool.

"I walked over to the wooden lattice that surrounded the porch and peered through its holes. I figured this would be a great place to hide, since it was sheltered from the sun and had an abundance of spiders and insects for the lizard to eat. However, the lattice was still intact, without any sign it'd been disturbed by anything.

"By then, my shorts and T-shirt were getting pretty damp from sweat. Shielding my eyes once more from the sun's intensity, I moved over to the pickup's sun-baked remains, knowing I didn't have long before I became totally drenched. The grass and weeds grew tall around the faded red vehicle, which still sat on the very same cinder blocks from when it was condemned to the backyard many years before. All four tires had long since been removed and most of the truck's body was devoured by rust. The windshield had been broken by an errant fly ball off my brother's bat during a neighborhood game of baseball two summers earlier, and most of the glass was still lying in shard fragments on the torn vinyl front seat.

"Once I was within a few feet of the truck, I got down on my knees to try and get a good view of the pickup's undercarriage. I could hardly see through the undergrowth that engulfed the bottom of the truck. I briefly considered reaching my hands underneath the pickup until I remembered the lizard's mouth was full of pointed sharp teeth.

"Thinking it might be there, I decided to eliminate other possible hiding places first. I stood up and leaned closer to the pickup, peering carefully through the driver-side window. From the undisturbed dirt and cobwebs covering the inside of the cab, I could tell the lizard hadn't been there. Next, I scanned the twisted branches of a fairly large mimosa that stood next to the pickup. The tree was filled with swallowtail butterflies coupling as they flew through the air near bloom clusters that populated the tree's upper branches. The critter wasn't up in the tree either, but I wondered for a moment if the damned thing had chameleon characteristics and could blend in with its environment.

"Debating where to look next, I decided for the time being to walk over to the tire-swing that hung from our giant oak. That's when I heard a noticeable 'clank' and rustling sound coming from the pile of broken appliances sitting nearby. Immediately, my heart raced and pounded heavily in my chest. The skin on my neck and arms turned cool as I felt the gooseflesh rise. A moment before I was overwhelmed by heat and now, suddenly, I felt cold and clammy. Something sifted ferociously through the tall grass and weeds surrounding an old washing machine and the strewn-about guts of a discarded television set.

"I moved cautiously up to the washer, worried that the bait container wouldn't be enough to protect me. I noticed a deflated soccer ball a short distance to my left, and silently hurried over to it, ever mindful to keep an eye on the machine. I picked up the flattened ball and moved in closer to the raucous, holding the ball near my head so that it was ready to be launched.

"The disturbance grew steadily more violent the closer I came to the junk pile. Expecting to see the lizard in a highly agitated rage, I prepared myself for the worst. My hand holding the soccer ball wavered noticeably just as I reached the washer.

"Its weathered door sat slightly ajar from when it was pushed open a moment ago. The machine itself was lying on its side and the invader had managed to climb inside, the hollow pounding on the washer's sides easily giving its exact location away. I bent over silently and threw open the door. The startled animal came barreling out, revealing its dark frightened eyes and small horns as it headed straight for me.

"I gasped and fell on my ass for the second time that afternoon. Fortunately for me, the menace lurking within the old washer was none other than Banjo, my grandfather's billy goat. At first I thought he was going to bite me, his teeth bared as meanly as any farm critter could possibly do. Banjo'd been oblivious to my presence until I threw open the washing machine's door. As soon as he recognized me, he tentatively approached and started eagerly licking me on my arms and legs.

"I remember scolding him as I returned his affections, but I felt a wave of relief rush over me since it hadn't been the lizard leaping toward me. It made me pause and think seriously about spending the rest of that steamy afternoon in the better comfort and safety of our house.

"'Have you seen any three foot lizards out here, Banjo?' I asked him. He whimpered slightly in response to my question, though I'm sure he had absolutely no idea what I was talking about. Knowing Banjo's tendency toward skittishness, I figured he'd have been more than content to remain inside the washer if he could have.

"He continued to caress my hand with the rough edge of his tongue. Banjo's fur was black with brown splotches on his back and sides, and at that moment all of it was glistening. The heat was getting to him, too, perhaps even more than it was getting to me. I figured he was trying to find a cool refuge when I startled him. He whimpered softly again and looked directly up into my face, pleading for me to lead us both out of the sweltering sauna we were presently standing in. I took him with me over to the oak's shade, deciding to forego looking for the lizard anymore.

"I don't know if you've ever seen any pictures of it, Agent McNamee, but our oak tree was truly magnificent. Grandpa once told me it'd been there long before the farmhouse was built, and that'd been roughly a hundred and seventy years before, as I'm sure you know. The tree's long branches rose to dizzying heights, and if anyone stood directly below them while leaning their head back as far as they could without falling over, the upward view would momentarily take their breath away.

"Banjo and I walked together into the cool shade provided by the oak's thick foliage. Although the air was still muggy, the temperature seemed much cooler here. Banjo was relieved as much as I was and trotted over to a half-empty bowl of water near the oak's trunk.

"A thirty-foot ladder made of small boards nailed into the tree's trunk led up to a wooden tree house that sat within a large cluster of branches. One particularly thick branch protruded out from the tree house, and from it hung an old tire swing. I walked over to the swing, and then set the deflated soccer ball and bait container on the near-barren ground surrounding the oak tree's trunk and climbed up into the tire.

"After a casual glance back toward the pickup truck and our house behind it, I was soon flying through the air. My damp clothes pressed against my skin and my hair blew back away from my forehead. I'd finally found some relief from the heat, feeling I might stay outside a bit longer than originally planned.

"Riding the swing, I had an excellent view of the Palmer's place off to the right and a pretty good view of the Johnson's farm over to the left of the yard. An old stone wall just over six feet in height completely enclosed the backyard, and the back portions of all three properties were only accessible by a seldom-used dirt frontage road. That's why very few folks ever saw the sphere at the rear of our property.

"As I'm sure you'd agree, it was definitely an oddity. I believe the sphere was nearly fifteen feet in diameter. It dwarfed the wall and wrought-iron gate in front of it. None of us had any idea what it was made of. But the report you've got should answer that question, I'm sure. I remember its texture was very smooth, much like finely sanded marble or limestone, and its color was off-white, almost like a fresh chicken egg.

"They say the sphere drew some attention twelve years earlier. I was too young to remember, but the local folks in Carlsdale sometimes talked about the government scientists who made routine visits to our home to study the peculiar object in our backyard for almost six months. You're probably aware that for awhile they examined the sphere daily, often leaving it hooked up to various monitoring devices and using solvents in minute amounts to determine its exact chemical composition.

"Eventually, my grandfather grew tired of all the attention and lack of privacy. Somehow, he managed to get NASA to agree to take the sphere away from us. Since he was tight-lipped about this for years, I had to rely on the local rumor mill in Carlsdale to first learn what happened, and why the sphere was still there many years later.

"According to rumor, Grandpa arranged for some folks from NASA to come and carry the sphere back with them to Houston. In an effort to help out, he'd enlisted the assistance of a good friend of his who owned a construction outfit in nearby Demopolis. This friend brought with him a small team of men, along with a large loader, two tractors, and an industrial crane. The NASA people then arrived with a van and what looked to be a large specially designed semi-truck.

"The workers from Demopolis and the NASA crew worked together to secure a special net around the sphere, in order to lift it safely over the back wall. The loader was ready and waiting just on the other side of the wall, along with all the other vehicles and a hundred or so onlookers. The workers finally secured the net around the sphere and were ready to hoist it up, when a black limousine suddenly came flying up the frontage road toward the work site. Everyone stopped to watch the approaching vehicle until it screeched to a halt a few feet away from NASA's semi-truck.

"The driver of the limo rolled down his window and motioned for the leader of the NASA group to step over to the driver side of the car. Once the leader reached the car, the rear passenger window also rolled down and the driver motioned for the man to go on back to the window. Apparently he recognized the back seat's occupant, and after conversing with whoever it was for a minute or two, he returned to the group while the limo turned around and raced back down the frontage road to where it came from.

"The leader first addressed his NASA associates, and they immediately climbed back over the wall to remove the net from the sphere. The man then walked over to Grandpa and his friend from Demopolis. The three men engaged in a heated discussion that lasted several minutes, after which the leader of the NASA group backed away from Grandpa and his buddy, all the while motioning for them to calm down and take it easy.

"It was said that everyone present looked on in disbelief as the NASA van and truck backed down the frontage road, leaving the sphere still sitting in front of the backyard gate. After the last cloud of dust settled, they all disbanded and left my grandfather alone to assist his friend from Demopolis in packing up the construction gear.

"The event was eventually forgotten by most folks, as was the sphere in our backyard."

"Well, I can honestly say you should find the report I've brought very interesting indeed," Peter told him before taking a good-sized drink from his second cup of coffee. Jack took the opportunity to take a drink from his Coke as well. "Not meaning to distract you from your train of thought, but I want to reassure you that despite my awareness of your family's history, I'm totally enthralled by what you're telling me here. So, continue like you are, Jack. This is great."

"All right, then," said Jack. "I remember looking toward the sphere while I thought about this NASA stuff. The top of it was bathed in the sun's bright light, while its lower half was mostly shadowed. Nothing but bare earth surrounded the sphere. Even the hardiest and most stubborn weeds refused to grow anywhere near it.

"As I flew higher through the air on the swing, I lifted my gaze past the sphere and over to the area just beyond the backyard. The frontage road was overrun with tall grass and weeds, as was the field that lay on the other side of the road. From there, the terrain sloped steadily upward to a thick wooded hillside less than an acre away. Back then, the hillside was filled with towering pines, elms, and oaks. It was like looking at your very own private forest. Since these trees hadn't been raped by the lumber industry, many were nearly as tall as the very tree I swung from.

"I remember feeling strangely at peace as I admired the forest's pristine beauty. By then my damp clothes had dried some, and I became aware of a fairly large object bulging from my shorts' pocket. It startled me, and I reached down into my pocket, being careful to maintain a secure grip on the swing while I pulled out a ring sucker. I'd purchased the item that morning while at the local barbershop with Grandpa. The sucker was still in its wrapper and originally resembled a giant ruby ring, though it was now quite misshapen.

"Even in the shade, the prism-like candy glistened within its plastic wrapper. Being thirteen and all, I imagined the sucker taunting me to open the wrapper and pull it out—like a challenge to see if I could do that without the damned thing slipping out of my grasp in the process. For some reason, this made me think of the lizard. I immediately felt depressed. I glanced back toward our house and where I'd searched earlier, but there was still no sign of it. I was now convinced it'd left our yard.

"I decided right then to go back inside the house. I slowed the swing down, disappointed the colorful little bastard failed to reappear. I would've liked to capture and detain it, at least long enough to impress Jeremy. Instead, I'd have to settle for a mere description of it, which would certainly be greeted with either cold skepticism or ridicule, depending on my brother's mood.

"I scanned the backyard one last time as the swing continued to slow down. I wondered which of my neighbors were now host to the elusive critter. I glanced over the wall to my right into the Palmer's yard. Despite the fact I didn't care for them much, I felt sad I wouldn't be able to steal a peek into their yard much longer. Within the next two weeks, the plan was for me to move in with my Uncle Monty and Aunt Martha in Tuscaloosa. I was fond of my aunt and uncle, but I truly hated the idea of leaving Carlsdale. *Completely* hated it. Yet, the opportunity to attend St. Andrews Academy, one of the finest schools in Alabama, was something I couldn't pass up.

"Grandpa was unreceptive to the thought of me moving away as well, even though I'd be living with his brother and sister-in-law, just an hour away. He finally warmed up to the idea after I assured him that I'd come back to visit almost every weekend. There really wasn't much choice in the matter, since there weren't any other schools in the immediate area offering the same educational opportunity as St. Andrews.

"The swing stopped moving, with me gazing absently into the prism of the wrapped, melted sucker held tightly in my hand. A wave of nostalgia swept over me as I realized things would never be the same for me. I'd sorely miss my grandfather and even Jeremy quite a bit, despite the fact I'd still see them on a regular basis. But, that was the point of it. I'd soon be a visitor to the place I'd called home for as long as I could remember.

"My parents mysteriously vanished without a trace one summer afternoon just before my first birthday. Jeremy remembered them a little, but his memories were becoming like faded snapshots. As for me, I didn't remember them at all. Much of what either of us had to go by came from some photographs and letters to our grandparents. The rest came from the stories Grandpa told us concerning our folks—that, and the local rumor mill in Carlsdale.

"Much of the information we heard about our mom and dad, Frank and Julie Kenney—in case you didn't know their first names, Agent McNamee—was positive in nature. Mostly, these were stories involving only our mom. There were other stories concerning our folks that weren't so good. These stories came mainly in the form of whispers behind our backs, which we'd only catch bits and pieces of now and then. This was especially true whenever we accompanied Grandpa into downtown Carlsdale, which at the time consisted of a grocery store, post office, barber shop, two gas stations, and a local branch of the First Alabama National Bank. These stories were dark in nature, and dealt with our ancestral home and the sphere in our backyard. Apparently, Dad and Mom's disappearance and the sudden appearance of the sphere happened at roughly the same time.

"What I gathered from these stories was that in June of 1987, my mom and dad brought Jeremy and I with them to Carlsdale from Atlanta to spend a couple of weeks with my grandparents. Something went terribly wrong, though, and a week and a half after our arrival in Carlsdale, my folks were officially listed as missing. The only noteworthy clue concerning their disappearance was that peculiar sphere in the backyard, which turned out to be not much of a clue at all.

"I remember when I was little, I would spend many afternoons and evenings in the tree house, armed with my toy binoculars. I'd aim them out toward the woods looking for any sign of my parents' return home, because that's the last place anyone saw them alive, as they headed out through the back gate with a picnic basket. When I got older, I'd still find myself looking out through my upstairs bedroom window from time to time. Often, I'd do this during late fall and on into the early winter months, when the oak's leaves were completely gone and I had a clearer view of the woods.

"I would've ventured out into the woods long ago myself, but Grandpa absolutely wouldn't allow it, saying he wasn't about to lose anyone else out there. Jeremy managed to sneak out once, but he didn't even make it to the woods. He made it half way through the field and came scurrying back, practically landing on his face as he climbed onto the back wall and dived haphazardly into the safety of the backyard. He told me he'd almost stepped on a copperhead and felt something else slither close behind him, and wasn't about to stick around and get bitten.

"I was thinking about all this shit when a sudden breeze picked up and circled all around me, bringing me immediately back to the present. The breeze was strong enough to gently push the swing back and forth, but the real strength of the wind was moving through the upper branches of the oak tree. I turned my head upward, fascinated for the moment by the rising and falling sounds from the wind as it weaved its way through the branches, bending them and rustling the leaves like a conductor directing a symphony orchestra.

"As I allowed myself to get caught up in the wonder of this experience, I suddenly heard a low growling noise coming from directly below me. I jerked my head downward to face the direction the sound was coming from, awkwardly pulling the tire-swing in the process. The lizard had come out of hiding and was glaring menacingly up at me just a foot or so away from my feet! It crept closer to within a few inches of my toes, baring its needle-like teeth again. Even through my youthful naiveté, I could tell the little fucker was getting ready to bite me.

"Without wasting another breath, I pulled my feet up and scrambled on top of the tire. I began climbing the rope of the swing, and lifted myself another six feet above the ground in a matter of seconds. Undeterred, the little monster jumped onto the swing, locking its claws on the tire's sides, its sharp talons puncturing holes through each side of the tire as it pursued me.

"By now, I'd seen enough to realize I was in grave danger, and I thoroughly regretted ever pursuing the mother fucker to begin with. I climbed even higher and before long approached the large branch that held the swing's rope. I looked down to see the lizard scale the rest of the swing and wrap one claw around the rope. As if sensing the difficult task it'd face by climbing the rope, it stopped to look up at me and then glanced over at the step boards nailed to the oak tree's trunk. The lizard then looked back up at me, eyeing me in such a way as if to let me know it intended to scale the tree in order to get me, if need be.

"I looked back toward the house, but it stood in solemn silence, confirming for me that no one inside was aware of my predicament yet. I then looked over at Banjo's food and water bowls and saw that he'd vacated the immediate area. Upon second glance, I glimpsed a portion of Banjo's head peering out toward me from his hiding place just behind the oak's trunk. Even from this distance, I could see the fear in his expression, for his ears were down lower than usual and his head was drawn back upon his neck.

"The lizard hissed loudly and reared back as if ready to leap and attack my feet and legs. I don't know why I didn't just yell or scream for my grandfather to come to my rescue. Maybe I was too surprised or frightened. But in any case, just as the lizard flexed its muscles to jump, it suddenly froze. It turned its head toward the woods, as if once again listening to some inaudible command. Within the next few seconds it released its grip on the rope of the swing and jumped down to the ground. It turned its attention completely away from me and then raced over to the sphere.

"I released my breath in a slow shuddering sound of fear. At the same time, however, I felt really angry with the little bastard for scaring the hell out of me. Foolishly and hastily, I slid down the rope and jumped off the swing. I picked up the metal bait container and set out after the lizard.

"It was slipping further away from me. It reached the sphere and with very little effort jumped on top of the barren globe. It turned and waited for me to arrive, and then let out one last malevolent hiss, its forked tongue sliding in and out of its needle-toothed mouth.

"Perhaps I ventured closer than I should've dared. But at the time I couldn't resist doing so since I was far angrier than scared. When I realized the lizard was about to leave the backyard, I looked for something to hit it with. I truly wanted to send a message that said it was definitely no longer welcome in our yard. I thought about hurling the metal bait container, but then thought better of it since the container belonged to my grandfather. I looked around frantically, but I wasn't able to find anything suitable for the task. All I was left with was the melted sucker.

"The lizard turned to face the wall and its exit to freedom on the other side. It glanced back at me tauntingly, as if daring me to try and hit it. This enraged me all the more.I threw the sucker, hitting the little dragon squarely on the back of its head. The piece of candy made a solid 'thunk' sound before careening onward beyond the backyard, landing somewhere in the field across the way. The startled monster yelped in surprise and hissed even louder at me. It then leapt from the sphere and out into the overgrown grass and weeds on the other side of the wall.

"I guess I felt a mixture of sadness and relief. But, I didn't have long to contemplate either feeling, for another one quickly overtook my senses. I was being watched. Not by anyone in the house, as I was certain that if Grandpa'd witnessed the confrontation between myself and the lizard, he would've known I needed some serious assistance and hurried outside to help me. Rather, I felt certain that whoever was watching me was doing so from just a short distance away from where I stood.

"I was completely sure of this, yet I wasn't at all sure on what direction the unknown voyeur was observing me from. Pretty weird, huh? It was like being intensely studied from every possible angle. The hairs on the back of my neck began to stand and tingle while a chill ran along my spine. I whirled around, but still saw no one. I was completely alone in the backyard except for Banjo hiding nearby.

"I finally decided I'd had enough of this shit, and as the oppressive heat was getting to me again, I bravely started walking back toward the house. It was then that I saw something out of the corner of my eye glistening in the sunlight as it lay in the dirt in front of the sphere. I turned to look at it and at first glance it appeared to be a piece of broken glass. But as I moved closer to it, I was surprised to find it was nothing of the sort. Instead, it looked like it was made of gold.

"I walked over and picked it up. The small oblong object was heavy for its size, and my experience in helping Grandpa polish an old coin collection from time to time helped me ascertain the object was indeed made of gold. I turned it over and over in my hands studying it, barely aware of the dark storm cloud coming toward me from the west. The front portion of the cloud was just then peeking over the majestic treetops at the edge of the woods, and I looked up only briefly in response to the soft rumble of thunder that filled the air in front of me. Satisfied it was just a light midsummer storm on the way, I immediately turned my attention back to the strange object in my hands.

"I was truly amazed at all of the little symbols and unusual designs that covered each side of the object. I stood where I was, totally mesmerized and unable to remove my eyes from it while I continued to turn it over in my hands. All at once, I felt very weird and dizzy... The next thing I remember was Grandpa calling out to me.

"'Jack! Jack!!' his voice shook me out my trance. 'What in the *hell* are you doing out here in the rain??'

"It was raining, all right, and by the looks of things, it'd been raining for quite some time. I was completely soaked with rainwater dripping from my head down onto the golden object. I was surprised to find that I still held it tightly. In fact, so tightly that my knuckles were ghostly white.

"Nervously, I cleared my throat while I fidgeted with the strange item, as I wasn't at all sure what to do with it. I looked over my shoulder and smiled sheepishly at my grandfather and absently shoved it into the depths of one of my shorts' pockets. 'Oh...nothing really, Grandpa,' I told him. 'I'm just trying to find out where that lizard took off to. I guess I look pretty silly just standing here, huh?'

"I'm sure I did from the look he gave me. I looked away from him, letting my eyes survey the glistening sphere and the muddy ground that surrounded it, until at last my gaze rested upon my drenched sneakers. I lifted one of my feet and was immediately surprised at how deep it'd sunk into the mud. The shoe made a low puckering sound as I raised it out of the muck. How long had I been there like this? It didn't seem like even a few minutes had passed since I picked up the object, and yet from the looks of my surroundings, I'd been standing there for more than an hour or two.

"'Well...are you going to just stand there all day hoping to sprout some roots, or do you think you'd mind if we went back inside the house, son?' Grandpa's voice betrayed his irritation, and who could blame him? He stood a few feet away from me, impatiently moving from foot to foot as though he were ready to sprint back to the farmhouse at any moment. The only protection from the rain he'd brought with him was that morning's newspaper, folded over and already soaked and dripping as he held it just above his head.

"'No...not at all, Grandpa,' I said. 'I'm ready to go in now.'

"He motioned for me to follow him as he turned and ran to the shelter of the oak. My legs felt like rubber as I chased after him. I wondered again as to how long I'd been standing in the rain. I could only venture a guess since the sun was completely blocked by the dark clouds above. Besides, my wristwatch was now missing. I felt completely disoriented and confused."

"That had to be very intense for you, Jack," Peter said, his eyes nearly back to their original clarity. They sparkled in a way that let Jack know he was definitely interested, absorbing every detail of his story so far. "Can you remember the intricate details on the golden object you were holding in your hands?"

"I wish I could, but I don't think so," he replied. "But, I'll bet I'd recognize them in a heartbeat if I ever saw them again."

"At a later time, I'd like to show you some early American artifacts we have in our Archives Center," Peter advised. "I'd be most interested to see how similar they are to each other."

"I'd definitely be willing to do that," Jack told him.

"Good. Let's keep this wonderful story of yours rolling," encouraged Peter.

"All right. I arrived at the base of the oak a moment after my grandfather did, and I walked over to where he stood. He eyed me sternly as I approached, the soaked newspaper held to his side with one hand while he petted Banjo with the other. 'Why were you just standing there, Jack?' he asked. 'What was so damned interesting that you'd completely ignore me calling you? Surely you must've heard me, didn't you?'

"Several different images crowded my mind. Everything from hunting the lizard throughout the backyard to simply standing in the rain as I held onto the mysterious golden object. All I could do in response was smile weakly and shrug my shoulders. 'I'm sorry, Grandpa,' I said. 'I don't know what came over me. One minute I'm chasing that lizard and the next minute I'm standing in the rain.'

"He raised his eyebrows as he continued to study me, although more compassionately than beforehand. He looked beyond me, back toward the area we both just ran from, and then shook his head. He smiled and chuckled to himself. 'Come on, son,' he said. 'Shall we make another mad dash for the porch? I'll race you!' He gave me a playful wink and then grasped me by the shoulder, guiding me over to the edge of the oak's heavy foliage. Water cascaded from the leaves above, forming several puddles just in front of us. On the count of three, we raced to the porch as the heavy rain pelted us mercilessly.

"Once we arrived soaked on the back porch, the rain storm immediately decreased its assault. Before my grandfather and I entered the back door to our farmhouse, the rain had nearly stopped, with only a light drizzle still lingering in the air outside.

"Grandpa had me remove my grimy shoes and leave them on the porch just outside the screened door. He did likewise before opening the door for us to go inside. I was glad to be indoors again as the strong aroma from dinner cooking on the kitchen stove quickened my senses and alerted me to my stomach's emptiness.

"The heat inside the kitchen was still stifling, even though a pair of floor fans stayed busy sending a cross breeze gathered from the main floor on through the kitchen itself. After checking on the status of that evening's meal simmering on the stove, Grandpa advised me to go on upstairs and change into dry clothes. He then headed for his own bedroom on the main level to do the same, with me following not far behind him.

"I headed upstairs, and as usual, the second, fourth, and seventh stairs squeaked loudly, despite my best effort to walk softly up the old mahogany staircase. Once I reached the second floor, I nearly ran to my bedroom at the southern end of the house. Even during the day, it was pretty creepy up there, especially along the hallway to my room.

"When I got to my bedroom, I walked over to my dresser and emptied my pockets of a few coins and the golden object. I set all of these items next to my parents' photographs and then took off my wet clothes. After leaving them in a small pile near the foot of my bed, I glanced out my bedroom window, which I mentioned earlier faced out into the backyard. The rain had completely ceased and the summer sun was in full force again. I started to turn back toward the door, but I noticed the time on my alarm clock read 5:31 pm. I couldn't believe it! I'd actually been standing by the sphere for almost three hours.

"No matter how hard I tried to search my memory, I couldn't account for the missing time or events. I finally had to let the matter rest, for Jeremy would be home at any minute and I was in danger of missing the start of dinner. I ran to the bathroom, and once I finished taking a shower, I put on a pair of clean jeans and a T-shirt. I grabbed the golden object off my dresser and shoved it into my pants' pocket, and was now prepared to head downstairs for dinner.

"I could already hear my grandfather talking to someone downstairs in the kitchen. A loud burst of laughter let me know that Jeremy was home. I started down the stairs, when suddenly I remembered my wristwatch was missing. I ran back up to my room and tried to locate it, checking all of the usual places, for I forgot that I'd last seen it when I was on the swing in the backyard. As soon as I sensed my brother and grandfather growing restless downstairs, I decided to search for it later.

"'Jack! What the hell's taking you so long up there?' Grandpa shouted from the bottom of the stairs. 'Supper's waiting and we're fixing to start eating without you!'

"I yelled back that I was on my way, and then hurried over to the top of the staircase. I was just in time to see my grandfather walking back to the kitchen. I clamored down the stairs, jumping past the bottom two before landing with a thud in the foyer. I headed straight for the kitchen as the creaking floorboards announced my rapid approach toward the dinner table. The full bodied aroma of spaghetti and meatballs filled the main floor, which kindled my raging hunger so much that I nearly forgot about the heavy object threatening to tear the fabric of my jeans' pocket. I steadied it with one hand to keep it from doing damage to my pants and walked into the kitchen and on over to the table already set for our evening meal.

"Jeremy leaned up against the kitchen counter, smoking his last cigarette before dinner. Tall, dark, and extremely good looking—at least that's what the ladies have always said—he'd be seventeen in September and already had a job lined up working full time for the local saw mill in town. Grandpa reluctantly agreed to allow him to drop out of school following the previous school year at Demopolis High School, since he'd nearly flunked out due to apathy anyway. 'What a waste!', Grandpa'd say, especially since Jeremy had shown such promise scholastically just a few years before. But, ever since he blew out his right knee playing football the previous fall, he'd pretty much given up on his education.

"Even as he leaned against the counter, the powerful build that had made him an all-state halfback was on display and hard to ignore. I often felt weak and puny in comparison to my older brother. Nonetheless, like many folks, I couldn't help but stare in admiration at his physique and rugged handsomeness.

"He, on the other hand, felt uncomfortable being so adored and idolized by me, and would meet my absent stare with a cold, icy glare. He allowed his piercing green eyes to cut through me like a pair of lasers as they peered out from behind his curly black shoulder-length hair. 'What the hell are you looking at, you little pecker head?' he asked me.

"As was often the case, I was unaware of my obvious adulation. 'Oh...u-uh nothing really, Jeremy.' I stammered. 'I-I was just wondering what you'd been up to today.'

"'Is that so? For a moment I thought you were wanting to kiss me or something like that,' he sneered. 'I thought I was going to have to come over there and kick your ass, little brother.'

"'Jeremy! Damn it, son, that'll be enough of that kind of talk!' Grandpa scolded him. He moved closer to the table, never taking his eyes off him as he made sure the two of us remained physically separated from each other. 'You'll not be ruining supper tonight, 'you hear? And, don't you dare think I won't enforce my words on you, son. I'll do it right here and now if I have to!'

"Jeremy looked over at Grandpa, whose icy glare was far colder than his own. He smiled and shrugged his shoulders as if to say 'I was only joking, man', and then took one last drag from his cigarette before mashing the remainder of it into a small ashtray sitting next to the sink. All the while, he never took his eyes away from Grandpa's unwavering gaze, until he finally glanced back over to me while I gave my best effort to pretend my feelings weren't hurt.

"Grandpa knew otherwise. 'Jeremy,' he said, 'you owe your brother an apology, and as soon as you do that, we can all sit down and start eating. 'You reckon you can handle that?'

"A slight, smug grin suddenly appeared upon my brother's face and he slowly nodded his head. I believe this was partly in amusement and partly in admiration for our grandfather's talent in manipulation. He considered resisting the obvious coercion, but his growling stomach strongly suggested he do otherwise. He gave in to his hunger. 'Sure, Grandpa,' he said softly, but still insolently, and then smiled directly at me. 'I'm sorry, Jackie, if I offended you in some way. Just don't patronize me so much, man. Okay?'

"'*Patronize?*' I thought to myself. That was such a big word for him to be using, though I actually liked him a hell of a lot better when he let his intelligence rather than his vulgarity shine through. 'Apology accepted,' I replied.

"With that taken care of, all three of us converged on the kitchen table, which was already set with steaming hot spaghetti and meatballs, buttered bread and fresh salad from Grandpa's garden. After a quick grace from him, we all dug in. At first, there was very little conversation among us, other than the usual 'please pass the whatever' and the obligatory 'thank you'. But after our initial hunger subsided, the scope of the conversation broadened considerably.

"'So, what've you been up to today, Jackie?' Jeremy asked. 'Grandpa told me you were trying to catch some strange looking lizard out in the backyard. What about it, little brother?'

"Ah...the moment I'd been anxiously hoping for had arrived! It was a very rare thing for me to capture center stage with my loquacious big brother around. I cleared my throat as I straightened myself in my chair, and checked one last time to make sure both my brother and grandfather were truly interested in what I had to say. Then, I began telling them about my backyard adventure that afternoon.

"Grandpa listened politely, occasionally rubbing his chin as if pondering how much of my narration was the actual truth and how much was an exaggeration of the facts involved. Jeremy, on the other hand, couldn't hide his complete disbelief in my story.

"It was pretty obvious to both myself and Grandpa that Jeremy thought most of what was coming out of my mouth was a load of fabricated bullshit. He finally looked away from me, turning his attention instead to the new décor in our recently remodeled kitchen. He seemed genuinely interested in the new cabinets, ceramic tile, and appliances, as well as the ancient crown moldings Grandpa had just finished restoring to their original beauty. All the while, the pompous smirk on his face broadened until he let out a sarcastic chuckle. Finally, he could contain himself no longer and completely gave in to a roaring fit of laughter.

"I immediately stopped talking, the wound from his blatant disrespect bringing an abrupt end to my story.

"Grandpa was obviously pained by my most recent hurt, and greatly annoyed by my older brother's rudeness. 'I'd like to know what you find so damned funny, Jeremy??' he demanded. 'You can be one insensitive horse's ass, you know?? *Well*?? What's up with that crap, son??'

"Not the least bit disturbed by Grandpa's rebuke, Jeremy continued to laugh until his face turned beet red. With the icy stares of Grandpa and myself upon him, he managed to regain his composure and soon told us both what he'd found so amusing. 'So, Jackie, you're telling us that you saw a lizard that looked like a miniature dragon??' he said. '*Ple-e-e-ase!!!*' He slapped his hand open-faced upon the kitchen table, rattling the plates and dishes as he did so. Again, he laughed uncontrollably until he struggled to keep his breath and tears formed in his eyes.

"'Are you sure it wasn't Barney or Puff the Magic Dragon out there in the backyard?' he taunted me. 'Maybe it was one of the Palmer kids' stuffed-animals being pulled on a string or something. *Oo-o-o-oh!*' He held his hands out in front of himself in mock fright, all the while ignoring my indignant pleas and Grandpa's growing anger, which was evident in the sullen redness spreading rapidly across his face.

"'I'm telling you the *truth*, Jeremy!! It was the coolest thing I've ever seen around here!' I cried. 'I wish you'd seen it yourself, because then you'd quit being such an asshole about it!'

"Both Jeremy and Grandpa eyed me sharply, for up until that time I'd never cursed in their presence.

"'The *truth??*' Jeremy mocked, and then stood up from the dinner table, walking over to his cigarettes and ashtray still sitting next to the kitchen sink. 'You're telling *me* the *truth*, Jackie?? Let me state here and now what likely *is* the *truth!*' He tapped out a smoke from the cigarette package and lit it before going on, signaling to Grandpa he was done with dinner.

"'Here's what I think happened,' he continued. 'I don't think there was *any* 'dragon-lizard' at *any* point or *anywhere* in the backyard, Jackie. I think this little story was no more than a lame cover-up of yours. It's just an excuse for getting caught jacking off by that sphere out back. Hell, Grandpa says he found you holding something just below your waist while you were standing out there in the rain. I'd bet a hundred dollars against a stale doughnut that the thing in your hands was just your 'pre-pube' tool!'

"Grandpa was now completely mortified for me, and was about to severely upbraid Jeremy once again. But, I stood up to him before Grandpa had a chance.

"'I'm not the one with the sticky-paged porn magazines stashed underneath his bed!' I said, daring him with a look to come over and shut me up.

"'*Fuck you, you little dweeb!!*' he shouted at me. Jeremy was about to come after me, and likely would've punched my lights out if it hadn't been for Grandpa's bear-like grip restraining him. As it was, he nearly knocked the remaining spaghetti and meatballs to the floor while trying to get me.

"'Boys!' Grandpa shouted. 'I've had enough of this shit! *Both* of you sit down—*nowww*!!' He eyed us both evenly, but soon focused his attention on Jeremy alone. The weight of his icy stare forced my brother back down into his seat at the kitchen table. He then motioned for me to sit down as well.

"A tense and uncomfortable silence settled upon the kitchen. None of us were hungry any longer. I fidgeted nervously while looking down at the half-eaten meal on my plate, as I waited for the horrible silence to end. Unwilling to look up, I could feel the searing heat of Jeremy's stare as he attempted to melt me into a molten puddle right where I sat. My story, which I'd hoped would impress my grandfather and especially my brother, had failed miserably.

"'What *were* you doing, standing in the rain over by the sphere anyway, Jack?' Grandpa finally asked.

"I looked up slowly, cautiously peering at both of them. The perturbed and angry looks from a moment ago had changed into more pliable and open looks of guarded curiosity. I took this as the perfect opportunity to play my 'ace in the hole' and reveal my hand to them. I stood up and carefully removed the golden object from my pocket.

"'Like I said, I wasn't playing with my privates out there,' I told them, and glanced coolly toward Jeremy before continuing. 'I was looking at this thing.' I cleared a spot amid the dishes of cold spaghetti and rapidly congealing tomato sauce, and set the object within the open space on the table.

"They both slowly stood up and leaned down toward it, a look of shocked fascination on Jeremy's face and one of surprised horror on Grandpa's. The object glowed softly on the table, surrounded by the remains of our foregone dinner. Its brightness seemed to slightly increase as the two of them leaned in closer to get a better look.

"Jeremy reached for the object, his hand wavering as if he expected it to disappear at any moment. It did. Just as he reached for it, Grandpa snatched it up off the table. He brought it close to his face as if to confirm and then reconfirm the reality of what he held in his hand. Jeremy stood dumbfounded, scarcely believing the old man's reflexes were that quick.

"I felt vindicated to some degree, although my grandfather's behavior was making me nervous. He kept turning the thing over and over in his hands while muttering under his breath. Before long, the crimson color returned to his face, deepening steadily until the veins in his neck began to throb.

"Both Jeremy and myself prepared ourselves for the rising anger we could see simmering to a boil within him, though he rarely got upset unless Jeremy purposely pushed him into a rage. There was something different about his demeanor this time, and it took us a minute or two to identify what it was.

"Grandpa began pacing aimlessly back and forth across the kitchen floor, whispering to himself as he wiped a bead of sweat from his brow. He seemed momentarily to have forgotten our very presence. That's when we recognized what we'd never seen in him before: fear. He was truly frightened.

"'Oh, my God. M-my God! Oh-h, m-my *God!!*' he stammered, gingerly passing the object from hand to hand as if trying to avoid any contamination from it.

"'What's wrong, Grandpa?' Jeremy asked him, moving ever so close as he tried to take the glowing object out of his hands.

"'That's close enough, Jeremy!' he warned. 'You have no idea what you're dealing with, son!' He tightened his grip on the thing, which seemed to make it glow even brighter.

"'*Come on*, Grandpa!' Jeremy pleaded, a slight adolescent whine creeping into his tough guy persona. 'I just want to look at it, that's all!'

"'I'm sorry, son, but whatever look you've gotten of it is going to have to suffice!' Grandpa told him.' This thing's an abomination, and I'll be damned for sure if I allow it to remain in our house for another minute!'

"The veins on the side of his neck truly looked like they were ready to explode. Suddenly, he turned toward the kitchen door and ran over to it. Just before opening the door he turned to face me. 'Where exactly did you find this thing, Jack?' he asked. 'If you've got it in your mind to tell me anything but the truth, don't do it! I need to know the specific spot where you found it.'

"'It was lying in the dirt, Grandpa, just in front of the sphere,' I replied. Although he strongly discouraged us from going near the sphere, it was far too late to lie about it. After all, he'd found me standing next to it while I was clutching the mysterious object in the rain.

"A deep dark cloud of sadness settled upon him as he heard these words. For a moment, he just stood where he was near the back door as if reconsidering his reaction to the situation at hand. He started to say something, but suddenly the rage returned to his face in full force. He threw open the kitchen door and stormed out onto the back porch. The screened door slammed behind him, the sharp crack of wood on wood piercing the air around us. Before either Jeremy or I could react, we heard his heavy footsteps going down the porch steps and out into the backyard. Alarmed, we ran outside in pursuit of him, the old screened door slamming again—twice this time—to announce our intentions.

"'*Stay right where you are, boys!!*' he yelled back to us. He'd already reached the trunk of the majestic oak and was about to disappear from our view. He motioned angrily for us to go back inside, yet without waiting to see if we obeyed him he continued on over to the sphere.

"Jeremy and I ignored his orders and followed him out into the backyard, where we pursued him from a safe distance. Moving as quietly as possible, we soon were able to close the gap between our agitated grandfather and ourselves. We came around the base of the oak in time to see him stoop down to set the strange object directly in front of the sphere in the fresh mud.

"Once he finished doing this, he stood back up and turned toward the farmhouse. The fading sunset formed a bizarre silhouette that I'll never forget, with the sphere and the glowing object before it. He took a step or two away from the sphere, but then suddenly stopped and whirled around to face it once more. In the next instant, he went back to the object and scooped it up out of the mud, hurling it over the stone wall toward the woods across the way while shouting something like 'Stay the hell away from here!'

"Neither myself or Jeremy wished to face any more of his wrath at this point, so before he turned around again we both bolted back toward the porch. We didn't stop running until we were safely inside the house.

"The stifling heat inside the kitchen had cooled down considerably during our short absence. Jeremy immediately moved over to the kitchen window and peered through it in order to gauge Grandpa's progress. I stood on the tip of my toes to get a clearer look over Jeremy's shoulder just as Grandpa climbed the last step leading up to the back porch. He swung open the screened door as he pushed his way into the kitchen, the door swinging back with another loud 'snap' as it slammed against the door frame again. He was obviously still very upset about this situation, but instead of encountering his anger, we were greeted only by his tears as they streamed down his face.

"'What's wrong, Grandpa?' I asked, alarmed but trying to broach the subject as tenderly as possible. I was shocked and saddened to see him crying, and could tell by the appalled look on Jeremy's face that he was just as surprised to see this. I couldn't remember a time when I'd seen anything like this, although I imagine he privately shed some tears from time to time when no one else was around.

"In answer to my question, Grandpa could only shake his head as he continued weeping. He momentarily looked away from us as he closed the storm door for the first time that day, turning the latch and dead bolt until they clicked into place as he glanced through the door's window to the backyard. He seemed apprehensive as he did this, as if expecting something to come out of its hiding place outside. I even wondered if he'd seen the lizard or one like it at some previous point in time, because it certainly appeared he was looking for something out there.

"I stood motionless next to my brother, watching Grandpa as he gazed out the storm door window, wiping his face and eyes with his shirt's sleeve. After a few agonizing minutes spent like this, he finally backed away from the door and looked over at us. 'Jeremy, go get the Winchester from the living room,' he instructed. 'I'll get the shotgun from my bedroom. We'll need to bring them both out here in the kitchen.'

"'What in the hell for, Grandpa?' Jeremy asked.

"Grandpa eyed us both tenderly and then gently shook his head. For the moment, he refused to answer Jeremy.

"'*Well??*' persisted my brother. 'Come on, Grandpa, you're starting to freak me out with this shit!'

"'Go upstairs, Jack, and close all the windows. Oh, and turn on the a.c. on your way back here,' Grandpa told me, for the moment continuing to ignore my brother.

"'Yes, sir.' I obediently replied. I sensed apprehension in Grandpa's voice, which only added to the growing exasperation threatening to overtake Jeremy. I alternated glances between the two before turning around to leave the kitchen. Jeremy reached out and grabbed my arm, preventing me from leaving just yet.

"'What the hell's going on here, Grandpa??' he demanded. 'Why do we have to close the windows, and what the fuck do you need a shotgun and rifle for, anyway??'

"Grandpa shook his head sadly from side to side before answering him. Likely only a minute or so passed while he did this, but it seemed like an eternity to me. When he tried to answer my brother, he seemed at a total loss for words. This only made the uncomfortable air around us thicken.

"He walked over to the sink where he reached out and closed the kitchen window, securely latching it. Then, he walked back over to the storm door and peered through the door's window once more, carefully scanning the porch and backyard for a second time. 'It's the 'Season', boys,' he finally said.

"Jeremy and I looked at each other for clarification as neither of us knew what he meant by this.

"'The '*Season*'?' Jeremy asked incredulously.

"'Yeah, Grandpa,' I chimed in. 'What kind of 'Season' do you mean?'

"'Just go close all the windows first and make sure the doors are locked upstairs, Jack. Jeremy, you and I will check everything down here on the main level. Once we've got the place completely secured, I'll tell you both a little bit about the 'Season',' he replied. 'Oh, and Jeremy, remember about the Winchester. Make sure it's loaded.' As soon as he finished delivering these instructions, he motioned for us both to move on out of the kitchen. 'We'll all meet back here when we're done. Jack, don't forget about the a.c., now.'

"'I won't, Grandpa,' I assured him.

"'Jeremy, you be sure to check the windows on the north and west sides of the main floor,' he reminded my brother. 'I'll check the windows on the south and east sides.'

"'Got it, Grandpa,' said Jeremy.

"The three of us left the kitchen to close the windows, with Jeremy shrugging his shoulders after I gave him a look that asked if he had any idea why we were doing this. Both he and I were very much bewildered by our grandfather's peculiar behavior and strange request, though we both were relieved that the air conditioner would finally be allowed to run throughout the old house.

"I ran upstairs and moved swiftly from room to room in order to finish my task as quickly as possible, despite the ever present spookiness of the second floor. Meanwhile, Jeremy started in the dining room and steadily worked his way to the living room, where he grabbed the Winchester and ammunition from the gun case.

"Grandpa was waiting at the kitchen table with his shotgun when Jeremy joined him in the kitchen. He told my brother to set the rifle next to the back door after first confirming the weapon was loaded. About the same time, the air conditioner kicked on and I'm sure they heard me running down the hall toward the kitchen.

"'All done, Grandpa!' I proudly announced.

"'Very good, son,' he told me. 'We're all set to defend ourselves should we be needing to do so.' Although always a handsome man, he looked like he'd aged ten years since dinner. His light gray eyes were still red from his recent tears, but the calm steadiness one could usually expect from him was rapidly returning.

"'Defend ourselves? From *what*??' Jeremy demanded again. He truly hated the vagueness of Grandpa's responses and was in no mood for any more mysteries. He was ready for the facts, and only the ones that pertained to why we were sitting in the kitchen with a pair of loaded weapons and every door and window in the house closed and secured. He knew it had everything to do with the strange gleaming object I'd placed in front of them on that very table less than an hour before, but this alone wasn't enough for him.

"'Let me begin by saying I'm truly sorry for breaking down like I did in front of y'all,' said Grandpa. 'The events of this evening have truly upset me. I honestly don't know what I'd do if something bad happened to either of you boys.' He paused for a moment to take a deep breath before continuing. 'I'll cut to the chase here boys, but first

I'm asking that you both stay away from the woods. For the time being, this includes the backyard as well.' He paused again and regarded us both very seriously.

"'Grandpa, what in the *hell* are you talking about??' asked Jeremy, disgusted by our grandfather's behavior as much as he was confused by the strange events of that evening. 'First of all, you go throwing that thing Jackie brought in here tonight out into the woods somewhere—and, it could've been worth a fucking fortune for all we know. Then, you bring up some shit about the 'Season' and whatever the hell that is. Now, you're telling us to stay away from the woods—which, if you'd stop and think about it, you'd realize neither one of us has ever even visited the woods out back. I mean, *you've* never even taken us hunting back there, ain't that right? We're always going to some place or another near Tuscaloosa or Demopolis for that type of shit. And, what's up with the backyard? Why in the hell do we have to stay out of there, too? Have the aliens finally come back for their fucking sphere, or something?? I mean, *come on!!!*'

"I remember Grandpa sat there glaring at Jeremy, sizing him up before responding to his barrage of insolent questions. After spending a moment sifting through his biting tirade, as well as recognizing the true worry underlying his questions and comments, he looked away from him and over at me. As for myself, I sat wide-eyed in my chair, still overwhelmed by the day's wonderful events and ever hopeful he'd somehow help me make sense of all that'd happened so far. He smiled at me before turning his attention back to Jeremy.

"'Perhaps you're right about the sphere, son, or maybe you're not,' he said. 'I reckon I've spent thousands of hours wondering if it had anything to do with the 'Season', or if it did come here from outer space, or any of a hundred other places—I don't really know. All I do know is that the 'Season' has been an event around these parts for a long, long time. I mean a very long time...long before that damned sphere showed up in the backyard, that's for sure.'

"Grandpa hesitated as if he suddenly realized he was about to divulge more information than he wanted. He paused thoughtfully and then continued, carefully selecting his words as if screening them before they escaped from his mouth. 'The legend of the 'Season' is very old, as I said, and the foreshadowing for it is often some sort of token that is easily recognized as not being from these parts. That thing Jack brought in here? 'Could be something like it, or maybe not. Regardless, knowing the 'Season's legend was all the reason I needed to get rid of the damned thing. It didn't feel right, keeping it in the house. I mean it felt *evil*. Even if y'all don't agree with me right now, perhaps someday you both will look back and realize I truly did the right thing.'

"Tears were beginning to well in his eyes again. The tip of the iceberg was all he'd divulged to us—I believe we both knew that. But, since this brought such obvious emotional pain to him, I knew he wasn't going to reveal much more to us that night.

"I didn't wish to upset him further, so I didn't ask any more questions. But I was extremely curious to know more about the 'Season' and its legend. I was especially interested as to whether the lizard, the golden object, and the sphere were all somehow connected to one another, as well as to my parents' sudden disappearance thirteen years earlier. It made sense to me, but I wanted to hear confirmation of this from Grandpa.

"'Grandpa...does this so called 'Season' have anything to do with Mom and Dad's disappearance?' It was Jeremy who broached the subject, and obviously, I was only slightly disappointed he'd done so.

"Grandpa regarded us both thoughtfully for a moment before he answered him. 'Perhaps,' he offered, 'but, I don't know for sure. It might, though—I'll be honest with you on that. It should make a stronger case for y'all staying away from the woods and the backyard for the present time.'

He scooted his chair back and stood up from the table. He walked back over to the back door and peered through the door's window once more. Outside, the early evening light was rapidly fading into twilight. It would be dark soon, and if there really was anything sinister lurking about our place, he surely realized the opportunity in gaining the upper hand was disappearing as quickly as the day's light. 'Jack', he said, still staring out through the window. 'Tell me once again about the lizard you saw today.'

"Before responding to my grandfather, I glanced cautiously at my older brother. Being ridiculed once fulfilled my daily quota for embarrassment tolerance, I'd decided, and I was willing to wait it out until Jeremy gave me his assurance that he'd be courteous and merciful to the storyteller this time.

"'*What??*' Jeremy snapped, again unnerved by me staring at him. 'What in the hell's up with you now, Jackie?'

"'I think Jack's expecting some common courtesy from you, son, before he starts telling his story again,' Grandpa explained. 'You'd be wiser to let him finish uninterrupted. I know *I'd* appreciate it.'

"Jeremy sighed and rolled his eyes. 'Let's just get this over with quickly, all right?'

"Grandpa and Jeremy looked over at me once more, and this time Jeremy did seem more interested in what I had to say about the strange lizard in the backyard. I would've relished the moment if this had been the first time I told my story. As it was, I could hardly wait to finish. This only exasperated my grandfather, who made me repeat several points and give him more specific details. Finally, once I'd finished my second narrative, I leaned back in my chair at the kitchen table and awaited the critical reviews, fidgeting quietly again as my audience stared back at me in silence.

"Grandpa spoke first as Jeremy looked on. 'I was hoping to see if the critter you saw today matched anything else that's ever been reported around this area, Jack', he said. 'I don't think I've read or heard about any lizards or anything else quite like that. I mean, I've heard that the Indians around here used to trade wild stories now and then about giant leeches and serpents living in or around the Tombigbee River, but no unusual lizards. At least none that I know of. I should've gotten up off my lazy butt earlier and taken a good look at the damned thing when it was sitting on the porch. But, that other thing you brought in here this evening...'

"He again looked outside into the growing darkness and then switched on the porch light as well as the backyard flood lights for a better view. Once he was satisfied there wasn't anything amiss for the time being, he shrugged his shoulders and turned his attention back to us, as we were both still seated at the kitchen table. I recall that Jeremy stared blankly at the wall behind me. He was as quiet as a church mouse, and I would've bet my life's savings he was wondering where exactly Grandpa had thrown the mysterious object.

"'Well, if I do catch sight of anything like what you saw earlier today, I intend to fill its sorry hind end with buck shot,' Grandpa advised as he moved back over to us. 'I reckon it'd be better, though, if the damned thing just stayed away from here. *Period!* Anyway, I'm taking the shotgun with me to the living room as I'm sure either one of you boys can handle the Winchester just fine if that lizard or anything else tries to come through the back door.'

"He headed for the dining room, which sat adjacent to the kitchen, glancing back toward us just before disappearing from our view on his way to the living room. 'On second thought, why don't you boys join me?' he asked. 'I'm sure we'll be up to the task of responding if needed, and I do believe the Braves are on television tonight. One of y'all should go ahead and bring the rifle, so that we'll have it handy.'

"I stood up and noisily pushed in my chair toward the kitchen table, drawing yet another look of irritation from my brother who stood up at the same time. I caught up with Grandpa and followed him into the living room. Jeremy lingered in the kitchen for a few minutes longer as he needed another cigarette. But once he was done clearing a few dishes from the dinner table, he grabbed the Winchester and joined us.

"Are you still with me so far, Agent McNamee?" Jack suddenly asked. "I'm probably boring you to death with this shit."

"Not at all, Jack," said Peter. "Are you ready for another Coke? I see you're done with the one you've got in your hand. I'm afraid that poor can's about to be split in two, by the looks of it."

"Yeah, I guess it is," Jack replied, smiling sheepishly again. "I might have another one in a little while, but I'm okay right now. You sure you don't just want the 'Cliff Notes' version of my story instead, to speed this up a bit?"

"Definitely not, Jack," Peter assured him, chuckling warmly. "On the contrary, your story seems to be working fine this way. You've got a captive audience sitting here before you, so please continue."

"All right, then. The living room was by far the largest room within our farmhouse, bearing much of the same design it was originally built with so many years ago. The ceiling stood nearly twelve feet high with hand engraved moldings similar in design to those in the kitchen, dining room, and most of the main floor. As I mentioned earlier, Grandpa had done some recent remodeling in the house, and the living room received quite a facelift. Grandpa kept the large mahogany gun case that had been passed down for generations, and he left a large oak bookcase that had belonged to his mother. Almost everything else was new. Although he was determined to keep our home's rich heritage intact, he spared no expense in redecorating the room with new furniture, draperies, rugs, and designer lighting to go along with a large home-theatre, sight and sound system.

"Jeremy came into the living room and found that Grandpa and I had taken our preferred places: Myself on the right side of the overstuffed sofa and Grandpa in his recliner-rocker, already with a magazine in his one hand and his pipe and tobacco pouch in the other. Jeremy took his own spot at the far left end of the sofa. Neither of us cared much for the middle, as a portrait of our great-great-grandmother sat above the sofa. The antique brass-framed mirror that hung above the mantel across the room leaned inward just enough to provide whoever was sitting in that unenviable spot with a clear view of her sullen stare. My brother and I tried to get Grandpa to get rid of the picture, or at least move it to another room, but he wouldn't do it. He told us he wasn't ready to part with his grandma's portrait. I think now he simply enjoyed watching our reaction whenever we caught a glimpse of her looking at us.

"'The game may be on already, boys,' I remember Grandpa saying to us. 'Why don't one of you turn on the television and find out for sure.'

"Jeremy picked up the remote control from the coffee table in front of the sofa and turned on the television, while I confirmed in the satellite guide that the game had already started. An instant later, our quiet living room was filled with the sound of the roaring crowd at Turner Field, along with the announcers' animated play by play. Within minutes, this single event had at least temporarily displaced the recent bizarre events, as Jeremy and I were soon engrossed by the game while our grandfather slowly leafed through his chosen magazine for the evening. Occasionally, he would look up to verify the score and current inning.

"Despite his seeming indifference, Grandpa got up from the recliner once thirty minutes had passed since we'd left the kitchen. He didn't return to the living room for a good ten minutes, indicating to me that he'd thoroughly surveyed both floors of the house before reclaiming his pipe, magazine, and favorite chair again.

"He maintained this routine for nearly two hours before I began to nod off. After he was reasonably certain we were in no immediate danger from anything that might still be lurking outside the house, he encouraged me to head upstairs to bed. Despite my sleepiness, I managed to flick on every light along the way up to my bedroom. I despised the upstairs spookiness, and often wished that either my grandfather or my surly brother would join me, at least until I'd reached the safety of my bedroom. But, since Grandpa's bedroom was downstairs and Jeremy rarely went to bed before the wee hours of the morning each night, I'd learned to cope with the shadows, bumps, and noisy creaks as best I could—regardless of the fact I was by then a teenager and no longer a mere child.

"After stopping briefly in the bathroom to brush my teeth, I moved swiftly to my bedroom, opening and then closing the bedroom door the very instant I was safely inside my room. Even in darkness, this was my sacred hideaway. This was my refuge, as none of the spookiness or creepy feelings that existed in various points throughout the house ever followed me there.

"I remember the moon was one night shy of its fullness, and beams of white light poured into my room, clearly illuminating everything around me. I got undressed, but before I crawled into my bed, I walked over to my window and looked out toward the majestic oak in the backyard. During the summer months, all I could usually see was the great expanse of the oak and its dense foliage. Only in fall and winter, like I mentioned earlier, was I apt to find a clear view of the woods rising beyond the backyard's rear wall.

"That night, however, I was able to see part of the wood's tree-line glistening in the moonlight through the gaps in the oak tree's leaves and branches. A gentle breeze pushed the branches back and forth, revealing even more of the woods' beauty than I'd expected to see, thanks to the brilliant light from the moon. At least that's what I originally thought it was.

"I pressed my face against the glass pane of my window for a better look at the light. It wasn't 'white' like the moon beams were. The light was golden in color and, through the small gaps in the oaks' branches, I could tell this unusual light was extremely bright. It seemed to grow even brighter by the second and soon rivaled the very brightness of the sun. The entire oak became a darkened silhouette in front of this magnificent light.

"I stood in awe at this strange spectacle and at first couldn't move. I wasn't even aware my mouth had fallen open. Nor was I fully aware of the soft moaning sound coming from deep within my throat. I finally managed to look away, but not before I heard my grandfather calling to me from the bottom of the staircase.

"'Are you okay, Jack?'

"'Yeah, Grandpa. I'm fine!' I replied, and moved quickly over to my bedroom door. I was just about to open it, when all at once the golden light that'd begun to fill my bedroom suddenly receded, and nearly disappeared altogether within the next few seconds.

"I walked over to the window and peered out into the backyard again. All that remained of the mysterious light was a much softer glow hovering near the edge of the woods where my grandfather had thrown the strange object earlier that evening. I stood there wondering what I should do next, as I wasn't sure if I should alert Grandpa and Jeremy about the light's presence. I didn't want to upset my grandfather again and I was certain that my brother would've climbed over the wall and tried to retrieve the object that most likely caused the strange light. Yet, if I didn't tell anyone about this, what could happen if the light was more sinister than beautiful?

"The light continued to dim, and since Grandpa was likely on one of his surveillance rounds when he called up to me, I decided to let the matter rest. I figured it could probably wait until breakfast the next morning, unless Grandpa or Jeremy encountered something unusual before then. I seriously doubted either one had seen the magnificent light, for I would've surely known it by now.

"I stood at the window for a few more minutes until the golden light completely disappeared. All that remained was the natural glow from the moon as it continued to bathe the earth below in its light. Satisfied that my home was safe for the present time, I moved over to my bed and quickly crawled under the covers.

"Once comfortable, I peered out toward the window once more. The light from the moon filled my room, illuminating nearly everything around me including the cherished pictures of my mom and dad that I kept on top of my dresser. I drew comfort from having those photographs close by, and never gave up hope my parents would someday be found alive.

"I laid there awhile thinking about them and all that had happened that day, until finally I drifted off to sleep. I remember thinking I heard a wild animal like a wolf crying from somewhere in the woods. Soon after, I was drawn into a night of strange dreams.

PART III

The Appointed Journey

"I must say, Jack, what I've heard so far has already made this evening's visit worthwhile!" Peter enthused. "There are quite a few references to the "Season" in the books I brought, by the way. Perhaps there'll be other things in your story that will tie in with each volume as well."

Jack smiled wanly. Although intrigued by what the agent told him, he still wondered if he was really doing the right thing. Retelling his story seemed to revive painful memories buried deep within his psyche.

"Well?" said Peter after Jack sat in silence for nearly a minute. "Are you ready to continue?"

"Yes. I think so," said Jack, drawing in a deep breath and releasing it slowly.

"Do you need to eat something first?" Peter asked him. "It's that time, I believe, and your mention of a spaghetti dinner got me thinking about food. Your grandpa must be a pretty good cook then, huh?"

"He's the best, in my biased opinion."

"Indeed... Well, are you hungry?"

"I am," said Jack. "But, I want to get this over with first."

"All right. I believe I can wait until then as well," said Peter. "Proceed."

"It'd been a restless night for me," said Jack. "The next morning I woke up clutching my pillow near the foot of my bed and I felt really tired. I remember lying there, stretching and yawning while listening to the throng of birds that sang noisily in the oak tree out back.

"'Hey, Jack! Get up son! Your breakfast is getting cold!' Grandpa called from downstairs.

"I could hear the clanking of silverware, plates, and dishes along with the muffled voices of my brother and grandfather down in the kitchen. I hurriedly got myself dressed and ran downstairs.

"'Good morning, Jack,' Grandpa told me. 'Your breakfast is already on the table.'

The aroma of eggs and bacon filled the air as my grandfather set the last steaming plate of scrambled eggs upon the kitchen table. Jeremy looked up from the sports page of the morning newspaper just long enough to nod an acknowledgement to my continued existence.

"'Good morning, y'all,' I said, and walked up to the table and sat down. As was usually the case, a short row of cereal boxes was lined up near my place setting. Grandpa handed me a small plate of bacon and eggs and I poured myself a bowl of cereal to go with this. I felt unusually hungry that morning and I eagerly dug into my food, wiping my eyes with my free hand to remove the last remaining traces of sleep from them.

"'How'd you sleep, son?' Grandpa asked me. 'Looks like you'd rather have stayed in bed and slept awhile longer.'

"'I'm fine, Grandpa,' I assured him. But as I sat there eating my breakfast, strange images kept racing though my mind—*very* strange and terrifying images. I was remembering bits and pieces of my dreams from the past night. I knew they all related back to the lizard and the mysterious golden object from the previous day.

"While I sat there at the table, I caught glimpses of a magnificent city with large buildings that reminded me of ancient ruins in Mexico and South America that I'd seen pictures of during the past school year. The images faded quickly from my mind, but for the moment, I lingered on a small group of uniquely handsome men and beautiful women standing near the top of a massive gold pyramid. I stood near the bottom of the pyramid's steps, looking up toward this group as they gazed back down at me in amusement.

"Suddenly, several streams of blood began to pour down the steps, splattering me where I stood. One member of the group, a male with long flowing white hair, threw something fairly large down toward me, smiling wickedly as he did so. I stepped aside just in time to watch the object slam against the steps nearby, splattering me further with more blood.

"The headless torso of a small child now rested carelessly across two of the steps. Sickened and horrified, I looked back up in time to see yet another object speeding toward me. The object splattered rain-like droplets of crimson upon me as I tried to protect myself. Once the object was within ten feet of me, I saw that it was the missing head from the child's body.

"'Jack, are you all right?' asked Grandpa. 'You look like you're a million miles away. What are you thinking about, son?'

"'Oh, nothing really,' I replied. But, I was startled by his voice. The images were gone completely. I would've thought they were gone forever, but after I recovered from the concussion I received two days later, I eventually remembered them.

"'Yeah, right, Jackie. I'll bet you were thinking about that goddamn 'Barney the Dragon' thing from yesterday,' taunted Jeremy. 'I'll bet you wonder if it wants to play with you again today, huh?'

"'I wasn't even thinking about the lizard.'

"'You were so.'

"'I was *not!*' I whined, glaring at him.

"'*Boys!*' Grandpa shouted. 'That's quite *enough!!*' He leaned in toward us both, and you could've easily heard a feather hit the floor at that moment—a truly rare occurrence at our home. He paused momentarily and then said, 'I'd prefer strongly that we not start this day like yesterday ended. Now, I want you both to leave the issue of the lizard Jack saw yesterday alone for now, and to completely forget about that other thing he brought in here last evening. Is that understood?'

'Jeremy and I looked away from him and briefly at each other before giving him an affirmative nod.

"'Good! And you can promise me now you'll both be staying away from the woods. Right?'

"'Yeah, Grandpa,' Jeremy sighed sarcastically. 'I can think of a thousand other things I'd rather do than battle a copperhead or whatever else is out there. You certainly won't be catching my ass anywhere near the woods!'

"Grandpa nodded thoughtfully as he studied my brother, perhaps debating again whether or not to rebuke him for his smart mouth. Since he received the general response he wanted, he turned his attention to me. 'What about you, Jack? I want you to swear to me that you'll stay away from the woods, *and* out of the backyard until further notice.'

"'I swear it, Grandpa,' I promised. It didn't seem like a big deal. I'd never visited the woods behind our home, and spent less time lately in the backyard.

"'Well, I reckon we've reached an understanding then!' Grandpa announced. He seemed quite pleased and resumed eating his breakfast. He motioned for us to do the same, so I returned to my cereal and Jeremy returned to his coffee and newspaper.

"After breakfast, my brother went to Demopolis to spend the day with Freddy Stinson. I helped my grandfather load up the dishwasher and then went upstairs to finish getting ready for my day. After combing my hair and brushing my teeth, I ran back downstairs and was about to run out the front door when Grandpa called to me from the kitchen.

"'Where are you running off to, son?' he asked.

"'I'm going over to Lee's house,' I told him. 'Is that okay with you?'

"'That'll be fine, son. Just make sure you're back here by four o'clock. All right?'

"'All right, Grandpa.'

"Lee Horne lived less than a quarter mile up the road from us and I hadn't hung out with him for the past few days. I was really looking forward to spending the day with my closest buddy. I looked down at my wrist to make note of the current time and realized I'd forgotten to put my watch on.

"'I'll be right back, Grandpa,' I told him as I ran back upstairs. 'I forgot something.'

"'What'd you forget, Jack?'

"'My watch. I'm going to go get it and then I'll go on over to Lee's.'

"'That'll be fine, son.'

"I couldn't believe I'd forgotten it. As I ran up the stairs again, I remembered missing it the previous evening as well, but forgot where I'd last seen it. I ran into my bedroom first, and after tearing my room apart, I checked the bathroom. Of course, the watch was nowhere to be found.

"I regretted not looking for it harder the night before. The watch was less than a week old, and was a birthday present from Grandpa. He'd wanted to give me something special that year since I was moving away soon. I'd had my eye on an expensive timepiece at a department store in Demopolis, so he bought it for me. The watch was loaded with all kinds of gadgets. My buddy Lee admired it and asked his folks if he could get one just like it when his birthday came around again in January. It'd be hard to replace and I prayed I hadn't lost it.

"I'd given up looking for it and was on my way downstairs to tell Grandpa the bad news when I suddenly recalled jumping off the swing when I last glanced at my watch. I figured it must've fallen off my wrist somewhere between the swing and the sphere. Relieved, I ran the rest of the way downstairs. My grandfather was sitting in his recliner, smoking his pipe as he read the newspaper.

"'Well, did you find it?' he asked without looking up from the paper.

"'Yeah, Grandpa, I found it,' I lied. 'I'll be back later.'

"'Four o'clock,' he reminded me, looking up just as I moved out from his direct view.

"'Four o'clock,' I confirmed, and swung open the front door, letting it slam behind me as I ran outside. It was noticeably cooler that morning, as the previous day's downpour had cleared much of the stifling heat and humidity from the air. I stood for a moment on the front porch, admiring as I often did the handsome beauty of the front yard. While the backyard was littered with a variety of junk, the front yard looked as if it belonged on the cover of some home improvement magazine. The lawn was perfectly manicured with several flower gardens, including two small gardens that encircled a pair of large maples set on either side of the long walkway that led from the front door up to Lelan's Road, the main road that ran along the front of our property.

"I set out immediately to retrieve my watch from the backyard without my grandfather finding out about it. He'd normally expect me to take the walkway to the road, although it wasn't unusual for me to occasionally cut across the lawn instead, going up at an angle toward the road. If I did that, it would put me near the southeastern corner of the Palmer's property.

"I moved across the lawn as inconspicuously as possible. Once I neared our yard's northernmost maple tree, I cut sharply over toward the Palmer's house, staying low to the ground to avoid Grandpa's detection. Once I reached the vegetable garden sitting adjacent to the Palmer's front yard, I quickly worked my way over to the stone wall and wrought-iron gate that led into our backyard.

"The gate was nearly identical to the one in the backyard where the sphere sat. I quietly went up to it and lifted the latch ever so slightly, but it started to groan loudly. My only option was to climb over the wall itself. I quickly scaled it and quietly jumped down to the other side, landing in a clump of weeds Grandpa left for Banjo to nibble on.

"I crouched down as I surveyed the backyard. So far, so good. Only the birds and insects were with me at the moment—especially the birds, as they covered the oak and chirped just as loudly as they had earlier that morning. I ran over to the tree, and just as I reached its outer branches, the birds flew off in a squalling flock. I thought for sure their cries would pull Grandpa from the comfort of his recliner. Fearing he'd venture out onto the back porch, I searched madly around the swing for my watch. As soon as I confirmed it wasn't there, I scrambled over to the side of the oak's trunk facing the woods. I peeked around the corner at the house, but Grandpa hadn't stepped outside yet. Relieved, I intended to resume the frantic search for my watch.

"The birds continued their clamorous departure from the oak, and I watched their hurried flight toward the west. Once they passed over the woods, they suddenly veered to the north as if they'd ran into an invisible wall. I couldn't believe it, so I continued to watch them, fascinated by their cries to one another as they changed direction in mid-flight. It amazed me that the tree, as large as it was, could've held so many of them just a moment ago.

"Soon, the birds were far enough away for me to start searching for my watch again. I groped through the weeds and grass near the tree's base, and around Banjo's food and water bowls, but there was still no sign of it. I was about to give up looking for it when I heard an animal whimper in pain near the sphere. I considered going back to the house for my grandfather, but knew I'd be in big trouble for breaking my promise to him. Even then, there was no telling if he'd feel the mysterious whimpering was worth looking into.

"The urgent cries of the animal told me I didn't have long to decide what to do. Despite my fear of what would happen to me if Grandpa caught me back there, I took a deep breath and ran to the sphere. I'd only taken a few steps when I suddenly froze in my footsteps, staring in disbelief at the scene before me. The previously immovable object had been rolled away from the wrought-iron gate and Banjo was now stuck between the rusted rails, crying and kicking his legs frantically into the air. My concern for him easily overrode the part of me that was surprised and frightened by what I saw. Once Banjo recognized me, he calmed down a little. I tried to pull on his legs, but he was wedged in tightly. In desperation, I started pushing on his butt. He finally slid to freedom on the other side of the gate, leaving a small cloud of black paint and rust flakes spiraling toward the ground.

"He stared back at me from the other side of the gate. I immediately panicked, and worried even more when I saw the gate had a large, rusted and bent, steel padlock holding it securely shut. I needed to get Banjo back inside the backyard before he ran away. Since the gate was too tall and awkward for me to climb over, I dropped to the ground and managed to squeeze my body through a space underneath it just big enough for me to crawl through.

"Banjo stuck his nose in my face and began licking me eagerly. I stood up, grimacing as I wiped his slobber onto my shirt. Undeterred, he jumped up on my chest to lick me some more. That's when I noticed the golden object from the night before. It was secured to his neck by several thin intertwined strips of leather, which I soon realized were the torn and frayed remnants of the wristband from my watch!

"Carefully, I removed the object from his neck, and as I did so I found my watch resting underneath it. I checked my watch thoroughly and was grateful it hadn't been harmed in anyway. It was still running with what likely was the correct time of 9:20 that morning.

"Next, I examined the object itself, which started glowing the moment I removed it from Banjo's neck. It certainly looked like the very same item Grandpa had thrown toward the woods the past evening. As I held it in my hands I soon felt dizzy again.

"Meanwhile, Banjo trotted away from me. I only caught a glimpse of this, but it was enough to shake me from the trance I was falling under. My heart pounded like a racehorse once I realized what'd almost happened again to me, and it pounded even heavier when I watched him push through the tall grass and weeds on his way to the woods.

"I shoved my watch into the right pocket of my shorts while I considered the fate of the golden object. It shimmered as if alive in my hands. I thought about throwing it deep into the woods where hopefully no one would ever find it again. But, since Grandpa had already tried to do that, I decided to hold onto it until I knew for sure what to do.

"'God...*please* don't let Grandpa find out about this!' I whispered to myself, and then slipped the thing into the left front pocket of my shorts. The object's weight threatened to tear the pocket. I had a hell of a time keeping it from bouncing out while I ran after Banjo.

"The grass and weeds rose up above my waist, and by the looks of things, no one had been in this area for quite some time. Only a weather-beaten washboard along with an exposed edge from its rusted tub was visible in the untamed field. This, along with the absence of any previous footprints in the rain-softened earth, made me wonder even more as to who had moved the immense sphere aside.

"Banjo hesitated just before disappearing into the woods. I ran as hard as I could to catch up to him, following the trail of broken weeds and grass he'd created. I tried not to think about the poisonous snakes and whatever else might be lurking about. By the time I reached the woods, Banjo was moving farther away from me, scaling the tree-covered hillside with ease. I was beginning to wonder if he was really worth it, but I pressed on behind him.

"'Banjo, stop!' I called after him. 'Come here, boy!! *Come here!!!*' He did stop, but only long enough to cast a brief glance at me before climbing further up the hill.

"'*Damn it!*' I hissed in frustration. I scrambled up the hillside, pulling up a few saplings in the process. I nearly toppled down the hill twice, grabbing onto a strongly rooted fern in order to steady myself. I could hear things slithering about in the thick underbrush near the ground, but I kept moving. To be honest, I was more concerned by what might come after me if I stopped than what I'd briefly encounter as I ran nimbly through the area.

"Before long, I reached the top of the hill, panting heavily as I glanced back toward the farmhouse. I was surrounded by the woods' unspoiled beauty, and in the sparse light that penetrated the trees' thick canopy, I finally spotted Banjo feeding nearby. I ran toward him, but once I closed in on the ornery animal, he scampered off again, moving deeper into the woods where even less sunlight could penetrate.

"I was clueless as to where he'd run off to next, and felt really nervous in the deepening darkness of the woods. I headed for the spot where I'd last seen his white-tipped tail. Suddenly, Banjo's voice echoed shrilly from an area just ahead of me to the right. Not able to see very well, I tripped on a fallen branch and went tumbling down a small embankment. I lay there momentarily in the cool moist undergrowth far below the towering trees. I remember a strong breeze rustled through the treetops. Once I heard Banjo calling out again, I got up and followed his cries.

"After moving through this dim-lit environment for a few hundred feet, I reached a steep embankment. There wasn't an immediate way around it, so I cautiously scaled it, praying to God Almighty that I didn't grab anything that could move or bite me. When I reached the top, Banjo was feeding on a clump of moss nearby. I brushed off my clothes, all the while scolding him. But, he still didn't respond. Instead, he moved even deeper into the woods.

"Mystified by Banjo's defiant behavior, I ran after him, shouting every obscenity I could think of to get him to stop. As I ran, I began to hear the faint rush of water, which steadily grew louder and louder until it became a loud roar. Banjo finally stopped at the edge of a clearing, where the morning light poured through brightly upon the ground below. I caught up with him and instinctively looked down. Below me was a drop-off of a few hundred feet. Luckily, I was able to grab onto a nearby branch that kept me from losing my balance. Clinging tightly to the branch, I carefully peered over the cliff's edge. A roaring river raged along its banks directly below me, crashing loudly against a series of large boulders as it made its way through a beautiful sprawling valley.

"I'd never seen anything like this, for the valley was filled with grove after grove of large fruit trees. Separating the groves from one another were huge meadows full of colorful wildflowers. The valley seemed endless, stretching for many miles in any direction.

"As my eyes followed the vast expanse of the valley, I was soon confronted with something massive shining within its midst, a mile or two away. I felt overwhelmed by wonder once I realized what I was looking at. An enormous spike-shaped tower of gold shimmered brilliantly in the morning sunlight. It stood majestically like a grand mountain and appeared to be encircled by a crystal wall, the top of which glistened just above the surrounding treetops.

"'*Wow!*' I whispered in awe. 'Will you look at that, Banjo...*Banjo?*' I whirled around. The goddamn billy goat was on his way down a flagstone path carved into the cliff's side. I chased after him, but due to the steepness of the path and Banjo's sure-footedness, he was getting away.

"'Isn't this just great!' I thought grimly, moving as quickly as I could toward the river below, and wondering how I'd ever get us back home. '*Banjo, stop!*' I yelled at him. '*Hey, wait for me!!!*'

"At the bottom of the cliff the path turned sharply toward the river. Banjo hesitated just long enough for me to catch up. I reached out to grab him, but he trotted off again! He was really pissing me off. I dove at his feet to stop him, but he still avoided my grasp.

"I scrambled to my feet and ran after him. I didn't catch Banjo until he trotted up to an old woman sitting on a rock beneath the shade of a large willow next to the river. He wagged his tail as if he knew her, and she extended her hand to pet him.

"I walked over to the woman, wondering who she could possibly be. I stepped under the drooping branches of the willow and was greatly surprised to find she wasn't old at all. It must've been her long white hair that at first glance threw me a curve. Now that I was within a few feet of her, I saw she was young—not more than a year or two older than Jeremy was.

"I soon realized I was staring at her, but couldn't help myself. She was stunningly beautiful, as pretty as any female I'd ever seen. Her features were perfect, with the most striking feature being her eyes. They were as blue as the morning sky—so blue that they seemed to glow from within her head. In fact, when I first stepped into the willow's shade, I thought her eyes were completely blue, without any trace of whiteness in them at all.

"The young woman smiled at me, perched on top of the rock and dressed in a long black satin gown that was tied with a matching sash at her waist. The combination of her hair, eyes, and dress would've intimidated a lot of folks, I figured, but I felt strangely comfortable and unthreatened in her presence.

"'Hello, ma'am,' I said shyly, raising my voice to be heard over the river's roar. 'My name's Jack.'

"'I know all about you, Jack Kenney,' she replied,' and, I know all about your brother, Jeremy, and your grandfather, Marshall Edwards, as well.' Her voice was strong and yet sweet as honey. For the moment, she remained seated upon the rock.

"'How'd you know my last name, and my brother and my grandpa? Have we met before?' I asked, surprised and now deeply curious.

"'I know a lot of things, Jack,' she replied. 'You might say it's a 'gift' I have. Just don't let it frighten you, okay?' The young woman chuckled lightly, the warm smile never leaving her face.

"'What's your name?' I asked. I was already completely captivated by her.

"'My name is Genovene.'

"'And your last name?' I asked, smiling sheepishly. 'You do have a last name, don't you?'

"'No, I don't have a last name,' she laughed. 'I've actually never needed one where I come from.'

"'Where's that?' I asked her.

"'When you were up on the hill, did you see the golden tower in the distance? That's where I live. That's my home, Jack,' she said.

"'*Wow!* It must be *so-o-o* cool to live there!' I said. Suddenly, I thought about my promise to Grandpa and my reason for being there in the first place. 'Maybe I can visit you again sometime, and you can show me where you live,' I told her. 'I need to get back home before my grandfather finds out I'm not at my friend Lee's house. Besides, Banjo's likely to run off again at any moment.'

"Genovene chuckled and pushed aside the willow's branches closest to her. 'He already has, Jack,' she said, pointing to a large meadow across the river. 'Banjo is playing over there as we speak!'

"Sure enough, when I turned around, Banjo was gone. I looked across the river and saw that he was playing with several other animals: a fawn, a rabbit, a raccoon, and a fox. I couldn't believe my eyes! The animals should've had nothing to do with one another. A bigger concern, though, was how he ever got there without me knowing it.

"'You see,' she said. 'Banjo's having a good enough time, don't you think? Besides, your grandfather's been busy tending the garden on the north side of your house for the past ten minutes. As you know, he'll likely be working in the yard until it's time for your supper, Jack.'

"I thought about what she told me. I assumed she was using her 'gift' to give me this information, since it was true Grandpa often worked in the yard for hours at a time. But, what about my last words to him, when I said I was going over to Lee's place? What if he found out I wasn't there?

"'Did you tell Lee you were coming over today?' she asked me.

"'Well, no,' I said. 'At least I don't think I did.'

"'Well, then, there's your answer, Jack!' She leaned forward, looking intently into my eyes, the deep blue luminescence of her own eyes glowing in sharp contrast to the lightness of her fair hair and skin. 'Why not come and see my place today? It won't take long to get there from here. You and Banjo will be back home before anyone misses you.'

"I thought about this for a moment, carefully weighing the pros and cons of taking her up on the offer. In the end, I found it impossible to resist her charm. I shoved my hands nervously into my pockets and tentatively nodded 'okay'.

"She stepped down from the rock and straightened her gown. At that moment, a gentle breeze swept through the area, gently lifting and pushing the willow's branches. She was slightly shorter than my brother, but still stood six inches taller than me.

"Genovene looked away from me, turning her attention instead to a nearby bridge. From the instant she stepped down from the rock, I watched her. I couldn't help myself. Her figure was as stunning as her face, and the way she moved, so sultry and graceful, stirred something deep within me. I even thought for a moment my heart had skipped a beat. My grandfather would've likely described her as 'divinely endowed'. I didn't think my brother would be quite so nice in his compliment, although his assessment would've roughly been the same as Grandpa's. She would be the ideal female for Jeremy's pet phrase of being built like a 'brick shithouse'.

"She suddenly turned back toward me, raising her eyebrows in a knowing way as if to remind me that she could easily read my thoughts. '*Men!*' she whispered in mock exasperation.

"I was so embarrassed. My face and the back of my neck immediately felt warm, and a ring of sweat formed quickly along my hairline. I looked down at the ground and for the moment wished I was a million miles from there.

"'Don't worry about it, hon',' she assured me, gently grasping my arm to pull me closer to her. 'After all, you're only human. Surely you've heard that every good boy gets his just dessert. Perhaps this could be your lucky day!' She smiled and playfully winked at me. I smiled back, overwhelmed by the typical hodge-podge of emotions most boys that age battle with.

"'You'll have a great time, Jack, I promise you,' she said. 'Now, there's one thing you'll need. Did you bring your talisman?'

"I had absolutely no idea what she was talking about. 'What do you mean, a talisman?' I asked.

"She studied me intently for a moment. 'Why, of course,' she said. 'I suppose you might not know what a talisman is if you'd never seen one before. But, I do believe you've seen one, and I believe you've seen it very recently. It's important that you have yours, Jack, or you'll never make it through the gates to my home.' She pulled out a golden object from a concealed pocket in her gown. 'It looks like this.'

"My eyes grew wide. The golden object she had in her hand was identical to the one I had in my pocket. I excitedly pulled it out and showed it to her.

"'That's it!' she enthused. 'Go ahead and hang onto it for now, and let's be on our way!' She took my hand and led me out from under the willow tree and back into the bright summer sunshine. I noticed now that her hair wasn't completely white after all. Instead, it was more like the color of white opals, with rainbow-like highlights that shimmered as she moved.

"We walked over to the bridge. The roar from the river grew louder as we approached the stone structure. The rushing water pounded the bottom of the bridge relentlessly, lifting the Spanish moss and thick green ivy that hung down along its sides. Each individual stone on the side of the bridge had intricate designs etched upon them, forming an ornate pattern that covered the entire bridge wall.

"The bridge was just wide enough to accommodate one person at a time, so Genovene got on first and I followed her. I found it hard not to stare at her shapely butt and slender long legs through the sheerness of her gown. If it hadn't been for the brief glimpse I caught of something gleaming in the water next to the bridge, I might not have ever been able to pull my gaze from her lovely backside. As it was, I was just in time to see what looked like an extremely large snake moving under the bridge. It was bathed in a brilliant array of blue, green, silver and red colors.

Suddenly, a thunderous roar shook the bridge to its very foundation. Terrified, I turned to run off the bridge. For I knew there was no way in hell the roar I just heard belonged to some snake. Genovene reached out and grabbed my arm to prevent me from fleeing.

'Please don't let her scare you,' she told me. 'The serpent below is harmless. Her name is Vydora and she protects our land from any unwanted intruders.'

"'That's a *serpent?*' I asked, still poised to flee at any moment.

"'Yes,' she said. 'Perhaps your people would rather call her a dragon of sorts.' She chuckled softly as if this was a private joke, but I sure as hell didn't think it was funny. 'Oh, come on, Jack. *Lighten up!*' she teased. 'I swear to you that Vydora would never harm you!' Her seductive smile quickly won my trust again. She moved up close to me, clasping my hand with hers once more while locking my gaze with her own. Right then, my fear and apprehension melted away. Still holding my hand, she turned around and led me to the other side of the river.

"Once across the bridge, we moved onto a smooth gravel path that divided the sprawling meadow into two large sections. On either side of the path stood a pair of small figures dressed in black cloaks covering their entire bodies except for their hands, which were ivory-white and bore long transparent fingernails. These figures looked a lot like small children hiding beneath the cloaks, and when Genovene talked to them, they spoke in animated high-pitched voices and in a language completely unfamiliar to me. After she'd finished speaking to them in the same language, they bowed before her and then retreated into the tall grass and wildflowers of the meadow.

"'These are my servants, Jack,' she said, 'and I've just told them to take care of Banjo until you return from visiting my home. I assure you that he'll be in good hands. Besides, he's having a great time with his new friends.'

"She was right. Banjo did appear to get along nicely with his newfound buddies. He looked over at me briefly and then went back to playing in the meadow, the five animals frolicking together under the watchful eyes of Genovene's servants. I couldn't get over how ridiculous this scene looked, but I felt Banjo would be all right there.

"'No offense intended, Genovene, but are your servants dwarves?' I asked. 'I mean, they seem like little kids.' I figured they were deformed, since their clothing covered them up and their voices were so shrill.

"'No offense taken,' she said. 'They are like children in so many ways.' She laughed softly and then grew silent, as if seriously reflecting on my observation. 'Actually, Jack, they're very different from most people,' she told me. 'You might say they're a unique race of mankind, and you'd probably be surprised to learn that they've been here in this region for many years. No, they're not midgets or dwarves—at least not according to what you're used to. The Indians of the southern nations call them '*miahluschkas*', and for centuries they've guarded the sacred places throughout America.'

"I turned to look again at them as they stood in the meadow near Banjo and the other animals. They in turn, looked over at me. I knew instinctively they studied me, perhaps reading my thoughts and feelings just like Genovene could do. It was pretty creepy since their hoods completely shaded their faces.

"'Come along, now,' said Genovene as she gently tugged on my arm. 'We need to be going so you'll have enough time to see my home.

There'll be other things on the way to my village that I'm sure will fascinate you as well.'

"Just then, seemingly out of nowhere, a ball of brilliant light appeared less than a hundred feet in front of us. The light bounced back and forth through the air, thickening into a rainbow-like band as it drew closer. Once it was less than twenty feet away, the band spiraled directly toward us, and then changed into a swirling swarm of colorful butterflies.

"I couldn't believe my eyes, stopping to watch the graceful insects circle above our heads and then speed off toward the bridge. I turned in time to see them veer skyward at the river's edge, where the butterflies changed back into their light-like form.

"'See what I mean?' said Genovene, obviously pleased by my reaction. 'We have so much here to delight you—many incredibly *wonderful* things that you'll experience before this day is over. Just remember, there's no need to worry about Banjo, Lee, or your grandpa. Everything will work out just fine!'

"We walked along the path through the meadow and talked about my carefree summer days and the upcoming move to Tuscaloosa. I could scarcely believe the beauty and wonder that surrounded me, for I'd never seen any place like this in Alabama before. For that matter, I'd never seen pictures of a place like this anywhere else, either. You're probably thinking I should've known I was headed for trouble after what I'd already experienced up to this point. But my mind was already clouded by desire, both for Genovene and for an adventure any teenage boy would die for.

"We soon reached a large grove of enormous fruit trees standing at the western edge of the meadow. Almost all of the trees were at their fullest maturity, and each one stood between forty and fifty feet high. Their thick branches were nearly overloaded with purple fruit that looked like giant tomatoes.

"'These are somila trees and have been part of my homeland for hundreds of years,' Genovene told me and then motioned for me to stop walking. 'Sh-h-h! Listen closely and tell me what you hear.'

"I did as she asked. Almost immediately, I heard something low and rhythmic, but it took me a moment to figure out what it reminded me of. 'I guess it sounds like someone's breathing,' I finally told her.

"'Very good!' she enthused, and seemed surprised that I guessed correctly. 'According to legend, the sound we're hearing now is the collective breaths of all the trees at sleep,' she went on to explain. "When I was a little girl, my brothers and sisters and I spent a lot of time in this grove playing hide n' seek, or simply enjoying the peaceful environment that the grove provides.'

"Now that I was aware of the sound, I could scarcely believe I hadn't noticed it when we first entered the grove. Not that I wasn't already impressed with the unusual size of the trees. I couldn't recall ever seeing fruit trees this tall, and definitely none that had trunks anywhere near as thick as these were. Every one of them was at least eight to ten feet in diameter. The trees lined both sides of the path and extended quite a distance in either direction.

"Genovene motioned for us to begin moving again, and as we moved deeper into the grove the trees grew closer to one another, eventually allowing only trickles of sunlight to seep through their dense foliage. We walked in silence, listening to the trees breathe while they 'slept'.

"Before long, we reached the end of the grove, where the trees were much more widely spaced apart. Suddenly, I felt like I was being watched from all angles, like I did the previous day in my backyard. I even looked over my shoulder several times, but didn't see anyone—not even the tiny miahluschkas that served Genovene.

"'Are you okay?' she asked, frowning slightly as worry crept onto her face.

"'Yeah...I guess it's just a little spooky in here,' I replied. My male pride had been triggered by my aroused libido, and I didn't want her to think I was a puss. So, I tried to change the subject by asking a question I'd been thinking about for the past few minutes. 'So, Genovene, how many brothers and sisters do you have?'

"'There's two of each, actually' she said. 'I'm the oldest child, and therefore the most privileged. But, each of us have an equal role in ruling our village and the surrounding areas for our father.'

"'Where are they now?' I asked.

"'My sisters and my oldest brother are visiting another grove,' she said. 'My youngest brother is presently at home in our village.'

"I nodded that I was satisfied by her answers. I then asked the question I've since learned most women loath. 'How old are you, if you don't mind me asking?'

"She started laughing again, apparently amused by my persistence to learn as much as I could about her. 'Let's just say I'm old enough, and wise beyond my years,' she said. 'But, I'm still young enough to thoroughly enjoy the companionship of someone like yourself.'

"I blushed as soon as she said this, and wished I could control my reactions better. She moved swiftly to ease my awkwardness by lightly massaging my shoulder.

'Enough questions,' she said. 'Save them for later, sweetie.'

"I found that I truly enjoyed her presence and attention, as several times so far she had brushed up against me, her shapely form pressing up and lingering against my body. Genovene's invasion of my personal space thrilled and excited me, even though the powerful and untamed emotions she stirred made me nervous.

"We exited the grove side by side, and the path took us downhill into another meadow. This one was even larger than the first we encountered. In the midst of this meadow lay a large pond, with two schools of ducks and geese swimming through cattails and lily pads near its shore. A number of weeping willow trees dotted the pond's shoreline, and a long wooden bridge stretched across the pond from the path to its continuation on the other side.

"I could clearly see the immense gold tower looming majestically less than a mile away. The tower dominated the area so much that it reminded me of a postcard my uncle once sent me depicting Mount Rainier in Washington state, except in this case, the shimmering golden sides of the soaring edifice replaced the glistening snowcaps of the mountain. I was in such awe I slowed to a near halt. Only the gentle prodding of Genovene brought me up to the pond's edge.

"The bridge over the pond was an unusual rope and wooden suspension structure. The roped portion was double-twined together and then interlaced through the floor and walls of the bridge, while the wooden portion appeared to be made from a sturdy grade of oak. The entire bridge was covered with intricate carvings very similar to the ones on the stone bridge we'd crossed earlier.

"Genovene stepped onto the bridge and I followed close behind her. The structure creaked and swayed noticeably as we traveled to the pond's other side. When we were nearly a third of the way across, I leaned over the side and looked down into the water below. It was so clear I could see almost everything, including the very bottom of the pond. It was like looking down on top of a huge aquarium, as the pond was stocked full of fish in all sizes, shapes, and luminous colors. A few of the larger fish moved near the surface, their sides gleaming brilliantly as they swam. One of them eyed me in such a way that I grew quite uncomfortable and was forced to look away.

"'Did you know, Jack, that your mother and father once visited my village long ago?' Genovene suddenly asked me, completely catching me off guard.

"'Wha-a-at?? Th-they *did*??' I gasped. For the moment, I forgot all about the fish. 'When was that??'

"'I believe it was twelve years ago,' she said. 'I was just a young girl then. But I remember them both clearly, as if it were only yesterday.'

"'Tell me about them...*please!*' I begged her. I knew so little about my parents, despite the stories my grandfather, as well as my uncle and aunt had told me. I probably looked like a starving puppy begging for table scraps to her, but I desperately wanted to learn everything I could about them, no matter where it came from.

"'Well, I only met them once,' she said. 'So, I didn't know them personally. I do remember both of them being really nice people. Your mother, as I recall, was a pretty, sweet, and intelligent woman, while your father was quite charming and witty, as well as very handsome.'

"She turned and looked at me, slowing down her pace as she did so. She smiled compassionately at me, for I couldn't hide my hurt and sorrow given the fact I missed my parents terribly. I appreciated her gentleness in telling me this information about my folks. But, there was something in the way she looked at me—something barely discernable in her eyes—that told me she hadn't revealed everything she knew about my mom and dad.

"Genovene reached back and gently took my hand before turning her attention to the shoreline on the other side of the pond, picking up her pace slightly, which I absently responded to. Nothing more was said between us until we reached the shore and were back on the path again. In the meantime, I let my thoughts drift back to the fish I'd encountered a few minutes before. It was more of a hungry look it'd given me, I finally decided. *Very* hungry.

"The gravel path lasted for another hundred yards or so, steadily heading uphill until it ended at the foot of a large rock formation with a grand staircase cut into the middle of it. She led me up to the staircase, pausing briefly at that juncture before continuing our ascent.

"'Once we climb the stairs before us, we'll be on the final walkway to my village' she said. 'We should be there in the next few minutes, Jack!' She was filled with such enthusiasm, such girlish giddiness, as she wrapped her arm inside mine. Lifting her gown slightly, she began walking up the stairs with me drawn tightly to her side. I was again distracted enough to think of nothing else, including the fish, the recent mention of my folks, and the growing heaviness of the talisman in my pocket.

"As soon as we reached the top of the staircase, we stood at the edge of a long corridor of colossal trees. I thought these mammoths were quite similar to the giant redwoods of northern California I'd seen in pictures, although these trees were much more unique. Genovene called them carnacs, and they were completely green. They sort of reminded me of giant stalks of broccoli and they soared almost two hundred feet above us with trunks that were easily twenty to thirty feet in diameter.

"The path resumed once more, but it was now a smooth floor of polished white marble. It gradually widened along the corridor, allowing the necessary space to accommodate the breadth of the massive trees, whose long lofty branches formed a connective canopy across the corridor. Long slender vines and Spanish moss hung down from these branches. What really captured my attention, though, was a pair of magnificent golden gates less than a quarter of a mile away.

"'There's the entrance to my home, Jack!' said Genovene as she pointed to the gates. 'See, I told you it wouldn't take long!' She literally beamed with excitement, so much that for a brief instant I could've sworn she actually *glowed*! For the first time, I felt a little freaked out about all of this. I mean, the enormous trees, the gates, and now her unearthly appearance—not to mention the incredible tower and all. It seemed like I'd stepped into some children's storybook. I immediately rubbed my eyes, and then thanked God when I looked at her again. She appeared normal, and I believed my eyes had somehow played a trick on me.

"I remember I was still staring at her when suddenly something scurried up the tree next to me. I turned to look, but whatever it was disappeared before I could clearly see it. Then, it happened again. Only this time, whatever it was scampered across the marble floor on its way to the other side. It quickly vanished behind the trunk of one of the carnac trees.

"Genovene directed my attention to the treetops, where at first I didn't notice anything unusual. Once my eyes adjusted to the corridor's dimness, I spotted a pair of nest-like huts perched high up in the trees. In each sat several miahluschkas, their hooded faces shrouded as they watched us move closer to the village entrance.

"'How'd they get up there?' I asked.

"'Like that,' she advised, and then pointed to a nearby tree. A pair of miahluschkas scaled the tree from the ground to the very top at incredible speed. She next pointed to the treetops just beyond the pair I'd already noticed. More miahluschkas were swinging from tree to tree using the vines that hung down from the highest branches to propel themselves. Like agile tree monkeys they moved effortlessly. I watched another one descend from its hut to the floor in a matter of seconds.

"'They're really *amazing!*' I told her. I scarcely could believe they possessed such incredible agility.

"'They're the only guardians we've ever needed out here,' said Genovene. 'They're able to swoop down on any unwelcome intruders when needed.'

"I remember how this puzzled me. 'That's a little hard to believe,' I told her. 'Obviously, I see how quick they move. Don't you think anyone with a gun could mow right through 'em?'

Despite their unusual athleticism, I couldn't picture them stopping a fierce intruder unless by sheer numbers alone.

"'You'd be surprised, Jack,' she said. 'The miahluschkas have very sharp teeth and claws. I've seen them tear apart a pack of wolves before. It wouldn't be a good idea to underestimate our little guardians.'

"She smiled and playfully winked at me once more, but I could tell she meant for her words to be taken very seriously by me. I hoped I hadn't offended her. Meanwhile, more and more miahluschkas came out of their hiding places while she continued to lead me closer to the village entrance unperturbed. I looked up toward the treetops and saw the hut-like nests were becoming more abundant. The miahluschkas' shrill calls to one another echoed loudly throughout the corridor, which made me consider further Genovene's warning.

"The twin gates soon came into clear view. Each one was spectacular in its own right, rising more than two hundred feet into the air and stretching at least half that wide across. The crystal wall encircling the village was just as tall as the gates, and behind the wall, I could see some of the village buildings shimmering in the sunlight. I truly wished Grandpa and Jeremy were there to see this with me, I was filled with such wonder.

"'Is it not marvelous, Jack?' she asked.

"'It's *totally* awesome!' I agreed.

"She nudged me forward until we stood directly in front of the massive gates, and then she led me up a short flight of marble stairs that brought us right up to them. I moved up to the left gate and touched it. The gate was warm, but not like I expected it to be, gleaming as if it absorbed the sunlight. I let my fingers caress the soft metal and the lines and curves of the intricate designs covering the gate.

"As I let my hands follow and trace the gate's designs, I looked up and noticed three sets of huge rings, that resembled door knockers, attached to the gates from between twenty and eighty feet above my head. I wondered what they were intended for, since only a mythical giant would be suited to use them to open or close the gates.

"Genovene stepped over to me and asked me to take my talisman from my pocket. I noticed that the designs on it were the same as those on the gates.

"'Your talisman is a key to the gate before you,' she told me, whispering softly in my ear. 'We've taken great pains to make sure our glorious village remains a secret. Only a select few ever get to see it. Can you imagine the stories you'll have to tell, along with experiences the vast majority of people will never share with you? You're truly special, Jack. Enjoy the moment. It's *your* special day. Now, come follow me.' She pulled away from me, holding her talisman as she walked over to the right gate and stood directly beneath the huge ring on that side.

"'Take your talisman and come up here to the other gate. Then, wait for my signal,' she instructed. 'As soon as I count to three you must put your talisman into the slot located below the gate's handle.' She followed my progress with her gaze as I walked up to the left gate again and located the slot, which was nearly a foot above my head. I pulled my talisman out of my pocket and looked over at her. She regarded me seriously. 'Remember, the talisman is your only ticket to gain access to everything that awaits you beyond these gates,' she admonished. 'So, be sure to insert it into your slot at *precisely* the same instant I put mine in.'

"'Okay,' I told her. I remember I tried to slow my breathing so that my excitement wouldn't get the better of me.

"'One...Two...*Three!*'

"A single 'click' sounded as both objects were inserted into the gate. With a loud groan, the massive gates of gold slowly opened. We backed up out of the way, and the bright glow from the village poured out into the corridor, completely bathing us in golden light. Genovene gently took my hand and led me just inside the village entrance. For the moment we just stood there, surveying the surreal beauty of the village while the gates slowly closed behind us."

PART IV

The Golden Village

"Agent McNamee, I do believe I'm ready for another Coke," said Jack.

"Sure, no problem." Peter stood up and moved over to the small refrigerator and opened it. "Let's see...there's still three left after this one, but I'm sure I can get more if we need it." He removed one of the cans and brought it over to the table.

"Have you heard enough, yet?" asked Jack after he opened the can and took a healthy swallow. "I'll be more than happy to shut up about this shit if you'd rather."

"No, don't stop," said Peter. "You keep forgetting that I want to hear your *entire* story. I know you're thinking most folks would consider this stuff as crazy, but remember I'm not your average audience."

"Well, I need to advise you that some pretty intense stuff is about to come your way, which may prove to be a lot harder to digest—even for you," Jack advised. "My personal involvement may make it really tough to share everything with you, Agent McNamee. But, I'll give it my best shot."

"Good. Let's hear what else you've got." Peter relaxed back into his seat once more.

"All right," said Jack. "Once the gates closed behind us, Genovene and I started walking along this golden road. A variety of shops lined both sides of the road amid tall juniper trees and mature magnolias. There were a number of weeping willows as well, with golden park benches beneath their shade.

"Many of the buildings stood several stories high and were made of marble, with snakes, dragons, and other critters etched in gold upon their walls. The buildings tapered inward on each level as they towered upward, similar to ancient structures in South America and the Far East that I'd once seen in pictures. Each of the inset doors, window shutters, and even the shingles on each roof appeared to be made of gold. Some buildings had symbols that were completely foreign to me etched above their doorways.

"The area was filled with beautiful women and men that were unusually tall. I remember they laughed loudly and traveled together in small groups, as I watched them come and go from the shops closest to us. The language they spoke seemed stranger to me than the one spoken by the miahluschkas. I asked Genovene if they were part of her family.

"'No, they're not,' she replied. 'The people you see around us are the caretakers of my village. You'll see them everywhere today.'

"They were all nearly seven feet in height and would surely be a basketball coach's dream. But they'd seem pretty strange to most folks. They all wore colorful robes and tunics, and a ton of gold jewelry. Olive skinned, their long braided hair was so dark it looked purple. Their eye color was like most folks—you know, everything from gray to brown, but flashing with a luminance unlike what you'll normally see. Despite their exceptional height, the villagers' movements were surprisingly graceful.

"'Are you getting hungry, yet?' Genovene asked me.

"'I am a little,' I replied.

"'Good, I've got just the thing for us!' she said. 'There's a candy store just ahead. Come on!' She enthusiastically pulled on my hand, intending to lead me over to the shop closest to us. But I resisted her. I didn't budge at all.

"'What's wrong?' she asked.

"'I don't know... I'm thinking I should get back home, Genovene,' I told her. 'Grandpa's probably wondering where I am by now. He's pretty good at figuring things out.' Truth is, I'd been fine up until a moment before, when a feeling of terrible dread suddenly overwhelmed me. I could've sworn I'd also heard a soft voice warning me that I mustn't stay—that I should leave *immediately*.

"'*Nonsense!*' she declared. She seemed hurt by my words. 'Shame on you, Jack Kenney, for not trusting me yet! I told you earlier your grandpa would be busy for a while, and that you'll be back home long before he comes looking for you. I know you're dying to see the rest of my village, so what've you got to lose? You've already come this far!'

"Her lip quivered as if she might cry. Perhaps she also sensed the invisible presence nearby, for she gazed beyond me and squinted angrily as if trying to focus in on something difficult to see. My apprehension suddenly dissipated as quickly as it had first come over me.

"Genovene seemed relieved, and soon was back to her vivacious self. But I couldn't help wondering about it. Was something trying to protect me? If so, from whom or what? But it was like that inner voice we all ignore at times, then wish we had paid attention. Know what I mean?

"She didn't give me long to think about this, invading my personal space once more. With a naughty smile she eyed me seductively and slid up close to me, her breasts pushing against my right collarbone and shoulder through her gown. "'Jack', she whispered. 'If you really want to leave, you can. I'd be sorely disappointed, but I won't stop you...won't you at least first accompany me to the candy store? You're hungry, right?'

"I nodded this was true.

"'Come share a small treat with me,' her voice as soft and sultry as the mythical Siren. 'After that, if you still would rather not stay, then I'll take you back home immediately. Should you decide instead to continue your visit here a while longer, I'll make sure you have the time of your life.'

"I was finding it harder to hide my arousal. She giggled softly and stepped away from me, giving me the space only a small part of me wished for. She turned her back and extended her hand for me to take. Once I took her hand in mine, she led me to the candy store, swinging her hips back and forth ever so slightly. 'What would it hurt?' I told myself, ignoring the dangerous compromise my hormones were forcing upon my ability to reason clearly.

"The candy store was an elaborate two-story structure, whose walls were encrusted with a variety of dazzling gemstones that stood out sharply from the white marble walls and gold trim on the building's outside facade. Above the shop's front door was an enormous gold ring with an even larger ruby glistening on top of it.

"I recall how I just stood there, not believing what I was looking at. The garish decoration looked an awful lot like the strawberry sucker I'd pulled from my pocket yesterday while swinging from the tire-swing. It wasn't half-melted like that sucker and at least a thousand times bigger.

"'Come on in, Jack!' Genovene said, pulling me up the stairs and through the building's entrance while I continued to stare at the huge ornament above us. She locked her arm around mine, and before I could protest further, we were already standing inside the store.

"The internal décor was just as garish as its outside facade. In a way, it reminded me of the 'Mrs. Smith's Candies' store at a strip mall my grandfather had recently taken me to in nearby Demopolis, only it appeared as if someone had dipped all of the metal components and wooden furniture in gold. The walls and counters appeared to be made from the same brilliant white marble used on the building's exterior.

"The ceiling was embossed with elaborate designs that were once again similar to the talisman I'd carried earlier. A unique system of running lights that were lavender, green, and white in color stretched along the border edges separating the walls from the ceiling itself. I followed the lights with my eyes, trying futilely to trace their exact path, while a tall dessert chef dressed in a gold and white outfit worked hurriedly behind the main counter pouring fresh chocolate into a large vat.

"'What you see before you is the finest chocolate in all the land,' Genovene purred softly. 'Go ahead...pick something that looks good to you.' She pointed to a vast crystal display case, which was loaded with a wide variety of chocolate candies, cakes, and cookies. I figured I'd try one of these items and then be on my way back home.

"After a moment's deliberation, I pointed to one of the fudge cookies sitting near the bottom of the case. The chef stopped what he was doing and quickly moved over to the case. Within seconds, he'd reached in and grabbed the cookie and handed it to me, wearing the warmest of smiles on his face. Before I could even say 'thanks' to the chef, Genovene beat me to it.

"'Thank you, Kolarre,' she said. 'I would like one of those as well, and then that will be all.'

"The chef did as instructed, and then bowed to her before retreating to his chores from a moment ago. I was surprised at the level of authority she seemed to have over him. I decided to wait to eat the cookie until after Genovene and I walked outside and were on the golden road again.

"'Go ahead and taste it!' she urged.

"I took a small bite, and the instant I swallowed it I felt lightheaded. The sensation soon subsided, and with it my immediate desire to return home.

"'This is really *good!*' I told her, surprised at how enamored I was over such a trivial thing as a chocolate cookie. I'd never tasted anything like it before and quickly devoured the rest of the cookie, still hungry for more. 'Would you mind if I had another one?'

"She chuckled softly, but grew silent as she considered my request. 'Why don't we wait, Jack,' she finally told me. 'I'll save my cookie for you to nibble on later if you'd like, but we mustn't spoil your appetite. It won't be too long before the Celebration Feast starts. As it is, I've got just enough time to show you around my village.' She slipped the cookie into her gown through a slight opening near her neck, and seductively moved her shoulders back and forth, allowing the treat to slide between her breasts where the ridge of the cookie's edge soon disappeared. My train of thought vanished with it as I watched her do this.

"'A 'celebration feast'?' I asked, when I regained my composure. A strange euphoria now flowed throughout my being. 'What's that?'

"'I forgot to tell you, didn't I?' She raised her eyebrows in mock surprise. 'Our village is having a special dinner today that you're especially invited to attend. Do you have any idea why?'

"I shook my head no, fighting to maintain my concentration while the euphoria gained strength.

"'This feast is for you,' she said. 'It's in your honor.'

"'It *is?*' I asked. I couldn't prevent the wide smile I felt spreading across my face while the strange blissful feeling continued to envelope my senses.

"'It most certainly is!' she said, beaming with delight. 'Now, let's get started on your personal tour. Shall we?' She held out her arm for me to take and we moved deeper into the village.

"At one point, I pulled out my watch to try and see what time it was—strictly out of curiosity, as I no longer cared about getting home on time. The crystal face glistened in the near noonday sunlight, and for the first time I noticed the crystal had been scuffed up a bit. This made me sad, though I had absolutely no idea why. At least I could still read the time clearly enough, which I knew was important for some reason. It was 11:30 and I felt good that I still had plenty of time available to me. '*Available for what?*' I wondered.

"Genovene watched me in my struggle as I'd nearly stopped moving. Her smile remained as radiant and alluring as ever, with a slight hint of tenderness emanating toward me from her luminous eyes. 'Jack, you shouldn't worry about what time it is. I won't forget what time your grandfather's expecting for you to be home. Before your stay is over, I *do* hope you learn to trust me some.'

"I just wanted to check the current time, that's all,' I told her, and then slipped the watch back into my short's pocket while meeting her intense gaze with my own subdued one. I couldn't get over how very beautiful she was, and the worst part for me was that her allure was growing stronger by the minute.

"More and more villagers appeared around us, until they threatened to overrun the entire road. Like swarming insects they seemed to come out from everywhere, quickly crowding us while we moved deeper into the village. I felt suffocated by their presence. Suddenly they all froze in their footsteps, looking back nervously toward the village entrance.

"At first, I saw and heard nothing and openly wondered what they were distracted by. Then, the loud groaning of the village gates announced the massive doors were reopening. Once the groaning stopped, another sound soon filled the air, growing louder and louder as it echoed throughout the area. The sound of horse hooves and wagon wheels clicking against the road's golden flagstones moved swiftly toward us.

"The villagers scattered off the road and Genovene steered me over to one side, barely avoiding a speeding stagecoach as it raced passed us. It was pulled along by what I believe were four white Arabian stallions driven by a ruggedly handsome man with long flowing white hair. The man's lustrous mane and flashing blue eyes were very similar to Genovene's, and he was dressed in a black cloak trailed by a long black cape. The carriage itself was a brilliant white, laced in gold trim and decorated with gems covering the reins and restraints used to guide the horses.

"The driver smiled and waved to us, his cape and hair floating and whipping around him as he flew by. Blown back by the wind from the passing carriage, I watched it as it disappeared around a corner in the road ahead, a shimmering white blur on its journey to whatever destination it had. Once it had safely passed, the villagers crowded back onto the road, raising their voices joyously and waving their arms above their heads. They then chased after the speeding carriage as an excited mob, leaving only a few stragglers in the immediate area as the village gates slowly closed again.

"'Who was that?' I asked.

"'That was Malacai, my brother,' said Genovene in admiration. 'He's always in such a hurry!'

"'How many brothers and sisters do you have again?'

"'Two of each,' she confirmed for me, 'and, they're all looking forward to meeting you, Jack!'

"I couldn't help but smile again, flattered at being treated as so important. Genovene affectionately massaged my shoulder before sliding her hand down to mine again. We then stepped back onto the golden road, following the excited mob chasing after Malacai in the distance ahead of us.

"'Where are they all headed to, anyway?' I asked.

"'They're on their way to the plaza leading to the tower,' she replied. "Did you see how excited they are about the Celebration Feast? It should be quite an event this time!'

"'Do you have these feasts often?'

"'Not often enough, I assure you,' she told me. 'We all love a good party around here, and today's the perfect opportunity for one!' Again, she seemed barely able to contain her excitement. It seemed her hair and gown turned translucent in the sunlight. But it was no longer possible for me to know for sure whether my eyes were playing tricks on me, or whether that fact was even important.

"'There's an amusement center just ahead of us that I think you might enjoy. Our arcades are truly unique. Would you like to see if there's anything you might want to try your hand at?'

"What kid wouldn't? I could only imagine how cool an arcade around there would be. I imagined every kid on the planet would love to trade places with me right then if they could. 'Sure,' I said. 'That sounds great!'

"She led me off the road to our right, and we soon stood in front of the wildest arcade I've ever seen. The building was incredibly gaudy in some ways and at the same time incredibly cool, like it belonged to Universal Studios in Orlando, or some place like that. Layers upon layers of twinkling jewels crowded the outside walls of the building in chaotic designs. The walls themselves were made of purple marble that was trimmed in gold, with hideous holographic monsters depicted in violent battle scenes upon each wall. The entire building stuck out like a sore thumb amongst its more elegant neighbors.

"A pair of tall golden pillars framed the entrance of the arcade, which was a high-rounded archway rising some thirty feet above us. Once we walked inside the building, I allowed my gaze to wander from wall to wall, taking in the multitude of games and other amusements situated beneath a burgundy colored ceiling that featured more monstrous images in holographic form. The dark green walls of the enormous room were covered with similar effects.

"At present, only a few villagers were there in the arcade, since most everyone else in the village had chased after Malacai. The excited laughter of these few jovial folks echoed against the lofty walls and ceiling, making it seem like a lot more people were in there with us.

"Some of the games in the room were familiar to me, such as a long row of pin-ball machines standing up against the wall nearest to the main entrance. Yet, most of the other games were completely foreign to me. Genovene led me further into the immense hall while everyone turned their heads to acknowledge her presence, though only for a brief moment. The allure of whatever game or amusement they were involved with soon recaptured their complete attention.

"As the two of us neared the center of the room, we came upon a lovely female flanked on either side by a handsome muscular male. All three were gathered in front of a mahogany game table that featured a horde of interlaced serpents carved upon its four legs and along its sides. The table was circular, but similar to a pool table, with its mesh-like pockets stationed at various points along the circumference of the table and red velvet covering its top. This was the game's only similarity to anything I'd ever seen. Sitting on top of the table were five large golden vipers with intricate purple, red, and black patterns covering the top portions of their slender bodies. At the moment, they hissed and thrashed violently upon the tabletop.

"'Come on over, Jack,' said Genovene. 'They won't mind us getting a better view of their contest.' She led me to the left side of the table. Both males held a loose bundle of large white marbles in one hand. In their other hand, they each held onto a single marble, apparently from the bundle. They leaned over the table with the vipers snapping their jaws at them, a mere foot or two away.

"The female standing between the two males threw a sapphire ball, slightly larger than the marbles, into the vipers' midst. All five snakes converged upon it, where finally the smallest and quickest of them captured and swallowed the glistening blue ball. No sooner than this snake finished swallowing the ball, the largest viper devoured it. The other three snakes immediately retreated to the sides of the table.

"At that point, the two males crouched just above the table's surface, each placing their marble between their thumb and forefinger. Suddenly, the sapphire ball came flying out of the largest snake's mouth. It ricocheted against the sidewalls of the table and the vulnerable bodies of the group of vipers still sitting on the table. An instant later, the male villagers carefully aimed and flicked their marbles onto the table. One of the marbles slammed into the careening sapphire and sent it into a mesh side-pocket.

"The male closest to me shouted gleefully while thrusting his hands into the air. The other male frowned, slapping his palm down upon the table in frustration. The girl seemed mostly unaffected by any of this.

"'This game is called 'Torens', and you probably can guess the objective,' Genovene explained. 'Rumus won this match, but Mina'ri has won his fair share of matches, too. Phletrea, the pretty girl standing between them, is here to keep them both under control. Actually, she's better at this particular game than either of them.'

"The snakes moved back into the center of the table with the smallest one crawling out of the largest one's mouth. A moment later, all five were hissing and thrashing again as the two villagers prepared for a rematch. Genovene gently tugged on my arm, directing my attention to what appeared to be a waterfall flowing from an unseen point in the middle of the air down into an ornate gold basin secured upon the floor.

"The six-foot wide band of water flowed swiftly and continuously, crashing toward the arcade's floor from its origin nearly twenty feet above us. I was completely intrigued by this illusion, far more than the table of snakes or anything else I'd seen so far in the arcade. I moved over to the waterfall and thrust my hand into the rushing water. To my utter amazement, my fingers not only got wet, but were also thrown downward by the water's force as it sprayed out upon us.

"'Careful, Jack!' she laughed. 'It's a lot more realistic than you expected, isn't it? Most of the games and amusements in here are like that. I'll bet you've never been in an arcade quite like this before, have you?'

"I nodded in agreement, still stunned and forced to rethink my earlier assessment of the table of snakes along with several other games I'd seen.

"'You've got to see this game over here in the corner!' said Genovene, turning my attention to a large red and black rectangular box standing near the rear wall of the room. 'It's called 'Thunder Knight' and I think you'll absolutely *love* it! Come on!" Her enthusiasm was by then irresistible to me, and under the spell of it I followed close behind her as she moved over to the game.

"At first glance, 'Thunder Knight' looked pretty much like the video games I'd seen at the arcades that Lee and I frequented in Demopolis. But once I moved up closer to it, I saw clearly that it was quite different from anything I'd ever seen. It didn't contain an actual video screen. It was just a big fancy red and black box with 'Thunder Knight' inscribed across the top and sides of it. Where the video screen would normally be found was a large hole flanked on either side by a pair of gold handgrips.

"A brilliant orange glow emanated from a six-inch space between the game and the floor beneath it, illuminating the bottom portion of the game. The enamel of the predominantly red and black metallic paints glistened richly in this light, adding a lustrous sheen to the seven-foot box. It appeared the box was floating, though more than likely, I realized something beneath the box held it up. I bent down in front of the game to verify this, but the light was too damned intense for me to see through it once I pushed my face up to the space between the floor and the game.

"I stood back up and decided to peer down into the hole in the game box. Immediately I felt extremely disoriented, as the hole seemed infinitely deep. I staggered back from the game.

"'This *can't* be possible,' I whispered in astonishment. I looked at the front of the game once more and estimated the floor was a mere four feet from where the hole began. If the hole continued through the floor of the arcade, then where was the light coming from? I looked over at Genovene, and she encouraged me to check under the box again. I got down on my knees and tentatively reached my hands and the rest of my arms' length into the space, feeling the coolness of the room's marble floor beneath my fingers. There wasn't a hole of any kind. I stood back up, completely baffled.

"'It's quite different from what you're used to, eh?' she confirmed. 'To play this game, you must stand as close as you can to the hole and brace yourself with the handles. Then, close your eyes. That's it!'

"I peered down into the bottomless hole. It seemed so dangerously deep, like if I got too close it might just suck me down into its impenetrable darkness. To steady myself, I took a deep breath and exhaled slowly. I placed both hands tightly upon the handgrips and closed my eyes as Genovene instructed.

"All at once I heard wild animals calling out to one another, as wind rustled through branches high above me. The air around me was filled with the pungent smell of pine. I slowly opened my eyes and was genuinely surprised to find I really was in a forest. Large fir and cedar trees, along with smaller ferns and shrubs, surrounded me. The songs of birds and chirping insects seemed to be everywhere and sunlight streamed down in misty rays shaped by the trees' dense foliage. The game box, Genovene, and the rest of the arcade were nowhere to be found.

"Suddenly, everything went deathly quiet. A sound like thunder approached me from the distance to my right, gradually growing louder and louder. Soon, I heard battle cries and the neighing of horses. I ducked for cover behind a thick mulberry bush, getting out of the way just as a medieval cavalry dressed in red and white armor came pouring through the forest, while more horsemen dressed in blue and gray armor pursued them. The second cavalry soon caught up with the first one before they reached a nearby clearing, and a bloody battle ensued. I was both sickened and badly frightened, as I watched the bloodbath through the branches and leaves of the mulberry bush.

"The men in blue prevailed, completely obliterating the red cavalry. The victors walked through the forest amid the fallen horses and soldiers, finishing off any surviving red and white clad soldiers who were still alive. The sound of the heavy swords hacking and tearing at the bodies, along with the pleading cries for mercy from the doomed and dying men, nearly caused me to faint.

"I was especially disturbed by the fate of one dying soldier. The man fell just a few feet in front of me on the other side of the mulberry bush and was mortally wounded. He wheezed from a gaping wound in his rib cage, struggling in vain to stand back up. The soldier raised his sword in a last valiant attempt to fend off another soldier in blue and gray who was walking stealthily up to him.

"Without saying a word, the advancing soldier closed in, and in the blink of an eye swung his broadsword from his side, severing his unfortunate victim's outstretched arm and hand, along with the top half of the man's head, armor and all. The arm and attached hand flew through the air, landing less than a foot away from me. Horrified, I looked down at it, the severed muscles still twitching beneath the bloody remnants of the soldier's glove and chain mail. The victim's body fell over, landing in the front side of the mulberry bush, a stream of gore soon running to the base of the bush as the man's blood and loosened brain matter poured out.

"I barely stifled a scream. I desperately wanted out of whatever nightmare this was, so I stood up and ran from the mulberry bush in pure panic, frantically trying to find a hidden doorway or some other way to leave the game and its bloody forest. My efforts failed to locate an exit, as nearly every direction I turned led deeper into the forest. I sprinted for the clearing, but soon the blue and gray army came after me, shouting in anger with their swords drawn high above their heads.

"Just before I reached the clearing, I tripped over an exposed tree root and tumbled to the ground. When I tried to get back on my feet, I slipped on some loose soil near where I'd originally fallen, which gave my pursuers the opportunity to catch up to me. Grimacing with unbridled malice, the soldiers bore down upon me. I thought for certain I was about to die, but just then, an enormous knight dressed in red and black armor stepped in between us. Another fierce battle took place, from which this knight arose victorious. He whirled around to face me, roaring with a terrible voice while he drew back his sword to strike me. I screamed as loud as I could.

"I awoke lying flat on my back upon the floor in front of the game box, shivering in cold sweat and fearing my heart would jump out of my chest at any moment.

"'Are you all right, Jack?' Genovene knelt beside me, peering down into my face. Her eyes revealed what I believed was true concern for me, although there was a glint of amusement as well.

"'Yeah, I'm okay,' I replied, still trying to clear my head of the gruesome images from a moment ago.

"'What did you think?' she asked.

"'It was pretty cool,' I said, not sure how to respond since the game honestly frightened me. 'But if you don't mind, I'd just as soon skip anything else like it.'

"'That'll be fine, since we need to leave anyway,' she said, chuckling softly. She helped me to my feet and then led me to the main exit from the arcade. On the way out, I saw a few villagers playing other games similar to 'Thunder Knight'. I watched them as they closed their eyes and clung tightly to the handgrips. Immediately, their bodies convulsed until they collapsed upon the floor, just as I'd done earlier. I couldn't believe the entire experience lasted no more than ten to fifteen seconds.

"Once we returned to the road, she pointed to a large magnolia just ahead of us, where the road turned sharply downhill. I almost stumbled on account of how steep the incline was. We were several hundred feet above a huge sprawling plaza bordered on each side by two magnificent gardens. High above the plaza was a long marble bridge connecting the gardens to each other, its shadow spread across much of the plaza floor beneath it. The bridge was covered with intricate artwork along its entire length with all of it outlined in gold. Carved serpents seemed to peer through thick dark green vines that hung over the side of the bridge.

"The bustling plaza was filled to capacity with the men and women of the village. They surrounded what looked like street venders, some who pushed their overloaded carts along while others waited upon the crowd from within small colorful booths. Just beyond the plaza was another grand staircase much larger than the one Genovene and I had climbed together earlier. It rose nearly a hundred feet from the plaza floor up to an extended courtyard. The staircase was as wide as the plaza and sat between a pair of gargantuan fountains that were actually statues of both a man and a woman. Like most everything I'd seen so far in the village, the statues appeared to have been cut from white marble, with strange symbols and designs etched in gold along the edges of their tunics, headbands, and other jewelry.

"The male statue carried a golden sword held within a sheath attached to its waist, and wore a warrior headdress similar to, what I later learned, the Inca and Mayan warlords had once worn upon their heads. These items, along with the female statue's headband and waist sash, were further adorned with enormous jewels. Each statue was roughly the same height as the staircase and both cast their gaze down to the plaza from where they stood, near the middle of the stairs. Matching waterfalls descended another fifty feet from atop the marble pedestals they stood upon. Even from where we were, I could hear the crash of the water as it reached twin pools located in the plaza gardens.

"The courtyard was about the size of a football field. On its left side, near the female statue, sat an imposing step pyramid with a stone table sitting on top of it. A fire burned next to the table, and I could see smoke-streaked flames billowing up into the air. The entire pyramid was made of gold and I figured it was at least two hundred feet in height.

"As I looked at this pyramid, I became more and more uneasy. Panic threatened to overtake the strange bliss I was presently immersed in. The pyramid seemed *very* familiar to me, but at the time I couldn't remember where I'd seen it before. Perhaps I might've figured it out if I could've only focused my thoughts for another moment or so. But where my gaze landed next took care of that.

"I can't adequately describe the tremendous sense of awe and wonder that overwhelmed me once I saw the massive tower glistening beyond the plaza. I'd never seen anything remotely like it, just like the other 99% of mankind, I'm sure. It dwarfed everything in the courtyard and plaza. The tower's base alone stood several stories high as it rose up from the courtyard. From the base, though, the golden obelisk shot up at least another couple thousand feet into the air.

"The tower appeared to be filled with numerous windows stretching along its length. They looked like a million diamonds as they sparkled in the sunlight from where we stood. I was truly overwhelmed—so much so, that the obvious question again of 'Why haven't I known or at least heard about this place before now?' didn't really occur to me. I couldn't pry my eyes off the thing as we started down the steep path to the plaza below.

"Genovene had been quietly observing me. She was obviously pleased and she laughed softly. 'Watch your step,' she advised. 'For now, it might be better to pay closer attention to your feet so you don't fall.'

"I pulled my gaze away from the tower and watched my feet, slipping slightly on the road. I reached out for her and she steadied me as we walked down the hill together. The air grew thicker once we neared the plaza, probably due to the high amount of moisture rising from the waterfalls and streams in the area. It was really beautiful, and the gardens were larger and even more spectacular than they'd first appeared from up above.

"Within each garden, a wide variety of flowers were arranged in elaborate mazes. I saw everything from daisies to roses, even my grandfather's beloved buttercups. Many of the flowers I didn't even recognize. A light breeze swirled within the plaza carrying the sweet floral aroma with it.

"The two of us moved through the plaza, passing through the crowd and the venders who were busy handing out white pastries of some kind. All the while, the villagers laughed and played merrily with one another, the look of ecstasy never leaving their faces. It was like they couldn't get enough of the stuff. Yet, distribution of this food was so efficient that no lines formed. I was amazed, since it was so much like ants or bees, but so different from how people usually behave. I wondered if the pastries contained something that made them act this way.

"'It's more than that, Jack,' Genovene explained, intercepting my thoughts. 'Yes, their hunger is insatiable and the manna they're eating heightens their senses. However, the reason for their joy and synergy is the Celebration Feast. They're especially excited since today's event coincides with our 'Festival of Life' holiday, which started yesterday.

"'Festival of life'?' I asked.

"'Yes, it's the holiest time that my village celebrates. It's like your Christmas and Easter rolled into one event. All of us join in a festive party in the plaza, and each person brings gifts for one another to share. But, the best part is when the feast starts. That's when this place will be rocking with energy, Jack, and it's set to happen *very soon!*'

"Her excitement got the better of her again and she looked away momentarily. When she looked back at me, she was more serene and pulled me close to her, gently clasping my hands with hers. 'There's still so much to see here and so much I'd love to show you,' she said softly, and more controlled. 'Time is passing quickly and we need to be moving along. Let me take you on a quick stroll through one of the gardens and then we'll go on up to the tower from there.'

"She took me to the garden on the left side of the plaza, passing through the ever-thickening crowd of people—many of whom had the manna's powder smeared upon their faces. Once we reached the garden's wall, Genovene stretched her hand over the top of the wall and waved something very small back and forth. It was too tiny for me to make out what it was, but an instant later the wall melted away, forming a space just wide enough for us to pass through. She led me into the garden, and as I turned around to look, I saw the wall repair itself.

"Almost immediately we were embraced by the most lovely aspects of nature. It made the plaza we just left look drab in comparison. Gone for the time being were the noises from the crowd less than ten feet away. The plaza's fanfare was completely replaced by the gentle songs of birds and insects, the soft breeze rustling through the branches of several willow trees, and the rushing and gentle gurgling of the water as it moved steadily downstream.

"It was so tranquil. The beauty and serenity in the garden made it difficult for me to compare anything to it. If there had been any animals there, I might've expected Adam and Eve to show up at any minute. I looked around, and suddenly noticed a variety of exotic plants and fruit trees I could swear hadn't been there a moment ago. I looked over at Genovene and she was eyeing me, knowingly. It made me uneasy.

"She chuckled and pulled me even closer, her ample bosom brushing up against me once more. 'You're actually right about those trees and bushes. Both gardens are magical and respond to the hidden depths of a person's mind and spirit,' she said. 'This particular garden responds to a person's positive thoughts, hopes, and dreams. The other garden across the way responds to a person's negative thoughts, fears, and nightmares. If you'll take a moment, you'll notice every plant, tree, and the very grass you're standing on are things you either have a fondness for or bring you peace. Do you see any spiders, or insects other than butterflies and ladybugs? Any vicious snakes or ferocious animals?'

"'No...I guess you're right about that,' I replied while I looked around. It was amazing. The lush green carpet of fresh-cut grass was indeed what I loved to see. It even smelled like it'd been cut just minutes before. I decided to test just how much of a magical garden it could be. I said, 'I don't see any animals, Genovene. I suppose you've figured out by now that I've always liked animals. So, why ain't there any dogs and cats here?'

"No sooner than I said this, a high-pitched growl emerged from a fern bush I was standing next to. A white tiger cub came pouncing out from behind the bush and playfully attacked my leg. 'What?? Whoa—hold on there, boy!' I cried out while trying to back away from it. 'Uh, Genovene...it won't bite me, will it??'

"'No, sweetie, it won't,' she told me, laughing while I attempted to climb over the wall. 'I'm sorry...but how's that for a kitten?' Still laughing, she walked over to me and picked up the tiger cub, setting it down a few feet away from us. She patted the animal gently on its behind and watched it disappear into the bushes. She then turned her attention back to me, chuckling softly with an amused look upon her face. 'Will you believe me now, Jack Kenney, oh 'ye of little faith', in the things I tell you?'

"I nodded silently and smiled shyly at her. She reached out and took my hand again, leading me to a path that ran through the flowerbeds and plants. We followed the path until we reached the waterfall that fed the garden's stream. Once there, we sat down together upon a golden bench nestled beneath a pair of willow trees. It overlooked a pool which had a waterfall that emptied into it and then forming a stream. As the deafening roar from the rushing water obliterated the sound of anything else in the garden, Genovene leaned into me again, speaking loudly so I could clearly hear her above the water's din. 'This is our wishing pool,' she told me. 'If you'd like, take a look down into the water, but be careful not to fall in.'

"I leaned over the edge of the pool and saw hundreds of gold and silver coins, and even some copper, steel, and nickel coins from more recent years as well, including a couple of quarters and a half-dollar lying near where we sat. The water was so clear that it looked like I could simply reach in and scoop the coins up with my hands.

"'Be careful, for the water is a lot deeper than you think!' she warned. She bent down and stuck her arm into the water all the way up to her elbow, but it seemed like she'd barely broken the water's surface. She then looked back at me. 'See what I mean?'

"'Yeah, I would've never figured that,' I agreed. 'I mean, everything in the pool looks real close!'

"'Things aren't always as they seem, or how we want them to be,' she said. 'Like this pool, for instance. Some wishes come true for those who make them here, and yet, many other wishes don't. Perhaps, as some say, it has a lot to do with the purity of the heart and soul of the person making the wish. I, for one, believe it has more to do with pure luck. Why don't you make a wish for something you truly long for, Jack?'

"I thought about it for a moment, and almost declined to wish for anything at all. Yet, the thing that mattered most to me and haunted every waking moment I had wouldn't let me pass up this opportunity. Even if it was a far-fetched desperate attempt for an answer or resolution to whatever became of my parents, I was willing to try anything. I needed to know what happened. I didn't feel I could formulate a true purpose for my life until this issue was known once and for all, even if it meant finding out my folks were dead.

"I pulled a dime from the deep recesses of one of my pockets and kneeled down at the edge of the pool. I then flipped the coin into the clear water, watching it slowly drift to the bottom until it rested on a pile of other coins. This felt like such an exercise in futility, and I felt more sadness at that moment than I ever recalled feeling before.

"I stared absently into the pool, barely aware of the waterfall's mighty roar. Genovene soon gently massaged my shoulders, so I knew it was time to leave this spot. I stood back up and she led me away from the stream, heading toward the garden wall nearest the staircase. We walked together quietly through more exotic plants and flowers, and soon found ourselves directly below the colossal statue of the woman. It towered in splendid elegance far above us. I stretched my neck back to get a better look as it sparkled in the sunlight, thinking this must be what it feels like if you're a bug about to get squished by someone.

"The feet alone were nearly as big as my bedroom. The statue was an amazing work of art, more so than any structure I'd ever seen before. So many minor details, like the striations on the toenails and small lines around the knees were plainly visible from where I stood. Even details that I couldn't quite see must've been carved into the torso and head of the statue, because it really did seem like it was looking down at me.

"From the head, arms, hands, torso, and knees surged jets of water which alternated and crossed one another in a variety of patterns. The affect of the sunlight reflecting off the water, along with the marble, gold, and jewels of the statue created a multicolored halo that surrounded it. I figured it must've taken years to make something like this.

"'You'd be surprised at how long it *didn't* take,' offered Genovene, reading my mind and chuckling softly once more. She led me to the garden's wall and waved her hand above it again. As before, the wall melted away and we moved back into the noisy plaza. I looked back to see if I could watch the wall mend itself, but it'd already finished.

"We soon reached the staircase and began our ascent to the courtyard. Realistic battle scenes were skillfully carved onto the side of each step. The scenes featured soldiers and warriors from different eras throughout North American history, as they fought against skeleton-like creatures. The higher the stair, the further back in history was the battle scene. I saw everything from soldiers of the American Revolutionary War to Spanish conquistadors to the North American Indians. As the stairs' scenes continued further back in time, they soon included Indians looking more like those once living in Central and South America.

"Once we reached the top of the staircase, the stairs depicted primitive people living in ancient jungles. They fared the worst out of all the warriors and soldiers, and their severed heads and limbs were hoisted high upon the monsters' spears and swords as trophies.

"My preoccupation with all of this greatly slowed our progress to the courtyard. She let me linger a moment longer and then pointed to the male statue on our right. 'This statue represents the brave warriors who have protected my people from the adversaries you see portrayed on the stairs,' she explained.

"Up close, the warrior was really something to see. Like its sister on the other side, it stood within its own sprinkler-fed rainbow. The realistic detail was frightening, for the warrior seemed to stare sullenly down upon us.

"'You're wondering why they look so real, aren't you?' observed Genovene. I nodded I was. 'With so much that's magical here, our personal icons must be believable,' she said. 'We call the male statue Morylan, and he represents courage and our continual search for excellence. The woman is called Lavonia, and she represents our proud heritage and emphasis on true beauty.'

"We soon reached the courtyard, where my eyes were drawn to the golden pyramid to our left. I'd guessed its height fairly accurately from the hill, but it turned out to be a lot wider and deeper than I'd originally thought. A long row of steps led from the courtyard to its very top, where the billowing smoke from the fire obscured that portion of the structure. Inscribed along the pyramid's sides were rows of hieroglyphs.

"Several fountains featuring gold nymphs sat within the courtyard. The floor was tiled in white marble squares that were bordered in gold trim. A crimson carpet that was fringed with gilded tassels ran from the top of the staircase to a pair of crystal doors in the tower's base.

"To the right of the carpet sat a long wooden table covered with serpent carvings similar to the ones on the game table from the arcade. This table was flanked on either side by a dozen high-backed chairs featuring the same designs carved in the wood. At the head of the table near the tower's base sat a large throne chair that was by far the most ornate furniture piece here. Its elongated back was covered in crushed velvet of the deepest purple I've ever seen, with what looked to be diamonds, sapphires, rubies, and emeralds embedded in the fabric.

"A long white tablecloth that had lavender tassels and was embroidered with dark green and gold vines covered the table, which was already set with golden plates, utensils, and large goblets. Elegant napkins were folded and stuffed inside the goblets, and large golden trays that were nearly overloaded with a wide variety of fruit were placed on each end of the table.

"To the right of the table stood a row of twelve, tall and narrow, juniper trees—all of which were decorated with gold and lavender ribbons. They sort of reminded me of Christmas trees that'd been stretched thin and stripped of the usual lights and ornaments.

"'As you can see, it's almost time for the festival to start,' Genovene told me, slipping her arm around my waist. The courtyard was filled with busy servants hustling back and forth from the tower to the area surrounding the table. 'I've saved the best for last, Jack! Are you ready for the final phase of our tour, to visit my house?'

"'Are you kidding? I'm definitely ready for that!' I told her. I was really excited. But I was also a little nervous, despite the presence of the strange euphoria I still felt. The main thing I'd hoped to do all along was visit the magnificent tower. Ever since I first saw it, I'd been intrigued by what it might be like inside, and now I stood on the threshold of finding out.

"Twelve steps led up from the courtyard to the colossal building. On the way to the entrance, I heard the sound of horses snorting. I looked toward the far end of the tower's base on my left and saw Malacai's carriage and horses. The carriage was unattended for the moment, and its door stood wide open with a footstool resting beneath it. Even from this distance, I could see the plush red and gold interior of the carriage.

"A high cupola that was supported by a row of marble columns ran along the length of the tower's base. Two huge muscular guards stood at attention on either side of the doors, and as Genovene and I approached, they bowed before her while pulling the doors open.

"We walked inside the tower and the guards closed the doors behind us. It took a moment for my eyes to adjust to the dimness, although it appeared the center of the enormous room was illuminated brightly from above. The walls and floor of the room appeared to be made of dark granite that was polished to a high-gloss sheen, which glistened despite the near darkness concealing much of the room.

"We moved toward the light. When we reached that portion of the room, I instinctively looked up toward the ceiling. The immense base opened up directly into the hollow spike of gold soaring to dizzying heights above us. I couldn't even see the top from where we stood. It was as if the tower had grown much taller since I'd last taken a good look at its peak from atop the plaza.

"I started to lose my balance, so I reached for Genovene to steady myself. I then looked up again. The spike was truly spectacular. Not only was it incredibly high, but also several hundred feet in diameter. A gold and marble staircase lined its sides, spiraling up as far as I could see. The rails and banisters of the staircase appeared to be made of solid twisted gold, and the crystal windows I'd seen earlier followed the staircase's ascent. Like prisms, they channeled sunlight as a rainbow within the shaft of the tower.

"A crystal tube stood in the very center of the room, running from the floor to what I assumed was the very top of the spike, since I couldn't see its end from where we presently stood. The entire length of the tube glowed.

"When I looked over at Genovene, a smile of sweet contentment was upon her face. 'Welcome to my home, Jack!' she joyfully exalted, the echo of her lovely voice bouncing from wall to wall as it rang throughout the temple base. She began to shimmer again.

"'This is really your...*house?*' I asked incredulously.

"She nodded this was indeed true, and pulled away from me. She then swung herself around with her arms out and her fingers pointed away from her body. She threw back her head in ecstasy as she twirled around me, dancing as a skilled ballerina might've done. Her gown floated lightly above the floor as she moved. She spun around me several times and then relaxed into a curtsy directly in front of me. Slowly, she raised herself up, eyeing me coyly. After a moment of silence, she spoke grandly, like she was in some Shakespearean play. 'Jack, this place is the temple of my people just as surely as it is my home!' she proclaimed. 'It's been my house longer than you could *ever* imagine, and is my father's creation!'

"She paused, making sure I followed her words. 'My father's name is Talusha, and he is the protector of my people! He's the one who gives us *life!* He keeps us content and happy, providing us always with an abundance of energy, food, and pleasure—and ensures that no one hurts us, *ever!* That's why very few have ever heard of us and our wonderful village!'

"I stood speechless, trying to fathom the significance of what she said and wondering why she was acting so strangely. She nodded and smiled,

"Genovene moved closer to me, sauntering without releasing me from her gaze. 'This is, as I've said, our temple,' she said, drastically reducing the volume of her speech to a sultry whisper. 'The people here worship Talusha as their lord and savior—their *god*! In this hallowed place, they let their voices ring out in adoration for him, because they know that without him, our very existence would end!'

"'Okay' I thought, 'she's fucking crazy after all!' A 'god' other than the One I prayed to every night for my mom and dad to finally come home? I seriously doubted that Reverend Meyers, the preacher at the local First Baptist church Grandpa sometimes took me to, ever heard of 'Talusha'. But, then I thought about all of the amazing things I'd experienced up until that moment. Surely something unnatural was going on, right? Still, it seemed ridiculous to consider Genovene's daddy was worshipped like that.

"'Jack,' she said, interrupting my thoughts. 'It doesn't matter if you believe in the divinity of Talusha or not. Before today is over, you *will* know him. I assure you that I speak the truth!' Her smile never faded despite my possible insult to her father. A feeling of uneasiness briefly touched my awareness and then quickly subsided. Other than the intense sadness I experienced at the garden's wishing pool, I still wasn't able to hold onto any feeling for long or my reasons for having them. They easily slipped through my mind's grasp along with my questions from a moment before.

"She moved closer with her consistent disregard for my personal space. I thought she might kiss me as she closed the gap between us to less than an inch. My manhood began to respond, and I was embarrassed she'd notice. The smile on her face turned mischievous and she took a step back from me. She deliberately looked down at the hefty bulge in my shorts, but only for a moment. Awkwardly torn between self-consciousness and the raging fire of my adolescent desire, I was mostly relieved when she looked away from my crotch and turned her intense blue eyes back to meet my own.

"'There's some unfinished business between you and I that'll need to be addressed before much longer,' she said. 'For now, follow me to the chalube'at. It'll take us up to where you'll see the most incredible view in the world!'

"She turned to lead me over to the crystal tube in the middle of the room, laughing softly to herself again. When she realized I hadn't moved yet, she stopped walking and looked back at me over her shoulder with a mock pout upon her face. 'Would you rather take the stairs, sweetie?' she asked, and then winked at me.

"Genovene awaited my response with her hands on her hips and her shapely bottom upturned ever so slightly. She was driving me nuts. Since the moment I first laid eyes on her, I'd been enraptured by her physical beauty. But, now I felt something else. I felt like my brother Jeremy would feel, as I was overwhelmed with tense excitement and incredible horniness. I wanted to fuck her badly and I wanted to do it right then and there on the temple's floor!

"She straightened up and waved her index finger at me tauntingly. 'Not *now*, my dear boy!' she laughed. 'Just remember what I told you earlier, that if you're a good boy you'll get your just dessert. Keep that in mind while we finish our tour.' She glanced one last time at my noticeable erection. 'Are you ready?'

"Cruelly, my lustful feelings suddenly gave way to one of shame, and I'm sure my face was beet-red. Despite this confusion that I feared might steer me to insanity if it kept up much longer, I followed her like an adoring puppy over to the crystal tube, or 'chalube'at' as she called it. I allowed my gaze to follow the tube's length, craning my neck back as far as I could. But like the very top of the tower where it supposedly led, the tube's end remained invisible to my eyes. I looked down at the chalube'at's base, wondering how it worked since there wasn't a visible doorway for getting in and out of the tube. Nor for that matter, was there any place to sit inside it.

"I felt apprehensive about getting inside the tube, but walking up the spiral staircase wasn't something I wanted to do either. Especially since the top couldn't be seen from where we presently stood. Regardless of which option I chose, I worried that I might pass out from either fear or excitement. I figured it'd be better for me if I were near her if that happened.

"She moved up to the chalube'at, and then quickly crossed her hands in front of herself with her palms facing inward toward her body. The tube suddenly separated into a series of panels that folded and crossed on top of themselves, forming a narrow doorway. This happened so swiftly and silently that if I'd not paid close attention, I'd have missed seeing it completely.

"Genovene stepped inside and motioned for me to follow. As soon as we were inside the tube, the panels quietly slipped back into place. I looked closely at the tube's wall, but couldn't detect the slightest seam or line. It was as if the doorway had never existed. She moved to one side of the tube and directed me to stand across from her on the other. 'Hold on tight!' she cautioned.

"'To *what?*' I wondered.

"In the very next instant we were jolted into the air, flying up the tube at an incredible rate of speed. The granite floor below us shrank rapidly until it vanished altogether from sight. With my feet dangling in the air, we rose higher and higher. For the first time, Genovene looked a lot like a witch, although a very beautiful one with her hair blowing in the air, her eyes a pair of flashing sapphires, and her black gown tapered to a point just below her feet.

"The thrill from this experience was indescribable, as you can surely imagine. I embraced the rush of excitement that filled my entire being. Suddenly, our ascent slowed dramatically when we neared the top. The refracted sunlight obscured the view below us, which was just as well, since I doubt we'd have seen much beneath us anyway. Once we reached the spike's ceiling, a hole opened up directly above us and we were slowly pulled through it into near blinding light. As soon as we were safely above the hole, it immediately closed beneath our feet and we landed gently upon a solid floor where the hole had been only a moment before.

"We remained inside the tube until Genovene stepped away from the wall and moved toward the center. I could only vaguely see her outline in the brilliant light, but I thought she was motioning for me to join her there. I moved toward her and once I reached the center of the tube, the panels slid open again, although I could only sense this. The heat from the intense light soon enveloped us from all directions. She then firmly grasped my hands and led me out of the tube. My legs felt like rubber, for I was afraid of being dropped back down the endless cylinder until we were lifted to safety. I was grateful for her steady grip to assist me until normal feeling returned to my limbs.

"The light remained extremely bright around us. I could barely see in front of me, and then only if I squinted painfully to do so. Genovene let go of my hands and moved a few feet away from me. I glimpsed her outline again while she appeared to be moving her arms over her head in a circular motion, like she held a pair of invisible lassos and was getting ready to rope some unseen steer with them. As she did this, the light dimmed until it reached the point where it no longer hurt my eyes and I could see my surroundings clearly. I found myself standing within a hollow crystal cone roughly sixty to seventy feet in diameter.

"The floor was a golden circle with engraved symbols on one half of it while the other half was smooth. The chalube'at was somehow joined to another large triangular-shaped crystal that bisected the floor. It reminded me of the sundial that stood in one of Grandpa's gardens, only this one was incredibly spectacular as the sun's rays poured down upon the crystal and floor in a brilliant array of colors.

"Genovene walked around the room surveying its contents and watching me do the same. 'Some ride, eh?' she finally said, moving over to me. 'I'll bet you've never been on an elevator quite like that before, have you? Just wait for the trip back down!' She laughed and led me to the west side of the crystal cone. 'This room is the power center for the temple, energized by the sun's radiation,' she explained. 'At times it can be almost uninhabitable in here, like it was when we first arrived, and especially during clear days when the sun's at its highest.

"'The triangular crystal and the golden plate it sits upon operate as a passive battery that continually absorbs energy from the atmosphere around us, even at night or during the coldest extremes of winter. The amount of energy stored up here is more than ample to support our temple, village, and even the surrounding groves and meadows. But if ever this power center were to fail us, we have a far more powerful source of energy that's located beneath the temple courtyard.'

"I looked out through the crystal wall of the cone. My head immediately began to swim from dizziness. I'll bet I was at least three to four thousand feet above the ground and everything below looked so minuscule and far away through wispy clouds surrounding the tower's peak. The entire village could easily have fit inside the edge of my pinky nail from where we currently stood. Toward the west of us, I saw endless forests and lakes stretching into the distance until they blended with the deep blue of a majestic mountain range. Confused, I moved to the north side of the cone and saw even more forests, lakes, and rivers, with a much larger body of water sitting further in the distance.

"When I moved over to the east side, I again saw nothing but forests and rivers until my view reached the great ocean beyond. *What in the hell was going on here?* I then ran over to the south side of the cone, said a quick prayer and looked. All I could see for miles were vast green forests penetrated only by more rivers and lakes that eventually emptied into yet another ocean. I saw a sliver of gold light glowing from many miles away toward the southwest that bordered the ocean's shoreline. I knew instinctively it was another tower, just like the one I was presently standing in.

"'Where'd my home go, Genovene?' I asked, my growing anxiety causing my voice to crack. 'It's gone! Where in the hell are we? Everything's *gone!!*'

"Gently and affectionately, she put her arm around my waist and pulled me close to her. 'Jack, do not be alarmed or afraid,' she said softly. 'What you see before you isn't the world as it is today, with all of its crime, overpopulation, and blatant disregard for nature. Instead, you're seeing the world as it was originally intended. It's the world from many hundreds of years ago before mankind overran this wonderful garden you see all around you. The distant locales you've just seen have been brought much closer by the powerful magnification of the crystal in this room.

"'The present day world is still with us, which I will show you soon enough. But, to understand my people and our purpose, you must at least have some knowledge of where we started. I can't show you everything, and we don't have time to go back all the way to our very origins. Nevertheless, I think when we're through up here you'll be glad you came.'

"I wasn't so sure of that, but my anxiety abated. She stepped away from me, placing her hands on the side of the cone that faced south and closed her eyes. Immediately, the crystal material began to re-shape itself and a short table-like ledge suddenly grew out of the cone's side and into the room. It was roughly the size of a small desktop, and she motioned for me to come over and take a closer look.

"I moved over to her and looked down into the ledge. At first, it was as clear as the crystal cone itself. But, once she showed me how to guide and operate it, I found that it worked like an up-close viewing screen. I could see detailed images of various locations in the primitive world far below us. The ledge could be moved in any direction and would grow smaller if I brought it forward, or larger if I pulled it back. I was puzzled by the fact it remained fully connected to the cone's wall at all times. Yet, when I moved it around in different directions, not a single seam or crease appeared. It was as if the crystal material in the wall and ledge reconfigured themselves in unison from one moment to the next.

"I held the object straight ahead and saw the deep green treetops of a lush ancient forest down below. On display in front of me was an aerial view about twenty feet above the trees. I raised it ever so slightly, and the images flew by as I did this. When they stopped, I had a bird's eye view of a large fluorescent blue snake moving through the undergrowth of the forest floor. I nudged the ledge a tad more and saw the close-up details of the snake's scales as it wreathed its way along the forest floor.

"I decided to try another view and pulled back a little. All at once I was staring into a nest of baby finches that appeared to be less than a foot away from me, as my view had retreated into the midst of a large fir tree. A small beetle with bulging green eyes suddenly landed on a branch less than an inch from where my view began. It completely obscured the images of the finches for about a minute as it walked across the branch. I got a better look at its colorful underbelly than I would've liked as it left slimy gray droppings on the branch while it passed by. In disgust, I pulled back further until my view was a few hundred feet above the forest.

"'This is oh, so *cool!*' I whispered in amazement, wishing once again Jeremy, Grandpa, or even Lee was there to see this. I turned the ledge around in a variety of directions, and in just a few minutes time I scanned everything from the Gulf of Mexico to the identical golden tower near the Central American coastline. I even dared to 'dive' into the Mississippi River, but apparently its water had been just as murky as it is now. I remember laughing in my excitement over all of this and Genovene laughed along with me.

"'The other views are very similar in what they have to offer,' she advised. 'We've just enough time for one more and then we must return to the main level, for the Festival Of Life is set to begin shortly.'

"I started to move toward the west side of the cone, for I'd always wanted to see the Rocky Mountains. But then I hesitated. I thought about my grandfather, and although I knew the thought would disappear in a moment, I wanted to make sure he was okay before the impulse to do so was gone again. 'Genovene...I'd rather see the present-day world instead of the one that's no longer here,' I told her. 'Would you mind if I go over to the east side and do that?'

"She pondered my request and her lovely smile faded briefly from her face. 'I suppose that'll be fine,' she said. 'But, only for a minute. All right?'

"'Sure,' I agreed.

"We walked together over to the east side of the crystal cone where she set caused the ledge to appear once again, and then she retreated to the center of the room. She squatted down and put one hand upon the crystal triangle while she placed her other hand on the smooth golden floor. She closed her eyes, and as she did this, I watched the world outside change. A moment later, the world I knew had returned.

"I could still see a good distance through the cone's wall, but the available viewing area had diminished significantly. The overall view was perhaps no more than a hundred miles in any one direction now, which was still pretty impressive even if it wasn't near as spectacular as the ancient view had been.

"Genovene stood up and reminded me that I didn't have long to check on my grandfather, as we needed to leave soon. I positioned the object to where I could see my home, and before long, I found him working beneath one of the large maple trees in our front yard. Grandpa was busy clearing out some pesky weeds from around the flowers that grew in a ring-shaped garden that encircled the tree. I watched him as he paused for a moment to wipe the sweat from his brow. He then looked up toward the sun before going back to clearing more weeds.

"Satisfied he wasn't worried about my whereabouts just yet, I pulled back, retracing the journey I took that morning to get where I now stood. The images flew by quickly, but I paused long enough to check on Banjo to make sure he was okay. He was still playing with the other animals in the meadow under the watchful eyes of several miahluschkas, whose faces remained shrouded by their hooded robes.

"I pulled the ledge back until the revealed images were from our immediate area, and out of curiosity positioned it upon the area directly below me. I then pushed forward just a hair, and the bustling temple courtyard zoomed into focus. The servants hurried about in their last minute preparations for the feast. I focused the viewer on the long dinner table, as it was now filled with bread, assorted pastries, and other entrees. Only a fairly large space remained in the center of the table, which I figured was reserved for the main course. Without lingering any longer, I shifted the view screen over to the pyramid.

"I followed the steps from the bottom on up to the very top of it. A large gold platter currently sat upon the stone table that earlier had been bare. Steam and smoke poured forth out of a large hole sitting next to the table. I pushed the crystal flap a little more in order to get a better look down inside the hole, and the view screen became completely filled with smoke and steam.

"Suddenly, I gasped. For, beneath the smoke and steam a brilliant blue mass was moving—*pulsing* as if it were alive and breathing. The mass was liquid-like and appeared to boil in some places and yet was literally engulfed by flames in other areas. Before I could look any longer, Genovene firmly grasped my arm, nearly hurting me. I looked back at her in surprise, shocked that this person who'd been so kind and gentle would do something like that.

"'Sorry, Jack, but we must leave *now!*' she announced sternly. She struggled noticeably to maintain her smile, but once I allowed her to guide me back over to the chalube'at, without any resistance other than the silent question of 'What in the hell's your problem?', she slowly regained her composure. I tried my best to pretend I hadn't noticed the drastic change in her demeanor, but doubt I was successful. All I knew was that I must've seen something I wasn't supposed to see, or even know about.

"'I'm sorry if I did something to offend you, Genovene...' I recall my voice trailed off, for I couldn't understand why she was so upset. She studied me for a moment, and then, as if she'd discovered some reassuring information from my thoughts or feelings, she began to relax once more. Before long, her radiant smile returned to her face and eyes, and she loosened her ironclad grip on my arm, sliding her hand down to mine again. As gently as before, she led me on over to the invisible entrance to the crystal transport tube.

"She paused in front of the chalube'at for a moment before moving directly ahead of me, motioning for me to wait where I was. Genovene went through her bizarre ritual once more and the tube's wall immediately produced another doorway. She reached back behind her at this point, gently grasping my crotch. Stunned and startled by this, I assumed she wanted my hand instead. She glanced over her shoulder, raising her eyebrows in a look of mild surprise, smiling mischievously. But without a word she accepted my hand and led me back inside the chalube'at.

"As soon as the panels closed, we barely had time to take our places opposite each other before the floor disappeared beneath us and we were dropped back down the tube. The trip to the bottom was even quicker than the trip up had been, and I thought for sure my stomach was going to come up into my mouth at any moment. I tried to scream, but couldn't do it. There was air, but I couldn't breathe. So I closed my eyes instead, which only made matters worse. I opened them again and looked across the tube at Genovene. Her hair was flying straight up above her head as she clutched her gown just above her knees in a determined effort to keep the garment from rising any higher.

"Suddenly, that mischievous smile returned to her face as her eyes flashed luminously at me. She allowed her gown to creep all the way up to her waist, which in a way reminded me of the famous picture I'd once seen of Marilyn Monroe. The only difference was that Genovene was completely naked from the waist down.

"I tried to look away, but couldn't. I was fascinated by what I saw. She seemed to enjoy my awkward response and smiled broadly before blowing a kiss at me. I forced myself to look beyond her at the blur of the staircase and crystal windows flying by. Right before reaching the temple floor, our descent suddenly slowed and we dropped lightly onto our feet again. For the moment, her gown concealed her nakedness as it stretched to the floor. Relief and disappointment filled me.

"She moved to the center of the tube while motioning for me to join her there. Once I reached the center, she grabbed and pulled me close to her, reaching with both hands between my legs. I was so nervous. I began to sweat while my heart pounded heavily in my chest. She gently massaged me while she penetrated my nervous and frightened eyes with a famished and predatory look in her own.

"Once the panels opened, she removed her hands from my crotch and reached for my hand again to lead me out of the chalube'at. I was under the intense assault of so many feelings. Wonderful and horrible feelings, such as ecstasy and guilt in a powerful but confusing mix with primitive emotions I didn't understand at the time. I was helpless to resist her ruthless seduction.

"She pulled me close behind her and led me away from the lighted area of the temple's base. We stepped into the shadows and soon the entire area before us was cloaked in thick blackness.

"'We've got a little time left before the Celebration Feast begins,' she said, her voice once more a sultry whisper. She pulled me up even with her and then leaned into me as we moved deeper into the darkness. 'No doubt, you're wondering where we're going now. I'm going to show you what very few have ever seen. All I ask is that you don't resist me. *Trust* in me. Will you do that for me, Jack?'

"I nodded, hesitantly but decidedly, since I knew I couldn't resist her anyway.

"'Don't let the darkness we're moving into alarm you,' she advised, 'for we will arrive at my chamber shortly afterward.'

"I couldn't see anything at all, not even Genovene, who was right next to me. Despite her closeness, I was aware of other unseen things moving around us as we headed deeper into the tower's base. Ominous and creepy things that were felt more than heard; however, I could've sworn I did hear a deep swishing sound along with a barely audible groan coming from the area just ahead of us.

"It seemed we'd walked quite a distance before I saw a light again, but since I no longer trusted my eyes, it may have only appeared that way. As we drew nearer to this light, it seemed to divide into two small spheres peering out from the darkness. The spheres lengthened and flickered, and soon revealed themselves to be a pair of fiery torches.

"The outline of a large doorway was now visible, standing between the torches, while slight movements on either side of the door indicated another pair of huge muscular guards hovering in the darkness just beyond the reach of the torches' light. With her hand maintaining a secure grip on my own, Genovene led me to the door. As before, these servants bowed before her. Then, one of the guards moved to open the medieval-like door, motioning for us to walk through it. The guard then shut the door behind us, as I heard the low groan and creaking of hinges straining to hold the weight of the wood.

"We were alone in darkness, but only briefly. Genovene stepped away from me, and as she did so, a dozen torches positioned throughout the spacious room suddenly ignited, along with a large array of candles that covered much of the floor and chamber tables, throwing their soft radiance upon everything in the room.

"Her bedroom was fit for a queen, with luxurious gold and lavender bed linens, tapestries, and draperies throughout. Massive and beautiful dark-wooden furniture that was traced and inlaid with intricate gold designs dominated the room. The centerpiece was the massive canopy bed that sat in the middle of it. It was a work of art in itself. All four bedposts were exquisitely hand-carved statues of well endowed naked men and voluptuous women facing inward toward the mattress and positioned so that a male and female faced each other. The mattress appeared soft and inviting with a thick comforter and many pillows. It made it hard not to imagine what I wanted to do with her there.

"Genovene sauntered slowly toward the bed with her back turned to me, while the reflection of the flickering candles on her satin gown enhanced her allure. My eyes followed her lovely form all the way to her feet as they padded quietly along the smooth white marble floor. She stopped once she reached the bed. Without turning around, she unfastened her gown, allowing it to fall to her ankles. She then carefully stepped out of the crumpled garment, leaving it on the floor as she turned around to face me.

"She was completely naked, and I was now completely aroused. My heart raced harder as my erection pulsed to full strength in my shorts. She was astonishingly beautiful, more so than any pin-up I'd ever seen in my brother's magazines. From the striking features in her face, to the full perfection of her breasts, to the soft loveliness of her sex, and even to her long slender legs and nymph-like feet, she was my fantasy. Not that I consciously knew it before that moment, but I've never forgotten it since.

"A knowing smirk tugged at the corners of her full lips as she moved stealthily toward me. She was like a cunning jaguar stalking a trapped young deer. Her eyes flashed in the firelight from the candles and torches, her breasts bouncing slightly as she closed in on me. She was almost too perfect, this voluptuous and sexually aggressive young woman. The excitement overwhelming my body along with the powerful euphoria I'd already been dealing with, kept me frozen in place, just inside the doorway.

"'Am I making you nervous, Jack?' she asked once she had closed to within a foot of me, the sultriness and immediate proximity of her voice sending a series of chills up and down my spine.

"'Ah, no. I mean...*yes*. At least a little, I guess,' I replied, swallowing hard. I felt strangely exposed and vulnerable to her.

"She glanced down at the hard-on in my shorts and then laughed softly before looking back into my face, studying my enraptured and nervous eyes. 'Good!' she said, and before I could say or think anything else, she leaned over and kissed me. Her kisses were soft and gentle at first as she caressed my mouth. But once I finally opened up to her guidance and more aggressive prodding, she kissed me fervently, pressing her body against mine while bringing my trembling hands up to touch and fondle the pointed nipples of her breasts.

"Genovene rubbed her pelvis against my crotch, stroking me to the point I thought I might erupt in my underpants. Passion finally had conquered the last of my reservations, and I gave into my desire. Returning her kisses with my own urgency, I began squeezing her ample breasts, at which point she removed her mouth from mine and pushed my face directly into her bosom, smiling broadly as she did so.

"'Do you want me?' she asked softly.

"I looked up from her breasts and nodded eagerly that I did. Without another word, she pulled me away from her, but only to re-attend to my mouth with her own, although not for long. Heading downward, she lifted up my T-shirt and kissed me on my chest and stomach. Then, with one quick swipe, she pulled my shorts and underwear down below my knees.

"I looked down at myself, naked and ready, and less than an inch from her face. She gave me a moment to anticipate her next move, winking playfully up at me once that moment was over. Then, she launched an assault on my virgin organ, caressing it with a flurry of licks and kisses while alternately stroking it with her hands.

"The pleasure I experienced was more intense than anything I'd ever known up to that point in my life. But once I gave into it, moaning as I rode this wave of physical ecstasy, I found I couldn't control the wave's momentum. When I came, I did so recklessly, throwing my seed into her face. Most of it landed near her mouth, though she raised herself up when I reached the last thrust, collecting a small stream between her breasts.

"She stood and pressed her mouth to mine again, forcing me to share a taste of myself with her. She then massaged my crotch again, stroking and caressing my relieved organ. To my amazement, it regrew rapidly into another raging hard-on. Grasping it firmly, she raised herself up and placed it inside her, teasing me as she only allowed it to remain inside her momentarily.

"'We don't have time to fuck right now,' she whispered huskily, as her own passion threatened to conquer her own self-control. 'But, perhaps they wouldn't mind if I fucked you on the celebration table before we ate. Who knows what they'd think of that?'

"I pictured the space in the middle of the table where the main course would be set once dinner was ready. A cold shudder ran through me, although at the moment I had no idea why it happened. She, on the other hand, cocked her head to one side as she studied my eyes and reaction, a hint of concern appearing in her own.

"'Who are 'they', anyway? Is she referring to her family?' I wondered to myself, somewhat horrified by the implications and images brought to my mind by her words.

"Before I could ponder the matter further, she pulled me out of her, and began working my dick fervently with her hands again. She bent down to her knees and smiled mischievously as she glanced up at my surprised face. Then, she shoved it back into her mouth, stroking it firmly and thoroughly along its entire length as she pushed it toward the back of her throat. Intense pleasure overtook me again, only this time I felt like I was leaving my body. I experienced the distinct sensation of rising upward toward a blinding light. Suddenly, the light faded and I was sucked down into a void of utter darkness. I floated aimlessly in this deep sea of blackness, feeling empty and lonely, and yet at the same time, warm and comfortable.

"From somewhere nearby, Genovene moaned passionately, the sound of her lilting voice growing steadily louder until it surrounded me completely. It so encompassed my being that it seemed to fill me from the inside out, saturating every cell and molecule I could claim as my own.

"'Give in to me, Jack, for now is the time,' her voice told me, the moan suddenly softening to a mere whisper. 'Things must work out as they should. True darkness is drawing near and the bright light of day will soon fade forever into evening, deepening from there to pitch blackness even deeper than that which you find yourself in now. It's best the nature of things in our world continue as it always has. For the sweetest and most meaningful moment of a day is the sunset, marking the inevitable surrender of daylight to the night's ominous power.'

"All at once, I was standing before her, spewing forth the final remnants of my seed into her open throat. Genovene moaned again as she collected the last drop. Then, she removed me from her mouth and pulled up my underwear and shorts, but only just above my knees.

"She stood up and looked directly into my eyes with her own, taunting me with her eyebrows slightly raised and another mischievous grin on her face. While sizing me up one more time, she deliberately licked her lips, finishing this process with a light smack. 'M-m-m-m!' she enthused. 'Oh, the *sweetness* of youth! The younger the sweeter, that's for sure!'

"She turned around and moved toward the bed, leaving me standing in my semi-nakedness near the door. Genovene purposely swung her hips back and forth to torment me further. Her arrogant swagger was all I needed to realize I'd been nothing more than her latest sexual conquest. The only salvageable thing for me was my awareness of this fact told me the chocolate cookie's strange hold on me had ended.

"'*What the fuck is going on here?*' I wondered in horror to myself. '*What in God's name have I just...DONE??*' I looked down at my nakedness and hurried to pull up my underwear and shorts. I could feel the blood rush to my face again along with the heat and cool sweat of the most extreme embarrassment I've ever experienced. I was humiliated—*completely* humiliated, and as I ran the hazy play by play of the experience through my mind, I teetered on the edge of a much more dangerous feeling of despair.

"'Oh, come now, Jack!' Genovene playfully chastised me as she walked over to a large armoire located near the head of the enormous bed. She opened it and pulled out a lavender cape and gown, setting them both upon the bed. She seemed at ease in her nakedness, addressing me as one would a familiar lover or spouse. The strange euphoria might be leaving, I thought, but her telepathic powers seemed to be right on top of my growing unease.

"'You've got that right, Jackie boy!' she teased. 'You were very enjoyable. You've got a great young body, a beautiful face and a *nice*, big cock for your age! What more could a girl want?' She laughed, but the insensitivity and arrogance in her voice were unmistakable. The sweetness and compassion from earlier were absent. I was definitely ready to go back home immediately!

"Genovene stifled her laughter. Suddenly, she dropped what she was doing with her gown and cape and studied me. A wounded and worried look soon replaced her giddy pompousness. 'Jack, forgive me, *please!* I was just trying to have a little fun with you! Besides, I did only what you've been wanting all day... My desire is to make you happy!' she concluded with a pout.

"In an amazing turnabout, the sweetness returned to her demeanor. I was truly confused now, not knowing which side of her was real and which was a facade hiding the other. I hoped this was the 'real' Genovene, but I wasn't at all sure about that and didn't think I ever could be.

"She moved back toward me, her naked beauty stirring my manhood again, although the wanton thoughts from earlier were long gone.

"'Look, Jack. I'm truly sorry for teasing you a moment ago. I *really* am' she told me. 'But I'm not sorry for bringing you into my bedchamber, nor am I apologizing for wanting to touch you either. I still want for us to be friends. *More* than friends, if that's possible. Okay?'

"I hesitated before accepting her apology. But I relented and accepted, mostly because I had wanted her. But I didn't have her...she had me. Regardless of the fact she appeared sincere, I intended to keep my guard up around her from then on.

"I hated what'd happened, but decided to stick around for the Celebration Feast in order to be polite to Genovene's family, and ensure she really kept her promise to lead me safely back home. I also vowed silently to flee immediately if anything else happened.

"'Very well, then,' she said. 'You can go home whenever you like. I only pray you won't hold my moment of indiscretion against me forever.' She seemed truly penitent as she turned away from me again, walking back toward the outfit she'd placed on the bed. She raised her hands above her head and clapped them together loudly. An instant later, the pair of muscular guards who protected the main access to her sanctuary opened the door and stepped into the room.

"'Urei and Quan, please escort our friend here back to the temple entrance,' she instructed them over her shoulder. She then addressed me as well.

"'I'll be along shortly, Jack. Wait for me at the celebration table in the temple courtyard.' She then motioned for the three of us to be on our way, seemingly unashamed in her nakedness before us all. 'Make sure you're ready for when the feast starts at three o'clock, Jack!' she called after me.

"'*Three o'clock??*' I responded, greatly alarmed. I pulled my watch from my shorts pocket. Under the torchlight's glow just outside her doorway I saw that my watch read 2:32. 'Genovene, I need to be on my way home *now!*' I told her. 'I can't afford to be late getting home today—Grandpa'd kill me for sure!'

"'Jack, *please* trust me!' said Genovene. 'You won't be late getting home, but the celebration feast for the Festival Of Life starts promptly at three—not a minute before or after. It's always been this way since for as long as I can remember. You and I won't stay long, but we need to make an appearance since you're the grand guest of honor!'

"'That's not going to leave me enough time to get back home!' I countered, unable to control the stress in my voice. 'It took at least an *hour* to get here from my house, and I've got to be home by *four*— .'

"'*Jack!*' she snapped, interrupting me. 'Look, I know a shortcut to your Grandpa's place. In fact, I used it yesterday when I first delivered the talisman to you. I *guarantee* that I'll have you home well before four o'clock this afternoon. Please, *trust me* on this—if for no other reason than the amazing things you've witnessed here, thanks to me! Please...*please* promise you'll join me at the grand celebration table outside. *Please*, Jack!'

"I wondered briefly about her reference to the talisman's delivery to me. But, her incredible charm and the commanding urgency in her voice overpowered my concern of getting home on time. Besides, it was plausible she knew a shortcut. 'All right, I'll stay for the beginning of the feast,' I agreed. 'Just remember I've got to be home *by* four. Okay?'

"'Fair enough,' she said, and turned her attention to her two guardians standing behind me. 'Urei and Quan, as soon as you've led Jack to the courtyard, please return here promptly. I'll be ready for you to escort me to my place next to him at the celebration table,' she instructed, moving over to pick up her gown. She then addressed me one last time. 'Why don't you wait for me by the temple steps, Jack? Better yet, if you'd like to look around the courtyard, feel free to do so. Just don't wander too far from the celebration table as we will get started right at three o'clock.'

"I told her I'd do that, and then she motioned for me to join Urei and Quan. Doing so, I glanced one last time at this gorgeous woman standing in the middle of her bedroom with her naked backside facing me. One of the guards—I had no idea which one was 'Urei' or 'Quan' at this point—closed the door and then motioned for me to lead the way into the darkness, while he and the other hulking servant of Genovene followed close behind me. I peered up into their emotionless faces before I lost the benefit of the torchlight's' glow, noting their dark eyes and strong features. Their thick black hair and reddish-brown skin made me wonder if they were of Native American descent. They were much larger than any people I'd ever seen before, including the other villagers. I figured if they were as strong and fierce as they looked, they'd certainly make a whole lot of money playing any professional sport they chose.

"Without the comfort of Genovene's warm presence next to me, the deep thick blackness we moved in seemed so much worse than it had when she and I walked through this area. I focused my attention on getting through it unharmed and bravely moved forward. Before long, I glimpsed a faint light in the distance that steadily grew stronger. A moment later, I realized the light was actually from the chalube'at. Seeing something I recognized gave me a little comfort and a direction to move toward.

"I picked up my pace, but once I did this, the slithering presence from earlier began to stir just ahead of us. Whatever it was, the unseen thing seemed to move very quickly from the front and then on over to the back of us, growling loudly at various points as it circled us while we crept along in the darkness. The menace suddenly came closer to us, and from the sounds and depth of its movements, I could tell the thing was quite large. Its steady advance and near proximity greatly unnerved me, fear forcing me to stop walking altogether.

"As if mimicking my abrupt stop and mocking my fear, the thing ceased its aggressive movements. It seemed to wait for my next move. A sickening, almost metallic smell, like old rust on a tin can, soon filled the air around us. I tried to identify the acrid smell, but struggled to do so. While I thought about what to do next, I realized what the odor could be.

"Blood. It was fucking *blood*, man! It was that and some rotting carcass of a dead animal, or animals. But how in the hell did the awful smell suddenly appear one minute when it wasn't there the minute before? It certainly wasn't present when Genovene and I came through the area earlier.

"A hot stinky breeze blew toward us from our right. To my horror, the source of both the stench and the wind draft was none other than a large mouth—a very, *very* large mouth. To think this massive orifice was hidden in the darkness just a few feet away, hungry and opened wide, was more than I could bear. I turned to run back to Genovene's chamber. Before I could do so, Urei and Quan grabbed and spun me back around to face our original destination toward the tower's main entrance. They prodded me toward the chalube'at, which was now just a couple hundred feet in front of us.

"'Don't be afraid,' one of them advised, their deep voice resonating deeply throughout the area. 'Keep moving, Jack. You'll reach your destination shortly and safely.'

"'Well, at least they speak English,' I thought to myself, not sure if I should really take comfort from that fact or not. 'What's out there, anyway?' I asked them.

"'The personal pets of Talusha,' the same guard replied. 'They are merely curious at this point.'

"'Could they hurt somebody?' I inquired further, knowing the answer was obvious, yet needing to hear a firm 'no'.

"'Only if you were in this place by yourself,' the guard responded, chuckling in amusement. His rumbling voice caused my gooseflesh to rise again.

"I summoned up my courage and headed for the light, moving swiftly while my companions kept pace with me. At first, the immense circling, menacing, and invisible brood continued to threaten our progress. But as we ignored them, they eventually became disinterested, drawing back deeper into the shadows once we reached the light.

"I was greatly relieved. A few trickles of cool sweat streamed down my back and sides, confirming just how tense things had been until a moment ago. Bathed in the bright glow from above, I craned my neck backward as far as I could, but still was unable to see the top of the magnificent tower. I looked over at my companions standing a few feet away.

"'Are you ready to continue, Jack?' the other guard asked me.

"Now that I got a good look at both of them, I was even more amazed at their massive size. Their physiques were quite imposing, with huge muscles that would make most body builders extremely envious. Being as handsome as they were, I wondered if either had ever experienced an intimate encounter with Genovene. It was hard not to picture them crushing her slender frame while in the throes of physical passion.

"'Jack,' the guard repeated, his voice rumbling as deeply as his companion's had earlier. 'We need to move on now.'

"'I'm ready,' I said, and the guards moved to either side of me. We made our way past the chalube'at gleaming in the center of the room, and headed for the main entrance. When we reached the building's foyer, I noticed a small group of servants hurrying back and forth from the tower to the courtyard. The temple guards held the crystal doors open for these servants as they carried more trays loaded with bread and fruit for the celebration feast. Some of the servants carried golden utensils, goblets, and large wine carafes.

"One servant in particular caught my eye, as she carried a hat-sized, square white box that was decorated with elaborate gold designs and trim. As this servant approached us, the box suddenly slipped from her grasp and tumbled onto the floor. A small door-like opening on the side of the box swung open and a stream of voices seeped out. At first, these voices sounded like murmuring. But after dropping the box again when attempting to pick it up, the crying voices became a roar that echoed loudly throughout the tower's base.

"'*Help me!! Get me out of heeerre!!!*' shrieked a young woman's voice. '*Save us, someone!!*' an old man's voice cried out. '*Release us from here!! Pleeease!!!*'

"The servant dove for the box, reaching for the little gold door in a desperate effort to close it.

"'*Where are you, Genovene?? I want my mommy and my da—.*'

"The terrified voice of a small child was cut off as the servant shut the door. I was deeply afraid and stood motionless next to Urei and Quan, as if nailed to the spot where I stood. The servant looked up, smiling nervously as she listened to my escorts. One of them scolded her in the language of the villagers. The servant's smile was quickly replaced by a look of fear and worry. She bowed low, and without looking back at any of us, she whirled around and ran to the tower's entrance, where she disappeared into the sunlit courtyard with the box securely tucked under her arm.

"'Please excuse this unpleasantness, Jack,' said the one who had scolded the careless servant. He was still upset, and his voice betrayed an underlying tension. 'The, um...house servants know better than to leave our village amusements unprotected. The one you saw a moment ago belongs in the arcade. It should've never been here in the first place.'

"Although plausible, I didn't think what he said accounted for the chilling desperation I heard in the distraught voices, nor did it account for why Genovene's name was called out so emphatically by some little girl's voice. I looked up into his face, wondering if it was Urei or Quan that had spoken to me. I was about to ask a question about the box, but the other guard spoke up just as I opened my mouth.

"'Jack, it's time for Quan and I to go back for Genovene,' Urei said. 'I hope you've brought your appetite, for the celebration table is now ready.'

"At least I finally knew 'who was who' between the two giants. Perhaps Urei would've been pleased to know I'd certainly brought my appetite, as I was starving. Since I knew the time was steadily marching toward three o'clock, I walked over to the temple's entrance, being careful to avoid colliding with the growing number of busy servants along the way. Upon reaching the entrance, the guards who were stationed there bowed politely to me, and then pulled open the crystal doors so I could exit the tower.

"'Remember, Jack, Genovene will be here shortly,' advised Urei, calling after me. 'The servants will show you where your place of honor is. I believe it is now fifteen minutes until three o'clock, and if you'd like to take a quick look around the courtyard, please feel free to do so. Just remember to be seated at the table at three o'clock *sharp*, Jack. Don't be late!'

"'I won't be!' I called back to him over my shoulder, waving to both of them as their hulking figures moved back toward the shadowy darkness. I then walked out of the temple and down the steps to the courtyard. I pulled my watch from my pocket and confirmed the time was 2:46. Not a bad guess by Urei. But I wondered again how I'd ever make it back home by four o'clock. I just hoped and prayed Genovene arrived in the courtyard on time and that our participation in this feast would be brief.

"The sun had already begun its descent toward the western edge of the clear blue sky. The majestic pyramid was now to my right, and the nearly overloaded table was to my left. Scores of servants hurried about in their final preparations for the feast. Many of the people from the plaza further below had come up to the courtyard as well.

"As I moved through the crowd, I noticed several men and women dressed in beautiful hooded robes. I was fairly certain they were all related to Genovene, probably the brothers and sisters she told me about earlier. Each of them had the same beautiful long white hair and luminous blue eyes. All of their robes were satin and adorned with gold embroidered designs and small jewels. Each robe was a different color: royal blue, crimson, emerald green, and midnight black.

"The four of them walked back and forth through the crowd from the table to the pyramid. I watched the one in the blue robe with particular fascination, since I recognized him as Genovene's brother Malacai. He carried a long knife in a jeweled sheath over to the foot of the pyramid's steps where he laid it down. The person in the emerald robe, a female, followed him. She carried a box that closely resembled the one I'd just seen inside the temple. She set it down next to the knife and then walked back to the table with Malacai.

"It really made me wonder what kind of event this was. I mean, what purpose did the fancy knife serve? Did the box sitting next to the knife contain strange voices, too? I shuddered at the thought of hearing more voices plead for mercy, even if it was supposedly an arcade game.

"I looked at my watch once more, noting I still had over ten minutes left until the Celebration Feast began. Since Genovene wasn't there yet, I decided to go ahead and look around on the other side of the courtyard. I put my watch back in my pocket and walked past the table toward the row of juniper trees. The aroma from the array of fresh baked bread, side-entrees, pies, and pastries made my stomach growl. When I reached the trees, their pine scent was quite powerful—strong enough to provide an odd contrast with the smells from the nearby table. For some reason I suddenly felt nauseated, and the intense hunger I felt just a moment ago was gone.

"I decided to see what was on the other side of the trees, hoping to at least find relief from the nausea growing worse by the second. I stepped through the row and soon had a great view of the rest of the village. The terrain dropped off steeply beyond the tower, and I could see hundreds of golden rooftops from the multitude of buildings that filled the area. I figured this must be where the people of this village resided. Beautiful gardens, streams, and a large pond dotted the graceful landscape. Beyond all of this, a mile or two away from the tower and plaza, stood the enormous crystal wall encircling the entire village.

"I remember thinking how amazing the place really was. Despite my awkward sexual experience with Genovene and the few times I'd been truly frightened, I still felt privileged to be there. Since she would be arriving in the courtyard at any moment, I turned around to go back. It was then that I noticed a small stone shack sitting near the edge of the tower's steps, just beyond the juniper trees and less than fifty feet away from me. I stopped and stared at it, thinking how odd it was for such a thing to be there amid the lavish grandeur that surrounded me. All at once it hit me, and another chill raced along my spine. It was my grandfather's tool shed."

"You're kidding," said Peter. A look of both wonder and surprise spread across his face.

The sudden sound of Peter's voice was startling. Jack had begun to lose himself in the story. Answering Peter was a welcome distraction.

"No, I'm serious," said Jack. "At first I thought it only reminded me of the 'real thing' back home. I mean, how'd it get there if it was, in fact, the same shed?"

Peter smiled and started to say something. But he stopped himself, telling Jack to continue, and what he wished to say could wait until later. Peter motioned for him to continue.

"Are you sure?' asked Jack. 'I know this all sounds crazy, but I swear I've been honest with you. *Completely* honest. Do you still want me to continue this way, to be so detailed and graphic?"

"Yes I do,' said Peter. 'I realize sharing some of this is painful for you. I appreciate what you're telling me more than you know."

"Okay, then,' said Jack. 'I walked over to the shed, my curiosity wouldn't let me just turn around and forget about it. Its stacked stone walls were painted white and the roof was made using wooden slats—*just* like Grandpa's! Even the spots where the roof had recently been repaired were the same! I thought of how Grandpa refused to tear the goddamned thing down, keeping it functional even if it didn't look right anymore as it sat up against our farmhouse, its worn wooden doors usually locked tightly with linked chains and padlocks.

"I walked around it. When I reached the front, I found the only difference between Grandpa's shed and this structure—although, I'm sure you're already realizing what is later revealed to me—that I'm talking about only *one* structure. In place of the old padlocked doors was an open space with a counter, and a few feet behind the counter were rows of shelves filled with ceramic dishes and pottery. It was some kind of shop!

"A cheerful girl in her late teens was waiting to greet me from behind the booth's counter. 'Well, hello, Jack!' she said. 'I was wondering when you'd find time to stop by here!'

"'What an amazing place this is, *indeed!*' I thought to myself. It seemed everyone knew my name and yet I was still meeting folks for the very fist time. Strangely, though, I felt totally at peace in this person's presence. It was different from the warmth I'd felt from Genovene. It was more like meeting a long lost friend.

"'It's so nice to see you, Jack,' she told me, and then reached over the counter and extended her hand for me to shake. 'I can't tell you how much I've been looking forward to this moment!' Her smile seemed so natural. To me she was absolutely beautiful, with hazel eyes and dark auburn hair that flowed in ringlets as it framed her dimpled face. A small patch of freckles dotted both cheeks, and with the laced up dress she was wearing, I thought she looked like she'd just stepped out of a Grimm's fairy tale and into the village.

"'Hi...it's nice to meet you, too,' I responded, trying hard not to stare, but unable to resist. 'What's your name?'

"'My name's not important at the moment, but very soon you'll know who I am,' the girl replied.

"The feeling of familiarity was growing stronger by the moment. I knew her from somewhere else, I was certain of it. But, since it would be impolite to keep staring at her, I glanced around the booth instead. It was set up as two separate rooms with the counter and its merchandise located in the front of the structure and a smaller room in the back.

"As I said a moment ago, everything on display was created in ceramic clay—splendid stuff that appeared to have been painted by hand. Their elegance and simpler beauty stood out sharply in contrast to the gold and crystal vessels I'd seen so far.

"'If you'd like to take a closer look at anything you see, just say so,' the girl said, before she turned and walked into the back room. 'I'm extending to you the special privilege of coming behind the counter.'

"Once she disappeared, I heard the squeaking noises of a pottery wheel spinning in that other room. I was completely enraptured with her, but in a safe way. Despite her earthy beauty, there wasn't a physical attraction. Rather than a sexual longing, I simply wanted to know this person, to speak with her and learn all about her. What about specifically? I didn't know yet. I just felt compelled to do this.

"The counter itself was wooden with a latch that allowed the countertop to be pulled up in order to let someone enter and leave the booth. It was slightly taller than my mid-section, so instead of lifting it, I bent down and slid under it to the other side. A lot more pottery and other items were stored underneath the counter, including a small silver box with a scene skillfully etched onto its face depicting a trio of angels descending upon the earth from heaven. The wings of the angels were inlaid with tiny sapphires and diamonds, and the eyes were emeralds. This was the only thing I readily saw that compared to the extravagance throughout the rest of the village.

"'It's beautiful, isn't it?' the girl called out from the back room.

"'Yeah, it sure is,' I agreed while continuing to examine it. I especially liked the way the jewels made the wings appear as if they were in constant motion. 'It's *very* beautiful.'

"'Why, thank you, Jack! It was a gift from someone very close to me,' she said. 'Come on back here for a moment, and bring the little box with you.'

"I went over to the doorway that led into the back room and peered inside. The room was completely bare except for a spinning wheel with a large lump of clay sitting upon it, and a pair of wooden chairs. There was also a small door next to a narrow window, which let in minimal light. The pretty girl sat upon the chair nearest to the wheel and she motioned for me to come and sit down in the other chair across from her.

"As soon as I sat down her appearance began to change. It was subtle at first, but as I stared at her in shock, the changes in her appearance became more dramatic and profound. She was aging before me and she was filling out somewhat as well. It was like watching one of those age progression programs you see on TV for missing kids. Less than a minute later, the beautiful young girl was still beautiful. But she was now twelve to fifteen years older and possibly twenty pounds heavier. I was sitting face to face with a person previously known to me only through photographs.

"'*Mom??*' I couldn't believe it! It was too good to be true, and for a moment I feared I'd stepped into some cruel illusion in the village. But the love exuding from the smiling woman sitting across from me, along with the strong feeling within my gut, told me this person was indeed my mother. As improbable as it seemed, here she was, very much alive and no longer a ghostly image in my head.

"'*Mom!!*' I cried out with joy, unaware for the moment I might damage her eardrums. She seemed unaffected by the loudness of my rapture. Only the emotion itself touched her and she smiled broadly with tears welling in her eyes.

"Unable to resist the urge, I stood up and she stood up to meet me. After hesitating only for an instant, this woman—my *mother*—and I reached out for each other in the kind of embrace that only two people separated for an unbearable length of time could ever understand. I buried my face in her shoulder, unable to control the waves of emotion that shook my soul to its very core. I released the burden of sadness and longing I'd carried with me for as long as I could remember in racking sobs.

"The warmth and softness of her being enveloped me as she returned the tightness of my arms' grip with her own. She was flesh and blood and not the cruel illusion I feared. To further confirm this, she loosened her hold on me and reached her hand under my chin to raise my face up to her own. Her eyes glistened as they released a pair of small imperfect streams upon her cheeks while she fought to control her breaths heaving within her chest.

"'Where have you *been* all this time?' I asked, struggling to keep my words from speeding out of my mouth. 'Where's Dad? Boy, Grandpa and Jeremy will be so happy! I can't wait to tell—.'

"'*Sh-sh-sh!*' she interrupted me, her index finger trembling as she motioned for me to be quiet. She was still smiling, but now shook her head as she sobbed in her joy. I broke down again as well, my shoulders shaking violently to the point I would've collapsed before her had she not tightened her grip to support me until the overwhelming swell of emotion ebbed enough for me to regain control of my balance.

"She gently pushed me away from her, motioning for me to sit down again while the tears streamed down her face. I sat down again, although I didn't allow her to leave my tear-blurred gaze as I did so. My mother brought her chair closer to mine, and as we sat together she dabbed my eyes with a handkerchief she pulled from her dress, stroking the side of my face softly, admiring the boy she'd missed seeing grow up.

"Like I said, I knew this was real. Regardless of all the strangeness I'd experienced, *this* was different. But despite the reality of my mother's presence sitting next to me, there was an underlying incompleteness to the event. It was as if some ominous feeling of sadness was also present and determined to keep it so. The very air around her held within it a condemnation or sentence of impending doom, despite any intentions on my part to make this complete and permanent.

"'Oh, how I've longed for this moment, Jack!' she said. 'I've dreamed of it for a very long time. There's so much I'd love to share with you...to tell you. But, there isn't enough time.'

"'What do you mean??' I asked indignantly. I didn't like the way she said this. The unpleasant feeling in the air grew heavier and more oppressive, which in turn filled me with dread.

"'*You* don't have time, Jack,' she told me. 'Listen closely and I'll quickly tell you what you need to know.'

"I wasn't sure what she meant by this. She seemed to sense my confusion and raised her eyebrows in anticipation of my questions that were sure to come.

"'You mean the dinner, or feast or whatever it is, which Genovene says is being held in my honor?' I asked.

"Surprised at this particular question, she laughed and said, '*Heavens* no, son. I wasn't referring to that at all. Yes, I know all about that, too, and we'll get to it in a moment. But, what I'm referring to is the fact your grandpa—*my* father—Is very worried about your whereabouts as we speak. He found out about twenty minutes ago you weren't with your friend Lee, and to be quite honest, he's berating himself for not keeping a better eye on you—especially after last night.'

"My mouth dropped open. 'How'd you know about that?'

"'Jack...Genovene isn't the only one around here who knows where you've been and what's going on around you,' she said. 'As a matter of fact, this is the only time since you first saw the talisman yesterday she hasn't known your thoughts and exact whereabouts. They're hidden from her now, but only for a short while. She'll soon discover you're here.'

"The sordid implications of my mom's words hit me full force. Images of my dick inside Genovene's mouth flooded my mind, and I was mortified now much more than before. *What did she think of that?*' I wondered. More important, though, was what she thought of *me*, her son.

"'My son, please understand that I'm also aware of the truth in the situation you found yourself,' she assured me. 'Genovene can be physically as beautiful and seductive as any male will ever encounter. Remember the cookie you ate? You never realized it was laced with a powerful aphrodisiac. As a result you were overmatched, without any chance of resisting her. I've always been proud of you, Jack, and *nothing* that happened today changed that. *Please* understand this.'

"I smiled weakly, for the moment staring down at the ground and still very much ashamed. At the same time, I was truly grateful that the person I'd always hoped would be proud of me actually was.

"'Now, listen closely,' she continued. 'You think Genovene's your friend, I know. But, besides the ruthless seduction we've now discussed, you've been given other clues about what she's really like. You've been given clues about the nature of this place as well. Let me start with things you'll easily understand. About the box in the temple— those voices you heard?'

"Yeah, what about them?

"'Urei lied to you,' she said. 'That was no game or amusement. Those voices belong to the spirits of people just like you who've been lured for centuries to this trap. Besides the first box and the one you saw placed near the pyramid's steps, there are hundreds of other boxes like it in the village, each with the souls of Genovene's victims trapped inside.'

"I was horrified by what she told me. Despite my reluctance to believe this about Genovene, my mother's words rang true. From deep within me, I felt Genovene's capacity for cruelty and wickedness just as clearly as I somehow knew the innate goodness of the woman sitting next to me. I suddenly felt panic, for I had no idea how we were going to get back home.

"'My mom smiled compassionately, and the warmth from her being radiated toward me. 'Do not fear,' she said, 'I have a plan. If you hadn't made your wish at the pool in the garden, I might not have been allowed to intervene.' She suddenly sat up straight, arching her neck and tilting her head slightly as she listened for a moment. She then grew serious and leaned closer to me. 'Jack,' she whispered, 'Genovene's coming out of the temple. She will start looking for you, in earnest, within the next few minutes.'

"I'm sure my eyes grew wide, as I completely forgot all about the starting time for the feast. I pulled my watch out again, noting the time was 2:57. Surprised, I brought the timepiece closer to my face, confirming what I saw was accurate. The words of Urei and Genovene echoed in my head and I realized I was about to be in a world of serious shit!

"'Jack, *please* pay attention to me!' My mother scolded me, letting her voice rise above the whisper she spoke with a moment before. '*Please* heed everything I'm telling you! You *must* flee from here and follow the golden road back out of the village. Then, you must take the same path you took in getting here, in order to get back home. You'll have to trust me that you'll be protected. Do not, I repeat, Jack, *do not* stray from the path or you'll make our task so much harder!

"'Genovene may try and convince you to stay for the feast, and I'm aware of the fact you're struggling with some sense of obligation to her. *Don't* give in to that feeling, my son! You *mustn't* do it, no matter what she does to try and convince you otherwise. Son, this feast is *not* for you, but rather, you're the feast!'

"She paused for a moment and looked down at the ground. Slowly, she raised her head, looking back into my eyes again. Tears were welling once more in her eyes. 'They plan to sacrifice you to Talusha, the blue demon of Karachi,' she continued. 'I know you saw the bubbling and burning thing when you were up in the temple tower. Well, you caught a glimpse of the essence of Talusha. To please him, they plan to give him your heart. Then, once that's done, they'd spend the rest of their celebration eating what's left of your body, after first sending your spirit into a box. Did you not see the altar on top of the pyramid, the knife lying next to the box at the foot of the pyramid's steps, and the empty space in the middle of the celebration table?'

"I nodded again to confirm I did, now gripped by terror.

"'Genovene and her tribe consider you a fine prize,' she explained, 'and they've had their eye on you since you were an infant. The details as to why this is so are not important enough for us to discuss at this time. Just be aware that your soul's energy would serve them well if they ever managed to capture it through your sacrificial death.'

"'Jack! Oh, Jack! Where are you?' The now familiar voice interrupted, calling out to me.

"Genovene was searching the courtyard and we both froze in silence. She was at least a couple hundred feet away from us, and her voice was faint. But a moment later her calls grew louder. She was moving toward us.

"I looked at my watch again. The time was now 3:02. I was late to the celebration feast and definitely now an official member of Genovene's shit list. I absently placed my watch back into my pocket as I again turned my attention back to my mother and her instructions.

"'Jack,' she whispered,' we only have a moment longer. Hand me the box, please.'

"I gave her the silver box and she turned it around so that the angels faced me directly.

"'Open it gently,' she instructed.

"I did. Inside the box sat a gray colored oval stone with a sword carved onto its face. The sword bisected a star and a circle, with smaller designs carved beneath them.

"'Go ahead and pick it up,' she urged me.

"I did as she asked, and held the stone within my hands.

"'What I'm about to tell you now is of the utmost importance, Jack,' she said. 'Keep the stone with you, and for God's sake don't lose it! On the left side of the main gates to the village as you leave this place, you'll find a golden lion's head protruding from the crystal wall. You must insert this stone into the lion's mouth in order to get out of the village. You got that, son?'

"'Yes ma'am,' I said. The stone was light and carried some warmth with it. I placed it inside my other pocket to keep it separate from my watch.

"'Jack!! Where *are* you??' shouted Genovene.

"I guessed she was now within forty feet of us, and I could hear the anger in her voice. In panic I stood up, for I felt compelled to leave the booth. My mother quickly grabbed my arm, effectively restraining me from doing that. She told me to stay put with her in the back room.

"'One last thing,' she whispered. 'You need to keep in mind that Genovene isn't what she seems to be. Nor is the village and all of the wonders along the path outside the village. They're real, but not in a permanent sense. They're superimposed upon your world, Jack. Again, there's no time to explain this more clearly right now. But here's something that'll enable you to see Genovene as she really is, to see what she truly looks like in her natural state.'

"My mom pulled out a small red satin bag with a leather strap from in between the laces of her dress near her bosom. She opened the bag and poured out a gold and gray colored dust upon my head, which disappeared the very instant the sparkling dust particles touched my scalp. 'This mixture is made from the very gold of this village, along with the charred remains of its many victims,' she told me. 'May it reveal to you the deception and the truth about Genovene, for she is far more cruel and wicked than any other person you've ever heard or read about in recorded history. I pray you escape without feeling the fear and pain of her wrath.'

"'*Jaaacckk!! This is a very poor way to treat someone who has taken the time to arrange a feast for you, and as the guest of honor you are now way past rude!!! Come out from there nowww!!!*' Genovene suddenly shrieked.

"Although we couldn't see her from the back room, I saw her shadow from the afternoon sun hitting the floor as it stretched across the doorway leading from the front room to the back room. Gone was the beautiful young woman from earlier. In her place was a tall gangly thing with what looked like a slender spine-like tail whipping back and forth behind her. I started to scream, but my mother covered my mouth and spun me around and over to the very back of the room. She opened the small door and quickly pushed me through to the outside.

"'Remember, my son, stay on the path!' she pleaded. 'Be very brave in spite of what you'll see. No matter what happens, we'll all be with you—remember that!'

"'*Mom!!!*' I shouted back through the doorway. 'Why aren't you following me out here? You're coming with me, right?? *Hurry!!!* Hey, come on, Mom!!! Get out here before it's too—.*"

"'No, Jack!' she interrupted me. 'The immediate opportunity is *only* intended for you! I can't be released from this place unless you make it out of the village alive! Now, *go!!*'

"I stood bewildered and confused just outside the chest-high doorway, but only for a moment. A loud crash suddenly came from the front of the booth along with the sound of a great struggle amid the breaking of the wooden shelves and the ceramics as they spilled onto the floor.

"'*Mom!!!*' I cried out, and then tried to re-enter the shack's rear room in an effort to come to her aid and rescue. I was forced back out the doorway, as somehow she managed to easily push me back through it and out of the shed once more, slamming the door shut this time and locking it behind her.

"'*Run, Jack!!! Run, nowww!!!*' she screamed.

"Reluctantly, I obeyed her command to leave, for instinctively I knew I didn't have any more time to waste. I offered a quick fervent prayer for her safety, and then ran along the row of juniper trees, trying to get to the staircase that led down to the plaza and the golden road beyond as quickly as possible."

PART V

The Race Back Home

"Man, are you all right?" Jack asked Peter, whose eyes glistened again. "Seriously, I can stop talking about this shit if you want me to."

"I'm fine, Jack—really, I am," he said. "I want you to continue telling me your story. If this Genovene and her kind had anything to do with Bobby's disappearance, which seems likely, then I'm left to conclude he's dead."

"Like I said, man, we can forget about doing this—."

"*No!*" said the agent, interrupting Jack more forcefully than he intended. "We're not going to forget about anything! I came here to learn everything you can tell me about what happened back then, Jack! I'll be all right. Just keep on like you've been, and I'll get through this just fine. If you can handle reliving it, then please go on."

"All right. But if you change your mind, just tell me and I'll stop," said Jack, pausing until Peter assured him again he was ready to continue. "I ran as hard and fast as my wobbly legs could carry me. Once I reached the top of the grand staircase, I saw that the plaza below was still filled with people playing and laughing merrily as before. I started to go down the stairs, when I heard a roaring shriek behind me.

"'*Jaacckk!! Stop right where you are and proceed no further!!!*'

"The voice was eerily inhuman and difficult for me to know exactly where it came from. Was it fifty feet? Twenty? Or, was it just a few feet behind me?

"'*Turn around!! Noowwww!!!*'

"The intense rage in the voice was unmistakable. Slowly I tuned around, shaking very badly. What I saw next has stayed with me ever since. It will likely haunt my nightmares for the duration of my life. Genovene stood less than thirty feet away from me. She no longer was the beautiful young woman I'd spent the better part of that day with. What stood before me now was a hideous thing that must've been there all along, lurking dangerously behind the alluring disguise of her gorgeous hair, face, and body. The only thing about her that was recognizable were the eyes, as the two huge blue glowing orbs gazed contemptuously at me from where she stood.

"She was dressed in the lavender outfit she'd picked out earlier, which was just like the ones her brothers and sisters wore in the courtyard. The cape hung loosely from what must've been her shoulders, since her body had changed dramatically. She was much taller now, and her head and body were gnarled and skeleton-like, and covered with a pink and gray gelatinous substance that pulsed when she moved. A long snout and jaw protruded from her head, and her mouth was full of sharp pointed teeth. Her long arms and legs were almost insect-like, with hooked claws at the end of each one. All in all, she reminded me of a grotesque giant praying mantis.

"Her claws scraped against the marble floor of the courtyard as she moved toward me, quickly closing the gap between us. When she was about ten feet away, I noticed several deep-red splotches that glistened on her robe, and feared for what became of my mother.

"'*What have you done to my mom, you goddamn fucking bitch??*'

"'Shall I give you the details? It'd be so much better if I left it to your active imagination to give you a graphic 'play by play' instead, you ungrateful *brat!!*' she hissed. She took another step forward and was within five feet of me. 'You almost ruined everything, you *worthless piece of shit!!!*' she shrieked, and closed the gap to a mere foot. I could smell the stench of rotting meat and decay on her breath as she spoke. She leaned down directly into my face and I thought for sure I would pass out or piss in my shorts.

"The pink and gray shit on her face oozed and recollected itself as if it had a life of its own. 'Now, Jack...you can either come back with me of your own free will, or I can take you there myself in *pieces!!*' she sneered, a blast of her nasty breath spraying my face as she bared her sharp teeth at me. 'Which do you prefer?'

"Part of me—the brave part, that is—wanted to run back to the shed and check on my mother. If she were alive, I'd try to save her and get her to leave the village with me. But it was much too late for that. I figure even she knew the fate awaiting her for intervening on my behalf. All I could do now was tremble before Genovene, for I was too frightened to speak.

"'Very well, then. I'll carry you myself!!' she snapped, and reached for me. Repulsed by her slimy touch, I jerked away from her. I lost my balance and tumbled down the staircase until I grabbed hold of a stair nearly fifteen feet down from the top. I was bruised and scraped up, but the pain shook me from my fear. I stood up wincing and ran down the stairs as swiftly as I could. Genovene screamed at me to stop, and I glanced over my shoulder to check on her progress down the staircase. She was having a hell of a time navigating the stairs, and the distance between us quickly widened.

"'*Stop him!!! He's getting away!!!*'" she roared.

"I hoped to increase my lead once I hit the plaza. But, just as soon as I reached it, the crowd suddenly stopped and turned their full attention upon me. As a group, they cocked their heads toward her, as if waiting to confirm her command.

"'*Seize him, nowww!!! If he escapes, there'll be hell to pay for every one of you!!!*'

"They immediately organized themselves into rows and marched toward me, their eyes completely black and their mouths contorted into menacing scowls. Genovene was now within a few feet of the plaza, along with her four siblings who'd undergone a similar transformation. I was nearly surrounded. Without anywhere else to turn, I spun around and ran over to the waterfall directly to my left, climbing onto the ledge that faced it.

"Below me was the pool that fed the stream which ran through the garden sitting opposite from the one Genovene and I visited earlier. '*So much for sticking to the golden road!*' I jumped into the pool twenty feet below. The water was hard and bitterly cold, which left me gasping for air once I resurfaced. Shivering and determined to stay low to avoid detection, I let the water's current take me down into the stream itself. After passing over some small rapids and then sliding underneath a thick moss-covered bough, the stream carried me into the very heart of the garden.

"The current slowed enough to where I was able to swim. I headed for the shoreline closest to the garden wall, knowing it was nearest the golden road. Once out of the water, I found myself standing in a jungle. It looked as vibrant as the other garden across the plaza, but there was something different about this place. All I immediately cared about, though, was no one had pursued me here.

"Moving along the stream's bank, I followed what I hoped was the main path through this place. My plan was to walk along the path for a hundred feet or so, and then cross over to the garden wall and sneak behind the crowd in the plaza.

"I hadn't walked far when it occurred to me what was missing from this tranquil place. It was *too* quiet. There wasn't any sound other than the steady rush of the stream. I'd yet to hear a single bird or insect calling from anywhere within the garden, and found the near perfect stillness unsettling. Not to mention every normally fragrant flower I'd encountered carried no scent at all. Other than plants, there were no other signs of life in the garden. On the edge of my memory sat something very important.

"All at once I figured it out and a new wave of panic swept over me. I remembered Genovene said this particular garden responded to a person's deepest fears—the opposite of the other garden across the way. I immediately slowed my pace and glanced around myself warily.

Just ahead of me, the path suddenly took a sharp turn deeper into the garden, next to where a clump of large sumac trees stood across from an immense lilac bush. Just as I reached this curve, I was greeted by the foul odor of rotting flesh.

"Cautiously, I took a step. No sooner than I did this, I was face to face with a series of giant webs attached from the lilac bush to the very last of the tall sumacs near the stream. The path was completely blocked. I tried to remain calm, but my fear had the upper hand. Aside from having to find another way through the garden, I worried where the maker, or makers, of these enormous webs might be.

"I raised my hand to wipe a trickle of sweat from just above my brow, and lightly brushed up against the sticky web. Instinctively I jerked my arm away from it. The sudden movement sent a tremor through the web and I heard a rattling noise above me that sounded similar to wooden blocks tumbling in a copper pan. I looked up and saw the skeletal remains of an unfortunate conquistador trapped between two of the webs just a few feet away. I was horrified! The remains were still clothed in full armor, which had long since turned green and black from oxidation. The flanks of the outfit displayed several large holes from the deteriorating affects of time, the elements, or something's very large fangs. The victim's bones were picked clean, and the skull was contorted to where it clearly depicted the last moments of terror this unlucky person endured.

"I stepped away, unable to remove my gaze from this gruesome sight. I moved closer to the sumacs standing near the stream's bank. Here, the stench was worse and seemed to come from the trees' trunks. I looked down and nearly hurled what was left in my empty stomach. Lying in a haphazard pile were the skulls of roughly another thirty victims. There was nothing left of their bodies, other than a stray femur and a few finger fragments. The only other items near the skulls were a Native American headdress and set of chest beads, along with a rusted musket barrel and the torn and tattered fabric of an early American officer's coat and cloak.

"I was surprised I hadn't noticed this scene when I first came round the curve. It was nearly impossible to miss, either by sight or smell, though partially concealed by thick cocoon-like webbing near the base of the trees. I bent down to get a better look at the skulls. A few bits of maggot-infested flesh clung to five or six of them, which was the likely source for the noxious odor. This puzzled me, since if the remains were as old as they appeared, how could there possibly be any decaying flesh left on them?

"That question would remain unanswered as suddenly I heard the creaking and snapping of branches from high above my head. I looked up in time to see a massive black spider with glowing orange eyes and long gray fangs descending toward me. The giant arachnid landed with a heavy thud only a few feet to my right. I leapt from the path, running as fast as I could back over to the stream. I was about to dive back into the chilly water, and hesitated just long enough to notice an unusually large cottonmouth slithering near the shoreline by me. Once the snake saw me it wriggled swiftly to the shore.

"Meanwhile, the spider crawled swiftly toward the stream. It stood a lot taller than I did at the time, as its prickly legs were a good two feet higher than my head. It eyed me hungrily and suddenly leaped into the air toward the spot where I was. I tripped and nearly fell backward down the embankment, and I almost tumbled headfirst into the gaping jaws of the water moccasin.

"Somehow, my clothing became entangled in a scrub bush sticking up from the ground. I tried desperately to free myself while the spider landed just inches away from my left shoulder and stumbled a bit. It quickly righted itself and began to raise its head in order to take a tasty bite out of me, its milky venom dripping from its twitching fangs that were primed and positioned to puncture my trembling body.

"I really thought this was *it*. The end of my brief life, and the horrible failure of my efforts to not only save my own skin, but to try and fulfill my mother's wish for me to escape the village alive. I was ready to give up and just let this goddamned duo have their way with me. As I prepared to die, part of my mother's last admonition to me blasted loudly through my tired mind. '*Be very brave in spite of what you'll see! No matter what happens, we will be with you—remember that!!*'

"With the cottonmouth slithering up the embankment toward me, I ripped the portion of my shorts snagged on the branch, freeing myself just as the water moccasin arrived and the spider was in the process of bringing its poisoned fangs down upon me. Encouraged by my mother's words, I somehow managed to avoid both creatures by rolling away from them and quickly getting back onto my feet. I then noticed a small space between the webs near the bottom of one of the sumac trees. I ran and dove into the space, dragging a thick sticky strand of web with me.

"The snake's jaws snapped madly at the empty air where my sneakers had been only a moment before, while the spider's sharp fangs bore into the ground not far from the snake's head. Both rebounded quickly and again set out after me just as I was pulling my feet through to the other side of the web. The snake slithered toward the hole while the spider snapped off its embedded fangs to free itself from the ground's hold, letting out a pained and angry screech as it spun around on its hind legs and set out after my ass in a rage.

"In its determination to get me, the spider knocked the water moccasin out of its way just as the snake reached the gap between the webs. It tried to squeeze its enormous body through the hole while tearing frantically at the only obstacle between it and myself. Fortunately, it only got its head halfway through the space while its body became wedged in tightly, gripped by its own sticky trap. For the present time, both menaces were safely detained.

"I didn't dare squander this opportunity. Hastily I stood up and ran through the flowers and thick shrubs in the garden. It was only a matter of time before the spider freed itself and found some other way to get to me. The snake was possibly on its way already, as I heard the rustling sound of leaves coming up fast behind me. Terrified, I picked up my pace, running harder and faster until I didn't hear the noise anymore.

"Hoping I'd at least temporarily eluded the water moccasin, I moved back onto the path again and soon neared the end of the garden. I began to look for a way out and took a fork in the path that led directly to the garden's wall some seventy feet away. The fork was lined on both sides with tall exotic ferns and abrasive thistles, which I tiptoed past quickly until I reached the wall.

"Once there I immediately tried to climb over it. As soon as I was halfway over, an invisible force threw me back into the garden. Surprised and a hell of a lot sorer, I struggled back onto my feet and moved back to the wall. I sought desperately to remember what Genovene had done earlier when she opened a passageway in the other garden. Tentatively, I stretched my hand across the top of the wall. I was barely able to push through the invisible barrier before my hand was violently thrown back, nearly knocking me down and sending a surge of sharp pain throughout my arm.

"I dropped to my knees and searched along the side of the wall for some kind of switch or lever, but didn't find one. While doing this, I heard a low menacing growl coming from the area where the fork began. An enormous white tiger soon emerged from behind the ferns and ambled onto the path. It headed straight for me. When the tiger closed to within forty feet, it suddenly sprinted toward me with its sharp teeth bared.

"All I could do was shrink against the wall in terror, searching the ground with my hands for rocks or anything else to throw at the animal. Finding nothing suitable, I suddenly remembered the oval stone in my pocket. I dug it out and was about to hurl it at the savage beast, but it was too late. I felt the tiger's hot breath and heavy weight crash down on top of me.

"Just as I was pinned to the ground, the stone in my outstretched hand touched the tiger's chest. Instantly, it disappeared. I stood up in disbelief and looked around me, but the tiger was truly *gone*! I started to relax and smile until I heard the slithering noise of the cottonmouth moving through the ferns and thistles. I looked up in time to see the spider's body cast its enormous shadow near the path's fork and knew I wouldn't likely fend off both of them at once.

"In desperation I turned to the wall and waved the stone in front of it. It melted away, and by the time I scurried through to the other side, the snake and spider arrived. I heard a screeching whine behind me that abruptly ceased. When I turned around, the wall was intact again, without any sign of the snake and spider. All that remained was the serene beauty of the garden, resting quietly on the other side.

"Gradually, the sound of the bustling plaza around me returned. I noticed then that I was bleeding. The tiger had torn a painful gash in my shoulder. I winced, but knew I had to keep moving. I was surprised Genovene and her cohorts were still congregated at the other end, facing the very spot from where I'd jumped down into the pool, as if time stood still while I was in the garden. Gingerly, I moved across the plaza to the steep incline of the golden road. In less than a minute I was on my way up the hill, but the steep grade of the road caused me to slip slightly. My sneakers squeaked, which alerted Genovene of my new location. I saw her grotesque head whip around.

"'*After him!!!*' she screamed. '*Hurry, he's getting away!!!*'

"I scrambled up the hill, climbing it by hooking my fingers and the tip of my shoes in between the golden flagstones to keep from tumbling back down into the plaza. Once the road leveled out and I could stand up straight once more, I raced to the top of the hill. I looked back at the crowd following right behind me. They rapidly closed the gap between us, making weird clicking noises with their mouths as they scaled the hill.

"Back near the plaza's staircase, Genovene and her four siblings remained. They stood in a slight arc facing the statue called Morylan. She was performing some sort of ritual act or spell with her hands while Malacai pointed a long golden wand at the statue. The jets of water stopped and the massive warrior began to move, bending his head down toward the five monsters as if listening to them. The statue then turned his head toward me, drawing the golden sword noisily from the sheath tied to his side. Morylan raised the weapon high above his head and jumped down into the plaza from his pedestal, making a sound like thunder as he landed. He moved swiftly toward me, trampling and crushing the villagers in his way, and leaving a trail of gory footprints in his wake.

"I knew he would be upon me in a matter of seconds. I started to run toward the large magnolia on the left side of the road. I changed my mind when I considered the likelihood of the stone warrior checking for me there first since it was the nearest refuge to the road. Instead, I sprinted to the closest shop sitting on the right side of the road and hid behind that building. From there I could clearly see the enormous crystal wall encircling the village, as it stood less than fifty yards away. The shops sat closer to the majestic wall nearer the entrance to the village, and I took comfort in the fact I was moving closer to freedom. My chances of reaching the main gates safely seemed better if I stayed behind the shops, contrary to my mother's instructions to stay on the golden road. I prayed my close proximity to the preferred path would prove to be enough in the end.

"I kept moving, darting carefully from shop to shop while staying low to the ground. I was thankful the areas in front of me were deserted so far. Even so, the thunderous footsteps of Morylan grew ever closer, along with the insect-like noises from the villagers in pursuit. The ground shook so badly I nearly lost my balance, and I was forced to stop and brace myself against the back wall of the closest shop.

"The footsteps continued to grow louder until they stopped in front of that very building, which happened to be the one sitting directly across from the arcade. An enormous shadow loomed over the two-story structure and thickened as Morylan bent down toward me. 'He *knows* I'm here!' I worried to myself. " *What the fuck do I do now??*'

"I embraced the wall tightly in an effort to further conceal myself, trying to remain as calm as possible. One of the warrior's giant hands crept around the side of the shop to the very back of it. Probing and searching, the hand began to feel the grass and finger through some bushes nearby, pulling them out by their dirt-clodded roots with the same ease I could employ on a small dandelion. Two of the hand's fingers brushed noisily against the building less than two feet from where I was crouched in my attempt to merge with the wall. Absolutely terrified, I fought desperately to stay still and quiet, slowing my breath while my pulse throbbed in my chest and neck. The probing pair of fingers moved to within a few inches of me.

"Preparing myself for the very worst, it never came. Inexplicably, the fingers pulled back and the hand lifted, disappearing from my view. A moment later, the shadow lengthened as Morylan stood back up. The ground soon shook and then shook again and again, decreasing in strength and volume as the warrior moved up the road toward the gates. The wound in my shoulder ached terribly, although it didn't prevent me from using my arm yet. If anything, I reasoned the wound's presence helped me stay focused in getting the hell out of there.

"Listening to the fading footfalls of the warrior as it neared its new destination, I wondered what time it was and pulled out my watch. It was now 3:42. There were several hours left until nightfall, but I was going to miss Grandpa's four o'clock deadline and knew I'd have to answer for it. It got me moving and just in time, as the shrill clicking noises rapidly approached my hiding place from somewhere close behind me. I glanced over my shoulder while putting my watch back in my pocket. With no one visible yet, I peered around the building's edge where Morylan's fingers had been only moments ago. The area before me sat deserted.

"I ran to the rear of the next shop, quickly concealing myself behind a ledge. Cautiously, I looked back toward the spot I'd just vacated. I still didn't see anyone, but I heard a lot more of their unnerving noises coming from the road nearby. I moved over to the far edge of the shop and saw the immense golden gates were less than a quarter mile away.

"Morylan was already there, standing directly in front of the gates with his back to the entrance. He moved his head back and forth menacingly as he scanned the area before him, apparently looking for me. Small bands of villagers seemed to be also on the lookout for my whereabouts, and I knew it was only a matter of time before they extended their search behind the shops.

"'*What are you all standing around for?? Tear this place apart and find him!!! NOW!!!*' Genovene was somewhere nearby, possibly in front of the arcade from the sound of her voice. '*Whoever brings that fucking piss-ant to me will share the divine pleasure of tearing his heart out and eating it with me while he's still alive!!!*'

"Nothing like a threat from her to get me going again. I moved away from the back wall of the building and quietly concealed myself within a small magnolia tree close by, the leaves and flowers were thick and reached down to the ground. No sooner than I did this, a small band of villagers suddenly came behind the shop looking for me. They moved over to my hiding place from a moment ago, and for the first time I noticed their skin was beginning to peel away. Each one was peeling in a different area of their bodies, some along their legs and others along their torsos and faces. The same pink and gray gelatinous substance I'd seen pulsing hideously on Genovene and her kin shined through the gaping holes in their skin as well.

The group walked around my immediate area, making their godawful noises and sniffing the air as they came up to the very magnolia I was hidden within. One of the villagers came up and directly faced me. I stood completely still, afraid to so much as blink until I realized the fucker couldn't see me, even though it stared right at me while it sniffed the air in front of the tree. Nearly half of its face was gone, and while looking absently toward me, it pulled the rest of its face off by the hair first and casually dropping it onto the grass. The smell and the ripping sound of the skin detaching from the creature's body were real nasty. It made me want to retch again.

"At least I now knew what their real faces looked like. Their eyes were deep vacant slants and their real mouths were nothing more than small slits, which sort of explained the weird noises they communicated with. This was such an incredible contrast to the beautiful smiles and faces I'd seen earlier. Their bodies bore the same gnarled characteristics as Genovene, with that slimy goo and all. But they were nowhere near as tall as her, nor did they have long fingers and claws like her either.

"I heard a sharp 'crack' from somewhere to the left of me, and the entire group moved swiftly in that direction. This was my chance to move out from my present hiding place and find another spot closer to the gates. A larger magnolia stood roughly a hundred feet away.

Although it was less concealing than the one I was in presently, and it was a risk to get there undetected, I was certain I'd be discovered soon if I stayed put.

"I quietly slipped out from under my protective cover and bolted for the new one, staying low to the ground and sliding under the bottom foliage of the larger tree. Luckily, I again arrived unnoticed. It proved to be a fortuitous move, for a second small band of villagers soon converged on my recently vacated magnolia. They peered within the leaves and flowers, and surely would've discovered me despite their poor eyesight. After poking and probing for a minute or so, they stopped sifting through the tree and soon left the area.

"I knew I had to keep moving. About twenty yards away sat one of the last remaining shops I could use for cover and then reach the village gates. I remembered seeing the tall sign in front of that shop when I first entered the village. The candy store wasn't far from it and would be the very last building separating me from my intended destination. I reached into my pocket to make sure the stone was still there. It was. Just then, two more villagers came around the corner. But they acted like they suddenly heard something behind them, and raced back to where they came from. I didn't wait to see if they'd be back my way again. I sprinted from the tree's protection to the back wall of the nearby shop.

"The pesky pair soon returned. The branches of the magnolia were still moving near the very spot I had just been, which drew their attention. While they trotted over to investigate, I moved quietly along the back wall of the shop. Once I reached the other end of this building, I went ahead and moved past the next two shops.

"I was now more than two buildings away from them. They looked casually toward the area I'd just left and then over to where I presently stood. I didn't think they could see me hiding behind a thick shrub that grew hugging the wall of the shop that served as my current protection. I carefully peered through its leaves and branches at them. I even started to think they were no longer interested in finding me. But, I was wrong on both counts. They sniffed the air around them and looked over to my general spot. After a quick glance at each other, they sprinted toward the shrub. I scurried quickly over to the next building, which was the next to last one before I reached the village entrance. Rather than check on the pair's progress, I kept moving until I reached the far edge of this particular shop's back wall. From here, the candy store was less than a hundred feet away.

"The area in front of me was clear and between the two buildings sat a beautiful flower garden. The plants were large and loaded with more flowers than I'd seen anywhere else in the village. I decided to make a run for this garden, hoping it would provide enough cover for me to rest and catch my breath.

"Though I couldn't see them yet, I heard my pursuers' excited chirping and approaching footsteps behind me. I sprinted to the garden, diving headfirst between a row of chrysanthemums and large sunflowers, where I hurriedly concealed myself in their thick leaves and large blooms.

"The ground was cool and moist, and felt really good against my scrapes and other wounds from earlier. Yet, the tear in my shoulder's muscle throbbed with every heartbeat as it continued to bleed. I didn't think I'd get an opportunity to properly care for it any time soon. Nonetheless, I was extremely thankful to be sheltered from the sun's unforgiving heat, even if that relief was temporary.

"I peered through the leaves and flowers' protective cover just as the two villagers arrived in the area. They sniffed the air repeatedly as they approached my latest hideout. When they reached the garden's edge, the pair separated and began circling it. They crouched low and chirped like cicadas looking for mates, and I knew they were determined to pinpoint my exact location. All of a sudden, though, they stopped. They stood back up and looked across the garden at each other, and then turned and ran away, chirping even more excitedly. I wasn't sure how to interpret this. While I hoped they'd lost track of me, I worried they'd found me and were off to report my whereabouts to Genovene. Even so, I relaxed, for I was completely exhausted.

"Once I regained my breath, I knew in all likelihood I'd been discovered and Genovene would soon be on her way. Time was running out for me, and it was imperative I reach the gates as soon as possible. While planning my next step, I laid down on my stomach, figuring it might be harder for anyone to see me if I stayed close to the ground. I was grateful again for the coolness and for the fact I had a clear view of the immediate area. At least for now I had the entire moment to myself without another living thing present, other than the various plants and flowers. I'd allow myself a few more seconds to regain some strength, and then resume my quest.

"Suddenly, the ground began to shake violently and the moist earth began to crumble and break apart around me. Amazingly, the plants remained stable despite the fact their roots were soon exposed throughout the garden. The skeletal remains of several human beings began to rise up slowly on either side of me. '*Oh shit!!*' I whispered, paralyzed by terrible fear. I was struggling to maintain my nerve and courage, when all at once my arms and legs were seized upon by the vice-like grip of four bony hands. I screamed.

"I screamed as fucking hard as I possibly could. I didn't give a damn if all the villagers and Genovene heard me or not, as I was petrified far beyond rational fear. I didn't give a fuck if Morylan heard me either, even if it meant he'd come over and crush me into mulch for the garden. I was on the cusp of losing all sanity, my mind and spirit finally crumbling from the continual bombardment I'd endured over the past few hours.

"More and more skeletons began to fill the garden floor, and as they quickly populated the area beneath the plants and flowers, a stranger thing began to happen. The bones began to take on the soft earth as flesh and even as clothing! I couldn't believe my eyes, and for the moment ceased screaming, much to the relief of my weary throat and ringing ears. A warm breeze began to blow along the garden floor and I soon realized the breeze carried a sound with it as it circled throughout the area. It was melodious voices.

"They were faint at first, perhaps on account of the damage I'd just delivered to my eardrums. But as I lay there listening, the voices grew increasingly louder and much clearer. They were speaking to me, or rather *singing* to me.

"'He is here! It's Jack! The *honored* one! The *anointed* one!! Our *sa-a-a-a-vi-i-or*!!!' The voices continued their strange song while the hands held me securely on the ground. Then, as the appendages became warm and fleshed out, they steadily loosened their grip, finally releasing me altogether once they'd completed their bizarre metamorphoses. I slowly sat up on my hands and knees, carefully surveying the garden floor as I did so. The entire area was now filled with the completely fleshed-out bodies of people from a variety of time periods, cultures, races, ages, and sexes. Their moist-earth faces were turned toward me anxiously as they sang their song. Rather than the stark fear I felt just a moment ago, I was now filled with bewilderment.

"The earthen flesh and apparel of these people seemed so real— so much like normal skin, muscles, eyes, lips, teeth, hair, and clothes! I looked down directly below me and watched as the skeleton of a young child transformed itself before me. Within the next minute, a little earthen girl dressed in pig tails and an embroidered nightgown smiled up at me.

"'Hello, Jack!' she greeted me in a soft, sweet, surprisingly normal voice. The singsong din from the others began to fade as if they were all listening to her now. 'We've been hoping you'd make it here so we could formally meet you in person!'

"I was speechless. Here I was listening to a small child made from the soil beneath me. The fucking *soil*, for Christ's sake! I couldn't believe my eyes and ears. Yet, despite the calm demeanor of all the individuals surrounding me, I suddenly felt panicked, for I was certain my screams had alerted Genovene and the others to my definite presence in the garden. I started to rise up in order to take a peek through the flowers, fully expecting to find myself surrounded by them. The little girl grabbed my arm to stop me.

"'Don't do it, Jack!' she advised. 'Do you really think she knows you're here? I know, you think she heard all of your hollering a moment ago, and believe me, we're all grateful you calmed down and gained some reason to your thoughts. But if Genovene had heard you, she would've been here long before now, I assure you of that much!'

"'What about the other two critters that were just here?' I asked her. 'I'm pretty sure they figured out I'm here.'

"'Perhaps they did. But, we sure gave them a good scare to send them scurrying away, didn't we?' She chuckled for a moment, and then looked up earnestly into my face. 'Jack...aside from the help of her bumbling goons, the truth of the matter is Genovene hasn't been able to keep track of you since you spoke to your mom back in that pottery shack of hers—.'

"'*You know my mom?*' I suddenly blurted out, unaware I'd even interrupted her. '*Where is she now? Is she okay??*'

"She really had my attention now. The little girl frowned slightly, as if sorting her thoughts, and then in the next instant she smiled and spoke to me again. 'There's not enough time to answer your questions to your satisfaction. I know it's not what you want to hear, but it's true. Think of it this way, Jack. Both your mom and your dad are doing fine now, just like we are.'

"The earthen group lying around her verbally agreed to this assessment, with one lingering 'amen' that followed the rest.

"'When your wish at the pool was granted earlier today, your mom was able to force her way out of the spiritual bondage that's held us all up until now. Once she went, the rest of us followed her lead. As we speak, the boxes you've learned about are bursting at their very seams throughout this place. For now, every one of us is free to roam the village since Genovene remains largely unaware of this development. That's how we ended up here with our very own bones that were buried in this spot long ago. *You're hurt!*'

"She gasped and then reached up and touched me on my shoulder with her earthen hand. Instantly, the pain began to disappear. She then withdrew her hand from the wound, crossing it with her other hand upon her stomach. I looked over at my shoulder and was amazed to see the wound closing up. A moment later, both the pain and all evidence of the tear in my shoulder were completely gone! I smiled and laughed to myself in nervous amazement, grateful for the little girl's healing power.

"'We're all victims of Genovene, Jack,' she told me, 'and we'd love nothing better than to see you succeed. So, we'll be sending you on your way in a moment. Just be aware she'll be able to see or at least sense your location once you get within striking distance of the golden lion's head—yes, it does really exist—and you must avoid any direct confrontations with that witch or you're a goner for sure! Trust me, Jack. She's able to wrap her claws around your throat in a death grip faster than you could call to Jesus! I know, Uncle Ned, that's sacrilegious of me, but I couldn't help myself. The next thing you know you're on top of that awful pyramid, with your chest laid bare naked and ready for her and her kin to carve out your beating heart. You can bet, too, they'll go and show it to you just before they tear your head off and butcher the rest of—.'

"'That's enough, Allyson!' a young man's voice broke in. 'Spare him your fascination with that shit, will you?' The man was obviously irritated with her and sat up suddenly, just to my right. He didn't look much older than Jeremy, and his hair was nearly as long as my brother's, too. He looked like Huck Finn would as a man, in overalls, torn shirt, and even a frayed straw hat—all made from the soil of the garden, no less.

"'Sorry, Uncle Ned,' she apologized. 'I guess I got a little carried away. Anyway, Jack, consider this as you leave us. I've been stuck here for more than thirty years, and my great, great, *great* Uncle Ned here has been trapped in this place for more than a *hundred* years! Can you believe it?? Others, some of whom are with us right now, have been in this hellish realm for several hundred years or longer. Much, *much* longer.'

"Suddenly, they all looked toward the road, even though only a few of them could see it clearly through the thick plant foliage. An old man in a western-styled suit and broad-brimmed hat took this opportunity to address me. 'You need to be on your way, son!' he admonished. 'They're out there eliminating hiding places and will be by to examine this nifty hideout pretty soon. 'Got to hand it to that bitch, she's pretty thorough about most things. Hey, y'all! Let's clear a path for Jack... Yeah, that's it! There you go, son!'

"The earthen people did as the old man directed, and I scooted myself over to the edge of the garden closest to the candy store. The flowers and plants were lower on this side, and I stuck my head up amid a thick clump of dark red poppies to get a good look at the surrounding area. The area was still clear.

"'Goodbye, Jack!' the little girl said, and everyone else in the group chimed in. 'We'll be praying for you, and if there's any way for us to help out, rest assured we'll do it!'

"'Thanks,' I whispered, and then stepped out onto the grass again, crouching low as I prepared to sprint over to the candy store.

"'Tell Marshall that your namesake says 'hello'! Can you remember to do that for me, son?' the old man called after me.

"'Yeah, I'll tell him that for sure!'

"'Good luck to you, son!'

"'Thanks. I'm sure I'll need it! Goodbye!' I then raced over to the back wall of the candy store. I was baffled by the old man's words. What did he mean by 'your namesake'? It didn't make any sense to me, but perhaps it'd mean something to Grandpa. I only wished I had more time to talk with him and the little girl.

"I moved quickly along the back wall until I could see the village gates. They were less than two hundred feet away. Unfortunately, Morylan still stood in front of them, continuously surveying both sides of the road.

"While deciding on how best to avoid detection by the giant sentinel, a chorus of shrill screams erupted into the air behind me from the garden. Curiosity got the better of me and I quietly moved back toward that area to find out what was happening. Near the edge of the building were a pair of juniper bushes and a large empty gold vat that was lying on its side. I moved over to the vat and crawled into a space between it and the store's back wall.

"I had a clear view of the garden. Genovene and her evil brood had converged upon the area. They'd pulled up nearly all of the plants and had strewn the bones of the earthen people all over the lawn. I winced while watching Genovene shake the fragile body of Allyson, which nearly disintegrated in her claws. All that remained was a decayed skeleton and the little girl's shrieks as they echoed through the air.

"Genovene laughed with delight and threw the lifeless bones on the grass. She crushed and ground them with her claws until a small pile of dust was all that was left of the little girl. Genovene then sent a gust of her foul breath upon the pile, scattering the dust in every direction. *'That'll teach that little daughter of a whore to mess with me and our kingdom!'* she roared. *'Make sure you treat the rest of them in the same manner!!'*

"Her siblings immediately stepped up their assault on the other earthen people. Terrible cries and moans soon filled the air, and as I agonized over the painful reality that once again I couldn't save anyone but myself, I prepared to leave my latest hideout. I started to crawl backward when the vat moved. It only moved a fraction of an inch, but to my horror, it squeaked noticeably. I prayed no one noticed and pulled my legs up to my chest. I closed my eyes and tried to remain as still as possible. But, I soon heard the fast approaching footsteps and excited whispers of Genovene and her kin.

"The vat was suddenly lifted up. I opened my eyes, expecting the worst, and was horrified to find all five standing over me with a crowd of villagers behind them. I was a goner for sure, just as Allyson had warned. Genovene seemed very pleased, giggling with delight as she bent down toward me. I felt really nauseated from her stench and repulsiveness, and feared she and the others planned to eat me right there. But suddenly the backside of the candy store's roof caved in, spilling debris in every direction. They all immediately backed up to avoid being hit, and I realized this could be the last lucky opportunity I'd ever get.

"I scrambled to my feet while gold and marble debris continued to fall, and the dust from the roof's contents rose as a small cloud in the air. I ran as hard and as fast as I ever had in my life, speeding along the back side of the candy store's building and beyond without even pausing to check if anyone was waiting for me there.

"*'Stop him, damn it!!!'* shrieked Genovene. *'After him, you fucking imbeciles!!! Stop him NOW!!!'*

"Morylan was on his knees and in the process of standing back up. I raced toward the golden lion's head, which I could finally see protruding from the crystal wall on the right side of the village entrance. I glanced over my shoulder and was shocked to discover it was the giant sentinel that'd inadvertently come to my rescue a moment ago. Morylan had just lifted his enormous hand up from the roof of the candy store, and was still flicking his fingers free of debris.

"Meanwhile, the angry mob of villagers were rapidly gaining on me, threatening to overtake me at any moment. To make matters worse, Morylan now lifted his left foot off the ground as he prepared to turn around, and the wind from this simple maneuver blew me off course. I nearly fell to the ground, but somehow managed to maintain my balance. With the chirping villagers about to catch me, I pulled the oval stone from my shorts' pocket. I was almost to the lion's head, and I lunged forward with my arms stretched out in front of me. I held the stone in my left hand with my palm thrust outward in order to feed it directly into the lion's mouth.

"The dark shadow of the immense foot descended quickly upon me, thickening as it announced the impending arrival of the warrior's crushing footstep. Like the terrible slowness in a dream, I watched myself approach the lion's head at a snail's pace, even though I was running full speed. The foot was just above me when I leaped for the lion's head with both arms outstretched in front of me like a diving outfielder making a last-ditch effort for an errant fly ball. In one swift graceful move that completely surprised myself, I angled my body in midair and then spread my arms apart, deftly depositing the stone inside the lion's mouth. I managed to avoid a direct collision with the crystal wall, but I still landed hard on my ass, just as the giant's foot slammed onto the ground a mere six inches away from me.

"The power from that footstep shook the ground mightily, and though I was already knocked off my feet, the force of this pushed me face up against the wall. Another deep rumbling sound soon filled the area, and I realized the wall itself was trembling. I immediately backed away from the wall and stood up, though it was extremely difficult to do so.

"Morylan and the villagers ignored me. Instead, this rumble that grew stronger as it threatened to overrun the village distracted them. The magnificent golden gates groaned open, and the splendid buildings and crystal wall of that wonderful place began to crack and crumble. The villagers all scattered in a screeching panic, like beetles whose nest had just been exposed to the light of day. As they scurried about looking for a safe place to hide, the golden road began to rise and buckle from the earth's upheaval.

"Genovene and her loathsome brood suddenly loomed again before me, blocking the sunlight as they drew ever closer. Just when I thought I might've seen the last of her, she found me yet again. But before she and the others were able to finally get their claws on me, the very ground the monsters stood upon gave way, sending each one sprawling and screaming into a large sinkhole. '*God damn you, Jack!!!*' she cursed me. '*God damn you and everything you love to HELL!!! Do you hear me?? TO HELL!!!*'

"Bravely, I edged on up to the rim of the sinkhole and peered down into the earth. The bare roots of a large magnolia swayed gently back and forth near the spot Genovene had been a moment ago, along with several gold flagstones and a few crumbling dirt clods. I started to feel dizzy from the sheer unending darkness of the hole and pulled myself back, though I couldn't help but smile. She was finally gone! That goddamn bitch and her wicked cronies were *really gone*!

"Now all I had to deal with was a remaining handful of villagers and Morylan. I turned toward them. They still ignored me just as they had before, this time preoccupied by the deepening fissures that stretched along the sides of the buildings and along the entire length of the crystal wall for as far as my eyes could see. It was then that I noticed a bright swirling mist of rainbow-like colors hovering just inside the village gates, now completely open.

"The mist swirled faster and faster, gaining momentum as it traveled between the two gates. It lengthened and twisted so that it soon looked like a cyclone measuring the same height as the gates themselves. A high-pitched sound similar to a teapot whistling filled the air. Interspersed with this sound were voices speaking to me again. I glanced once more at Morylan, and after noting his own fascination with the strange mist, I decided it was safe enough for me to get a closer look.

"'*Thank you, Jack! You did it, son!! We knew you could do it!! Thank you! Thank you!! Thank yo-o-u-u!!!*'

"The voice of my mother, along with a multitude of others, rang out into the crumbling village and seemed to hasten the destruction of the buildings. They collapsed in upon themselves. The massive crystal wall was soon to follow, but I couldn't take my eyes off the swirling mass. The souls of the village's countless victims filled the air in front of me, and I could see their radiant smiles mingling with the intense light shimmering throughout the cyclone.

"'You must leave now, Jack,' a familiar voice told me from somewhere nearby. At first, I couldn't tell if it was behind me, in front of me, or from either side. For all I knew it could've been coming from inside my mind. The only thing I knew for sure was it belonged to my mother. 'Your journey has just begun, my son. Come on.'

"Her voice moved through me, from front to back, until her unseen spirit gently prodded me from behind, pulling and pushing as she guided me through the open gates of the ruined village. I stood atop the steps that led directly down into the corridor that Genovene and I had walked through earlier. 'Be brave, Jack,' she said. 'Be very brave and stay on the path you see before you. They'll collect themselves and be after you soon, while others lie in wait. Remember we *are* with you as well, and will do everything possible to ensure your safe return home. Go quickly!'

"I felt several unseen hands upon my back, and then I was shoved through the gateway out into the world of freedom, or at least freedom from the village. Once I reached the bottom step, I heard the mournful cries of Genovene amid the enraptured voices of her emancipated victims. I couldn't believe she made it back so quickly from the seemingly bottomless pit she fell into.

"I turned around in time to see the cyclone lengthen and rise above the village wall. It then disappeared in a bright blast of light speeding through the sky toward the late afternoon sun, taking with it the grateful multitude of voices. Heeding my mom's latest warning, I didn't wait to see if Genovene, Morylan, or any other fiends were on their way after me. I raced down the long corridor, determined to make it back home before it got dark.

"The first few hundred feet were easy. I'd completely forgotten the miahluschkas because I didn't see them right away. I soon heard their high-pitched voices sending an alarm to one another that rang shrilly throughout the corridor. I looked up as I ran, but still didn't see anything. Suddenly, a wave of darkness appeared high in the treetops, moving up quickly from the village ruins behind me.

"The wave passed over my head and started moving down the massive carnac trees ahead of me. Once the wave neared the ground, to my horror it was made up entirely of miahluschkas, whose faces remained shrouded by their hoods. I tried to run past them since none had ventured onto the marble floor yet. As I ran, I cast a quick glance over my shoulder. Seeing no one behind me I picked up speed, returning my line of vision to my front. Shocked by what I found waiting for me, I nearly hurled myself into the air, I stopped so fast.

"An army of several hundred miahluschkas stood waiting less than twenty feet away, completely blocking the marble pathway. I couldn't believe they had moved into position that fast. They removed their hoods, and a stray beam of sunlight settled upon many of their pale frightful faces. Every one of them had long white hair as brilliant in color as Genovene's had been while in her human form. They glared at me malevolently, their pupil-less gray eyes devoid of any warmth as they pulled back their lips far enough to reveal sharp jagged teeth. They spread out and soon surrounded me, scooting up ever closer as drool ran unchecked down their dark robes.

"I had absolutely no idea what to do next, and my mind raced wildly as my panic deepened. As they closed in tighter around me, I thought again of my mother's words. Maybe it was the hubris of youth, but I felt since mom's earlier admonitions had saved me once they could do it again. I decided to meet my aggressors head on.

"With the miahluschkas brushing up against me, I began screaming uncontrollably while throwing my arms and legs in every direction. The entire group froze and seemed unsure how to respond. They soon backed away from me, as confusion replaced the malice they'd originally greeted me with.

"Since this strategy seemed to work, I intensified my body's chaotic movements and inadvertently kicked a pair of them. They went flying into the trunk of a nearby carnac, splattering there before sliding down to the tree's base where they slumped over onto each other, dead. Once the rest of them saw this, they quickly disbanded, screeching shrilly as they ran away from me.

"What a pleasant surprise!. But I wasn't given long to enjoy it, as a heavy crash rocked the area behind me. Morylan was now on his way after me, the loud noise caused by the golden gate on the right side of the village entrance tumbling to the ground. The angry giant proceeded to tear down the left gate, and the last few villagers poured out into the corridor.

"They ran toward me with Morylan lumbering right behind them. His powerful footsteps easily obscured their chirps and other gibberish. The ground shook beneath me, but I forced my protesting legs to move and ran again. My lungs and sides burned terribly, and I feared I wouldn't be able to prevent my pursuers from catching me.

"I didn't realize at first the thick vines and moss hanging from the trees slowed Morylan's progress. He couldn't run after me effectively and I saw frustration on his face once I glanced over my shoulder. He began using his sword to cut the vines, which only made matters worse. The vines now hung even lower and were a greater nuisance.

"He stopped cutting the vines and started using the massive sword on the trees themselves. But since the sword was actually made of gold, it became more bent and mangled with each whack. Finally, he threw down the now useless weapon and pulled the tree until it snapped near its base. Dark green sap flowed out into the corridor, which formed an additional sticky mess for him to step through. Completely frustrated, Morylan suddenly stopped, picked up the sword, and threw it at me.

"I just happened to see him do this and was able to avoid the flying sword. I sprinted to one side of the corridor and dove headfirst into the tall grass and wildflowers growing between the immense carnacs. The sword careened down the marble floor, crushing the leading villagers before skidding on up to the very end of the corridor, where it rested precariously over the side of the stone staircase.

"The rest of the villagers slid on the gooey mixture that a moment ago had been their comrades. One by one they toppled to the ground, falling on top of each other as they looked back anxiously at Morylan, who quickly bore down on them all. In the midst of this confusion, several miahluschkas gathered around me. I immediately got back to my feet, and they cautiously moved away from me. They were now far more fearful of me than I was of them.

"Once I was back in the corridor, I started running again. The marble floor was slippery with blood and gore, and I eluded the grasp of at least one villager that tried to tackle me. I was soon in the lead again.

"The gap between us steadily increased and I kept running until I reached the sword, which still hung over the top of the staircase. I crawled underneath the huge, twisted blade, carefully avoiding the gore that clung to it and which had collected in puddles upon the stairs below it. When I was far enough away from the carnage, I scrambled as quickly as possible to reach the bottom. I jumped down onto the gravel pathway and immediately raced for the pond. By then, I had a huge lead over everyone else. The villagers seemed unable to look past the liquid remains of their comrades trickling down the stairs. It wasn't until Morylan caught up to them that they finally ran after me in earnest.

"The marble giant bent down to pick up his useless sword, nearly dropping it before snatching it up into his hands. For some reason, he wouldn't pursue any of us down the staircase. Instead, he glowered in anger while fidgeting back and forth as if he wasn't sure what to do next. Obviously, his maker never believed anything that ran from him would ever be able to make it past this point.

"I noted most of this from over my shoulder as I ran. I soon reached the bridge to cross over the pond. After I climbed up onto it, I paused to take another look behind me. For the moment, the villagers didn't seem as interested in me. They were fascinated instead by something in the water just to my left. I took a quick look as well, glancing over the side of the bridge while maintaining my guard. At first, I couldn't see what caused the air bubbles in the churning water. But I did notice they were moving swiftly toward me. My heart began to feel the now familiar panic as the ducks and geese suddenly flew away from the pond in fright.

"The disturbance in the water caused the bridge to sway suddenly, and I lost my grip on the railing and fell hard on my ass. I wouldn't need another look, and certainly wasn't foolish enough to take one either. I only hoped the immense fish I just saw wasn't able to bite through the wood and rope of the swinging bridge to get me.

"Cautiously, I got back on my feet again, crouching below the railing. I thought about getting off the bridge, but the villagers had already climbed on and were pursuing me from a safe distance. I had no choice but to move ahead. Even though the villagers hadn't been a very large threat as of yet, I took nothing for granted in this place. Once I neared the middle of the pond, I peered over the edge and saw that the fish were getting even bigger. Their cold and hungry eyes seemed to follow my progress from just below the water's surface.

"Suddenly, several of the fish flew into the air above the bridge, snapping their jaws wildly. I now had my first good look at them. They were horrifying. When their jaws opened, I saw row upon row of sharp jagged teeth. They could easily suspend themselves in the air with large red fins that fanned out into wing-like appendages with razors on the ends. I barely avoided being filleted by one of these monsters as it came at me. It missed, but caused me to fall. Meanwhile, my pursuers used this opportunity to make up the lost ground between us. They crept within a few feet of me, and I was forced again to resume my trip across the bridge.

"I hadn't made it far when one particularly large fish crashed onto the bridge directly in front of me. It flipped around with its teeth gnashing at my legs and feet. Unfortunately, I was left with little room to maneuver, since I could hear the excited clicking noises from the bastards coming up right behind me.

"The fish flipped itself toward my chest. At the same time it flew up, I dropped and rolled under it, the fish's sharp fins grazing the back of my T-shirt, easily ripping it with its razors. The villager right behind me wasn't so lucky. The fish flipped upward again and latched its deadly jaws onto its face. Blood and some grayish goo squirted everywhere as the surprised fucker howled in pain, falling to its knees in a desperate effort to free itself.

"This struggle kept them all at bay for a few minutes, and I used this advantage to gain a sizable lead. After dodging past two more flying fish, I finally neared the other side of the pond. That's when I heard a tremendous roar coming from the stone staircase nearly a quarter of a mile behind me. I turned to look and saw Morylan swing his bloodied sword wildly above his head. For whatever reason, he remained where he was just above the staircase, bellowing angry and nonsensical sounds at me. Then, he took a step back and hurled the sword in my direction one last time. The heavy weapon landed just beyond the middle of the bridge, twisting and snapping it into two pieces. The terrified villagers screeched loudly as they fell into the water.

"I made it to the pond's other side just before my side of the bridge was pulled underwater by the force of the blow delivered to it. I might've been all right anyway, for the fish paid little attention to me, choosing my adversaries instead that were conveniently gathered in the middle of the pond. I climbed up the grassy bank overlooking the pond and sat down, trying to catch my breath again before moving on. Beyond the pond, I saw Morylan fall down to his knees atop the staircase. With his headdress now removed, he buried his face in his hands. Beyond the towering trees behind him stood what was left of the golden spike, looming only fifty feet or so above the tree line.

"I needed to get going. I stood and walked over to the path leading to the grove of fruit trees I'd visited that morning with Genovene. I hadn't gone far when I heard another huge rumble coming from behind me. Looking over my shoulder, I didn't immediately see anything different from a moment ago. But then I saw Morylan look up toward an enormous black cloud hovering above the remnants of the golden spike. Bolts of lightning flashed around it as the cloud rumbled again. The last of the spike melted away until it completely disappeared from view. As it did, the cloud steadily grew larger before moving toward me.

"I couldn't fucking believe it. I mean, it was like there was no end to this shit! I started running for the grove. A gusty breeze soon blew through the meadow around me, bending the tall grass and wildflowers to the ground. The wind continued to get worse until I stepped inside the cool expanse of the grove.

"I was again impressed by the huge fruit trees that Genovene had called Somilas. I remembered the gentile breath-like sounds they had made earlier. They were quiet now, and like everything else in this hellish place, what was once benevolent was now presented with an ominous evil. The trees were awake.

"I slowed my pace and warily looked around. The dim stillness made the grove a hell of lot spookier than it'd been earlier, and the deeper I moved into it the less light there was. Suddenly, I heard something move to my right. I quickly turned my head but saw nothing. Then something moved again, only this time it was on the left side of the path. I stopped and looked over there, but again detected nothing out of place. Maybe what I heard was the trees' fruit falling to the ground. Yes, that was it...some ripe 'Somalian' fruit dropping.

"That logic began to comfort me, until I glimpsed a tree's root rise out of the ground and take a step forward. I was only a quarter of the way into the grove, and I considered turning around and going back. But that meant I'd be dealing with other unknown dangers while I tried to find some other way home. What if Morylan had somehow followed me and was waiting for me just outside the grove? 'What' would I do then? Maybe even Genovene was there, too, hoping I'd panic and frantically run back out of this place. Hell, even if neither was there, what about the dark cloud I saw?

"A loud thud resounded from behind me to my left. As soon as I looked in that direction, another loud thud came from my right side. I whirled around, peering as best I could into the dimness. The decision I'd just debated over had now been made for me. Seven trees had closed in around me, leaving only the path ahead presently unblocked. Another tree approached the path, and I could tell it intended to close me in."

Shaking his head, Jack softly addressed Peter again. "You know, Agent McNamee...I was pretty fucking frazzled by this time. I was weary and exhausted, and so goddamned tempted to simply collapse upon the ground and go no further. But just as I felt this suicidal urge, sudden warmth enveloped me. I didn't physically hear a voice this time, but I felt something powerfully impressed upon my mind. It was like, 'don't give in, Jack—the path will protect you!'.

"I mustered up my courage and took a few steps forward. The eighth tree lifted a root from the ground and crashed it across the path in front of me, shaking the very earth as it met the gravel surface. Within the next few seconds the tree would completely block the path. I bravely sprinted toward it just as it lifted another root to pull itself around and directly block me. In the very instant it lifted its root, I dove and rolled underneath it. The root slammed down where I'd been just a split second before.

"I was now behind the trees. I stood up and ran, hearing a loud, meaty, breath-like sound coming from behind me. I glanced over my shoulder and was surprised to find what I'd originally thought was the back of the tree I'd just slipped past was actually the front. There was a face on the trunk, and it sneered contemptuously at me. The eyes, nose, and mouth were clearly defined, though if these features hadn't been moving, I might've never detected their existence. It rumbled as it spoke something to me, though I couldn't figure out what it said. It must've been an order to stop me in some way, because the other trees in the grove started moving toward the path.

"Other trees tried to halt me with their branches, but I kept running. When I was within a hundred feet of the grove's exit, they crowded the path along its remaining length. One stepped in front of me. I moved to the right as if I was going to try to really move in that direction. When the tree went for the fake I ran to the left instead. Despite my dexterity, I narrowly escaped in one piece, receiving a reminder of just how close it'd been as a long scratch from a branch drew blood along the outside of my right leg.

"I was just about to leave the grove when I happened to look over to my right. Immediately I stopped moving. Banjo and his playmates were suspended in the air within a circle of five trees less than eighty feet away. They were hanging from the trees' branches. A sixth tree moved within the circle and now approached the tree from which Banjo hung.

"He was putting up quite a struggle, kicking his legs desperately. A branch was wrapped tightly around his snout to keep him quiet while two others were wrapped around his mid-section and shoulders to keep him from escaping. The other four animals remained motionless, with strips of bloody flesh and fur hanging from their torn bodies. The middle tree closed in on Banjo.

"'*What the fuck am I supposed to do now?*' In my mind I knew I should just get the hell out of there, to save my own skin. But my heart wouldn't let me do it. I couldn't bring myself to desert my friend, even if he was just an animal.

"Fearing I'd surely regret it, I ran off the path and raced to the circle. After eluding the outstretched branches from more trees that pursued me, I reached the trees holding the animals, moving around the circle I finally came to the one that held Banjo.

"He was suspended nearly fifteen feet above the ground—obviously far beyond my reach. To make matters worse, the middle tree was in the process of positioning a branch directly in front of him, the twigs at the end of the branch contorted into a menacing claw. As it raised this branch to strike Banjo, I kicked the tree holding him. Sharp pain ripped through me, from my toes to my knee, and I cried out in agony. But, surprisingly this caused the tree holding Banjo to move its branch the instant before the middle tree's claw came downward. The claw missed Banjo by just a hair, crashing into the ground and snapping two of its twigs off.

"Both trees turned toward me as I limped out of their reach. Despite the pain in my foot I approached the tree holding Banjo again, bravely kicking it with my other foot. The tree swung around, trying to grab me with another of its branches. It missed me completely, but it hit the tree holding the dead fawn on its face. That tree dropped the fawn's carcass to the ground. To my surprise—and this is the honest-to-God-truth—it then swung a branch with its twigs all balled up in a roll-like fist and pummeled the tree holding Banjo on the face. It let out a rumble of pain and dropped Banjo to the ground, turning its full attention toward the other tree.

"As ridiculous as this sounds, an all out fight broke out between the two of them, and in the confusion that followed, I ran into the circle, picked up Banjo, and threw him over my shoulder as I dodged past the middle tree and the others now preoccupied by the tree battle. I then raced back to the path.

"The entire grove was in an uproar and couldn't organize themselves in time to stop us from leaving. All they could do was throw their fruit at us. Fortunately they had terrible aim, although one somila's fruit glanced off my shoulder and landed on the ground. When it did, it burst open and some acid-like shit poured out, sizzling and foaming as it burned a hole in the ground. I ran even harder.

"Once we left the grove, the somilas didn't pursue us anymore. When I was certain we were out of their range and truly safe, I sat Banjo down on the path and dropped to my knees from exhaustion. Every time I got tired, it was worse than before, and it took longer for me to recover. Thankfully, Banjo didn't move away from me this time, because I wouldn't have been able to stop him. He put his front hooves on my shoulder and eagerly licked me on the face, bleating repeatedly in my ear.

"I was relieved he was unharmed, despite his own ordeal. I scolded him for almost getting killed, wondering why he and his buddies didn't stay put in the meadow like they were supposed to. He just looked at me curiously while I petted him. I looked to the side of the path where I'd watched him and the other animals at play earlier. The ground was completely scorched and the grass and wildflowers were burned away from that entire portion of the meadow. Whatever had caused this, it had done so fairly recently, as smoldering flames burned the remaining grass near the path.

"I worried for a moment the somilas had done this, and that they might be coming for us soon after all. But, when I saw the damage to the meadow extended for several acres on either side of the path, I knew something else was responsible for this.

"I spotted a pair of crumpled and shredded robes lying on the ground not far from us, and I moved over to get a better look at the mangled garments. Lying next to them were the partially eaten and charred remains of the two miahluschkas Genovene had assigned to watch over Banjo. Their torn bodies were violated so badly, at first glance I wasn't quite sure what I was looking at. But once I stooped down to examine the half-eaten torso of one of the critters and its exposed internal organs, along with the shattered skull of the other one, I soon verified what they once were. I was surprised at how similar they were to the rest of the human race—unlike Genovene and the others.

"I moved back over to the path, keeping Banjo close by me. It didn't take long to find out what was coming next, for no sooner than we reached the path again, a solid gust of wind was there to greet us. An ominous dark shadow suddenly obscured the late afternoon sunshine that had so recently bathed us in its warmth.

"I grabbed Banjo and ran to the river. I didn't need to verify the cloud from earlier was above us. I looked up anyway just in time to see a pair of misty appendages grow from the cloud and reach for us, bringing more gusts of wind and bolts of lightning down into the meadow. The cloud was much larger now, and its wind fierce enough to throw me to the ground. Once I was able to stand again, I couldn't maintain my balance, falling a number of times while struggling to hold onto Banjo.

"The sheer force of the assault grew stronger and stronger until the powerful gusts finally knocked us down to the point where neither of us could stand up. I crawled toward the stone bridge while holding onto Banjo's collar, dragging the terrified animal with me. Even though it was less than a hundred feet away, I didn't think we'd ever reach the bridge.

"The cloud's darkening arms continued to solidify until they were clearly defined and muscular that included hands and lucid fingers. I swear to God I'm telling you the truth, Agent McNamee, but I can't blame you if you don't believe me. I know I scarcely believed I was really seeing this shit!

"Somehow we reached the bridge. I climbed on first and then

pulled Banjo up with me, being careful not to strangle him. The cloud's hands grasped the sides of the bridge, sending an immediate tremor throughout the stone structure. Powerful gusts blew across it, and torrid lightning strikes, which had been landing closer and closer to us, now crept to within a few feet. The crackling and sizzling sounds were near unbearable, but we kept going.

"Just before we reached the midway point, one of the clouds' hands let go of the bridge and tried to grab us. Since the bridge was very narrow, it couldn't quite get a grip on either Banjo or me. Still, I nearly lost my grip on the bridge's railing, forcing me to use my arms and elbows to keep from being tossed over the side into the raging river below. I couldn't hang on to Banjo, though he managed to wedge himself in between my legs.

"Moving along like this was tedious, but we managed to make progress anyway. We were nearing the end of the bridge when a powerful bolt of lightning slammed into the bridge floor only steps behind us. Besides singeing the hair on my right leg, it mortally damaged the structure, leaving a deep crack in the bridge where it hit. The crack soon splintered into smaller ones that quickly spread toward us, and I could tell the bridge wouldn't hold up much longer. It was about to collapse into the volatile water below.

"I pulled and pushed Banjo with my legs as I desperately worked toward the other shore, resolutely determined to cross the bridge before it crumbled into the river. When we were within fifteen feet of the eastern shoreline, the hand gave up in its pursuit of us and began whipping the water from the turbulent river onto the bridge. The water, acting as a powerful hammer, crashed heavily against the foundation of the bridge. It made it even harder for me to hang on, as the cracks in the bridge floor and walls quickly widened.

"The bridge finally began its collapse. Huge pieces of stone fell into the river from our rear. I clung to the stone railing with Banjo clinging frantically to my legs, and could feel a deep rumbling as well as the frightened trembling of my little companion. On account of our dire situation and my own desperate fear, we were still nearly ten feet from the shoreline.

"Another section crumbled into the river. I took as wide a step as I possibly could and I tightened my grip on Banjo. Right as the floor disappeared beneath us, I leapt with all my might while pushing him along side me through the air. The river's powerful current dislodged the bridge's foundation, pushing us closer to land. I grabbed onto a large clump of thistles growing along the water's edge with one hand. While ignoring the thorns piercing that hand, I secured my grip on Banjo's front leg with the other. I then watched what was left of the bridge crash into the river where it vanished in the rushing rapids.

"I pulled Banjo to safety atop the embankment above the shoreline. The cloud's hands and arms rapidly withdrew into the cloud, and the entire thing dissipated a moment later. The volatile water, in turn, slowed down to a smooth, peaceful current as the river returned to its original course through the woods. Feeling a little safer, I took a moment to remove the painful stickers from my bleeding hand, finding it hard to believe I'd actually hung onto the sharp thistles and Banjo without both of us tumbling down into the river.

"The late afternoon sun had returned, although it'd dropped deeper into the western sky. The sun's rays danced upon the river while the grove and meadow disappeared. In their place were the usual trees and plants typical for the woods near Carlsdale, like tall pines, oaks, and elms. Wild ferns and blackberry bushes were among the plants familiar to me that crowded the dirt path overgrown with tall grass and weeds.

"I felt ecstatic to be back in a world I readily knew and understood, where magic and monsters didn't exist. 'We did it, Banjo!' I shouted excitedly. 'We made it out of that hellhole alive!!! Can you believe it??' I kneeled down and hugged him, smiling despite my weariness. All we had to do now was get through the woods and we'd be back home. I stood up and headed for the hillside, with Banjo trotting along side me.

"When we reached the top of the hill, I surveyed the area one last time. The wilderness below was still impressive, although it was nowhere near amazing as the view I'd enjoyed earlier that day. It was as if I was looking out onto the vast, and for the most part undisturbed, forest for the very first time. Although unremarkable, it was home and it was beautiful. Relieved the adventure was over, I turned away from the hills' edge and led Banjo into the woods.

"We had just stepped into the deep shade of the woods when all at once we heard an incredible, almost ear-splitting roar which shook the entire hillside behind us. Since I wasn't expecting it, the roar was the most frightening thing I'd heard all day. I cautiously crept back up to the small hill's top and peered down at the river below. On the ground between the river and the path that led up the hill sat the biggest damn reptile I'd ever seen.

"As I told Sheriff McCracken later that night, I estimated its length to be at least seventy feet, and from the shiny colors on its scaly skin, I recognized it had to be the serpent Genovene referred to as Vydora. She was much larger than what I'd remembered seeing splashing around in the water underneath the stone bridge earlier. It took me a moment, but I soon realized I'd only seen her tail and not the rest of her body at the time.

"Vydora's appearance certainly matched her roar, for her claws were long and sharp. Her head was huge with gold horns on top of it, and her mouth was open to where I could see several rows of pointed sharp teeth. As I said earlier, she also had a pair of multi-colored fans near where her ears must've been. To me, she really did look like a cross between a *tyrannosaurus rex* and a mythical dragon—just like the sheriff's report stated. To her I must've looked like 'dinner', for as soon as she spied me peeking down at her, she roared loudly again.

"A long stream of fire flew out of her mouth, stopping less than fifteen feet below us and scorching a patch of tall grass. I now knew what had burned the meadow on the other side of the river. Even from where I was crouched down, I could feel the fire's intense heat.

"Keep in mind Vydora had one other physical aspect I failed to recognized at first glance. The wings I told you about? They were on her back and blended in perfectly with her scales. So unless they were extended, like they were right then, you might not notice them. Having a good idea what was coming next I quickly went over to Banjo, giving him a firm swat on his butt to get him moving.

"Vydora flew through the air and landed with an immense thud right where we'd been only an instant before. We ran into the woods, moving down the incline on the other side of the hill just as she reached its pinnacle. I turned and saw her colorful silhouette against the backdrop of the late afternoon sky, the sunlight glistening on her head and shoulders as it reflected off her horns and scales. Once she spotted us moving through the woods below her, she roared again and sprayed fire through the trees and plants aiming directly for us.

"The light and heat were extremely intense. I shielded my eyes and turned my back to her, running as fast as I could with Banjo keeping pace with me. She pursued us and closed the gap very quickly, crushing the trees—even the largest ones—in her path. Propelled once more by fear, we ran deeper into the woods where it was much darker and a lot harder to see anything. Vydora spewed another stream of flames that struck a group of trees standing nearby to our left, illuminating the woods around us.

"Banjo suddenly veered away from me toward the right, sprinting into the deep woods. Vydora continued after me and I knew I had no chance of outrunning her. She was about to overtake me, for I could hear her breathing and I felt the moisture from her snout spray upon my neck as she snorted. The sweltering warmth of her mouth cloaked my back and I smelled its sulfuric sourness. Visions of the miahluschkas' charred, half-eaten remains filled my terrified mind. Since I knew she could bite me in half at any moment, I stopped and changed direction, sprinting to the same area Banjo had fled.

"Vydora's jaws closed on empty air as she attempted snapping at me. She turned her head to follow me as I ran away from her, roaring in anger and spraying another long stream of flames at me. In desperation, I crawled under some thick undergrowth, where I was surprised to find a small cliff hidden beneath it. I grabbed onto a thick vine and quickly slid over the edge. There was a deep crevice beneath the cliff and I leaned into it as far as I possibly could, not even thinking about what could be waiting there for me. I felt a warm furry animal with bristly hair on its head and immediately backed away from it.

"I almost scrambled out of there, but then realized it was Banjo! He started to whimper. I put my hand over his mouth to shut him up, since I knew Vydora was somewhere close behind me. Several trees suddenly ignited nearby, and I tightened my grip on the billy goat's snout while we both trembled. The pounding approach of the dragon bore down quickly on our hiding place.

"The ground above creaked and started to give way as she stood right on top of us, sending clods of soft earth down upon us both. A low-pitched growl rumbled through the area and then the underside of her massive jaw appeared as she nuzzled her face into the space in front of our hideout.

"Fortunately, her head was at an awkward angle to where she couldn't see us hiding just a few feet away, although certainly she could smell us. Her loud snorts resounded repeatedly until suddenly she withdrew. I can only reason she did this because of the fire spreading rapidly toward us all. I let out a slow quiet breath I'd been holding, but didn't dare loosen my grip on Banjo's snout just yet.

"The ground above creaked heavily once more and then the thunderous steps moved away from us. I let go of Banjo and stepped out from under the cliff as the fire crept closer. I poked my head above the cliff's ledge and saw that Vydora was already a hundred feet away, and getting more frustrated by the minute since she couldn't locate me. She reared her massive head back upon her neck as she straightened her enormous body, which caused her head to disappear briefly in the treetops. She roared her displeasure and then sprayed fire into the very trees that concealed her. The scene was surreal as the ignited foliage burned brightly, casting eerie shadows upon her enraged features. I looked around frantically for a route out of there that wasn't on fire.

"I reached back under the ledge and dragged Banjo out. He whined terribly, but there wasn't time to calm him down. There was only a tiny gap left for us to escape the fire. I would've liked to check on Vydora's whereabouts one more time, but the smoke and heat made my eyes water terribly, and it was getting harder to breath. I pushed Banjo through the gap, praying that the fire wasn't worse on the other side, and followed after him.

"Once through the gap, I was relieved the fire hadn't spread through this area of the woods yet. Banjo immediately shook his body to rid himself of the ashes that'd landed on him, while I wiped my eyes with the inside of my T-shirt. We moved quickly. It was only inevitable before the fire spread toward us. At least it seemed unlikely we'd have to deal with Vydora again, because it sounded like she was moving further away, roaring angrily the entire time.

"I worried about Grandpa and Jeremy, as I was pretty certain the dragon was heading straight for our house. I needed to warn them, even though they'd surely heard Vydora's angry cries and seen the fire she'd caused. I grabbed Banjo and started running south as fast as I could, hoping I could exit the woods near the Johnson's farm. I soon saw the remnants of daylight ahead as the trees began to thin. Less than a minute later, I saw the green backside of the John Deere tractor in that photograph you have. I secured my grip on Banjo's collar and raced out of the woods.

"Perhaps you know this, but Ben Johnson's farm sat on one hundred and thirty acres, which bordered the woods on the west side and Lelan's road on the east. Fielder's Pond formed the southern boundary of the farm, while the northern border was my grandfather's place. I ran past the tractor, practically choking poor Banjo as I continued to pull him along behind me, and went directly to the Johnson's farmhouse. I intended to use their telephone to call Grandpa, and then the sheriff and fire department.

"Once we arrived at the house I went over and banged on the back door. There was no answer. I pounded again even harder, but still no answer. I ran around to the front door, but got the same response. After peering through the living room and kitchen windows, I confirmed that indeed no one was home.

"Just to be sure, I went over to the main barn that sat adjacent to the farmhouse. It was locked. I turned back toward the woods and was alarmed to see the area we'd just traveled through completely engulfed by flames. That left the old frontage road as the quickest way home. Banjo resisted me some, since this meant we had to head back toward the woods first. I was scared, too, and I half-expected Vydora to reappear at any moment. But there was no sign of her—only the fiery destruction she'd caused.

"The road wasn't so overgrown with weeds and such until our farmhouse came into view, just as we reached the last few acres of the Johnson's property. Suddenly, the air shook again as the dragon roared loudly from somewhere close by. I dropped to the ground, holding Banjo down with me and peering in the direction the roar came from. The fire still raged through the woods, increasing in strength, and yet it still hadn't crossed over into the field. In the midst of the fire stood Vydora's hulking figure. She seemed nervous, and as I watched her, she bellowed an anxious cry into the smoke-filled air.

"It made me smile a little as I stood up. Apparently, she'd boxed herself in with the very flames she'd created. She soon disappeared from view and her cries grew softer as she moved south through the woods. I finally felt relieved, and walked the rest of the way home after loosening my grip on Banjo.

"Grandpa and Jeremy were in our backyard, sitting on the oak's lowest limb. They both looked toward the woods. So far, neither of them noticed Banjo and me as we approached the gate. They didn't seem to notice the raging fire in the woods. I wondered why they weren't reacting to that or Vydora's distant roars.

"I heard my name mentioned once and then Grandpa looked toward the sphere and back gate with a look of worry and sadness, and more than a hint of irritation. I was pretty sure he knew I went where I wasn't allowed.

"'*Hey Grandpa! Grandpa!!*' I cried. '*I'm over here!! Hey, Jeremy, tell Grandpa I'm home!!! Jeremy? Grandpa??*' They couldn't hear me even though I yelled at the top of my lungs. They both looked nonchalantly toward where I was standing, and then away again. I realized they couldn't see me either!

"We were just a few feet away from the back gate. I started coaxing Banjo to go underneath the gate like I had earlier that day, so I wouldn't have to force him through the gate's railings again. The sky was beginning to turn into the deep purple of twilight when all of a sudden the earth shook again, throwing us both to the ground. A large hole opened in the earth, and Genovene in all of her hideousness came rising up through it. Towering over me, she bent down and placed her incredibly grotesque face close to mine.

"'So...you think you've won, do you?' she asked, sneering at me. 'You think *you've* defeated *me*, Jack Kenney?? THINK AGAIN YOU MISERABLE FUCKING CURR!!!' Her shrieking nearly split my eardrums. '*I shouldn't have played with you the way I did!!! I should've conducted business as usual and taken you when I had the chance to do so yesterday!!!*' she snarled. 'Mark...my...WORDS!!! *I'll never make the same mistake in dealings with you humans EVER AGAIN!!!*' She looked around, as did I. Silently, and desperately, I prayed that someone would see me and come to my rescue.

"'*Hel—!*' I tried to scream, but Genovene grabbed me, cutting off my words, and placed her slimy claws over my mouth. I thought for sure that I'd hurl my guts up when the gelatinous mess oozed into my mouth.

"'Well, Jackie boy...this day won't be completely wasted,' she continued, lowering her voice to a gruff whisper. Her breath was as foul as a ripe outhouse. 'I'm going to break your grandfather's spirit! I'll leave him your mutilated little corpse to discover, but I'm taking your heart and I'm claiming your soul!!! What do you think of tha—!'

"'*LEAVE HIM ALONE!!! LEAVE HIM ALONE, NOW, GENOVENE!!!*' a mighty, thunderous voice suddenly shouted from behind her. A brilliant white light filled the area, and a look of utter surprise spread across Genovene's frightful face. She backed up from me, reluctantly releasing me from her powerful grip as she slowly turned her sneering head toward the sphere. Upon it stood an angel roughly twelve feet in height.

"The angel was the most magnificent being I'd ever seen, and had a mixture of male and female features. Its hair was long and lustrous, resting as a full golden mane upon its broad shoulders. Its eyes, which were as green as emeralds, were soft and luminous in appearance with long golden lashes—as beautiful as any woman I'd ever seen. Yet, the rest of its face was filled with masculine features, such as a sleek prominent nose and powerful jaw line.

"The angel's body was slender and yet its arms and legs were defined by powerful muscles that flexed continuously beneath its bronze skin. It was dressed in a shimmering white tunic and its wingspan was incredibly wide. Deep lavender and white, yet iridescent, feathers filled both wings that extended outward and behind from its shoulders. Unlike pictures and paintings I'd seen depicting such heavenly beings, the wings on this angel seemed to have a life of their own, moving and twitching as it stood there gazing down at us from atop the sphere.

"I was so enthralled by the angel's appearance I didn't notice right away that my mom was also standing on the sphere in front of it. My mouth flew open in joyful surprise, and widened further once I realized my dad stood just to the left of her. He had his arm around my mom's waist, while she in turn had her arm wrapped around the shoulders of a pretty little girl who stood just to the right of her. They were all dressed in shimmering white tunics similar to what the angel wore.

"My mother looked like she did when I last saw her in the village, and I imagine this was how she looked when she and my dad disappeared so many years before.

"'*Mom? Is that really you, too, Dad??*' I cried in disbelief. Before either of them could answer, the angel spoke to me again.

"'Stand up, Jack, and come here!' it commanded, its voice so unusual, but at the same time pleasant to my ears despite its force. 'Bring Banjo with you!'

"I picked up Banjo and walked past Genovene, determined not to look up at her. I felt her heated stare as I walked by, but she didn't prevent me from obeying the angel. As soon as I reached the back gate, I looked up at the four figures standing on the sphere. The little girl spoke first.

"'Well, I see you made it Jack. I knew you'd do it! I just *knew* you would!'

"'A-a-allyson?? So that's you up there?' I finally recognized the little girl and was surprised I hadn't known who she was sooner. It might've been her missing pigtails that'd thrown me. More than likely it was the fact she no longer was an image made of garden soil. Instead, she appeared to be a living being of flesh and blood.

"'How do I look?' she asked. 'Quite an improvement from earlier, wouldn't you say?' She primped playfully as she curtsied before me, while the spirits of my mom and dad looked on in amusement. The angel, meanwhile, turned its gaze back toward Genovene. The brilliant light that seemed to stretch endlessly above us was rapidly filling with other angels of similar appearance descending toward the earth. Even though the brightness of the light was more intense than any I'd ever experienced before, it didn't bother my eyes. Nor did it hinder my perception, for I could clearly see everything around me. The army of angels soon hovered around the sphere, as if guarding all of us.

"'I told you we'd be with you, didn't I, son?' my mom's spirit gently reminded me as she nodded to my dad. He then addressed me himself.

"'We're very proud of you, Jack, and of Jeremy, too—though, you may wonder why, in your brother's case, sometimes,' he told me, chuckling lightly. 'We've been catching up on what we've missed since we last saw you boys. I'd say Marshall's done a helluva job raising you both.' He suddenly grew quiet and sad, probably reflecting on all he'd missed out on over the past dozen years.

"'Jack, we've only got a moment or two left before we must rejoin the others,' my mother told me. 'They're about to begin the initiation for us all as a group, since there are so many of us that were hostages in Genovene's world. Some folks were there for as long as eight to nine thousand years, believe it or not.'

"I tried to picture this 'initiation' she just spoke of, wondering exactly what she meant.

"'There's really no way to explain it to where you'd understand,' she said, obviously knowing my thoughts again. 'Someday you'll know what I'm talking about—I assure you. For now, all you need to know is everyone gets to experience this event. We all go through it when our work here's done. Your life has just begun, Jack, and you have many wonderful years to look forward to before it is your time to experience this. But, our wait was long and cruel because of Genovene.' She looked back at her. I could see anger filling my mother's face. Genovene seemed to take pleasure in this, hissing contemptuously as she smiled back at her. Mom's spirit looked like she was about to go after that fucking bitch and exact some revenge, but the powerful hands of the angel restrained her.

"'You must be diligent and finish instructing your son, Julie,' the angel advised, and then cast its own disdainful gaze down toward Genovene. 'We will deal with her shortly.'

"Mom nodded that she understood the angel's admonishment and then spoke to me once more. 'Listen closely, Jack. Put Banjo through the rails and then you must re-enter the gate in the same exact manner you left through it earlier today. Have you got that?'

"I nodded that I did and carried Banjo up to the rails of the wrought-iron gate, where I pushed him on through to the other side. As soon as I did, I laid down on my stomach and crawled underneath the gate. I stood up and brushed myself off once I reached the other side. I looked back at her and the other three smiling down at me.

"'Tell Papa we miss him, too, and that my mother sends her love to him as well,' Mom told me. 'She's doing fine, by the way, and looks forward to their eventual reunion. You might ask him if he feels her presence sometimes, because she visits him whenever he needs encouragement in raising you boys or to cheer him up when he gets down thinking about her... and about us,' she added with a tinge of sadness.

"Mom looked up at the angel who towered above her by a good six feet. It nodded to her and she turned one last time to face me. 'Be attentive to the knowledge and wisdom of your grandpa, for he has much to share with you and to teach you. He knows more than you realize, and has experienced a lot,' she said. 'But, you must tell him your story first. Don't be afraid, my son, and let this knowledge work to heal and strengthen all three of you. Even though we're moving on, please remember that we're only a whisper away and can readily hear your thoughts and prayers when you need us. We will always be with you in that way. Goodbye for now, Jack...*We love you!*'

"Tears filled her eyes and I noticed Allyson was sniffling, fighting back her own tears. My father's spirit stood by stoically, dealing with this painful moment in his own way, which I guess was so like him. The angel's compassionate expression never changed, as if this kind of moment was nothing new for it to witness.

"I wanted so badly for them to stay and not go, though I realized they no longer could be a part of the world I lived in. It was sinking in now that my parents had been dead for years—since the very day they'd mysteriously disappeared from Carlsdale so long ago. My shoulders shook uncontrollably from the wave of emotions I'd kept bottled up inside my heart since I was little. I'd always hoped for a happy, *lasting* reunion with my folks, and the realization that it wasn't meant to be was nearly more than I could bear.

"Drawing every ounce of courage I had, I managed to subdue this tidal wave of feelings for the time being, wiping the flood of silent tears from my face with the back of my hand. In that very instant, the three former prisoners of Genovene and her wicked village began to mutate, lengthening and dissolving until at last they'd completed their metamorphoses into three brilliant rays of light. A moment later, these rays shot skyward with many other rays from souls I hadn't even noticed before then.

"The angel and its comrades also watched this spectacle, but only momentarily. As soon as the ethereal beams of light left the immediate area, the magnificent angel stepped onto the wall and reached down using his incredible strength to roll the stone sphere back to its rightful place. I breathed a sigh of relief as the sphere obscured the wrought-iron gate once more. Then, all of the angels drew swords concealed within their garments and descended directly into the area where I'd last seen Genovene, with the angel that'd rescued me leading the way.

"An intense struggle ensued on the other side of the stone wall that went on for nearly twenty minutes. I heard terrible screams of pain as bones snapped and both fabric and flesh were gruesomely ripped apart. I began to worry why so many angels weren't able to swoop in on her and just wipe her out, but then realized her comrades must've joined the struggle.

"I nervously glanced back toward the oak. My grandfather and brother had just climbed down from their observation point on the oak branch. They still seemed unaware of what was taking place just a short distance from them. Jeremy headed back to the house while Grandpa stood where he was, looking glumly toward my direction as if he could see me. I confirmed once more that neither of them could hear or see me, yelling at the top of my lungs while jumping up and down like a lunatic. As these antics got no response at all, I reluctantly turned my attention back to the battle on the other side of the wall.

"The fight finally reached its climax. I heard the angel and Genovene shriek at each other in one angry voice that terminated in a loud clap of thunder. Sudden and complete silence then filled the entire area, lasting for nearly a minute. Gradually, the sounds of birds and insects, along with the raging fire nearby rang in my ears again.

"I stared at the wall and the fire consuming the woods beyond it. I didn't know whether to cry or laugh, or if I should feel sad, happy, or some crazy combination of both emotions.

"'There you are, Jack! Where have you—*what the hell?? Jeremy!! Call the fire department!!! There's a fire burning the woods down!!!*' Grandpa shouted while running over to me. He wrapped his strong arms around me and hugged me tightly. '*I thought we'd lost you for sure!!*' He started to cry, and then hugged me even tighter. I started crying, too.

"'*Grandpa?? What in the hell's going on here??*' cried Jeremy. '*Th-the fire. Where in Jesus' fricking name did all that shit come from, anyway??*' He staggered toward us nervously, obviously astounded by the fire that had engulfed the woods. I couldn't help but feel a little satisfaction at this. My big bad brother may really be bad, but he could still get scared shitless now and then.

"'*I mean...what the fuck?? Just a moment ago I looked out toward the woods and not a goddamn thing was going on!! But, hell, it looks like that motha's been burning for quite awhile!!!*' Jeremy couldn't pry his eyes from the blaze, and didn't even notice I'd returned home.

Grandpa looked back at him and sighed in frustration. 'I know, son, but call the fire department right now!' he ordered, his voice filled with urgency. "Hurry, let's get some buckets of water in case it gets any closer to the house!' He turned back to me and smiled wanly.

"Jeremy ran back to the house, but stopped just before he reached the back porch. He spun around and faced me as I stood next to Grandpa. 'How'd you get here, Jackie?' he shouted, clearly startled that he'd just now noticed my presence in the backyard. 'We've been looking all over God's creation for you—!'

"'Just call the fire department, damn it!! We'll quiz Jack later on!!!' Grandpa was growing increasingly irritated, but this time Jeremy heeded his request and hurried into the house and called the fire department. My grandfather now studied me, noting my cuts, bruises, and my torn and filthy clothing. He shook his head and whispered, 'My God...what have you been up to, son?'

"'It's a long story, Grandpa. I'll tell you everything—I promise—but, can I eat something first? I'm really starving!' I told him, still wiping the tears from my eyes. 'I hope you're not too upset with me, even though I let you down.'

"'Well, that all depends, Jack,' he advised, eyeing me thoughtfully. 'Your story had better be a good one.' He put his arm around my shoulders and motioned for us both to walk over to the oak together. 'We'll get you cleaned up and get some good food into that stomach of yours just as soon as the fire department arrives,' he told me when we reached the tree.

"Less than ten minutes later Carlsdale's fire department arrived. The entire department for our community, at the time, consisted of eight men and three trucks. And one of those trucks looked like it belonged in a museum.

"The fire never spread to anywhere else outside the woods, even though the grass and weeds separating the woods from Ben Johnson's farm and our place were fairly dry. Carl Peterson, who was our local fire chief back then, as you know, agreed this was very strange.

"At first, the largely volunteer group panicked when they saw how strong the fire was. This prompted Carl to call the Demopolis fire department for assistance. Within an hour of fighting the blaze, though, the fire miraculously died down, seemingly on its own. In a span of just under two and a half hours, the fire that'd destroyed nearly the entire wooded area beyond the frontage road was safely under control.

"Carl called his Demopolis fire-fighting buddies again before they'd gotten too far out of their own city limits, and they turned around and went home. He would've had them continue on out to Carlsdale, if for no other reason than as a precautionary measure. But, as the fire began to diminish quickly before disappearing altogether, without hardly any assistance needed from his small group of firemen, Carl didn't want to face any possible ridicule. Or, or worse yet, take the chance of jeopardizing any future assistance he might need from the western Demopolis team by not being taken seriously.

"Meanwhile, once Grandpa learned the fire wouldn't be difficult to contain, he had me go inside the house and get cleaned up. He also told me to let Jeremy know our supper would be on the table soon.

"As soon as I left him to go inside, Grandpa decided to put the dozen or so buckets of water he'd prepared to fight the fire with to good use. He coaxed Banjo to sit still long enough for him to secure the billy goat with his leash by the oak tree. Using the dog soap he kept on the back porch for the hounds he used to own at one time, he gave Banjo a badly needed bath. It only took a few minutes to do this, and once he was completely clean, Grandpa turned him loose again. He then waved to Carl and came inside our old farmhouse to finish fixing dinner, while Banjo ran around the backyard in the early evening twilight, shaking the excess water from his freshly cleaned body."

PART VI

Revelations and a Lesson in History

Jack grew quiet and looked down at the table. He remained silent for the next few minutes, waiting for Agent McNamee to respond to his story. But the agent sat in silence as well. Finally, Jack grew irritated enough to broach the question himself. "So...what do you think?" he asked without looking up.

"About your story? I find it very compelling, Jack. You should already know that," Peter replied. "I'm definitely convinced your experience and my nephew's disappearance are related to each other. Now, and don't take offense, memory is a funny thing, Jack. You were an adolescent when this happened. Given the trauma, and all the time that's passed since then, it's likely some of what you remember could be embellished a bit. I'd like to believe it all... But you've got to admit, Jack, trees with faces that talk; clouds with arms, hands, and 'lucent' fingers; and, statues that one minute are inanimate fountains and the next come to life are not just strange. They sound like pure fantasy. I guarantee you anyone else around here would find that sort of stuff, to put it bluntly, a load of shit.

"Still, the fact remains there is quite a bit of material to confirm most of what you've told me. Like the temple you described. There have been many legends throughout the world detailing similar golden structures. Even the name 'Genovene' has been referred to in several ancient manuscripts as a demonic entity. Furthermore, the description you gave me of the 'villagers' is very similar to some descriptions of alien life forms I've studied, and your angel description is strikingly similar to several accounts we have on file in Richmond."

"There's more," Jack told him, and then raised his gaze to meet

Peter's.

"I know that," replied Peter, matter-of-factly.

"Would you like to hear it then? I need to warn you there'll be wilder shit to come. Although, there'll be no more trees with faces that talk,' said Jack, able to laugh for the first time that day.

"Yes, I'd love to hear it."

"Are you sure?"

"*Yes*! That's why I'm here."

"All right, but first I've got to take a piss! That's one thing I've found to be true about soft drinks," Jack said as he stood up and moved over to the corner restroom. "It doesn't stay long in your system—that's for goddamned sure!"

"I've got news for you, Jack. Coffee works the same way. So, when you're done in there, I need to take a break as well," Peter advised, chuckling to himself over the baser facts of life.

As soon as both men had finished their 'calls to nature', Peter rejoined Jack at the table, stopping to grab another cup of steaming coffee along the way.

"I take it you're not interested in another Coke," Peter observed, once he noticed Jack without another beverage. "How's your stomach holding out? If you're about to describe another of your grandpa's home cooked meals, I'm not sure *I'll* be able to wait until your story's finished, Jack!"

"Well, I believe I won't be able to do my story justice without at least one more trip to Grandpa's kitchen," Jack told him. "I'll try not to spend too long on describing food, though."

"I'd appreciate that!" Peter teased, and then motioned for Jack to retake his seat. "Would you like a cup of water instead?"

"Nah, at least not yet."

"All right, then. Let's hear the rest of your story."

"I was so glad to be home again," said Jack, resuming where he left off. "As soon as I entered the back porch door and smelled the pot roast simmering in the kitchen, I felt safe and secure at last. I felt a twinge of guilt as well, since I knew dinner had been ready for the past couple of hours. A quick glance at the kitchen wall clock and the ready dinner table confirmed that fact. Curious to see if my watch was correct, I pulled it out of my shorts' pocket. The face bore several deep scratches that looked even worse due to the grime caked onto it. The time it displayed was within five minutes of the half-past seven reading on the kitchen clock.

"Jeremy continued the endless barrage of questions he'd launched upon me from the moment I was within earshot of the back porch steps. He finished his current cigarette and flicked the remaining butt onto a barren spot in the backyard and followed me inside. At first the exchange was amicable enough, although my answers were brief and to the point. But upon mentioning my trip to the golden village, Jeremy's response was a derisive snicker accompanied by his usual rolling of the eyes kept barely visible through his dark locks swung to one side. I was not amused, and sick of his dismissive sarcasm. I decided to end the interrogation right there. Leaving him standing in disbelief at my own brash indifference, I left the kitchen and headed upstairs.

"I trudged up the old staircase, scarcely aware of the spookiness always present. I didn't even think about it until I'd already reached my bedroom and removed the grimy clothes from my tired and sore body, throwing them in the upstairs hamper on the way to the bathroom. About the time my grandfather entered the house after giving Banjo his bath, I turned on the shower and stepped into it, allowing the warm jets of water and soap to rinse the dirt and fatigue away, while soothing my injuries. When I was completely clean and the water's temperature had gotten noticeably colder, I stepped out of the shower feeling refreshed enough to face Grandpa and Jeremy. After I dressed I moved gingerly downstairs, already feeling the soreness that was sure to get worse. Jeremy met me at the foot of the staircase.

"'So, what's the real scoop, Jackie?' he demanded. 'It'd be wiser for you to just 'fess up to what you've *really* been up to. And, please...spare me the bullshit about some 'golden village' this time. 'Think you can do that, peckerhead—.'

"'Lay off him, son!' Grandpa intervened. 'Let him eat something first, for God's sake! Jack's obviously got some explaining to do, but I'm sure we'll get the story of what happened in due time. Now, come on over to the dinner table, y'all. Supper's waiting and it'll get cold soon.'

"Jeremy regarded me suspiciously before relenting to our grandfather's words. Grandpa led the way to the kitchen, where we all converged on the table ready and waiting. I was famished since the chocolate cookie was the last thing I'd eaten. I literally shook when I pulled my chair out from the table, using the rest of my energy to sit down and pull myself up to my plate. Observing how weak I was, Grandpa placed some roast, creamed potatoes, and steamed vegetables onto my plate for me, and buttered a piece of warm bread, giving that to me as well.

"As usual, there was little conversation at the dinner table, although Grandpa and Jeremy briefly discussed the remarkable progress the firefighters made with the dwindling fire in the woods. After that, an awkward and tense silence pervaded the overall mood. Both my brother and grandfather kept a watchful eye on me throughout our meal together. I knew they were both anxious to hear my story, regardless of what Jeremy had said.

"The flashing red lights from the fire trucks parked just on the other side of the backyard's wall flickered eerily in the evening's deepening darkness, their reflections dancing on the kitchen walls as they trickled through the back porch door and kitchen windows. Frankly, I was surprised the emergency lights were visible at all from here, given the truck's location and the obstructions of the wall and oak tree. They presented an unsettling reminder of what'd happened that day.

"'Jack...*Jack*! Snap out of it, son!' Grandpa told me, jolting my mind back into the present. 'Go on and finish eating so you can tell us what's been going on with you.' He stood up and my normally aversive brother joined him in the early stages of clearing off the table. 'Do you want any dessert, Jack?" Grandpa asked me. "I baked an apple pie if you'd be interested in having any.'

"'No thanks, Grandpa,' I said. 'I think I've finished eating.' I felt much better, and not to be outdone by Jeremy, I stood up and brought my own dishes over to the sink. 'I might have some later,' I told him.

"'That'll be fine, son.'

"Grandpa motioned for Jeremy and I to go on into the living room. He said he'd join us after he finished clearing the dinner table first. Jeremy waited for me to walk with him, which I wasn't too keen about after the ruthless interrogation I'd endured earlier. But, he didn't say anything this time.

"Before long Grandpa joined us in the living room. He switched on the overhead lights so we could all clearly see one another. 'Why don't you boys make yourselves comfortable on the sofa,' he suggested.

"Jeremy and I went over to the sofa and sat down, taking our usual places on either end. My brother turned toward me, and I could feel his heavy stare while I gazed absently at the floor. Grandpa took his recliner and brought it over to where it directly faced me and then he sat down. After a moment of awkward silence he spoke.

"'Okay, Jack, let's have it," he said. "I'd prefer that you start from the beginning and work your way from there. Oh, and Jeremy. *Please* don't interrupt your brother. All right, son?'

"Jeremy shrugged his shoulders at Grandpa and offered a half smile to me. I took a deep breath and exhaled slowly. Then I began speaking to them of my incredible adventure. It was actually a lot easier for me to tell this tale than I'd figured it'd be, although at some points I lacked the words to adequately describe what I'd seen and gone through. I told them everything. Everything, that is, except for my intimate encounter with Genovene. Until this evening, I'd never shared it with anyone. I intended to keep that particular experience in the far corner of my mind, hoping that someday it'd be as good as forgotten. It's never happened, so I guess you're as good an audience as anyone, I reckon. Besides, you asked me to tell you as much as I possibly could. Hopefully it wasn't more than you bargained for."

"Absolutely not," Peter assured him. "On the contrary, sharing your most personal experiences in regard to all this gives me deeper insight into what Genovene's truly like. You couldn't ask for a more appreciative audience. Trust me."

"Well, all right." Jack grinned sheepishly again. "Jeremy listened, and surprised me in that he did manage to contain himself this time. In fact, at some points of the story, he actually looked genuinely amazed at the things I described, even though he never was frightened by the scarier stuff I talked about. He remained seated for the duration of the tale; smoking the last few cigarettes from the scrunched-up pack in his shirt pocket.

"Grandpa also gave his full attention to me, listening quietly in his chair and occasionally puffing on the pipe he'd lit soon after I began my story. He seemed very thoughtful and a bit more sad than usual, especially when I related information about my parents and Allyson, the little girl from the village. He raised his eyebrows and puckered the side of his mouth on his pipe while slowly nodding his head, as if those particular points especially captured his interest.

"Once I finished, we all sat in silence for awhile. Grandpa finally stood up and walked over to a row of portraits hanging on the living room wall of my grandmother and us, along with a larger family portrait that included our parents. Jeremy and I followed him with our eyes until my brother grew restless.

"'Well, Jackie. I suppose I owe you an apology for giving you a hard time about your 'golden village', man,' he said. 'I have to hand it to you, regardless of how much of what you told us is true or not, that was a good story. An interesting and *damned* good story, I'd say! There's just some parts that are pretty hard to believe, and would take some 'seeing' before I could believe it all.'

"I nodded, pleased he found any of what I said relevant, and in complete shock he'd actually apologize to me. By my count, it was only the second time in my life he'd ever done that. Jeremy let me know he wasn't finished talking yet, so I encouraged him to go on.

"'But that bizarre fire today, and the goddamned thing you brought in here last night...the talisman? I saw those things with my own eyes, and to be honest with you, Jackie, I may have seen something myself last night. I could've sworn I saw a light glowing out in the woods when I got myself a drink before I went to bed. It was gold and misty, and seemed to get brighter by the second.

"'Grandpa was out cold by then, snoring in the recliner. I woke him up and told him what I saw. We both ran out to the back porch to take a look, but whatever it was vanished by then. It just fucking disappeared, so I haven't got any proof. I'm pretty sure it *was* there, though I guess it could've been an optical illusion or some shit like that.' He shrugged his shoulders and opened a brand new pack of cigarettes, tapping out a fresh cancer-stick. He placed it between his teeth while he searched for his lighter.

"'I saw it too, Jeremy,' I said.

"Grandpa turned around to look at me, and Jeremy dropped the virgin cigarette out of his mouth, wearing perhaps the closest thing to true surprise we'd likely ever see on his face.

"'I saw it when I went to bed and looked out my window last night,' I explained. "I watched it till it died down. But y'all were still awake downstairs. Grandpa even called upstairs to make sure I was all right.'

"'Wait a minute,' said Jeremy, a look of confusion on his face. 'You went to bed before midnight, if I remember correctly, and I saw the light around one or one-thirty. Hell, it could've even been a little later.'

"All three of us reflected silently on this. Given the implied nature of the information we'd just exchanged, whatever caused the strange glow in the woods had done so more than once, maybe even several times throughout the night. Its source might've moved the sphere in the backyard while we slept, or while we conversed in the living room as we watched the baseball game, completely unaware something lurked outside in the backyard. Perhaps it crept up to the house and watched us sitting in the living room, or spied on Jeremy and myself as we stared at its strange glow, knowing what it planned for me the next day. I shuddered while Jeremy simply shrugged his shoulders again.

"Grandpa came back over and stood behind the recliner. He continued to smoke his pipe, leaning on the back of the chair as he eyed me directly. My brother and I both watched him, expecting him to say something profound at any moment. He waited awhile longer as if sorting his thoughts one last time, and then finally spoke.

"'I believe your story, Jack, and I believe it in its entirety,' he said, coming around to the front of the chair where he sat down again. 'This isn't the first time in my life that I've encountered the golden object you brought in here yesterday, as I'm sure you both could tell based on my reaction last night. But, it was the first time I recognized its importance right away, for it's an evil thing. I wish I'd realized that twelve years ago, and if I'd understood its significance when I'd first seen one of these things as a child, I might've learned what to do with it back then. Perhaps most of what has happened since could've been avoided.'

"He grew thoughtful and sad again, and then hung his head in silence for a moment or two. When he looked back up, tears welled in his eyes like they'd done the previous evening. He wiped his eyes with his shirtsleeve and then looked at his watch. My story had taken nearly an hour and a half and the time was now approaching ten o'clock.

"'It's getting late, boys," he said. 'I have a story of my own to tell that should shed some light on Jack's story. But it can wait till tomorrow. I want to take a look at the area you went to today, Jack. Jeremy needs...and so do I...to see where it happened. I think it will benefit us all.'

"I cringed as Grandpa said this. I definitely did *not* want to go back there. *Ever!*

"'Jack' he said, his voice soft with compassion. 'Don't be afraid. I think you'll find the area will look nothing like it did today. The 'City of Gold' you visited appears to folks only every so often. In fact, every time it's been sighted in my lifetime, it's vanished before it could be verified and investigated. It disappears so quickly that no one has even been able to photograph the place. You'll see. By the time we get back there tomorrow, the city will be long gone.'

"Of course, I'd already seen the area transform before my very eyes after I crossed the river and looked back. But what about the fire still burning in the woods? Granted, it seemed to be under control for the time being, but who could say it'd remain that way? Moreover, what if Vydora was still on the loose out there somewhere, just waiting for me to return to the river? What then?? I silently contemplated these things when the doorbell rang.

"'Well, who on earth could that be at this hour?' wondered Grandpa, as he walked over to the front door and turned on the porch light, then peered through the peephole. Carl Peterson and Sheriff Joe McCracken stood on the front porch, squinting in the brightness of the porch light.

"'Good evening, Marshall,' said Carl, after Grandpa opened the door for him. 'Sorry to bother y'all at this late hour, but we saw the living room lights on and figured someone was still up.' He looked genuinely pained to disturb us, but something in his eyes said it was real important for him to do so. He and Grandpa had been close friends since grade school, even though Grandpa was nearly four years older. As kids, he never minded Carl tagging along and their friendship grew from there. Carl was the best man at Grandpa and Grandma's wedding many years ago, and was present when Grandpa retired as manager of the local saw mill when I was ten. In fact, he was one of the few friends that remained true once the bullshit started about my parents' sudden disappearance.

"'Come on in,' Grandpa said, stepping aside to allow them entry into our home. Carl was quite a bit heavier than my grandfather, with thinning gray hair and pale blue eyes that stood out from his flushed complexion. Sheriff McCracken, on the other hand, was a thin, deeply tanned man in his mid-forties, with dark brown eyes and brown hair revealing slight touches of gray along his sideburns and moustache. Although Grandpa didn't know him well, he seemed to respect him.

"'Well, hello, boys!' Carl said, and then smiled as he extended a meaty hand out for both of us to shake, as we remained seated on the sofa. 'I don't believe either of you've met Sheriff McCracken.'

"'Pleased to meet you both,' offered the sheriff, who then extended his hand for us to shake as well.

"'So, what's the latest on the fire, Carl? It's still under control, ain't it?' Grandpa asked.

"'Yeah, it's definitely under control,' Carl sighed. 'There's not even a glowing ember remaining from it anywhere, and we've covered the area twice thoroughly. 'Nothing's left but smoke and blackened trees. It's by far the strangest fire I've ever been involved with. Almost like it started dying on its own once we got here. All I know is we encountered a few problems getting water flow from two of our trucks to work right, meaning we were operating at maybe forty- percent capacity. It turned out we didn't even need that much, since the flames died immediately once our few working hoses hit them. That's why we were able to tell the Demopolis boys to go on back home. Definitely, it's been one strange scene. 'Ain't ever seen anything like it—I mean *never* in the forty-six years I've been doing this for a living.'

"Carl paused, studying all three of us before turning to Sheriff McCracken. The sheriff gave him a slight nod and he turned his attention back to my grandfather. 'That's not why we're here, though, Marshall. At least not the main reason we stopped by.'

"Grandpa appeared perplexed, though Jeremy and I were pretty sure he wasn't really. 'Oh? What's up, Carl?'

"'Well, we're actually wanting to ask Jack a few questions, Marshall, if it'd be all right with you.'

"Grandpa hesitated before looking over at me to gauge my reaction. After indicating I'd be fine with that, Grandpa gave his okay. Sheriff McCracken took over at this point, after Grandpa offered him a seat in his favorite chair. He moved the recliner closer to me and sat down, removing a small notebook and pen from his shirt pocket. He leaned in toward me, lightly tapping his pen on the notebook. Grandpa and Carl moved over and stood behind him, looking on from either side.

"'Jack, you're not in any trouble,' the sheriff told me. 'So, let me start out by assuring you of that. What I've come to find out is this: were you anywhere near Ben Johnson's place this afternoon? If the answer's 'yes', did you see anything unusual?'

"'I walked by there with Banjo somewhere around six-thirty this evening,' I replied after only a moment's deliberation. I was determined to stick with the basic facts. No need for crazy tales about running for my life to escape an angry fire-breathing dragon at this point.

"'Well, you see, Pete Aderley confirmed he saw you and a billy goat about that time,' stated the sheriff. 'You know Pete, don't you? He owns the feed lot that sits next to the Johnson's farm, just south of their farmhouse and silo, up near the road.' He paused to allow me a moment to confirm I knew Mr. Aderley, which I did.

"Anyway, Pete only saw you in passing, but told me he noticed you were on your way to the front door of the farmhouse. A few minutes later when he looked again, you had moved over by the barn. This time, he watched you long enough to see you leave the area and head toward the woods. Again, since you weren't there long, we're not suspecting you of doing anything—believe me, son.

"'Pete went back to what he was doing, which was unloading feed from his truck into the storage bins in the small warehouse on his lot.

About ten minutes after he saw you leave the Johnson's farm, he heard a tremendous racket going on next door, along with what he thought at the time was a small earthquake. It was strong enough to knock a few bags of feed off the truck and down on top of him, pinning him underneath. From what he told us, he laid there terrified, listening to all the commotion and unable to crawl out from under the feed sacks.

"'Now, here's where it gets pretty weird, and it's where we could sure use your help, son,' said Sheriff McCracken. 'We need to know if you saw or heard anything, no matter how strange or crazy it may have seemed at the time. Pete swears he heard some god-awful roar, like from one of those dinosaur-action movies. Excuse me for saying so, but whatever he heard scared the holy hell out of him. I mean, it scared him so bad he literally *pissed his pants*! You know something pretty bad had to happen to scare a man enough to make him do something as embarrassing as that. I hate seeming so indiscreet, but I need you to understand the depth of his fear.

"'Right after he heard the roar, everything went completely quiet. Pete said it was like whatever made the noise stopped right in the middle of making it again, as if something, or someone, shut it off, like hitting the 'mute' button on a remote.' He stopped to look around and make sure we were still with him so far. To his surprise, I'm sure, Jeremy, Grandpa, and I were all straight-faced and fully attentive to what he was telling us. He smiled shyly.

"'I'm about to get to the point of this, and appreciate your patience,' he said. 'Pete's son, Sam, arrived about thirty minutes later to check on his daddy and was quite alarmed to find him hollering beneath the feed sacks. Sam uncovered him and then got him cleaned up. Pete's all right, by the way, with no broken bones—just a bruised ego, I guess you'd say!' He chuckled lightly and we all politely snickered.

"'Anyway, Sam and Pete decided to investigate the source of all the commotion at the Johnson's farm, and walked over to the farmhouse. They found out, as you must've earlier, that they weren't home— and thank the Good Lord for it! What the Aderleys also found was that the Johnson's farmhouse has been destroyed. I mean *completely* destroyed. The house has huge holes running throughout the main floor, and everything inside has been either crushed or ripped apart. Even the barn closest to the house, the one you went to, got ransacked. One side of it's now completely burned away, though the fire didn't spread to the rest of it for some reason. It's just like what happened in the woods. Carl here thinks whoever or whatever was responsible for all of this may have gotten spooked and ran off.'

"The sheriff suddenly looked down at his feet and fidgeted quietly in the recliner. The room grew very quiet until he couldn't stand waiting for some kind of response from me. 'So, Jack' he said, steadily lifting his gaze. 'Did you see or hear *anything* unusual this afternoon?'

"I thought carefully about his question and the best way to answer it. I was truly surprised to learn Pete Aderley could see me, and yet Grandpa and Jeremy couldn't until after I returned to our backyard. Of course, I knew what'd happened. Vydora finally escaped from the woods and followed my trail, destroying everything in her path. She was probably erased from this reality when the angels and Genovene reached the climax of their battle and disappeared from the area. I wasn't about to tell the sheriff this.

"I looked over at my grandfather, who seemed to sense my dilemma. I then looked back toward Sheriff McCracken, and was about to say I hadn't seen or heard anything at all, when Grandpa suddenly spoke for me.

"'Jack told us tonight he thought he saw a huge lizard-like critter that may have started the fire in the woods,' he said, perhaps figuring a partial truth was as decent as any place to go with this. I hoped his offering of a little information the sheriff already knew something about would keep me from having to run through the entire story again.

"'Is that true, son?' Sheriff McCracken asked me, surprisingly straight-faced as he leaned ever closer to me. I nodded 'yes', and he turned his attention back to Carl Peterson. 'Show him, Carl. Go ahead and show him what we found in the farmhouse rubble.'

"Carl walked over and showed me a large envelope he'd kept under his arm up to that point. 'We found this, Jack,' he said, and proceeded to open the envelope and pull out the same reptilian scale that's sitting here now. At the time, it was carefully sealed in a plastic bag to protect it.

'Jeremy's eyes got really big and he moved closer to get a better look at the strange specimen in the bag. I just sat there, unfazed and not at all shocked to see the small leftover from Vydora's visit to the Johnson's place. I even smiled slightly as I realized this was such a small part of the monster, perhaps no more to it than the dozens of body hairs people cast off each day. Grandpa watched my reaction to this, as did Carl and the sheriff. Even his eyes were lit up from excitement and wonder as he looked on.

"'We also found two enormous footprints in the mud around Ben's tractor near the woods,' Carl advised. 'We've got pictures of them that should be developed sometime tomorrow morning along with a few Polaroids that didn't turn out as well as we'd hoped. Plus, we're setting plaster casts right now to save the footprints before nature gets an opportunity to destroy them.' He shifted his weight from one foot to the other. In the meantime, Sheriff McCracken resumed his interrogation.

"'What did this 'lizard-thing' look like, Jack?' he asked. "I mean, how big was it and all?'

"'It was *very* big. Enormous is a good way to describe it,' I told him. 'You'll probably find this hard to believe, but it looked a lot like a *tyrannosaurus rex* except that it had horns on its head and was covered with those scales.' I hoped this was good enough. Telling him the critter could also fly and blow long streams of fire, as I stated to you earlier, seemed like such a bad idea.

"'So, you're saying, what...it was forty to fifty feet tall and Godzilla-like?' he clarified, unable to control a wry smile. It disappeared when he saw my expression. How could my description be so hard to believe when he'd seen the evidence?

"'It was at least that big,' I told him, confidently.

"'Um-hm-m,' he nodded. 'Where'd you first see it?'

"'I saw it in the woods.'

"'In the woods. When was that and what were *you* doing in the woods? Was this after the fire started or before?'

"'It was around five o'clock, I guess,' I said. 'I was chasing Banjo because he got out of the backyard and was running for the woods. I didn't catch up to him until he had already gotten pretty far. The fire hadn't started yet.'

"Believe it or not, Agent McNamee, I really hated lying, and was sorely afraid I was going to trip on my words. I looked over at Grandpa and saw he looked amused, perhaps even a little proud at my attempt to remain vague as possible. I knew he was certainly one who valued secrecy if the information being withheld wouldn't prove beneficial to whomever requested it. He'd protected us for years that way, especially in regard to the sphere and its origins. I guess he figured we'd know if, or when, we needed to know. I felt the same principal applied right then. They likely weren't going to find Vydora again, so why tell them more than was necessary?

"'Well, that explains the broken weeds and downtrodden grass in the field behind your backyard,' Sheriff McCracken advised. 'But, where *in* the woods did you see this thing?'

"'I don't remember exactly,' I told him. 'It came out of nowhere and I grabbed Banjo and tried to get out of the woods. I guess I got turned around and came out over by the Johnson's place. I ran to their house, hoping to get them to call the authorities. When they weren't there, I checked the doors to the house and barn, but they were all locked. So, I ran home to get help. By then, we all saw the fire raging in the woods and Grandpa had Jeremy called the fire department. I don't know how the fire got started—honest. I hope you don't think I set it. There's no way I would, or could, have started one that large and that quickly.'

"Even though I was new to the art of deception, I felt I was doing a good job. Quite a bit of my reply was true, and I started to feel pretty good about my chances of surviving this interrogation with my incredible experience intact and untarnished by anyone's ridicule. Other than Jeremy's, of course, which I figured I could live with.

"Sheriff McCracken sat in silence. After about a minute, he looked up at Carl, who shrugged his shoulders. Then he looked back at me, releasing a deep sigh as he concluded our interview. 'Well, your story definitely fits the facts we have so far,' he said. 'Sorry if I was a little rough on you, Jack. That certainly wasn't my intention. But, as you can imagine, we've got a pretty delicate situation on our hands. I've got to have some answers, or at least know as much information as we can gather on this event, and still keep things quiet around here. I mean, we don't want the media involved, because it could stir everyone around here into an awful panic. Already, the Palmers are snooping around out there. Carl tells me you've always had trouble with them.

"'Aside from a few folks like them, I'm sure y'all agree our community likes privacy and wants to uphold Carlsdale's reputation as a good community and a quiet town. We don't want a lot of curious types hanging around here, is what I mean to say. Let them join the other tourists visiting the space center or Gulf Shores and places like that. The last thing we need is some giant lizard running loose around here and becoming the state of Alabama's biggest attraction.

"'One other problem is we've got some explaining to do once the Johnson's come back from their Florida vacation and find their home in ruins. I suppose you know they're pretty temperamental folks as it is. Since I've got a close nephew that works for the FBI, I'm planning to contact him in the morning and see if I can fax the pictures to him. He might know of someone in the bureau, or somewhere else who can help us with this—especially if the critter comes back, which I fully expect. I doubt seriously it just vanished into thin air.'

"Sheriff McCracken eyed me knowingly, as if he could decipher the rampant thoughts racing through my mind. I waited expectantly for him to tell me what he really thought of my responses to his questions. But it never happened. Instead, he stood up and pushed the recliner back. He looked over at Carl, who motioned for him to join him at the front door.

"'I guess that's it for now,' the sheriff said as he looked back at the three of us. 'Sorry to have kept y'all up. If you don't mind, until we know how to better handle this thing, if anyone asks y'all what happened, please say it was just a brush fire. We'd sure appreciate it.' He nodded to Carl to confirm this. 'Jack, Jeremy, and Marshall...y'all have a good night,' he said, before turning toward the door. 'Take care.'

"I thought Carl and Sheriff McCracken were almost as tired as I was. The three of us watched them as they reached the front door and opened it to step outside. The sheriff stopped suddenly and turned back toward us. This time he was smiling. 'Marshall, how'd you ever get that big ole' round rock inside your backyard?' he asked. 'Carl tells me you and a bunch of guys put it there as a prank on your late wife, though he says it's a secret as to how you actually got it over the wall. Is that so?'

"Grandpa looked over at Carl, who gave him a wink unseen by the sheriff. While still holding Carl in his gaze, Grandpa smiled and answered the question. 'Yeah, Joe, that's how it got there, all right,' he said. 'Maybe some other time I'll fill you in on the details. Elsie was fit to be tied on account of it. That's for sure!'

"The three men joined in laughter while Jeremy and I looked on, half smiling and barely able to appreciate our elders' sense of humor. Once the laughter died, Carl and Sheriff McCracken said goodbye again before walking outside, closing the door behind them as they left us in peace.

"'Nice job, Jackie,' Jeremy said. A definite tone of admiration was evident in his voice as he drew out a fresh cigarette from the pack in his shirt pocket. He looked like he wasn't going to survive another minute without one. The two visitors had stayed nearly half an hour and he'd already been dying for another smoke well before their unexpected arrival. He quickly lit the cigarette, inhaling and then exhaling a long stream of smoke.

"'I thought for awhile old Joe McCracken was going to corner your ass and stick it to you with a red-hot poker. Man, I really did!' He threw his head back in laughter, but it ended quickly once he started to cough and had to take another long drag from his cigarette. 'But, you know, Jackie. You've got to wonder what did become of...was it Vydor? No, Vydora...yeah, that was it. Vydora. You've still got to keep an eye out for that thing because you didn't see her leave now, did you little brother?'

"I shrugged my shoulders and nodded 'no'.

"'I mean, I would've been very, *very* skeptical of all this since it's beyond weird,' he continued. 'But, there's no denying the concrete evidence available to support it all. And, Grandpa, what about that sphere, anyway? You know...you never have told us a goddamned thing about it, really. So, what's up with that? As a matter of fact, the most I've ever heard about it was tonight from Jack and Sheriff McCracken. You know, old man, now would be as good a time as any to come clean on the subject. Wouldn't you agree?'

"'Not tonight, son,' said Grandpa, much more weary than irritated. 'Definitely *not* tonight. I'm beat. I'm sure Jack is too, and we should all turn in before it gets much later since we've got a big day ahead of us tomorrow. I'll tell you this, though. I promise to tell you everything I know about it before tomorrow's over and done with. How's that sound?'

"'Sounds great to me, Grandpa!' I told him, but Jeremy hesitated before agreeing he could wait one more day.

"'All right, I guess,' he finally agreed.

"Grandpa walked over to the gun case and pulled out a semi-automatic pistol from the bottom drawer along with the very same Winchester he'd taken out the previous evening. After making sure both weapons were properly loaded, he brought them over to the recliner and sat them both down on the seat of it.

"'What are you doing, Grandpa?' I asked, more curious than alarmed.

"He stopped and looked over at Jeremy and I, regarding both of us evenly. 'Just preparing for the rest of the evening, son,' he said. 'The "Season" ain't quite over yet.'

"'What do you mean?' I was a little more alarmed now.

"'I could use some enlightening as well, Grandpa,' added Jeremy.

"'All right, then,' he agreed. 'Although I do believe everything you told us tonight, Jack, I think I should be considered a fool if I didn't prepare, just in case, for the return of the lizard-thing, this 'Vydora' you've spoken of. At night, especially, one can't be too careful about such things. Tomorrow when we visit the area around the river, I'll be packing some iron, too. Now, don't worry yourselves about this. I don't expect we'll find anything there to remind you of Genovene's presence, Jack, or Vydora's for that matter. But, that's tomorrow in the full light of day, and right now its nearing midnight. Who knows what could be out there in the night's shadows, hiding and waiting for us to lower our guard, regardless that a full moon's out tonight.'

"Grandpa had a faraway look in his eyes. Meanwhile, I wondered what good a gun would do on Vydora. As if reading my thoughts, he suddenly frowned. 'Well, regardless of what either of you boys think, I'm camping out here in the living room,' he said, 'Consider this strictly a precaution, since 'better safe than sorry' has always been my motto.' He smiled and pushed the recliner back over to its original position and placed the firearms on the floor beside it. He then obtained a warm blanket from his bedroom and headed for the kitchen. Grandpa didn't return until he found an unopened bottle of scotch whiskey.

"I knew he was now set up for the remainder of the night, and was planning to stay awake till dawn. Usually, whenever he did this he'd take a catnap for an hour or two until either Jeremy or myself got up.

"I wasn't afraid, but I felt a strong urge to keep him company for awhile. 'Would you mind if I join you, Grandpa?' I asked him.

"'Not at all, son,' he said. 'But, you'll need your rest. Why don't you sleep on the sofa, Jack.'

"'All right,' I told him.

"'Count me in here, too, Grandpa,' Jeremy said. 'I'll get my sleeping bag and set it up on the floor, though it'll be strange not having any female action to keep me company tonight—just kidding, y'all! I wouldn't *really* do that...at least not here!' Jeremy shot a wry smile toward Grandpa while winking at me. I couldn't believe the camaraderie we now enjoyed. We hadn't been like this to one another since grade school, and I secretly prayed it'd be a lasting thing between us.

"Jeremy left the living room and I caught up with him at the foot of the staircase. We went upstairs together to both get our sleeping bags, and returned downstairs to the living room a few minutes later. We set up the bags near the fireplace and told Grandpa we'd decided to give him the sofa to sleep on. He declined our offer, stating again that he'd be just fine right where he was, sitting in his favorite chair. He turned on the light next to the recliner, switching it to its lowest setting so as not to disturb us. I could tell he expected us to drift off to sleep once we got comfortable in our bags.

"My brother and I conversed with each other for another twenty minutes or so, discussing several different aspects of my story. In the meantime, Grandpa picked up a mystery novel he had nearly finished. Every so often he'd look up from his book, perking his ears as if listening closely for some suspicious noise hidden amid our whispered voices. He didn't have to do that for long, as his earlier presumption was correct. Jeremy and I did fall asleep.

"I found out later that he continued to read his book. After getting up twice to explore the premises and finding nothing out of the ordinary, he returned to his chair and opened the novel for the last time that night. By then, it was the wee hours of the next morning, and he later said he found it increasingly difficult to keep his own eyes open despite the fact he lacked just a few pages to the book's conclusion. Around two am he finally drifted off to sleep.

"When Grandpa awoke, around 4:30 am the morning of July 21st, he still held the opened mystery novel on his lap. Luckily for him, he managed to avoid a stiff neck this time, as he usually didn't when falling asleep in the recliner. Since Jeremy and I still slept, he sat the book down quietly on the floor and got up from his chair, leaving the living room for his bedroom and bathroom down the hallway. Once there, he showered and got himself ready to meet the day.

"He arrived in the kitchen not long after this, and was surprised to find Jeremy waiting for him at the kitchen sink, his first cigarette of the day nearly finished. He raised his cup of freshly brewed coffee to our grandfather in salutation.

"'Good morning, Grandpa,' he said. 'Coffee's nice n' hot, the way you like it.' Jeremy poured him a cup and handed it to him. Grandpa thanked him and eyed him curiously, probably wondering what the hell had gotten into his oldest grandson. It wasn't at all like him to be so agreeable and congenial this early in the morning.

"'Did you sleep all right, son?' asked Grandpa.

"'Yeah, I did,' replied my brother. 'I'd say better than I have in years. It may sound strange, and maybe even a bit sappy, but something about Jack's story really gets to me. I don't know for sure what it is, but maybe it's the stuff about Mom and Dad. All I know for sure is I *feel* better, Grandpa. I mean, I don't feel near as mad at the world, like I usually do. I know I can be a real asshole sometimes, and I'm sorry. I hope to God this feeling lasts!'

"Grandpa told me later he couldn't help but smile at this, and laid his hand on Jeremy's shoulder, which was another thing that would've been impossible to do up until then. Rather than flinch like he normally would, Jeremy seemed at ease as he returned Grandpa's smile.

"'Hm-m-m. I hope it lasts, too!' Grandpa told him. 'I'm glad you believe Jack's story, Jeremy, and like I said last night, I have a story of my own that should add to and support his account.'

"'I'm looking forward to hearing it,' said Jeremy, ' and I hope you can clear up the last few questions I have about all of this.'

"'Tonight I'll tell you everything you're interested in finding out about, as long as it deals directly with the subject at hand. In the meantime, I'm hungry,' said Grandpa. 'Want some bacon and eggs, son? Or, maybe some flapjacks instead?'

"'Anything's fine with me,' said Jeremy. 'Want me to wake up Jack?'

"'No, son,' Grandpa advised, moving over to the cupboard and refrigerator to get the necessary items to cook breakfast. 'Let him sleep a while longer. Another hour or two should be plenty, I reckon. If he doesn't wake up on his own, we'll get him up at nine-thirty. How's that for a plan?'

"'That's cool with me,' my brother agreed. 'What time are we going to check out the place Jack went yesterday, or are we still planning to do that today?'

"'We are. I thought just before lunchtime would be good, and I'll pack us a decent meal to take with us. Sound good to you?'

"'Sounds good.'

"Grandpa finished preparing breakfast for them. After they'd eaten, Jeremy went upstairs to get ready for the day. I continued to sleep soundly through all of this, while Grandpa began work on getting our lunch together. Neither one disturbed me until nine-thirty rolled around.

"'Hey Jack! Wake up!! *Wake u*—well, look who's awake, Grandpa! *Finally*!!' chided Jeremy. 'We thought you were going to sleep all day, Sleeping Beauty!'

"I looked up. He stood over me, smiling in amusement.

"'*Well*?? Get up, Jackie boy! Your cereal's on the table and your clothes are laid out on the sofa!'

"I sat up and stretched while I rubbed the sleep from my eyes. Then, I stood up and staggered to the bathroom. It seemed like every muscle in my body screamed for relief. At least I wasn't as tired as I thought I'd be. Once I finished my business in the bathroom I moved over to the kitchen. I plopped down into my chair before the usual row of cereal boxes, slowly pouring myself some corn flakes and milk in the bowl set in front of me.

"'Good morning, Jack! Looks like you finally got a good night's rest, even though I can see you're still a little sore,' Grandpa said. He gave me a wink and a warm smile. 'I'm packing a lunch for our little trip today, so I'll be busy by the stove if you need me for anything.'

"He looked happier than usual, so I figured he was really looking forward to this. After I was done with breakfast, I got myself ready for the day, wishing the whole time there was some way to postpone the trip.

"'Meet me on the front porch, boys!' Grandpa called out to us from the kitchen. 'We should be ready to go in just a few minutes!'

"I had gone upstairs and was on my way down to the foyer. Jeremy waited by the front door, smiling smugly as he watched my final descent. He held an unlit cigarette in his mouth while his lighter was primed and ready in his right hand, just waiting for the first permissible opportunity to feed his addiction. Usually, he could've cared less about lighting up a smoke once he technically was on his way outside the house. I really hoped this new version of him turned out to be a lasting thing.

"'You ready, Jackie?' he asked.

"'Yep,' I replied, following him out the front door.

"'*Whew!*' he said, immediately holding his arm up to shield his eyes from the morning sun. 'It's going to be fucking hotter than hell today. I hope this goddamned expedition is worth it, don't you?'

"'Yeah, I do,' I replied. Well, so he hadn't changed that much. At least he was being cordial to me, which allowed my fantasy of a new and improved older brother to continue. 'Actually, I was hoping we could do this some other time.'

"'Well, I'm not averse to visiting the place, except on a day like today,' he advised, pausing to take another long drag from his cigarette. 'Here's what I'm really interested in: If we meet up with this Genovene, and she looks as hot as your first description of her...well...I'd like to get her on her knees and suck me off good.'

"I felt an icy tingle race up and down my spine. All at once, I relived my most intimate moments from the day before. I never told him about my experience with Genovene, but here he was talking about that kind of shit! He immediately sensed my discomfort.

"'Hey, bro, I'm messing with you!' he assured me. 'Do you really think I'd want that monstrous bitch doing me with that hideous face you described last night? Even if she can make herself hot as a centerfold, damn I'd still know what's underneath! It ain't fucking happening—that's for goddamn sure, Jackie! Not even if she offered me a million bucks...although, I'd have to consider it for two—*just kidding!!*' He grabbed my shoulder and gave me the wink we'd both learned from our grandfather. At that same moment, Grandpa came barreling out the front door with the remaining supplies for our trip.

"'Come on boys!' he ordered us. 'I've got the Jeep ready and waiting!' He stepped off the porch and took the walkway around to the side of the house where the Jeep was parked, with Jeremy and me right behind him.

"The Jeep was old, with the faded paint once a much darker shade of green. Grandpa had already loaded two backpacks into the Jeep's rear, and added a third pack and a small cooler when we reached the vehicle. We all climbed in, with Jeremy joining Grandpa in the front seat while I settled into the seat behind them. After letting the engine warm up, Grandpa backed the Jeep down our long driveway and onto Lelan's Road.

"We headed north about a mile until we reached a fork in the road. Grandpa took the left fork, which is Baileys Bend Road, and followed it as it curved and twisted for roughly another mile before it straightened out again, bearing steeply downhill toward the west. Then, he slowed the Jeep down and turned left onto a dirt road heading south as it followed a large river. An old tattered and rusted sign that stood near the road's entrance read 'Black Warrior Road'. I asked Grandpa if it was the same river I saw the previous day.

"'Yes it is, son,' he said. 'I know you're familiar with other portions of it, since it's part of the Tombigbee River. This portion, however, was once confused with the Black Warrior River years ago—same as the rest of the river up north of us. The Tombigbee travels a huge distance from northern Mississippi to the southern-most reaches of Alabama. From there it feeds the Mobile River that empties directly into the Gulf of Mexico.

"'The road here used to follow the river from Tuscaloosa on through Carlsdale as it headed south. A host of other little townships once used this road as a major thoroughfare, but due to modern developments the road no longer extends past Carlsdale. It'll take us up to a bridge that sits near the path I believe you walked on yesterday, Jack. Even though it's longer this way, it's much safer than chancing a trip through the woods by our house, since there could be a few hot spots hidden under all the charred timber.'

"Are you sure you want to do this, Grandpa?' I asked once we approached the hillside with the path cut along its face. I immediately pictured Vydora peering at us through the treetops, ready to jump down from the hillside and land directly in front of the Jeep.

"'Yeah, I do," he replied. "And, I believe it's all right for us to be here today, Jack. Otherwise you would've fussed more to keep us away from here. Ain't I right about that, son?' He looked over his shoulder and gave me another wink.

"'Yeah, I guess so, Grandpa,' I said. 'I can't help feeling it's too soon for me to be back here.' Right when I said this, we pulled alongside the front of the hill. I drew in my breath as Jeremy whistled under his own. Grandpa simply looked on in silence. The entire hillside was laced with dark charred streaks from when Vydora unleashed her fiery wrath the previous afternoon.

"'Will you look at that shit!' whispered Jeremy.

"'The flagstone path along that hillside was laid more than two hundred years ago, boys,' Grandpa told us, ignoring Vydora's handiwork for the moment. 'In fact, this area has been settled by the likes of us since the early seventeen hundreds. Prior to that, this was the sacred hunting grounds and campsite of the Chickasaw Indians.'

"Me and Jeremy looked at each other, raising our eyebrows in surprise at our grandfather's nonchalant reaction to the fire damage on the hillside. When we looked back at him, he pulled his gaze away from the road long enough for us to catch the sparkle in his eyes and the excitement in his face.

"'Try not to let any of this make you uneasy,' he advised while turning his attention back to the road ahead of us. 'But if you boys are too uncomfortable with what we're about to do, and you want to turn around and go back home, I suppose we could do just that. I'd just be dropping you off, though.'

"'Dropping us off??' Jeremy seemed offended he'd even suggest such a thing.

"'Yes, dropping you both off,' said Grandpa. 'I'm going to have a look around here regardless of what either of you decide to do. Hopefully, now that we've taken the trouble to actually come here, you'll stay with me. If legends are correct, we won't be encountering any dragons, golden villages, or anything else of the sort since it's all gone and shouldn't be able to reappear. I'm highly curious about what might've been left behind, though. Perhaps we'll even find us a gold trinket or two—it's happened before!'

"Despite the potential danger, neither of us wanted to go back yet. The tantalizing mystery of what was left behind latched onto our curiosity almost as tightly as it had our grandfather's.

"'There's the bridge,' he announced. 'I'll park the Jeep over here against the hill, and then we'll head on over to the old fort.'

"I immediately felt a cold shudder run through me. The bridge sat in the exact same spot as the one that'd been there the previous day. Granted, it was an old rickety log structure, but the fact a bridge of any kind sat there was disturbing. I glanced a short distance down from the bridge to see if the willow was still there. But, the tree and any other remnant from Genovene's world were long gone. Only a large solitary fir stood near the bridge.

"'So, there's really a fort around here?' asked Jeremy. He eagerly looked out toward the bridge through the front passenger window. 'I thought that was just an old myth.'

"'No, it's real, all right,' Grandpa told him. 'There's not much left of it now, I understand.' He pulled the Jeep alongside the hill and parked it beneath a pair of medium-sized walnut trees that'd somehow escaped the fire. We all jumped out and moved to the back of the Jeep to get our supplies.

"Each of us grabbed a backpack, and Grandpa gave Jeremy the

cooler to carry. Once we were ready to go, Grandpa grabbed his rifle and placed it in his backpack, and then shut the Jeep's rear door. He reassured me again the firearm was strictly precautionary, and then the three of us headed for the bridge.

"'Be careful, boys!' Grandpa cautioned. 'The bridge should support us well enough, but y'all can't be bouncing up and down on it. The fort is about a mile up the road from here.' He climbed on first and we stepped on to follow closely. Along the way, I looked down into the deep water beneath us through gaps in the flimsy wooden floor of the bridge. I was thankful these spaces weren't large enough to fall through. But as the old bridge creaked and moaned in protest with each step we took, I became nervous.

"Once we stood on the other side of the Tombigbee River, I couldn't believe the dramatic change in the area's landscape since yesterday. The native trees and plants had completely overrun the area since then, and it appeared these woods hadn't been visited by anyone for many years. The wooded area before us seemed to stretch for several miles—all the way up to the nearby town of Paxton, according to Grandpa. It looked like a totally different place. The only similarity that remained was the western direction of the path.

"Within fifteen minutes we arrived at a clearing in the woods that spanned roughly twenty acres. Weathered, hand-hewn logs were lying on the ground throughout the area and most of them were at least partially hidden by tall grass and weeds. A few logs stood on either side of the path, and Grandpa said they were part of the main entrance to the fort at one time. Behind the entrance, nearly a hundred feet away, sat the ruins of a pair of small buildings.

"I was leading the way by then, and since I was really curious about these buildings, I ran toward them to get a better look. They were made almost entirely of stone, except for the splintered fragments of wooden doors and shutters. There were also the frayed remains of the wooden crossbeams that hung down from the open rooftops of each structure.

"Suddenly, I was forced to grab and pinch my nose as the area began to stink to high heaven with a noxious odor that smelled like rotten eggs. Holding my nose and breathing through my mouth, I moved up to the doorway of one of the buildings. Moss and algae covered the stone walls and thick cobwebs hung down from the few remaining ceiling boards. The dirt floor was overrun with weeds and an assortment of old beer and soda bottles. Near the doorway, I watched a large golden orb spider crawl steadily toward a monarch butterfly struggling desperately to free itself from the spider's near-perfect web. I shivered and looked away.

"My grandfather soon arrived and we waited for Jeremy to catch up to us. Once he did, he grabbed and pinched his nose as well. "'Pee-ewww! What the hell is that smell?' he whined in disgust.

"'Sulfur,' replied Grandpa. 'This is what's left of the first fort ever built in the region, called Fort Mullins. You've probably never even heard of it, since it didn't stay functional for long. The early settlers in this area tried to push it from their memories, if not from the local history books, soon after it was abandoned two hundred and seventy years ago,' he explained.

"'You know, my brother Monty and I used to play around here with Carl Peterson, along with a group of local kids,' he continued, smiling as he reminisced for a moment. 'We'd wade in the shallows of the river, chilling our legs and feet, and then we'd make a mad dash through the woods until we reached the hot springs just beyond the fort here, which I'll show you in a moment. We'd play 'hide n' seek' till it'd get dark and we all had to go home. The older folks back then said kids had been doing that kind of thing for years. The only time they weren't doing it was during the Civil War when folks stayed low or they'd likely get shot.'

"He looked away, gazing in the direction of the river. Then, he looked back at the fort ruins, chuckling quietly to himself. 'Monty and I came out here regularly,' he recalled. 'We even caught a young couple completely naked one time behind these buildings. Man, I've never seen two people fly out of here faster, both butt-naked and carrying their clothes—most of which they dropped along the way!' He laughed heartily for a moment before moving beyond the ruins. He walked over to a large rock formation sitting near the far-west edge of the clearing, still chuckling to himself. Me and Jeremy followed him and were soon greeted by the gurgling and swishing noises of water boiling nearby, accompanied by a small cloud of steam rising up from the top of the rock formation.

"'Here's what's stinking the place up, boys,' he told us. 'It's probably the only hot spring in this country unknown to the National Geological Institute or whatever outfit currently keeps track of these things. It doesn't even have a name—not even an Indian one I'm aware of. But it does seem likely someone would've had to refer to it by some moniker through the years. Watch your step and I'll show y'all something.'

"We climbed the dark-gray rocks and once we reached the top, Grandpa steadied himself on a large slab. He sat down and motioned for us to do the same. The gurgling-swishing sound was pretty loud from up there. The small cloud of steam hovered just in front and above the slab beneath it, sending out mist-like tendrils toward us. I turned to watch these vapor fragments rise higher into the air before they dissipated completely, some twenty feet above the formation.

"The smell was nearly unbearable, even though Jeremy and I were pinching our noses as tightly as we could. Grandpa, on the other hand, seemed for the most part unaffected by the smell and was soon ready to continue as our tour guide.

"'Boys, you'll need to be extremely careful,' he warned us. 'If you look down from here, you'll see a sight you're not likely to ever forget.' He leaned just barely over the slab's edge, while we did likewise. Peering through the rising steam, we saw the boiling pool of water in its brilliant turquoise basin, bubbling twelve to fifteen feet below us. The water pushed and surged its way over the far corner of the hot tub-sized pool, forming a stream that carved a path another forty feet downward until it emptied into another much larger pool. Steam rose from the larger pool as well, but it didn't appear to boil from where we sat.

"'The Indians, both ancient and more recent up until a hundred and eighty years ago, spent a great deal of time here,' explained Grandpa. 'We know this on account of the burial mounds and stone graves on the north, west, and south sides of the clearing. The water directly below us is scalding hot, as you can tell, but the water in the larger pool is much more pleasant. On average, it stays between ninety-eight and a hundred and seven degrees Fahrenheit all year 'round. The Indians must've bathed in it because I know we did growing up. I suppose the first white settlers to this area decided to build the fort here for the same reason, to have access to the hot water. If they needed fresh cold water, the river sits less than a mile away, as you know.'

"I stared into the bubbling pool below, as if charmed by the brilliant blue-green color of the water. I knew it was an illusion caused by the mineral deposits from the water encrusted upon the rock sides of the pool. Yet, the color and the big bursting bubbles reminded me of something... All of a sudden it hit me as to what it was, and I backed up quickly from the slab's edge.

"'What's wrong, son?' Grandpa asked, as a look of worry spread across his face. 'Is the steam too warm for you?'

"'Yeah, a little bit, Grandpa,' I told him. I really hated lying to him. The steam was hot, but that wasn't the reason I backed away. Rather, the bubbling water reminded me of the throbbing blue mass I'd seen in Genovene's village. It reminded me an awful lot of that hideous thing, and I now wanted to get as far away as I could from it. 'Can we go now, Grandpa?' I pleaded, and looked up at him with imploring eyes. 'I'm feeling kind of sick to my stomach from that awful smell.'

"'Are you sure, Jack?' Grandpa studied my face, seemingly torn between genuine concern and disappointment.

"'If you can hold off puking your guts, Jackie, I'd like to take a quick look into the other pool down there,' said Jeremy, moving quickly down the side of the rock formation to the ground below. 'I'll be back in just a minute, y'all!'

"Before either of us could stop him, he finished his descent and was on his way over to the larger pool of water. Large patches of algae covered boulders and smaller rocks that enclosed the pool. Jeremy leaned over the edge and looked down into the water. 'Hey! This is pretty cool down here!' he shouted up to us. He stuck his hand into the steaming water, swishing it back and forth near the surface. "The water's pretty clear down here, too! Nice and warm, though I'd have to say it's a little on the hot side!'

"My brother continued to inspect the pool from where he stood, smiling with the smug look that'd become his trademark over the years. Suddenly, his eyes grew wide with terror and he quickly withdrew his hand out of the water as he staggered back from the pool's edge. '*Holy mother of Jesus!!!*' he cried out. '*Fuckin'-A!! There's something moving around in there!!!*... Could be a goddamn poisonous water snake or some other shit-head, but whatever it is, it looks like one *big* motherfucker!!! Did you know if this thing has fish or snakes, Grandpa?'

"'No, son, I'm not!' he replied, the worried look steadily deepening in his ruddy face. 'You need to get the hell away from there *now*, Jeremy!!! We're on our way down! *Come on, Jack!!*'

"Just as Jeremy moved back over to us, the pool began to show ripples and waves as if some large creature was moving just below the water's surface. Suddenly, a heavy splash of water flew into the air and the shimmering body of the mysterious critter was briefly visible to all of us. To me it looked more lizard-like than a snake or a fish. Perhaps a miniature version of Vydora had managed to hide here. If it was, even her small size scared the shit out of me. Jeremy and Grandpa seemed to recognize the same thing, probably from my description the night before.

"Jeremy took off running and shouted over his shoulder for us to follow his lead and get the hell out of the clearing. At Grandpa's insistence, I scurried down the rock formation's side first, with him following close behind me. As soon as we reached the ground, a menacing murmur came from the pool. The motherfucker slithered out of it and dropped down into the camouflage provided by the tall grass and weeds that filled the clearing.

"'*Run, goddamn it!!! Run!!!*' Jeremy screamed. '*It's headed straight for you!!!*'

"Grandpa and I immediately sprinted toward Jeremy, who was already on the path that led out of the clearing. A heavy rustling sound followed us as we ran, but I never saw the critter itself even though I glanced several times over my shoulder. I could only see the quivering weeds and grass less than a hundred feet behind us announcing its pursuit. It was closing fast, and just before we reached the edge of the clearing, Grandpa suddenly stopped.

"He quickly removed his rifle from his backpack and aimed it in the direction the noisy thing was coming from and tried to squeeze off a shot, but the Winchester jammed up on him. He tried to get it unstuck, but it was no use. The unseen menace quickly bore down upon him. In frustration, he threw down the rifle and removed his backpack, literally ripping it open in the process. He reached underneath our lunch and uncovered his semi-automatic pistol, pulling it out from its holster while he motioned for me to keep moving toward Jeremy. 'Go on, son!' he urged me. 'I'll be along in just a minute!'

"Grandpa turned to face the lizard, which was now less than twenty feet away. He fired several shots into the dense grass and weeds. At least one of the bullets struck the thing. It let out a blood-curdling howl followed by an angry roar. Despite its obvious rage it refused to reveal itself, whimpering in pain and for the moment no longer interested in being the aggressor. Grandpa made the most of this reprieve, running as fast as he could to catch up with us while we anxiously waited for him near the entrance to the woods.

"'Did you kill it?' Jeremy asked.

"'I don't think so,' he replied, panting hard as he tried to catch his breath. He bent over for a moment to replenish his body's oxygen supply, all the while keeping a watchful eye on the area he'd vacated just a moment ago. 'I think I hurt it some...and it's not coming after us... At least for now.'

"He stood up and allowed himself one last look to survey the boyhood haunt he hadn't seen in years, and to talk himself out of his immediate desire to go back and retrieve the Winchester. Even though it was an heirloom from his father's side, he decided it presented too great a risk to try and recover it right then. He told us later that he intended to come back for it with Sheriff McCracken or at least one of his deputies in the next day or so.

"When he turned back toward us, I watched him intently, studying, in particular, his eyes. They were darker than usual and revealed his fear—same as they had just two nights before. The thing lurking in the clearing had truly frightened us all, but none as badly as Grandpa. I confirmed this by shifting my gaze to my brother's face. Even though Jeremy's sure-fire cockiness was nowhere to be found, I couldn't honestly tell if he was still scared. Surprised perhaps, but after the initial shock wore off, he seemed like his old self. Even as I thought this, I watched him reach for the cigarette pack and lighter in his breast pocket, confirming further that he was fine.

"As for myself, I felt more confused than frightened. I thought for sure everything magical, or supernatural for that matter, had disappeared with Genovene the day before. Now, I realized that assumption wasn't correct.

"'Don't plan on smoking just yet, Jeremy, because we need to get the hell out of here first!' Grandpa warned. Without waiting for a response from my brother, he firmly grasped us both by our shoulders, turning our attention to the nearby woods. 'I don't want to wait around here any longer in case that thing's got friends, or decides it's well enough to come after us on its own!'

"At his urging, we ran into the woods and didn't stop running until we reached the bridge. I remember the air was thick and humid, and rain clouds obscured the sun. The birds and insects seemed oblivious to both our presence and the impending weather, never ceasing their songs to one another. As I listened to them, I thought I heard something else. Something sinister? I wasn't sure. But there was something quietly stalking us. I didn't think it was the thing from the hot spring, because it felt different somehow. I was pretty certain Jeremy and Grandpa felt it, too.

"'Man, this place is creepy,' whispered Jeremy, loud enough to draw a responsive look from Grandpa and me. 'I can't imagine why you and Uncle Monty would want to spend as much time as you say you did here, Grandpa. It seems pretty fu—.'

"'*Sh-sh-h!*' Grandpa interrupted. 'I just heard something! Over there...just to the left of the bridge.' He pointed to a place where the woods came to an abrupt halt just a few feet from the bridge. There was no one there at the moment, and the ground was almost bare. Only a few clumps of crabgrass and a short spiny weed populated the spot.

"Suddenly we all heard an audible 'snap' in that very spot, as if some invisible person stood there and had shifted their weight from one unseen foot to another, inadvertently stepping on a brittle twig or something similar. Immediately, the entire wooded area grew quiet around us, as if every living thing picked up a predatory scent unavailable to our startled senses.

"The hairs on the back of my neck sprang to life, and the feeling of being watched hit me and then intensified. I gradually became aware of a smooth cool breeze in the area, blowing toward us from the clearing. The breeze picked up in intensity and as it did, I heard a sultry whisper pass just above my head.

"'Ja-a-a-ck. *Ja-a-a-ck*.'

"'Did y'all hear that?' I asked

"'Hear *what*?' said Jeremy, a look of profound concentration on his face. 'You don't mean the sound by the bridge, do you? We all heard that.'

"'*No!*' I said. 'Somebody's calling my name!!'

"'What do you mean 'somebody's calling your name'?' my brother retorted.

"'I mean...like *that!*" I exclaimed, hearing it again while I spoke. 'Can't you hear *it*? Can't *you*, Grandpa??' I was near panic, and after the adventure I'd braved the day before, it wouldn't take much to throw me into complete hysteria. All the while, the voice grew stronger and clearer, with longer drawn out vowels, as if taunting me.

"'Lovely Ja-a-a-ck. You're *mi-i-i-ne!* Lovely, beautiful *Ja-a-ack* is...*mi-i-i-ne!!*'

"It was Genovene. Her voice was so sultry and seductive. I realized then this was her favorite disguise. Perhaps only the unluckiest of her victims ever saw the real monster she is. '*Don't y'all hear that?*'

I implored, near tears.

"Grandpa looked over at Jeremy and then back at me. 'Son,' he said. 'I don't think either of us can hear it. I mean, what exactly are you hearing and where's it coming from?'

"I wanted to say the voice was coming from directly above me. That's where it'd been when I first heard it, although it now moved freely with the breeze that gently blew through the area. She was everywhere but nowhere.

"'Sw-e-e-e-t Jackie boy! I love the way you *ta-a-a-ste!*'

"The voice swooped in beside my left ear and then quickly drew away again, echoing throughout the area. I almost grabbed Grandpa's pistol to shoot my invisible tormentor.

"'I love you Ja-a-a-ck! I love your luscious *co-o-o-ck!* I *ba-a-a-dly* want to *su-u-u-ck* it and *fu-u-u-ck* it again and *again* and *ag-a-a-a-in!!*'

"'Y'all! Help!! Help me NOW!!!' I cried out, thankful they couldn't here the last words. I was on the brink of no return. Grandpa and Jeremy looked on helplessly, since there was nothing either of them could do for me. I couldn't believe Genovene's seeming immortality, given all that happened to her the day before. She remained as cunning and as powerful as ever, which was evident in the way she attacked me now. After all, we couldn't shoot what we couldn't see and only what I could hear.

"Tears began to well as I considered this. All the while, the verbal assault grew steadily worse. The wind increased its intensity as it blew against the trees and plants near the path, forcefully pushing them back and forth. At least my grandfather and brother could see this, as they anxiously looked around themselves.

"'Oh-h-h *Ja-a-a-a-ck!!!* Let me *su-u-uck* your big *thro-o-o-b-b-b-ing pe-e-n-i-s-s!!!* I need to *su-u-uck* you! I need to *e-e-ea-t* you! We *all* need to *e-e-ea-t* you, *Ja-a- a- a-ck-e-e Bo-o-oy-y!!!*'

"Right then, an invisible pair of lips kissed my cheek, while a pair of invisible hands gently grasped my crotch, immediately stroking me through my pants. That was *it!* I wasn't going to stand idly by and let this continue. I spun around and slapped at the unseen hands while shouting a string of angry obscenities. I must've looked like someone near a nervous breakdown to Jeremy and Grandpa.

"Like a bear running from an angry beehive, I raced for the bridge. I could've cared less if anything else waited for me there. My entire focus was on reaching the other side of the river as quickly as possible. I prayed that my brother and grandfather had enough sense to follow me.

"I ran across the flimsy structure and kept running until I arrived at the Jeep. When I stopped and turned around, I witnessed a strange and horrific transformation of the area for the second time in two days. Fortunately, Jeremy and Grandpa had hurried after me, crossing the bridge and reaching the Jeep shortly after I did. They were just in time to escape the magnificent metamorphoses that soon took over the other side of the Tombigbee River.

"Enormous pyramids were popping up everywhere on the other shoreline, and a narrow golden pathway now ran between two of these structures sitting closest to the river's edge near the old bridge. All of them were transparent with lavender and gold designs etched upon them, and each one appeared to glow from within.

"The trees and plant life on the other side of the river were not exempt from this incredible event, as more tropical foliage soon filled the area, giving the western bank of the river an Amazon rainforest appearance. Where once was barren ground just a moment ago, a pair of thick palm trees now stood up against the rickety bridge's foundation.

"Standing on the bridge and watching me in my amazement was none other than Genovene and her four siblings, as beautiful as they ever were and all dressed in long flowing lavender gowns. Once I noticed them, they smiled and waved at me. '*Y'all come back now, ya hear!!*' Genovene shouted, and then she threw her head back in laughter.

"'*Do you see that?*' I pleaded with the others. '*Look, damn it!!! Now, do you believe me??*'

"'Believe *what??*' Jeremy retorted again, letting his irritation slip through as he and Grandpa turned their attention to the other side of the river. 'What are we supposed to be looking at, Jackie?'

"'*THEM!!!*' I shouted, pointing toward the group still standing on the bridge. '*Them, and all of those pyramids behind them!!! They're right there in front of you, if you'd just look—.*' A horrible realization swept over me as I suddenly remembered the previous evening when neither of them could hear me shouting while I stood with Banjo at the back gate to our home. It seemed like the same kind of thing was happening again.

"'They are, huh?' said Jeremy, narrowing his eyes to indicate he was trying very hard to see what I claimed was across the way from us. 'Either you've got some special type of vision, Jackie, or I'm as blind as a fucking bat. I don't see a goddamned thing. Do you, Grandpa?'

"'No...I'm afraid I don't either, son,' he replied, and then turned his attention solely on me, his eyes worried. 'Who's 'them', Jack?'

"'Genovene and her kin,' I said. 'But it's the human version of them all that I described to you last night. In fact, I really don't think they plan to hurt us. At least not right now. Are you sure you can't see them?' I hoped I wasn't placing us in any real danger, but I didn't think I was wrong about what I felt.

"'Son, I don't see anything and I can't hear anything other than you two,' said Grandpa. 'It doesn't mean I don't believe you're really experiencing this stuff. I think we've all been through enough already to prove most anything is possible.' He sighed and looked out toward the bridge again. 'Perhaps Genovene and whoever's with her are visible and audible only to you,' he suggested.

"I felt desperate, wishing he was wrong, but fearing he wasn't. I wanted so badly for him and Jeremy to see her at least.

"'What did she say to you?' Grandpa asked.

"'Uh, she was saying my name over and over, and telling me she wouldn't let me leave. That they needed me,' I explained as calmly as I could. I purposely left out the sexual references.

"'Anything else?'

"'Uh, no. Not really, anyway.' I lied.

"'Hm-m-m-m. Are you sure?' asked Grandpa. He eyed me thoughtfully, like he often did when I was in some sort of trouble. Since I normally was a horrible liar, this was all it usually took for me to come clean. I'd gained some confidence since skirting around Sheriff McCracken's questions the night before. Yet, It was still hard to ignore the pain I felt from lying one more time to my grandfather. I guess it was a little like Saint Peter must've felt when he denied knowing the Lord three times following Jesus' arrest by the Romans long ago. I just wasn't ready to disclose Genovene's fascination with using and humiliating me sexually. .

"'Yeah, I'm sure, Grandpa,' I assured him. 'It was nothing, really, mostly just some unintelligible gibberish. The only thing I could make out was that the voice kept saying my name and asking me to stay.'

"I avoided his gaze by looking over at Genovene again. The smile on her gorgeous face suddenly dropped, as her lower jaw opened in an unnatural yawn. It looked dark and infinite inside, and suddenly I was shown a flash of her hideous snout and teeth. After revealing this she quickly shut her cavernous mouth and smirked. She slowly shook her head from side to side as she pressed her index finger to her lips. Then, she and the others turned around and walked off the bridge, disappearing into thin air as soon as they stepped onto the golden pathway. A moment later, the golden pathway, along with the surrounding rainforest and the ethereal pyramids, faded rapidly until all evidence of this event completely vanished.

"'Well, they're gone now,' I reported, my voice shaking. 'They just disappeared a moment ago.' I looked over at Jeremy, who shrugged his shoulders in indifference to the whole affair. Grandpa still seemed disappointed he wasn't able to catch a glimpse of them and their wonderful handiwork.

"'Are you boys getting hungry?' he asked, grimacing slightly once he removed his backpack from his weary shoulders. 'I think it's best if we just go home now. I'm sure y'all agree it wouldn't be such a good idea to eat lunch here after what's transpired. Besides, I believe it's fixing to rain soon.'

"'That's fine with me,' I said. 'I've seen enough of this place.' No lie here. I found myself wondering about the message Genovene had sent me a moment ago. My dream of never seeing her again definitely faded in the light of day.

"'How about you, Jeremy?' he asked.

"'Yeah, I guess so,' my brother said. 'I could sure use a smoke, and I've got some more questions for Jackie.'

"'Let's get everything loaded up first, so we can be on our way out of here.' Grandpa led the way over to the Jeep, and within a couple of minutes we had everything loaded in the back. Before we finished climbing back into the vehicle, the first raindrops descended upon us. Grandpa drove us back onto Black Warrior Road, and before we reached Baileys Bend Road, the dreary sky unleashed a torrid downpour on the area below.

"'It looks like we left just in time, boys, and all in all I'd say it's been worth it coming out here today,' said Grandpa. 'Though, perhaps Jack might disagree.' He turned and smiled at me. 'Sorry about your experience by the bridge, Jack. At least you and Jeremy have now had the opportunity to see what the area you visited yesterday really looks like—.'

"'But, Grandpa,' I interrupted, 'this isn't where the village was. It had to be a lot further away from here. It was probably way beyond those burial mounds over by the hot spring on the other side of the pool, maybe even a mile or so further into the woods.'

"He regarded me thoughtfully again. 'No, Jack,' he told me. 'I believe your village was right there by the fort and hot spring. Much of your story, along with certain events that've happened there through the years, lead me to believe that. I'll explain it to you later, tonight after dinner. I'll tell both of you everything I know about this stuff. All right?'

"'Okay,' I agreed. 'I may still feel like I do now, that the village was located somewhere further away than the area we went to today. Will you at least hear me out on this when you're done telling what you know?'

"'Of course I will.' He chuckled at my reluctance to take his unproven word on the subject. Grandpa told me later it reminded him of my mom, and even my grandma for that matter.

"We followed the old dirt road, which was rapidly becoming a sloppy mixture of squashed grass, weeds, and mud, without another visit from Genovene and her funhouse from hell. It was as if Genovene, that sagacious witch, and her magical environment were restricted to the area we'd just left behind, much like a ghost that's imprisoned by the dwelling it's forced to haunt. Before long, we were back on the weathered asphalt of Bailey's Bend Road, and heading back toward our home.

"'So, what was Genovene wearing today, Jackie?' Jeremy asked me. He'd been silent for the past ten minutes, and it was clear where his mind had been.

"'They were all dressed in purple gowns kind of like what Freddy wore for graduation back in May,' I told him. It was a half-lie this time, but an effective one. Nothing like a direct hit when you needed it, since I knew Jeremy regretted quitting school early. The mere mention of Freddy's graduation outfit should've, by itself, shut my brother's mouth. Also, depicting the voluptuous figure of Genovene clad in an oversized graduation gown would hardly qualify as sexy in his mind, and I knew this. If he found out about the sheerness of the tight lavender outfits she and her sisters wore when I saw them on the bridge, Grandpa and I would've never heard the end of it.

"'Hm-m-m...so that's it, huh?' he said, his voice lowered in disappointment.

"'Yeah, that's it,' I told him, almost chuckling. I was punchy by now, and picturing Genovene in a graduation outfit with one of those ridiculous hats was almost too much.

"We veered onto Lelan's Road, sliding slightly in the driving rain. Since we were almost home, Jeremy dropped the subject for the time being. Grandpa pulled the Jeep into its parking space next to the house, and the three of us jumped out and quickly unloaded our gear.

"Once inside the house, we headed for the kitchen, emptying the backpacks' contents onto the kitchen table. To avoid a return to the subject of Genovene's wardrobe and a possible link to the invisible sexual harassment I'd endured that afternoon, I offered an elaborate description of the pyramids looming just beyond the bridge, as well as the unusual designs etched onto their transparent sides. I did so awkwardly, interrupting the small talk between my brother and grandfather about how good a cold roast beef sandwich can taste when you're really hungry. As I blurted out my ramble describing the wondrous scene on the Tombigbee's western bank, Jeremy and Grandpa abruptly ended their conversation and turned their entire attention to me.

"It was if they'd decided to wait upon me to bring it up and didn't know how to broach the subject of what I'd actually seen, given my near hysteria by the bridge and my reluctance at that point to elaborate on what'd happened. Once I realized this was all they really wanted, I relaxed enough to clearly describe the environment that'd suddenly appeared by the bridge. After I finished, we all sat in silence.

"Jeremy appeared to bite his lower lip, as if forcing himself to keep a painful promise not to interrogate me further about Genovene's attire. Grandpa, on the other hand, stared out through the kitchen window, like he was reliving an experience from many years ago. He eventually turned his attention back to me.

"'Well, son, that makes three truly unique experiences for you in three days,' he said. 'I'd say there's never been a 'Season' quite like this one before—definitely not around these parts. I just hope what I've got to say tonight has relevance for you both, in light of this. If for some reason it doesn't, please feel free to stop me from boring y'all.' He stood up and pushed in his chair, picking up the condiments from the table and taking them over to the 'fridge. 'I thought we'd order a couple of pizzas tonight, boys, since I'm too beat to cook,' he advised. 'How's that sound to y'all?'

"'Sounds great!' I said.

"'I can live with that, I guess,' said Jeremy, standing up and pushing his chair in also. He then headed for the sink to get his ashtray, a freshly lit cigarette dangling from his lips. It sat there precariously, bouncing up and down as he hummed an Alice N' Chains' tune.

"'You know, son, if that damned thing falls on the floor and scorches the tile, you'll be responsible for cleaning it up!' Grandpa warned.

"'Don't worry,' Jeremy assured him. 'I've yet to drop so much as an ash on your pretty floor so far, have I not?'

"Grandpa glared at him for a moment. He then sighed and shook his head as he continued to clear the kitchen table of the remnants of our lunch.

"'Ah, hell. I just remembered I'm supposed to help Freddy fix his carburetor this afternoon,' Jeremy said. He carefully tapped the cigarette into the base of the ashtray, preserving most of it so he could finish it later. He then pulled out his truck keys and headed for the hallway. 'Why don't I get the pizzas, Grandpa,' he offered. 'I know what y'all usually like and there's a new place over in Demopolis. If y'all are willing, we could try it out.'

"'Sure,' said Grandpa, pleasantly surprised by Jeremy's offer.

"'I trust you,' I added. 'But, are you planning to tell Freddy what's been going on around here?'

"My brother frowned for a moment as if he was considering this idea for the first time. 'No, I don't think so,' he told us both. 'At least not until I get a better handle on what it's all about. I honestly don't know what to think. Like Grandpa here, I shared in some of what's happened and it's pretty much fucked up my way of thinking. That's all I can be sure of at this point.' He threw back his hair from his face and checked his breast pocket to make sure he had enough cigarettes to last the afternoon. 'Well, I better get going,' he told us, and headed for the hallway. 'I'm looking forward to what you've got to say tonight, Grandpa. Hopefully, it'll help me understand everything a little better. I'll see y'all in awhile. Is six o'clock okay?'

"'That'll be just fine, Jeremy. Don't go racing out there,' Grandpa told him. 'We'll see you in a bit with those pizzas.'

"'Oh, and don't forget to call Carl Peterson or Sheriff McCracken to tell them about that thing by the old fort and the hot spring,' Jeremy reminded him, just as he stepped out of our view.

"'I was just fixing to do that!' Grandpa called after him.

"Jeremy's slammed the front door as he left, and soon the heavy rumble of his customized truck filled the air outside our home until it faded as he pulled out onto Lelan's Road. I could still faintly hear his vehicle as it pulled onto Bailey's Bend Road on its way toward Demopolis and Freddy Stinson's place.

"'Well, I guess I better call Carl and Joe,' Grandpa sighed. 'Are you up for helping me pick some vegetables from the garden after while, Jack, if it stops raining?'

"'Sure.'

"'Good. I was thinking a small salad might be nice to go with dinner tonight.'

"'I'll be passing on that, Grandpa,' I told him, 'and you know Jeremy probably won't want one either. But if you want one, I'll be glad to help you with it.'

"'Actually, one of us will be enough to get the fixings if it's just myself who wants a salad tonight,' he said. 'You're still welcome to join me anyway, as I always enjoy your company.'

"'Thanks, Grandpa. I'll do that.'

"He excused himself from the kitchen and went through the dining room then into the living room. He called Carl Peterson to tell him about the latest critter we'd encountered. I was curious as to why he needed to make the call from the living room when there was a perfectly functioning phone in the kitchen. I decided it didn't really matter, despite the obvious hushed tone Grandpa was using once he got Carl on the line. After briefly eavesdropping in the dining room, I felt uncomfortable spying on him, and since I couldn't make out what was being said anyway, I gave up. As the rain had stopped and the sun now forced its way through the storm clouds, I went outside to wait for him on the back porch.

"The air was still thick with heat and humidity. I let the kitchen's screen door slam shut to alert Grandpa as to where I went. The backyard's vast array of insects had already resumed the daily activities they'd abandoned earlier on account of the weather. I smiled to myself at how resilient they were in the face of continuous adversity, and walked over to one of two chairs sitting near the steps that led down into the yard. I brushed a small spider web and a few stray leaves off the chair's seat and sat down.

"'Are you ready, Jack' Grandpa asked once he came out of the kitchen and onto the porch a few minutes later, letting the screen door slam again. He held a pair of buckets along with work gloves and a straw hat for himself. He'd also brought along an extra pair of sunglasses for me to wear.

"'Yeah, I'm ready,' I said, and stood up to meet him by the porch steps.

"'Carl told me he'll contact Joe,' he said.

"'What did he think of what happened today?'

"'He was a little surprised, I think,' said Grandpa. 'I get the feeling he still expects Vydora to re-emerge at any time. He hadn't considered checking for her at the old fort area, though. He said as soon as Joe can spare a moment, he'd like to go out there and take a look. But after what I told him, along with what happened yesterday, I do believe he won't be going anywhere near there unless he's escorted by Sheriff McCracken *and* a couple of his armed deputies.' Grandpa smiled and I couldn't help chuckling at what he just said. 'Anyway, since the sun's back out, I thought we'd go on out to the garden now while we have the chance,' he advised. 'It'll probably be a little muddy out there, so I'm going to put my old work boots on and you'll want to change into the pair of old shoes you have sitting by the back door.'

"I told him I'd rather wear the hiking shoes I already had on. I assured him I'd be careful to keep them clean. He told me that'd be fine, and then came over and sat down next to me in the other chair near the steps. He took off his shoes and exchanged them for a weathered and torn pair of low-top boots, and then left the nicer pair of shoes underneath the chair he was sitting in. He stood up and straightened his trousers while motioning to me that he was ready to visit the garden.

"'You may want to put these on, Jack, unless you'd rather wear my hat,' he teased as he handed me the sunglasses.

"'You can keep the hat, Grandpa,' I told him. 'I shouldn't need the glasses either, since we're only going to be outside here for a little while. Right?'

"'Well, I had a few other things to take care of,' he advised. 'You can go back inside once we get the garden stuff together. I'd appreciate it if you'd wear these until then.'

"I went ahead and put on the glasses while Grandpa wore the straw hat and work gloves. He then led the way down the porch steps and around to the front of the house through the wrought-iron gate. As I mentioned earlier, the garden itself sat right next to the Palmer's front yard. It was roughly a quarter of an acre in size and was enclosed by a waist-high picket fence. I ran up to it across our driveway and the slippery grass of the front lawn, opening the fence's wooden gate for us to walk through.

'The earth was still wet from the recent rain shower, leaving me to wonder why in the hell I actually agreed to do this. I stood on a thin strip of grass and one of the ornamental flagstones that bordered the garden. Once Grandpa realized he should've insisted on me dressing more appropriately, he told me to wait by the garden's gate, and that he'd hand me the buckets when they were full.

"'Sorry, son, I should've realized the garden would be like this,' he said as he glanced at his wristwatch. '*Damn*! It's almost three o'clock. We better get busy, here!'

"He gave me one of the buckets to hold, thinking it'd be easier to maneuver through the mud and muck with just a bucket at a time to fill up. Grandpa moved in amongst the well-kept plants, carefully avoiding the network of vines lying exposed upon the ground. The garden was filled with just about every kind of vegetable there is, like cucumbers, squash, carrots, and potatoes. There were several tall rows of corn, and shorter rows of cabbage, lettuce, and peppers—both hot and mild. There were even some fruit plants such as tomatoes, strawberries, cantaloupes, and watermelons. At the far eastern edge of the garden, there stood a pair of tall trellises full of concord grapes.

"'I'll be back in a moment, Jack,' he said. 'I'm going to start over there on the far end and work my way back here.'

"'All right,' I said. 'I'll be here waiting for you.' I found a fairly dry flagstone near the gate and sat down on it. Grandpa was nearing the eastern end of the garden, but from where I sat, I could clearly see his work boots and the bottom portion of his trousers through the gaps between the plants' leaves and stalks.

"The remaining clouds had nearly disappeared and the sun bore down unmercifully upon us. A medium-sized elm tree that stood in the Palmer's front yard and hung over onto our property threw its misshapen shadow into the northwestern corner of the garden. A gentle breeze swayed the branches of the elm back and forth, giving life to the shadow, and made it appear as if it had scrawny arms with grotesquely long fingers or claws at the end of these arms. I shuddered again, despite the intense warmth provided by the sun's heat, and turned to look directly at the tree, removing the sunglasses from my eyes.

"Nothing unusual. Nothing out of place. Just an old and very deformed elm tree. I turned back to face the garden, noticing my grandfather was slowly working his way back toward me. Suddenly, I became aware of someone standing nearby. At least that's how it felt, and the intensity of the unannounced visitor's presence, or stare, was enough to raise the gooseflesh on my neck, shoulders, and arms.

"I whirled around on the flagstone, but there was no one there. Only the elm tree pushed to and fro by the soft breeze. I looked over toward our backyard wall and gate, but there wasn't anyone over there either. Both our front yard and the Palmer's were completely clear, yet the feeling of being watched remained.

"I turned around to face the garden again. Grandpa sifted through the corn less than thirty feet away. 'Hurry, Grandpa. *Please!*' I whispered. It now seemed to take him forever to gather the ingredients for his dinner salad. He looked up briefly and smiled at me, unaware I was sitting on pins and needles.

"'I'll be done with this bucket in just a minute or so, Jack!' he called to me.

"'Okay, Grandpa!' I replied, silently hollering '*Please hurry!!*' The eyes of the unseen presence grew more intense, as if trying to burn a hole through me. I seriously considered getting my shoes muddy and joining him in the middle of the garden, when the same disconcerting voice of Genovene returned.

"'Ja-a-a-ck. Ja-a-a-ck!'

"'Hey, Grandpa!' I called to him. 'Would you mind if I come join you?'

"'*Ja-a-a-ck!! You can't ru-u-un! You can't hi-i-i-de!*

"'Son, I'm almost done, so there's no sense in getting your shoes muddy!'

"'I will *always* know how to *fi-i-i-nd* you!! I will always know where you *a-r-r-r-e!! Ha-ha-ha-ha!!!*'

"Grandpa bent down to reach for a few young hot peppers from the plant. In that very moment, I saw a shadow standing to the right of the elm tree's shadow. It loomed above the garden as the form that created it silently approached the garden's fence. The shadow appeared to be that of a giant misshapen insect, much like the repulsive appearance of Genovene the day before. I froze, while the shadow shortened and its image became even more misshapen. I realized in horror it was bending down toward me.

"It touched me.

"'*Grandpa!!!*'

"He looked up just as I stood and tried to run to him. The bottoms of my shoes were still slick from the wet grass, and I slipped on the flagstone. I fell headlong into the garden's mud, snapping three vines and crushing a small butternut squash against my chest.

"'*Jack!! Are you all right??*'

"I felt Grandpa's strong hands lift me up. I wiped the mud from my face and out of my mouth while I looked over my shoulder. Whatever had stalked me was now gone. Only the ugly elm tree loomed above the fence line a short distance away.

"'What in the *hell* just happened??' Grandpa demanded.

"'I-I don't really know,' I replied, determined not to alarm him further. 'I felt something crawl on my back and it scared the holy crap out of me, Grandpa. Sorry about that!' I tried to force the biggest smile I could muster to sell this. He smiled in return, but something in his eyes told me he wasn't completely buying it this time.

"'Come on, son,' he told me. 'Let's go inside and get you cleaned up. I believe I've got the fixings here to make a salad big enough for all of us if you and Jeremy decide to have some after all.'

"The two of us left the garden and headed back to the house. Once we returned to the back porch, we left our muddied shoes there and went on inside. It felt considerably warmer in the kitchen than it did earlier, despite the hard-working floor fans. Grandpa placed the bucket of vegetables in the sink and told me he was going to get cleaned up. We agreed to meet in the living room once I finished taking a shower, but before I started up the stairs, he stopped me and said he had something important to tell me first.

"'Son, you've been through quite a bit these past few days,' he said. 'But, there are some things you need to know. Number one, I'll always love you no matter what happens or what you do—that's the most important. Number two, I'm as proud as anybody could be that you're my grandson. Most folks couldn't survive what you've gone through, but I was already proud of you anyway. You're a good kid. Number three, and this is the last thing, Jack. I know a hell of a lot more than you think I do and you're *not* near as good a liar as you think you've become. Now, go on and get cleaned up and I'll see you down here in awhile.' He watched me walk to the top of the stairs before walking back to his own bedroom.

"I was pleased that the upstairs' spookiness continued to have little affect on me. But now I worried about Genovene's whereabouts. I kept imagining her jumping out from the shadows, and prayed fervently that she wasn't somewhere in the house.

"I quickly showered and put on some clean clothes, and then headed back downstairs to the living room. According to the mantel clock, it was a few minutes after four in the afternoon. Jeremy wasn't due home with the pizzas for another two hours. Grandpa stood on his stepladder near the front corner of the room, reaching for a dust-covered photo album that'd been barely visible atop the bookshelf. He looked over at me while hoisting the heavy book down from its resting-place. I'd never even noticed it before.

"'Hey, son,' he called over to me. 'Do you feel better now?'

"'Yeah, Grandpa, much better,' I told him. 'What've you got there?'

"'Oh, just a very old picture album,' he explained. 'I thought it might be kind of fun for you and Jeremy to thumb through this tonight.' He stepped off the ladder and carried the old and dusty book over to the dining room table, where it landed with a thick thump as he laid it down.

"I decided to follow him into the dining room, where I found him carefully dusting off the book's cover. Once he was done, he left it near the center of the table, straightening the table's embroidered tablecloth before moving into the kitchen.

"'I want to finish getting my salad ready for dinner and let it chill in the 'fridge,' he said once he noticed I'd followed him from the dining room. 'Why don't you find out if the Braves are playing again today? If they are, I'll get us a couple of sodas and we'll watch the game together.'

"'All right.' I went into the living room and turned on the TV. Sure enough, the Atlanta Braves were playing. I remember it was the top of the second inning, and they were playing the San Diego Padres. I let Grandpa know this and sat down on the sofa. Once he joined me, we watched the game together until Jeremy showed up a couple of hours later with the pizzas.

"It was just after six o'clock when he got home, carrying our dinner in a protective carrier he'd purchased that afternoon. Grandpa allowed us to eat in the living room while we watched the remainder of the baseball game. It was extremely rare for him to do this, and perhaps the only time he'd ever suggested it himself. The mood was lighthearted, and my brother and I were excited to hear what Grandpa would soon tell us.

"Once we were done eating, he told me and Jeremy to grab another soda from the kitchen and meet him in the dining room. We then waited for him at the table. Since spending time here was another rarity, usually reserved for special occasions, it only added to the intrigue that marked this evening's event. Grandpa soon joined us carrying an ice-cold bottle of beer, which commanded the immediate attention of my brother.

"'So, when did you buy the beer, Grandpa?'

"'A couple of days ago,' he replied, smiling in amusement at the wounded puppy look on Jeremy's face. 'The reason I got one out now is we're running a little low on cold drinks, and I decided to save the rest of them for you two.'

"'You know I'd rather have a beer!' whined Jeremy. 'Suppose I finish the soda I've got now and then helped myself to one. Would you really mind tonight if I did? That way, we could save the sodas for Jackie.'

"Grandpa frowned briefly, but it was replaced by an amused look on his face. 'Yeah, I guess that'll be all right,' he sighed. 'Just be sure to limit yourself to a couple... as in two, *not* four or five, son!'

"Jeremy grinned and promised he'd hold it to two beers. Grandpa then sat down at the head of the table, which was in front of a pair of large French-paned windows facing the backyard's appliance-junk pile. I always assumed the God-awful view was his reason to keep the curtains and blinds almost always drawn shut, like they were that evening.

"'It may take some time to do this, but I'll try and keep it interesting,' he said, smiling wanly as if he were having second thoughts about sharing his long-held secrets with us. 'As I told y'all last night, this was not my first encounter with the golden object, or talisman as Genovene called it in your story last night, Jack. I've seen one just like it before, back when I was a child.

"'I was a boy of about eight years old at the time, and I lived here in this very house, with my father, mother, and your Uncle Monty. My grandpa had died a few years earlier and Papa inherited the place even though grandma was still alive. She didn't want to live in this big old house by herself, and as I've gotten older I can understand why.

"'One day when I was playing by myself in the backyard, I stumbled across a shiny gold thing lying just inside the back gate, right where that stone sphere sits now. It glowed something fierce there on the ground, and I guess most any kid would've picked it up. I scooped it up and immediately slipped it inside my overalls' pocket. I didn't take a good look at it until later on when I was alone in the tool shed out back.

"'Once I did finally get a good look at it, all of the strange designs and inscriptions on it made me dizzy, just like the one Jack picked up did to him. I mean, both objects were probably very similar if not identical to one another. Well, just then Monty snuck up behind me, so I stuffed it back into my pocket. He saw me do it, and since he was three years older, he bullied me to make me let him see it. I knew if I did that he'd keep it and I'd never get it back, so I got away from him and ran out of the tool shed. Even back then he could never catch me.'

"Grandpa paused for a moment. A dreamy, far away look was in his eyes as he reminisced. He laughed softly. 'I ran around the backyard until I was far enough away from him,' he said, 'I vowed right then to give the damned thing to Lisa Ann Stratton as soon as I found an opportunity to do so. I had the biggest crush on her, and aside from picking flowers for her from my momma's flower garden, I couldn't do much else to show how I cared for her. This was going to be my ticket to her heart. I just knew it.

"'I made a beeline for her house, which is where Ben and Maggie Johnson now live—or used to, until yesterday. I squeezed through a narrow gap in the Stratton's picket fence and ran to the backyard where Lisa Ann was playing with her poodle named Scratches. Animals have always taken a liking to me, except I suppose that critter we encountered today. It definitely worked to my advantage with Scratches. As soon as she saw me, she came running up wagging her tail and trying to lick me. I looked up at Lisa Ann as she watched us play, smiling that beautiful smile.

"'I was finally able to break the ice with Lisa Ann on account of this, since she pretty much ignored the flowers and all, probably because she was a little older than me. To make sure I'd made a lasting impression, I pulled the golden object out of my pocket and handed it to her. It seemed to get brighter as she held it up close to her face, and the light made her braided blond hair and deep blue eyes look prettier than ever. She was quite impressed and ran inside her house to show it off to her parents.

"'Less than a minute later, her great uncle who'd been visiting their farm, came outside with the object in his hands. He walked down the back porch steps and right up to me. He was a tall, thin older gentleman who was dressed like a preacher in a black suit, with a wide-brimmed black hat and western-styled bow tie. His hair and trimmed beard were a brilliant white, which was a great contrast to his deeply lined, tanned skin.

"'He stood there and sized me up—more like bore holes in me with his steel-blue eyes. 'Where'd you get this?', he asked me. I told him I found it in my backyard. He examined the talisman right there in front of me, moving it around in his hands as if he could read its inscriptions. After doing that for about a minute, he said, 'So, you're the *chosen* one. Isn't that interesting'. I asked what he meant, but he shrugged his shoulders and said he hoped he was wrong about that. Now I was really confused. But he just stood there tapping the thing for another minute or so while he studied it some more.

"'When the old man finished doing this, he looked at me again and asked, 'What's your name, boy?'. I told him 'Marshall', of course, and he said, 'Well, Marshall, you need to return this thing to the very same spot you found it in'. I just stood there flabbergasted by what he told me. I guess he could sense my reluctance to take my gift back from Lisa Ann, because after holding on to it for another moment he said, 'Very well. I'll see to it that it's properly disposed.' He sized me up for another moment and then turned and walked back to the house, eyeing me one last time before going inside.

"Soon after that, Lisa Ann came back outside and we played together for a while longer. That day was the beginning of a great friendship between her and I that held strong till your grandma stole my heart away twelve years later.'

"'Grandpa, what happened to your talisman?' I asked, uninterested in hearing about his love life.

"'Don't worry, son. I'll get to that,' he replied. 'But first thing's first. That old man was known throughout the world as Dr. Nathaniel 'Jack' Stratton. I can't even count how many of his stories I used to tell your mom when she was a little girl. I always figured she named you after him, Jack. He was an anthropologist, whose specialty was researching lost American civilizations, both in this continent and in South America. He was in his mid-seventies when I met him, though he was still strong and virile as any man half his age.'

"The gooseflesh crawled on my arms again and the faint hairs stood on end. I remembered the earthen old man's words from when I hid in the garden in Genovene's village. *'Tell Marshall your namesake said hello'*.

"I couldn't remember if I told Grandpa and Jeremy about this encounter or not, but I sat enthralled at the dining room table for the next hour while Grandpa told us a few of Dr. Stratton's more daring expeditions. I pictured a younger Dr. Stratton similar to Indiana Jones. Surprisingly, Jeremy found these stories interesting as well, although not nearly as much as I did. Once he lost interest, he started drumming his fingers beneath the table.

"'Well, hell, I guess we've talked enough about Dr. Stratton's exploits,' said Grandpa, glancing at his wristwatch. 'Sorry about that, Jeremy. I'll try and stick closer to the stuff concerning us most this evening.

"Anyway, as time went on, Dr. Stratton taught Lisa Ann and me about the specific legends that dealt with the talisman, along with his own theories concerning its existence and purpose. He'd do this whenever he was in town, as he'd stay for a month at a time before heading back to his estate in Tennessee. Over the next few years, it turned out to be quite a bit of information.

"'He believed the Inca, Mayan, and Aztec cultures, among others, were patterned after a much older one, for he found numerous references to a mythical golden city that required human sacrifice to survive. Surely y'all are familiar with the temples and sacrifice rituals of ancient Mexico and South America? You boys learned that in school, right?'

"We both agreed we had.

"'Well, Dr. Stratton believed these civilizations imitated this earlier culture to try and obtain eternal life for their privileged members, such as priests, rulers, and aristocrats,' Grandpa explained. 'Obviously they weren't successful in that, but they managed to amass an incredible fortune in gold over the years, perhaps thinking this would attract the gods' favor.

"'Now, like most folks, Lisa Ann and I found this stuff pretty hard to believe, especially after we made the mistake of telling other folks about it and they poked fun at us. Eventually Dr. Stratton proved there was far too much evidence to be ignored. He even showed us a large chest filled with books he kept at the Stratton farm, detailing similar legends of the Native North Americans. This included our own Mississippian Nations, who left behind some amazing ruins throughout the state similar in many ways to those of their distant Mexican and South American cousins.

"'One notable legend I've always been fascinated by is one involving the ancient Incas of Peru. It's a little gruesome, but fascinating nonetheless. These Indians believed the sacred city of gold was once located on a mountain called 'Machu Picchu' near the modern city of Lima. According to Dr. Stratton, only sacred virgins and the Inca priests that'd lead them to their sacrificial deaths were allowed in this city.

"'The city itself was built on a ledge protruding from the mountain's side, which overlooked a large valley. Inca tribes from all over gathered in this valley to celebrate their feasts and sacred ceremonies. At daybreak when these events took place, a large disk made of solid gold was rolled out to the very end of the ledge, and then angled so the sunlight hit it in such a way as to make the disk look like a huge fireball.

"'When this fireball's light was at its brightest, an anointed virgin was sacrificed before the vast crowd of people below by a high priest or priestess. After tearing out her heart and decapitating the head, the remaining torso would be tossed into the midst of the throng to do with as they pleased.'

"Grandpa paused here to make sure he hadn't lost his audience. He hadn't yet, so he continued. 'Even though no one since has ever located the golden disk or the city it came from, other than the famous ruins located further up the mountain, a few periodicals over the years have reported the existence of a group of eclectic Indians who appear from time to time near the mountain's base. These Indians usually disappear from sight whenever modern people come within striking distance of them. A few stories I've read tell how the locals in Lima claim people either end up dead or simply vanish if they venture too close to the 'lost' city. I can tell by the look on your face, Jack, there are similarities between this and what you encountered yesterday.'

"'Yeah, there are,' I agreed.

"'There were other Dr. Stratton theories I found interesting as well. Like the idea the legendary city either moved from place to place, or that several such cities existed. He claimed he'd found plenty of evidence for this later notion within the written histories and oral traditions of both North and South American Indians. From Argentina to Missouri, he said there were as many as twelve different locations. I recall last night, Jack, you mentioned seeing another distant tower like the one you were in yesterday.'

"I nodded that was true.

"'Dr. Stratton would've been happy to have seen that, I'm sure. He had theorized the only way anybody would see the inside of one of these cities was to be invited. I remember he was very adamant about this, telling Lisa Ann and me that unless a person was given a sacred sign or mark, such as a talisman, they'd never get beyond the city's gates. He'd always remind us of the strange symbols engraved upon the thing I found in my backyard, and how he'd felt all along it'd been given to me on purpose.'

"'What happened to your talisman, Grandpa?' I asked again.

"'Son, I promise we'll get to that in due time,' he replied, chuckling at my unwavering persistence. 'Suffice it to say for now it disappeared from Dr. Stratton's room at his farm before he had a chance to dispose of it as he'd intended.' Grandpa paused to take a long drink from his beer. 'As I was saying,' he continued, 'his theories were quite interesting. But Lisa Ann and I remained a little skeptical, due to the ridicule we still endured from time to time.

"Our skepticism didn't fade until he taught us about our own sordid local history. We learned much of Alabama and Mississippi had provided a home base of sorts for one of these golden cities. The earliest evidence for this comes from the sixteenth century in southern North America and the evil Spanish conqueror Ferdinand Desoto. You may or may not be aware that on his relentless search for gold and other treasures, Desoto came through Alabama, leaving a path of bloody destruction in his wake. You and I know the Indians around here didn't have much gold, and that was pretty much the case throughout North America. Gold was only found in Mexico and South America at that time, as I mentioned earlier.

"On this continent, the Indians placed a much higher emphasis on spiritual things, like the idea of achieving oneness with Mother Earth and the Great Spirit. They didn't concern themselves with amassing gold and precious gems. Even so, most tribes still believed in an ancient and largely forgotten golden metropolis, and that its location could only exist upon holy ground. This usually meant a place where the earth's energy is closer to the ground's surface, where it's easily detected if one knew what to look for.'

"'You mean, like some place similar to the hot spring we saw today?' Jeremy suggested.

"'Precisely!' Grandpa was extremely pleased by his response, which told him my brother was still interested in what he had to say. 'Y'all can probably imagine what a madman like Desoto would do. He went on an endless search for this fabled city, thinking he could plunder it and make himself immensely rich and powerful in the process. Other than a rumor here and there, he never found it. Many innocent Natives died as a result of his frustration.

"'One tribe of Chickasaws lived not far from here, and Desoto heard they knew where the golden city was located. According to Dr. Stratton, many members of the tribe had recently seen a golden 'mountain' looming high above the trees near what would later become known as the Tombigbee River. When Desoto arrived at the Chickasaws' village, he'd just missed a sighting of this immense object the day before. Tishomingo, who was the tribe's chieftain, pointed him to the area the most recent event took place. The conquistador leader set off across the river and into the woods, ending up with his army in the very clearing we visited today, finding only the burial grounds and the bubbling hot spring and its pools.

"'Enraged, as he thought he'd been deliberately deceived, Desoto slew every man, woman, and child in the village, except for Tishomingo and his immediate family, whom he brought instead to the clearing. After his men brutally raped Tishomingo's wife and two daughters in front of him, he had them dropped to their deaths one by one into the scalding water of the boiling hot spring's upper pool along with Tishomingo's three sons. The Chickasaw chieftain was then thrown into the upper pool by Desoto himself after first running him threw with his sword.'

"I cringed as Grandpa said this, scarcely believing the brutality of Desoto, whose exploits were barely touched upon during my education.

"'What a way to go,' deadpanned Jeremy. 'I'll bet they all wished he'd just finished them off at the village like he did the others.'

"'Actually it was even worse than that,' Grandpa told us. 'The conquistadors waited around the pool below the boiling one, where that thing crawled out after us today. Eventually, Tishomingo and his family's remains drifted down into the pool and the conquistadors fished them out of the water and scattered them throughout the clearing for the wild animals and scavengers to devour. According to what Dr. Stratton knew on the subject, the intense heat from the water cooked them like you or I would cook stew meat, with the flesh eventually separating from the bones. It was an easy matter at that point to scatter the body parts throughout the area.'

"Now Jeremy grimaced as well. 'How'd anyone know about this, Grandpa?' he asked. 'It sure as hell wasn't mentioned when I was in school, and I'll bet not for you two either.'

"'It wasn't, just like most of the awful things that happened to Native Americans,' Grandpa said in a regretful tone. 'Apparently, though, one of the Chickasaw warriors survived and watched the awful event from a safe distance, probably ashamed he didn't have the guts to come to Tishomingo's family's defense and die valiantly with them. He was the only eyewitness to this gruesome event that we know of, according to Jack Stratton's records, obviously there are no written accounts available from Desoto or his men to verify this.'

"Suddenly, Grandpa straightened up in his chair as if listening to some sound unheard by either Jeremy or me. His expression grew serious and the worry that'd been lingering returned full force into his eyes.

"'What's wrong, Grandpa?' I asked him.

"'Probably nothing,' he said. 'I'll be right back.' He stepped over to one of the dining room windows and peered through the blinds. Then he walked past both of us, heading into the living room and on over to the gun case. He grabbed his shotgun and loaded it, and proceeded to go from room to room throughout the old farmhouse, shutting and locking every window as he went. A few minutes later, the sudden hum of the air conditioner broke the silence. Creaks upon the stairs told us we could expect Grandpa's return at any moment. He soon walked back into the dining room, armed and ready to protect his beloved home and family.

"'So, what was it?' Jeremy asked, now a little nervous himself.

"'Nothing, really,' said Grandpa. 'It's just a feeling, I guess. I thought I heard someone, or something, brush against these windowpanes from outside the house. I checked everything and brought this along just in case.' He patted the palm of his hand against the gun's butt, much like he'd done two nights before in the kitchen. 'Since I've still got a ways to go, I thought I'd tell y'all a few more things and then we'll break for a snack or dessert if you'd like. How's that sound?'

"We both nodded that'd be fine.

"'Sorry, boys, about the gruesome details on some of this stuff,' he apologized. 'I'll try and tone it down some, if I can. I've pretty much got to tell my story straight up in order to get it out after all these years.' His eyes grew misty and he helped himself to another long drink from his beer. After he finished it and wiped his mouth on his forearm, he sat the near empty bottle back down on the dining room table and resumed his story.

"'One thing I thought about while shutting things up around here were the 'miahluschkas' from Jack's story last night,' Grandpa said. 'Dr. Stratton mentioned them, too. But I'm not sure his miahluschkas and yours are the same ones or not. His miahluschkas were part of the legends of the Cherokee, Choctaw, and Chickasaw tribes. There could be other tribes that believed in them, too, I suppose.

"'The miahluschkas I'm familiar with are assigned spirits, if you will, who've been charged to protect sacred burial grounds and meeting places. They're supposedly the restless souls of deceased tribe members who either died dishonorably in battle, or who brought other shame upon themselves and their people. Hence, they're forced to walk the earth with their only redemption coming from the successful protection of the very souls they failed to honor during life. Which is to say they must guard the tribe's final resting-place and whatever artifacts were sent with them in death.

"'These spirits are bound to this arrangement until the end of time, or until the bones they're guarding are completely dissolved into Mother Earth. A lot of hauntings have been attributed to them. It happens when, whether by intent or even inadvertently, the sacred grounds are disturbed in some way—like the Bell Witch legend up in Tennessee that you once asked me about, Jeremy.

"'Anyway, Jack, your miahluschkas seem quite different from these others. Maybe their role's different in Genovene's world. The only thing that sounds similar to them is an old Cherokee legend about a race of tiny people living in Appalachia several hundred years ago. I forget their Indian names, but in English they were referred to as the 'moon-eye people' by the Cherokee, for their skin was as white as snow and their eyes completely gray. They couldn't see well in the full light of day as a result of their condition.

"'According to this legend, these people were forced to leave Appalachia by the Native Americans moving into the area at that time. Their existence was partially responsible for the lack of fear many southern tribes displayed when first encountering the European settlers, since most southeastern tribes had reportedly encountered these mysterious white people at one point or another.' Grandpa paused and shook his head. Then he smiled sheepishly at us. We were both still with him, although Jeremy had begun drumming his fingers again. 'Sorry once again about getting sidetracked, boys,' said Grandpa. 'Why don't we grab some dessert, and I'll get this story moving quicker.'

"'We all got up and went into the kitchen where Grandpa and I helped ourselves to a piece of pie, while Jeremy helped himself to another cigarette. When we were ready to return to the dining room, Grandpa and Jeremy grabbed a beer and I picked up another soda. We sat down at the table again and Grandpa continued where he left off.

"'All right then, so where were we? Oh, yes, the golden city,' he said. 'Dr Stratton felt that if the city had a permanent home in North America, it had to be in Alabama or Mississippi, since most of the folklore came from these two areas. As time moved on, the white and black folks in this country began adding stories of their own. He showed us actual written accounts of settlers seeing a golden light glistening just above the tree line from far off, only to find it no longer there by the time they reached the area. He even showed us a couple of very old plantation diaries, where the slave owners complained angrily that some of their slaves were lying to protect other slaves who'd run off. Several entries in these diaries were eerily similar, stating the missing slave or slaves in question were last seen sleepwalking into the nearby woods, while none of the other slaves could shake them awake or dissuade them from their course. These unfortunate folks were never seen or heard from again.

"'Most accounts centered around Natchez, Mississippi, and here in our own neck of the woods, although there hasn't been a reported sighting in the Natchez area since just before the Civil War, when the hot spring near the Mississippi River suddenly dried up. There's nobody left that even remembers exactly where it was located. Some folks argued vehemently years ago with Jack Stratton, saying that the hot spring never even existed—despite the documentation he'd tirelessly gathered and presented to the contrary.

"'Here in our area, there's been a steady stream of sightings and strange occurrences among non-Indian folks since the place was first settled nearly three hundred years ago. Even at the old fort, there were stories of people disappearing without a trace. Perhaps the fort was closed on account of this, but it didn't stop the phenomenon from continuing on up to the present day. It's definitely how we came to use the phrase 'The 'Season'' around these parts. I know my grandmother used it on several occasions when somebody from here turned up missing. She only jumped the gun one time I know of.

"'Oh, and about the talisman intended for me... Monty accused me of hiding it from him and was going to beat me up. I was afraid of him because even though I could outrun him, he was still much bigger than I was at the time. He screamed at me from the top of his lungs, he was so angry about this, demanding for me to hand it over to him. I finally had to tell him I'd already given it to Lisa Ann and she'd in turn given it to her great uncle. I cried, thinking he'd go ask for it back, but he didn't.

"'It may just be a coincidence, though I seriously doubt it. A homeless man named Virgil Hannah once hung out near the feed lot, which was in business even way back then. At that time, it was owned and operated by Pete Aderley's daddy, Shannon Aderley. Anyway, Lisa Ann said Virgil started keeping an eye on the Stratton farmhouse and acting real suspicious. This took place not long after Monty and I had our tiff, which was near the Stratton's yard when it happened.

"'A few days later, Dr. Stratton went to look for the talisman in his room. But, it was nowhere to be found. Folks didn't lock their doors around here back then since they didn't feel they needed to, so it would've been easy enough for anyone to take it. The talisman was never again seen by the doctor or anybody else. Neither was Virgil—not by anyone. He simply vanished from the area...' Grandpa's voice trailed off, and he remained quiet for a moment. A wan smile was on his face.

"'When I was twenty, my life changed forever,' he told us when he was ready to speak again. 'That's how old I was when I met Elsie Smith, your grandma. Lord, she was the prettiest thing I'd ever laid eyes on. I quite forgot about Lisa Ann Stratton, though we remained friends. I'm sure it hurt her that the romantic feelings I had when I was eight steadily declined until they died altogether when I was a young teenager. She eventually married, twice actually, but not before she was in her early thirties. Dr. Jack Stratton was long gone by then. He passed away during my senior year in high school. The funeral was closed casket, and for a long time a rumor persisted among the older folks in Carlsdale that he'd faked his death here in order to live out his final days down in Colombia, where it was rumored he had another estate.

"'I almost believed this, but it didn't feel right. My opinion now is he became a victim of the mysterious city he'd spent most of his life tracking down. I think he's the old man Jack met while hiding in the village garden yesterday.'

"Jeremy raised his eyebrows in surprise at this statement and finished his beer. Like me, he'd been following Grandpa's story closely. But this last bit caught him off guard, and he seemed to be searching his memory for the details from my story to verify what Grandpa just said.

"'I'll come back to this point if we need to, Jeremy,' Grandpa told him, since he knew I'd already made the connection. 'For now, I'd like to move on, so we're not sitting here till the wee hours of the morning. Is that all right with you?'

"My brother nodded and then looked over at me suspiciously.

"'Thanks, boys, I do appreciate it. We're about to enter some pretty tough territory for me. *Please*, bear with me if I struggle some with this. As you may be aware, Elsie and I dated for a good three years before I proposed to her. I remember being a nervous wreck on the day I asked her to marry me. Hell, it took me nearly six months to work up the courage just to do it in the first place! I don't know why I was so nervous because I knew she had wanted to get married for some time. As soon as I popped the question to her she cried '*yes!*' and threw her arms around my neck so hard I thought she might break it.'

"Grandpa laughed as he recalled this, and tears formed in his eyes. He smiled tenderly, wiping his eyes with the side of his forearm again. 'I think we both knew in our hearts we'd be married someday from the very moment we met,' he said. 'We officially tied the knot the following spring, and after we got married, we lived for a couple of years in a small bungalow across the tracks since it was closer to town. But Papa died when I was twenty-six and Momma needed help keeping this place up, especially since my grandma was still alive, though she was pretty feeble by then. She passed away a year later, while Elsie was pregnant with your mom.

"'Once Julie was born that summer, this house came to life like it'd never done before. She was truly something special, and as pretty as her mother with the same auburn hair and hazel eyes. Her smile seemed to light up her face and she definitely lit up a room the minute she entered it. She was smart, too, but I guess I'm getting away from the point of my story again.' Grandpa exhaled slowly in an attempt to maintain his composure and then finished his beer. He stood up from the table and asked us if we'd like another drink from the kitchen, since he was going to get himself another beer. We both agreed to that, and he left us for a moment.

"Since it was getting later in the evening, he turned on the kitchen light and walked over to the door leading out to the back porch. He turned on the outside lights as well, and briefly opened the back door to take a look outside. Satisfied nothing was amiss in the backyard, he closed and locked the door again. He grabbed another soda for me along with a couple more beers for himself and Jeremy, and walked back into the dining room.

"'Hopefully, I can finish this rambling monologue before we're finished with these,' he said as he handed us our drinks. He sat his bottle upon the table, and then turned on the room's chandelier. Suddenly he frowned, and moved over to the French-paned windows, peering carefully between the blinds.

"'What's up now, Grandpa?' I asked.

"'I don't know,' he replied. 'Maybe it's just paranoia or perhaps the fact I haven't slept well these past few nights. I keep feeling like someone's listening to us over here by the windows. It's not necessarily a bad feeling, and I've checked three times now and there's nothing going on outside that I can see.' He closed the blinds again, shaking his head as he returned to his seat.

"'I almost got one of these for you, Jack, but I still think you should wait a couple of years before indulging in this stuff. Hell, Jeremy had to wait until he was nearly sixteen before I agreed to let him have a beer in this house.' Grandpa nodded and gave me a playful wink.

"'That's okay,' I told him, thinking to myself how little he knew about my older brother's exploits over the past five years.

"'I intend to finish this before you boys are done with your drinks,' he said. 'Don't try and make a liar out of me, Jeremy, in order to finagle another beer from your dear old grandpa.'

"Jeremy smiled slyly, but neither Grandpa nor myself thought he'd take advantage of him this time.

"'There weren't any more encounters with a talisman around here, at least not for many years,' resumed Grandpa. 'Not until Julie was all grown up and married, and you two lads were among us. *Oh*, but wait. Let me correct myself. There was *one* encounter I'd almost completely forgotten about until last night. Jack, you know the little girl in the village you told us about, the one called Allyson?'

"Yeah."

"Your mom had a friend, her best friend, whose name was Allyson Carter. She disappeared without a trace when your mom was a little girl. Allyson lived on the other side of the Palmer place with her mom and older brother. There used to be a house sitting in the field over there, up until maybe twenty years ago.'

"'I'll bet anything it's the same girl, Grandpa!' I agreed, eager to learn what he knew about her.

"'I recall you told us last night that your mom's spirit seemed partial to her,' he said. 'She certainly seems to be the same person. For Jeremy's benefit, and to give you some missing information, Jack, I'll tell you both everything I know concerning her disappearance.

"'I remember Allyson's mom, Mamie Carter, told Elsie and me that her daughter wasn't acting like her normal self. This started about a week before she disappeared. She'd sit on her back porch and stare off toward the woods with a peculiar smile and faraway look on her face. In fact, now that I think of it, Mamie told us she heard Allyson talking quite a bit with an 'imaginary friend', if you will. I wish I could recall the name of that 'friend'. I'd be willing to bet it was Genovene, though. Mamie went on to say she overheard her little girl arguing with the pretend person, saying things like 'No, I can't go there. I'd get in big trouble', or 'My mommy says there's lots of things in the woods that'll hurt you if you're not careful'.

"'Your mom was devastated when Allyson disappeared, and the timing couldn't have been any worse as it happened just a week and a half before Julie's eighth birthday. We had to postpone your mother's birthday party on account of her being so upset over this. She would sit for hours out back on that old tire-swing, staring off toward the woods as if she was waiting for Allyson to return.

"'I've wondered if Julie saw anything like the golden object I found as a little boy in Allyson's possession, because one day while she grieved over the little girl's disappearance, she said something very strange. She said 'I told her not to listen to them!' When I asked her about this, she clammed up in silence and never told me what she meant by her words. She had said it absently and to herself, thinking no one could overhear.

"'Julie eventually healed from her loss and made new friends. She also became a lot more interested in school from that point on. Perhaps staying busy with her schoolwork kept her mind occupied enough to push the sadness away. I don't know... What I do know is she grew up to be such a wonderful young woman. She excelled in high school and was offered a Rhodes scholarship to Oxford, England, as you both know. She decided to stay closer to home, attending the University of Alabama on a full-ride scholarship instead. That's where she met Frank, who was from Baltimore and attending school on a football scholarship.

"'Now, I realize y'all have been told, and probably still remember, a lot of this stuff. Just let an old man tell his tale without interruption, okay?' We nodded and he continued. 'Your folks dated and fell in love while attending college, and shortly after graduation, they got engaged and moved to Atlanta, where Frank enjoyed a brief career in professional football playing for the Falcons as a reserve linebacker. They decided to get married the following spring, and did so in Tuscaloosa. *Boy*, what a fun time that was! I'm sure glad Elsie and I didn't have any other kids or we wouldn't have had nearly enough money to throw her that incredible wedding like we did!'

"Grandpa laughed again to himself, but then sighed deeply once more before going on. 'Your parents soon got their masters degrees at Georgia Tech in Atlanta,' he continued. 'Frank's was in journalism and Julie's was in bioengineering. You were already a toddler by then, Jeremy, since you were born four months after your folks got married. We had no idea your mom was pregnant until she was in her sixth month. Elsie thought for sure you'd be a sickly child. Thank God she was wrong about that, because you've grown up to be a strong and healthy young man.'

"Jeremy smiled smugly again, nodding his head slightly to confirm this assessment of himself. Meanwhile, I sat nearly motionless as I listened to Grandpa. I'd been starving for information concerning my family's history, and I was determined to store every bit of it in my memory.

"Grandpa paused and eyed us both seriously. 'I know I'm still beating around the bush a little, but we're about to get to the worst part,' he told us. 'The worst part for *me*, anyway. I'll get through it best I can. It will be hard, but I'll try to hold it together.'

"'That's all right,' I said gently, and then glanced over at Jeremy. 'We understand, Grandpa. You just tell us when you're ready.'

"'Thanks, boys. I mean it'. He took another few deep breaths. 'They were doing all right on their own, your mom and dad. You were soon on the way, Jack, and despite that, Julie managed to land a very lucrative position with a genetics-testing firm in Atlanta. They even allowed her to stay on and work flexible hours after you were born.

Frank had worked his way up in the sports department for a local television news station, and had been in that position for nearly four years. They paid for the bulk of his master's work while your mom's was paid in full by a fellowship she received while at Georgia Tech.

"'Twelve years ago this summer, your folks decided to finally spend a couple of weeks with us down here in Carlsdale. Frank hadn't been here since they were married, and your mom hadn't been here since she finished her schooling in Atlanta. Neither of you kids had ever seen this place since all of our family get-togethers had been held in Atlanta at your parents' home, so your Uncle Ned could be there, too. I guess they felt obligated to do everything with Frank's brother because he didn't like to travel anywhere—still doesn't, as you know. Frank felt he owed him, I suppose, being he was the one who raised your dad after their parents died in a horrible car crash some years back.

"'Anyway, we finally got to see all of you on our own turf. It was wonderful for the first week. Jack, I know you don't remember anything, though Jeremy, you should remember some. It was definitely a time to enjoy and remember. But, then your mom and dad started acting strange during their second week here with us. I mean, they both grew real distant from Elsie and me, as well as from you two boys. Your mom and grandma started snapping at each other—something I'd not seen them do since Julie lost Allyson, nearly twenty years before this... *I wish to God I'd paid closer attention!!*' Grandpa said louder than he intended. He lowered his face into his hands and lost control.

"Grandpa began to sob and fought hard to hold the tears back, shaking and gritting his teeth in doing so. He raised his head and looked at us with teary eyes that plead silently for understanding. Jeremy and I reached across the table, each one grabbing onto and clasping his hands. This surprised him, I think, especially coming from my brother, and he seemed to draw strength from it. 'Your mom and grandma kept on fighting,' he said, once he regained most of his composure. 'Even your dad grew hostile toward us. Frank was always quiet, but warm and friendly when you got to know him. Now, that warmth was completely gone, and he regarded us with suspicion no matter what we said or did.

"'On each of the last four days of their stay, they left you boys with us and went on picnics in the woods. This was very peculiar, and they would be gone for hours at a time. They seemed quite content with this ritual. In fact, on the day before they disappeared for good, your mom and dad were gone for nearly seven hours! Their bizarre behavior really had us deeply worried, and, to be honest, pretty ticked off, too.

"'I should've recognized the signs, but you know, I never thought even once about the golden object, the "Season", or any of the old stories and all of that—*not once! Not one fricking time, y'all!! I wish to God I knew why I hadn't!!!*' He sat up straight, closing his eyes and drawing in several more deep breaths. 'The night before that fateful day, Julie and Elsie had a major blowup,' he said. 'I never found out what it was all about. I only remember your mom shouting 'It's my life, Mother, and I'll live it exactly as I damn well please!' Of course, I got mad and hollered at her, and then your dad joined in and it got uglier from there.

"'Everyone went to bed upset that night, and your grandma and I tossed around and didn't sleep at all. The next morning, your folks were going out the back gate with their fully packed picnic basket again, and this time they had you boys with them. A horrible feeling came over me, so I grabbed Elsie and we stopped Julie and Frank just before they were able to get through the gate with either of you. They allowed you to stay with us, and both were actually quite pleasant for a change. After they left, I was thinking about Julie's strange smile she gave me right before going through the gate. It was faint and her eyes were absent of their usual glow. It wasn't until then I remembered seeing the look on someone else's face years ago... Alyson. By that time, though, they were already deep in the woods. I should've tried to cut them off along the road we took earlier today, but like everything else, that option never occurred to me.

"'Since I needed to pick up a few things from town, I decided to take you, Jeremy, along with me, and I told Elsie we'd be back in an hour or so. It was a beautiful sunny day when I left the house, without a cloud in the sky, and it took me roughly an hour and a half to get everything I needed. On the way home, I noticed a bad storm was blowing in from the west. So, I stepped on the gas in order to get us back to this old place before it hit. Once we got here I ran inside, thinking that Elsie and you, Jack, would be safe and protected from the weather. I soon discovered neither of you were in the house. I panicked and told Jeremy to stay put in the kitchen until I returned.

"'It'd just started raining hard when I ran out onto the back porch. I didn't see anything or anyone right away, so I ran down the porch steps and on over to the oak tree. The first thing I noticed from there was the sphere sitting in front of the back gate. I was so taken by surprise at the strangeness and enormity of the thing sitting in our backyard, I could only stop and stare stupidly at it. I finally noticed Elsie holding you, Jack, on her knees near the thing. Several bright flashes of lightning struck the ground between the oak and the sphere. I said a prayer under my breath, and ran over to where you and your grandma were huddled together.

"'I tried to get her to come out of the rain, but she wouldn't budge at all. She wouldn't tell me what'd happened, either. She just kept muttering about the 'angels and the sphere', and some other mostly incoherent stuff like 'they're gone' and 'protect the baby. Keep Jack safe'. She said this last phrase over and over.

"'I ran back inside the house and got a thick blanket. Struggling against the rain and a pretty fierce wind, I wrapped Elsie up in the blanket and took you, Jack, into my arms. I then hurriedly brought you both inside the house to safety.'

"Grandpa grew silent again and looked over toward the living room, where the light from the full moon poured in through the front windows. He shook his head slowly and turned back to our expectant faces. He smiled tenderly once more, but the deep sadness in his eyes spoke volumes as to the depth of his sorrow. 'Elsie never recovered,' he said softly, his voice straining just above a whisper. 'She might've been able to, but they wouldn't let her. *They just wouldn't do it!!!*'

"He dug his finger tips into the dining room table, nearly pushing the embroidered lace of the table cloth into the thick mahogany of the table itself. He grimaced painfully while fighting the torrent of emotions threatening to overtake him. Once the tempest subsided, he realized we were staring helplessly at him, unable to disguise our worry. Until then, he'd been the role model of peace and self-control for as long as either of us could remember.

"After an awkward moment in silence, Jeremy was the only one willing to push him further into his pain. 'What do you mean by 'they wouldn't let her'?' he asked, trying to broach the subject as gently as his blunt nature would allow. 'Who are *they?*'

"Grandpa regarded him evenly for a moment before answering him, perhaps deciding if his query was noble or not. '*They* are the ones who slowly drove your grandma down into the ground, twisting the disappearance of our most prized possession in the world, your mom, like a dagger through her broken heart and soul,' he told us. 'It wasn't enough that we'd never see Julie, or Frank for that matter, ever again. Almost immediately, other problems began to complicate what was already a nightmare—problems far bigger than we could've ever imagined at the time.

"'Anyway, that very day, I called Carl and some other close friends of mine to form a search party and head out into the woods. Of course, we waited first to see if your folks came back. But when they still hadn't returned to the house that evening, my buddies and I set out after them. We searched everywhere, including the old fort and hot spring. By then some of us got to thinking about the local legends concerning the "Season" and all. We even extended our search to the burial mounds and beyond, up to a mile in every direction. We didn't find a single trace of them, and that was with help from a small team of bloodhounds, too. We finally had to turn back and go home, where Carl and I contacted the state authorities. That's when our problems compounded and worsened.

"'Carl and the others were quite amazed by the sphere in the backyard, so were the state authorities when they finally came down to Carlsdale from Birmingham to investigate your folks' disappearance. They weren't able to keep the news of all that'd happened, especially the appearance of the sphere in the backyard, from spreading like wildfire throughout the local region. People drove up and down Lelan's Road trying to catch a glimpse of the goddamned thing! The most impertinent ones tried to sneak around to the backyard, or simply drove behind our place on the utility road. Some of them got to see the sphere, but I sure as hell ran them off once I caught them snooping around back there, using the very shotgun I'm holding now.' He lightly stroked the weapon's barrel while he stared off into space.

"'People came from all over,' he sighed. 'They came from as far east as Uniontown, on the other side of Demopolis, and from Lilita and Bellamy on the west side. They even came from as far north as Clinton and as far south as Myrtlewood. Elsie was a mess over this, I mean near a breakdown over it all! What she truly needed was peace to help her deal with the loss of Julie and Frank, because *she* knew they were dead and we'd never find their bodies. She'd tell me this all the time, largely on account of my stubborn resistance to the idea. Even so, I was gentle with her. What she got from everybody else, though, was a steady dose of insensitivity and downright rudeness.

"'The older folks were the worst. They continually chided us on account of the 'Season's legend. They said we should've known better, because some of them saw the drastic change in Frank's behavior that last week when he stopped by Max Reynolds' grocery store on several occasions. They couldn't get over how the nice young man from Atlanta had turned into such an obnoxious asshole, seemingly overnight. Even the younger, more reliable townsfolk stated Frank had got to the point where he was just damn right rude to everyone, most noticeably on the day before he and Julie disappeared for good, when he'd stopped by for the last time to pick up some picnic supplies.

"'But, the real trouble for us started once a few FBI agents from Atlanta showed up one day. They seemed cordial enough at first, but once they'd completed their own search of the area, their attitude changed. They asked a bunch of probing questions—personal ones about how good our relationship with Julie and Frank was. It didn't help none that Missie Palmer next door was sitting on her porch listening to Elsie and Julie damn near duke it out the night before your folks went on that last picnic outing.

"'It was like everybody else around here started changing toward us, too, except for Carl and a couple of other buddies of mine who've since passed away. Suspicion was cast entirely on us, like we made Julie and Frank somehow disappear. I'm not saying they thought we ran them off, either! Most everyone thought we'd killed them ourselves and buried their bodies in some unknown location, which the federal authorities were now here to find.

"'The strangest thing about all of this is that while they were turning their investigation's focus upon us, they were also becoming a hell of a lot more interested in the sphere out in the backyard. It seemed to me they were creating a diversion to get the growing national media and local interest *entirely* on us and our missing daughter and son-in-law. We found it quite disturbing when all the scientist-types showed up around here. Elsie, myself, and neither of you youngsters were allowed anywhere near the damned thing while they examined it. I mean, y'all wouldn't believe the amount of strange looking equipment these people brought into the backyard.

"'The stress from all this wore us both down, but Elsie took it the hardest. She seemed to age quickly from the loss of our only child. I tried to be of comfort to her, but I was dealing with the same thing as she. To be perfectly honest, I didn't know if either of us would make it through that time, though you boys' presence in our lives made a huge difference. Knowing you both needed us to hang in there helped a great deal, and if they'd have just let us be at that point, your grandma'd likely be here today!'

"Grandpa stood up and walked over to the dining room windows again. This time, he peered more cautiously through them into the backyard. The light from the moon above shone brightly, illuminating the entire landscape before his eyes. He smiled sadly, perhaps envisioning the way the yard once looked.

"'Grandpa,' I said, 'if you don't want to tell us any more, you really don—.'

"'*I need to finish this!*' he interrupted me, whirling around to face us. 'I've got to finish this *tonight! I can feel it!!*' he shouted. '*Now* is the only time I'll be able to talk about it all the way through!' He began to pace back and forth in front of the windows, his head bowed sullenly as he gathered his thoughts and resolve. When he was ready to address us again, he moved back to the table. 'Do either of you remember staying with your Uncle Monty and Aunt Martha?' he asked.

"'You mean when we visited them last summer?' I asked.

"'No, son. I mean when you were just a toddler,' he said. 'I'd say you were just over a year old back then and Jeremy was soon to be five.'

"'I remember, Grandpa,' said Jeremy. 'I celebrated my fifth birthday with them. We stayed awhile with them after that, didn't we?'

"'Yes, you did,' he said. 'At least six or seven months, possibly longer than that.'

"'I wish I could remember,' I said, trying to picture what that period of time had been like.

"'I barely remember it,' Jeremy added. 'Just bits and pieces.'

"'Bits and pieces,' Grandpa repeated thoughtfully. 'If only it had been just a visit. Monty and Martha probably never told either of you that y'all were taken from your grandma's and my custody—*forcibly* taken, I might add. Did they?'

"'No,' we acknowledged quietly, surprised by this revelation.

"'Well, you were,' he said. 'It happened while the investigation going on in our backyard continued. All the while, the police interrogations we endured became more and more intense. They never filed charges against us, though, since they were unable to produce any physical evidence suggesting foul play.' He studied us both intently, perhaps noting how disturbed we were by the bitter sorrow that drove him along.

"'Let me backtrack for a moment, because it's important to understand what actually happened the afternoon of your folks' disappearance before we go further,' he said, and then leaned toward us, tightly gripping the side of the table to steady himself. 'Elsie never told me herself, but she did tell a reporter quite a bit for some reason. Seems to me, she would've confided in someone she trusted and was close to, like myself. I've had a lot of time to think about this, and I now realize she needed to share her terrible secret with a stranger instead, since I was too close to the situation and our mutual loss.

"'The reporter she talked to was a young girl by the name of Gloria, though I've forgotten her last name. Hell, I don't even own a copy of the magazine article anymore since it brought me too much pain, and folks around here thought her story was a bunch of bullshit anyway!' Grandpa stood back up and resumed pacing again in front of the windows, while our eyes were glued silently to his every move.

"'According to the published story, Elsie told this Gloria that she was in the house when she heard a loud rumbling sound coming from the backyard. Since she was unwilling to leave you, Jack, in the house unattended, she brought you with her out onto the porch. She then said she saw a brilliant light coming from just beyond the oak tree. I guess she would've stayed on the porch, but she claimed to hear Julie calling to her from within this mysterious light.

"'Though Julie's voice seemed calm, Elsie instinctively thought she and Frank were in some kind of trouble. She ran down the porch steps and over to the tree with Jack in her arms. What she saw next is the stuff I figured only people experiencing religious hallucinations or visions and the like were apt to see, until your story last night. All around the back gate, including in the air and on the ground, were angels—and not so much the girlish kind you see in paintings or on Christmas cards and such. No, Lord, these angels were at least ten feet in height, and very muscular. Much like the angel you told us about, they were the perfect mix between male and female, with long beautiful hair and handsome facial features, as well as the large wingspan you described.

"The angels prepared the ground for the sphere, which was descending to the earth through a spectacular rainbow-like spiral that was suspended in the air. That's how the reporter claimed Elsie described it, anyway. These angels pushed and guided the sphere along until they positioned it in our yard directly in front of the back gate, calling excitedly to one another with their strange voices. Two of the angels walked up to Elsie and started talking to her. She was so terrified that she pretty much forgot everything they told her just as soon as they said it, other than the fact the sphere was placed here to cover up an ancient doorway between heaven and hell. After telling her this they turned and walked away. But one of them turned back to her one last time and told her she must 'keep the children safe', and especially to be sure that 'the baby was protected'—the same stuff she told me when I found her kneeling by the sphere with Jack in her arms a little while later.

"'According to this reporter, this Gloria, your dear grandma was completely overwhelmed by all of this. Yet, she managed to keep her wits long enough to inquire about Julie and Frank, since she knew something had to have gone terribly wrong for them that day. The one angel lowered and shook its head, at which point Elsie became hysterical. She grabbed the arm of the angel while pleading with it to tell her this wasn't so, that it wasn't too late to save them. To her surprise, the angel's arm pulsed with energy and what she soon recognized was unfathomable strength. This powerful and gentle being told her nothing could be done for either Julie or Frank, other than to pray for their souls. The angel then told her that our daughter and son-in-law would be all right if she did this, though we wouldn't see them again for a long time.

"'I guess this last part was what gave me the slim hope they'd find their way back here someday, that they hadn't actually died after all, but maybe were prisoners in some unknown world or reality. I believe this was partially true after hearing your tale last night, Jack. I guess I never wanted to accept what I always knew was true in my gut as well as in my heart and in my soul...that your folks *had* died that awful day and were never coming back.'

"Grandpa moved over to the southernmost window and peered through the blinds and the French panes, looking out into the backyard one more time. 'Elsie said the angels gathered around the sphere as a group and then suddenly disappeared in a bright flash of light,' he said with his back still turned toward us. 'The rumbling sound immediately ceased, and once her sight recovered from the light, all that remained in the backyard aside from the stuff that'd always been there, was the sphere. The storm that'd been gathering for the past half hour or so, began to unleash its fury on the entire area, sending torrents of rain upon the backyard and Elsie, who'd dropped to her knees with Jack here held tightly in her arms. That's when I found you both.'

"He turned to face us. Tears streamed down his face despite the fact he'd kept his voice in check, keeping his pent-up grief and sorrow largely at bay while he told us his story, which I hoped for his sake was nearly done. He tried to smile, his eyes clouded with tears and his mouth quivering. Somehow he mustered enough strength to complete the chronicle he'd started more than two hours ago.

"'When Elsie told Gloria her story, the magazine she wrote for quickly printed and released it in September. I'd say it's no coincidence that the authorities, including a man named Stu Johnson from the FBI, soon paid us another visit. They came out to the house a week or so later and placed us under 'house arrest'. They took you boys away from us that day and wanted to place you in a foster home. I was finally able to persuade them it'd be in your best interests to stay with a close relative.

"'Ned Kenney was given the first opportunity, but wasn't willing to shoulder the responsibility for you two. The thought of raising a young toddler was the thing that scared him the most. He seemed a little too unaffected by his brother's disappearance, which really irked us. I mean it was *his* brother and sister-in-law for Christ's sake! What more had to happen before he gave a damn??

"'We finally decided Monty and Martha's home would be the best place for you, and since they were immediately willing to help, they picked you boys up that night from the detention center. Me and Elsie were forced to share this place with a pair of U.S. Marshals, who guarded the front and back doors to the house to make sure we didn't run off, while a third one did all of our errands and grocery shopping for us. It was *horrible* being stranded in our own home!

"'Elsie was so distraught about this latest development that I knew for sure she was headed for a heart attack or nervous breakdown if things didn't improve quickly around here. The worst part was the charges against us were tenuous at best, since there was still absolutely nothing that linked us to your folks' disappearance. We even quietly discussed the idea of hiring a lawyer to force the state and federal government to either bring us to court and try us or let us go, but we kept thinking they'd surely realize their mistake and release us and give you boys back.

"'After a few months like this, we knew they weren't going to leave us without a fight, as more and more scientists came here to study the sphere. You'd have thought the media would've caught wind of this—at least a tidbit or two from the Carlsdale rumor mill. But, every time you'd turn on the television or radio you wouldn't find anything pertaining to it. Just the continued search for Julie and Frank and the police's suspicion we were involved. The same was true for the mainstream newspapers.

"'Finally we had enough, and contacted an attorney recommended by Carl, a Mr. Dwayne Stevenson from Demopolis. We arranged an appointment with him on the Tuesday afternoon right after Thanksgiving that year. He was a nice enough fella in his late forties and had lots of experience in criminal law; though he told us he'd never encountered a case like ours before. After meeting with him for a few hours, he left us both with a promise to get this whole thing resolved by Christmas. He said it was the gravest miscarriage of justice he'd ever seen and that he intended to contact the judge in Birmingham who'd signed the arrest warrant in the first place on the following day, since they both knew each other fairly well.

"'We said goodbye to Mr. Stevenson and had a good feeling about things for the first time since before your folks' disappearance. That was the last time we ever saw him. We waited and waited, thinking he'd get back to us. After we felt we'd waited long enough, we called and left several messages for him at his office number's voice mail. Elsie set out to find his home telephone number so she could give him a piece of her mind, she was so steamed about his apparent brush-off. She managed to obtain the number, and when she called it, Mr. Stevenson's wife answered the phone. Once Elsie told her she was looking for him, Mrs. Stevenson suddenly burst into tears.

"'Elsie, being as tender hearted as she was, felt bad for the woman—terribly bad, actually, when she found out what was going on. But at first she had no idea what to think of Mrs. Stevenson's behavior. Once Elsie was able to calm her down, she told Elsie that her husband had died a few weeks back. He'd been killed when his car ran off the road near a bridge on Highway Forty-three. The accident happened the morning after his visit with us, on his way up to Birmingham to visit the judge who'd signed our warrant.

"'We felt awful for Mrs. Stevenson's loss, and we sent her a sympathy card and floral arrangement to let her know just how saddened we were for her. Elsie was as determined as ever to get to the bottom of this, though, since we both agreed it was a horribly strange coincidence that Mr. Stevenson would suffer an accident soon after talking to us.

"'We weren't sure what to do next, but decided we'd be better off waiting till after the holidays before planning our next move. We decided this two days before Christmas. But the very next morning on Christmas Eve, the FBI agent named Stu Johnson came over to our house and told us we were free to go. That's all he said. No apology, no sorry about the mistake they'd made, no 'Merry Christmas', *no nothin'!!* He just collected the three U.S. Marshals on duty and left.

"'I had a good mind to say something to him about the whole goddamned affair, until I thought of Dwayne Stevenson and decided to keep my mouth shut. Meanwhile, Elsie ran out into the backyard. Sure enough, all the equipment, tents, and scientists had cleared out quietly the night before. But they'd left the sphere. They took our grandkids and our freedom, but they left us the rock! Grandpa paused to catch his breath and organize his thoughts again before going on.

"'Sorry, boys,' he told us, wiping at his eyes and nose. 'I see you've both finished your drinks. Just let me get through this. Five more minutes is all I'll need, if even that much.'

"We both nodded to him, although he really didn't need to ask us for this. We were completely absorbed by everything he said.

"'Well, we were finally free, Elsie and me. Despite the tremendous stress from all of this, I assumed things would work out for us. Later that morning, a representative from the federal courthouse in Birmingham came to visit us with some papers to fill out. The rep came with the social worker involved in removing you both from our care. We soon learned that even though our arrest was over, and despite the fact any and all charges against us were dropped, the state authorities didn't think we were fit to raise y'all. The only way for us to regain custody of you boys was to fight the state's decision through the courts. Mrs. Joyce Summers, the social worker, advised what I confirmed later that day, that the earliest court date available wasn't until late February. This also meant we had to wait at least until then before we could see you boys again, since we were still restricted from having any contact with y'all.

"'This was the final straw for Elsie, even though we were on our way out of the hell we'd lived through over the past five months. After our two visitors left us, we spent a very somber Christmas together. I did my best to cheer her up, but she seemed to get more and more despondent by the day. She'd even grimace now and then, so I knew her heart palpitations, which had grown more frequent since September, were getting worse. Without having you boys around, there just wasn't enough to get her through the grief of our first Christmas without our beloved daughter.

"'On the morning of December the twenty-ninth, just two days before our thirty-fifth New Year's Eve together, I found her lying on the floor upstairs just a few feet away from the top step. I think she woke up sometime during the night, probably to get herself a glass of milk downstairs. Maybe she thought it was indigestion, but I've tried to thank God that the heart attack that killed her did so quickly and quietly.

"'We buried her in the double plot she and I'd purchased some years back on the other side of town, over in Greenbrier Cemetery, as you both know. Then, in February I managed to get custody of you boys once again, and I've spent the last eleven years or so trying to raise you two as best as I can. But not a day goes by without me pining some for your mom and grandma—I'd surely be lying if I told you I wasn't.'

"Grandpa excused himself from our presence and left the dining room. We watched him go into the kitchen, weeping as he did so. When he reached the kitchen table, he leaned upon it and began to cry harder, his shoulders heaving as he could no longer contain the terrible pain within himself. I immediately got up from the dining room table to go over and give him a warm hug. Jeremy wasn't able to maintain his facade of coolness, and soon followed me over to Grandpa. All three of us cried together, as the deluge of emotion quickly spread from one to another.

"This was the onset of true healing for each of us, the seeds of which had been sown two nights before when I'd brought the talisman inside our old farmhouse. As we stood together in the kitchen, the years of silence, pain, and misunderstanding flowed out of us through our tears.

"When the tears subsided, Grandpa thanked us both for our support, telling us if it hadn't been for our presence in his life he would've never made it this far. Since we were ready to move on to whatever was next, he suggested we spend a few minutes checking out the mysterious photo album he'd set out on the dining room table. He told us he preferred to wait in the kitchen until we were finished looking through it. After Jeremy stepped outside the back door for a quick cigarette, my brother and I returned to the dining room.

"Jeremy pulled his chair next to mine while I brought the heavy book over to us. It smelled musty when I opened it, and I now noticed a small rip on the inside of the leather-bound album. The pictures near the front were old and yellowed. I glanced over my shoulder to where Grandpa sat at the kitchen table, listening to the radio on low volume while he smoked his pipe. The cherry almond aroma was my favorite, and I started to pick up the photo album to take it into the kitchen so Jeremy and I could join him there.

"'I'd prefer that you both keep that thing in there, if you don't mind,' said Grandpa, perhaps more sternly then he intended. 'It's important to me that you look through it without my hindrance.'

"Jeremy looked back at Grandpa quizzically, and almost said something. But after everything that had taken place that evening, he decided to go along with what Grandpa wanted. He and I returned our attention to the photographs on the first page.

"I recognized some of the images, since there were a number of pictures throughout the main floor of our house showing Grandpa and my Uncle Monty as youngsters. I was also familiar with the images of my great-grandmother and her mom and dad. As we moved through the pages, carefully turning each one over before going on to the next, the pictures grew more recent. I paused to point out a photograph of Dr. Stratton to Jeremy when I recognized the image of the old man I met in Genovene's village. Grandpa recognized that's who we were looking at from my excited comments, and he asked us to tell him when we reached the very end of the album.

"As we neared the end of the album, we found lots of photographs of our mom and a few that included my Grandma and Grandpa. They looked like a real happy family when mom was young, and I saw how she looked a lot like Grandma when she was a young woman. I lingered most on an image of our mom when she was a senior in high school, since it was identical to how she looked when I first saw her in the village the day before. When Jeremy saw what I was looking at he whistled and nodded approvingly

"'*Goddamn*, mom was a real looker back in her day, huh?' he cooed. 'Sorry y'all, but *man-n-n!* The only pictures I'd ever seen of Mom were when she was older. You know, the ones on the wall and that smaller photo beneath the coffee table in the living room. Oh, and the one on Jackie's dresser upstairs.'

"'She was definitely something to behold, that's for sure,' Grandpa agreed from the kitchen. 'She was just like her momma, though I'd say she got some of her good looks from her old man, too.' He chuckled softly, but then seemed to grow sad again. 'It's no wonder you kids turned out so handsome with parents like Frank and Julie…You should be just a few pages away from the end.'

"Grandpa stood up and slowly moved back to the dining room, where he leaned up against one side of the doorway. He motioned for us to finish while he puffed thoughtfully on his pipe.

"The next page featured pictures from my parents' wedding, where again Jeremy commented on mom's 'hot' look. Then again, our dad wasn't too shabby himself. There was even a picture of him in his Atlanta Falcon uniform diving for a football on the next to last page of the album. It was sad for my brother and I to go through these pictures, and we lingered on these pages a moment or two longer. But nothing here could've prepared us for the photos on the very last page.

"Four of the five pictures featured our mom and dad and looked like they were taken with a disposable camera, as the quality wasn't near as good as the other pictures All of the shots appeared to have been taken in the back yard near the oak tree.

"'That one was taken shortly after y'all arrived from Atlanta,' Grandpa advised, his voice a whisper as he stole a peek at the first photo over Jeremy's shoulder. 'Everything started out just fine…'

"Indeed, my mom and dad looked happy. My dad was holding Jeremy against his shoulder and my mom held me in her arms. To be honest, Agent McNamee, to this day I just wish we'd closed the album right then and called it a night. If I hadn't had the experiences with my mother's spirit the day before, the images of her and my dad contained within the ensuing photographs would've surely haunted me for the rest of my life. But we needed to go on. Information about our parents had always been scarce, so we were drinking it all in.

"It appeared that several other photos had been removed from this last page at some point. Of the handful that remained, three pictures featured my parents, and each revealed the steady progression of the personality change that defined their bizarre behavior during the last half of their vacation to Carlsdale. Each shot was taken in the same general area of the backyard. My brother and I were present in only one more shot with them. It was the last picture, and even though our beloved mother and father held us again, they were completely distracted. My dad's attention was drawn to the oak, which was to his left. Mom's gaze followed his. Even Jeremy was frowning, which made me wonder why in the hell Grandpa had kept this picture, or why anyone spent the effort capturing the shot in the first place.

"Jeremy squinted his eyes as he studied the picture more closely. Suddenly, he gasped slightly, pulling on my arm. When I looked at where he pointed, at first I didn't recognize the wispy image barely visible next to the south side of the oak tree. The image was barely detectable, but once I brought my face close enough to confirm what was there, my blood immediately turned cold. The image was of a face, which barely stood out at all. Yet, the blue eyes and sardonic grin framed by ghost-like hair were clearly recognizable once I realized what I was looking at.

"'Well, your reaction to that picture confirms what I've worried about since the other night when you first brought that talisman in here, Jack,' said Grandpa, his voice hushed as he moved between us to close the album. He pushed it back toward the middle of the table, and I silently prayed that it was the last time I ever saw Genovene's face. 'That's her, isn't it, Jack? Elsie said that was a face and not some defect in the film when we first got the pictures developed. She later told me about a young girl she saw swinging from the tire-swing, a week after your folks were gone, that had light hair and very blue eyes. But, until I heard your story last night I ignored what she said about that, even though I have seen the empty swing moving through the air as if someone was sitting in it from time to time. You'd think after everything I've personally experienced, including Julie and Frank's disappearance, that it'd knock some sense into my head. But for some reason it didn't. I wish I knew why.'

"Grandpa moved over to the dining room windows, peering through the blinds once more. The abundant light from the full moon was still at its brightest, and the backyard was illuminated nearly as much as when the sun is out during the late afternoon. He closed the small crease he'd created between the blinds and turned to face us again. 'I'd say we've spent enough time tonight in this room,' he told us. 'How about we forget about that album for now and go out on the back porch for a while? The full moon's out and it might be kind of nice.'

"'What about that presence you felt out there earlier?' I asked, thinking about my strange experience in the garden that afternoon. It didn't help matters that I had just seen a picture of the owner of the voice that had scared me so bad and sent me sprawling into the garden's mud earlier.

"'I believe whatever was trying to peek in on us has left now. I really do,' he advised. 'Just in case I'm wrong about that, I'll bring the gun with me. I've learned today that we can never be too careful.'

"'It's all right with me if we go out on the back porch for a while,' offered Jeremy. 'I can always use another smoke. Besides, Jackie, we can check that picture out again later. You saw the image of that face, right?' My brother backed up from the table and immediately reached for his breast pocket, while Grandpa led the way through the kitchen and on out to the back porch. 'Let's see what he has to say about this.'

"Jeremy motioned toward Grandpa, who sadly shook his head in response. Once we were outside, we all remarked on how it was so much cooler than normal for the time of year, especially July, and the strong scent of burnt wood filled the night air. But at least there was no sign or feeling that Genovene or any other menace was in the immediate area. Everything felt very peaceful, like it usually had up until three days ago.

"Grandpa sat down on the porch steps and looked out into the backyard with his shotgun cradled between his knees. He struck a match to relight his pipe and then allowed Jeremy to use the rest of the flame to light the cigarette he delicately balanced between his lips. Once that was done, Jeremy leaned up against the support post closest to the steps. I stood across from him on the other side of the steps, leaning on the porch rail as I watched the steady smoke stream from Grandpa's pipe rise into the air just above our heads, seemingly chased by the small row of rings Jeremy created with his cigarette.

"Grandpa had turned the porch and security lights off just before the three of us ventured outside, as there was no need for any artificial light. The entire yard was aglow from the brightness of the moon alone. Even the giant oak and the mimosas, along with the backyard's assortment of rusted junk, were fully illuminated. The stone sphere looked ominous and eerie as it sat in its spot near the back wall, though we could only catch glimpses of it through the oak's branches and leaves from where we were presently perched upon the porch.

"'Tomorrow, I'm going to start cleaning away all of this garbage back here,' Grandpa announced as he puffed on his pipe. 'It's finally time to get that done. I probably should've done it years ago, but I could never bring myself to care much about the backyard after Elsie passed away. That damned sphere has always reminded me of what's happened every time I've laid eyes on it. At least I'm not trying to have it removed anymore—I gave up on that after the NASA fiasco happened long ago. Yes, I can tell from both of your faces that you've both heard that story and are probably wondering why I'd do something that stupid in light of everything else that happened, as well as the 'Season' legend. Right?'

"We both confirmed it was a question for us, especially the reaction to call NASA after everything he'd been through.

"Well... let's just say that after all Elsie and I had to contend with, I was just so overwhelmed by grief that the only thing I could think of was getting the goddamned thing out of here,' he explained. 'But, I'll never try that again.' He smiled wanly as he said this. 'Now that I've learned my lesson, I hope wherever Elsie is now, she's happy knowing I'm finally going to take care of this eyesore.'

"Jeremy and I told him we'd help him get that done. That brought a warmer smile from him and he looked up toward the sky. Even though the moon was incredibly bright that evening, we were still able to trace most of the constellations and identify the nearby planets and bigger galaxies in the summer night sky. Grandpa quizzed us, as he sometimes did, on which constellation or celestial body was what and also on the various myths of the zodiac.

"We spent nearly an hour doing this, until we started getting tired as midnight approached. The three of us went back inside the farmhouse, the steadily growing noise from the crickets, tree toads, and cicadas no longer audible as we walked back into the kitchen and closed the storm door behind us. Grandpa turned the porch light and the security floodlights back on. Then he and Jeremy walked on into the living room to relax a little before retiring for the evening.

"As for myself, I was finally feeling the full affects of my adventure from the day before and decided to go immediately upstairs to bed. My brother turned on the television, and our grandfather moved over to his recliner. I told them both 'goodnight' and that I loved them.

"'Goodnight, Jack,' Grandpa called after me before I disappeared from view on the staircase to head upstairs. 'I love you, too, son and that goes for you as well, Jeremy.'

"My brother seemed uncomfortable and embarrassed by this, like he'd had quite enough of the sentimental spirit that'd pervaded the evening up until then. He mumbled 'ditto' under his breath and told me 'goodnight'. I heard him pick up the sound system's remote control and plop down upon the sofa right after that.

"Once I reached my bedroom, I found it was brightly illuminated by the moonlight. Rather than turn on the bedroom light, I left it off and walked over to my window and looked out into the backyard. Through the gaps in the oak's foliage, I saw the blackened remains of the woods as they glistened in the moonlight. I was amazed at the contrast between what I beheld now as compared to the same view only two nights before. I stood there for nearly a minute, and then turned away when I'd looked long enough.

"I felt so exhausted I just went over to my bed and climbed in, leaving half my clothes on. But I couldn't sleep, for I was still too excited about everything that'd happened. I remember how I laid awake for quite a while, staring up at the ceiling. In an effort to distract myself, I tried to think about other things aside from the events of the past few days, but even then my thoughts returned to the lovely face of my mom.

"As the night grew deeper, a warm presence began filling up my room, and soon after this I started drifting off to sleep. When I crossed from this world over into the world of dreams, I heard my mother's voice softly say, 'Remember, Jack, that no matter what happens, I will always be with you.' I forced myself awake again, hoping to capture the quiet warmth that now completely enveloped my bedroom.

"'Goodnight, Mom...wherever you are,' I whispered. A light chuckle came from somewhere near the window of my room and then, 'Goodnight, my son'. I smiled and closed my eyes, and immediately fell asleep."

PART VII

A Season's End

Jack sat in silence and leaned back in his chair, indicating his story was now finished.

Agent McNamee was so engrossed by Jack's story that at first he didn't recognize Jack's body language. Once he did, he straightened himself in his chair and leaned slightly across the table. "So, that's *it*?"

"Yep. Pretty much anyway," Jack told him.

"Then there's more. Correct?"

"Well, I guess if you're wanting information on the tornado and such, then there might be."

" Please tell me about that, too, Jack," said Peter, as he relaxed in his chair once more. "I've said all along I want to hear everything. That includes *anything* else you can possibly tell me about what happened back then. If you want to take a dinner break first, that's fine with me. I don't want to leave here tonight until you've shared all you know."

"I can still wait on dinner," Jack said. "But, before I tell you anything more, I need to know what you honestly think of my grandfather's story. I mean, do you believe it? Or do you think it's a load of bullshit?"

Agent McNamee pondered his response to Jack's question. "No, I don't think your grandpa's story is a load of crap," he finally told him. "Nor have I felt anything you've related to me this evening is a fabrication. All I was trying to stress to you earlier is that this stuff may not fly too well with the other agents listening to us now, or whoever reviews the transcript later on. Surely, I hope you realize if anyone from this agency can be your ally, it *must* be me. You've got to trust me, Jack."

Jack studied the agent's face, nodding slightly to confirm his belief in Peter's honesty. "All right. But, I warn you the rest of what I've got to say will remain on the other side of 'normal'—same as nearly everything I've told you so far," he advised. "Also, much of what I know of the tornado that destroyed our home came from a trio of other eyewitnesses—*not* the Palmers, by the way.

"So, there's nothing at all to add from the Palmers?"

"No, *definitely* not anything from those sons of bitches!" Jack told him in disgust. "*Hell, no!* The only eyewitnesses I'm talking about are Freddy Stinson, Jeremy's best buddy, and his little brother Kyle. Along with another of my brother's pals, Ronnie Holmes."

Peter frowned and picked up one of his journals again, paging quickly through it as he sought to confirm this latest revelation.

"It's not in there, I assure you," Jack told him. "None of them ever came forward. At first it was because they didn't want to be ridiculed for what they saw. Then, after Carl Peterson and Sheriff McCracken were murdered, they swore one another to secrecy. They finally told Jeremy almost two years later, after my brother first told them he'd turned his life around and quit carousing and smoking—cold turkey on both accounts. He'd just gotten his high school diploma and was already accepted into the University of Alabama. The clincher for his buddies came when he revealed his dream of becoming an archaeologist. They told him everything at that point."

"Then Jeremy told you. Is that assumption correct?"

"Yes. That's correct," said Jack. "The account I'm fixing to tell you is a mixture of sorts. Some of the information is from myself, along with Jeremy and Grandpa. The rest is from the stuff Freddy, Kyle, and Ronnie told Jeremy. Are you ready?"

"Yes," said Peter. "I'm ready when you are!"

"All right, then," Jack said, and straightened himself in his chair as he leaned forward again. "Sometime around two in the morning, after Grandpa and Jeremy had gone to bed, Freddy, Kyle, and Ronnie snuck behind our property. They were determined to verify the damage caused by Vydora. As you can probably guess, Jeremy wasn't able to keep his mouth shut.

"I don't imagine my brother figured his buddies would ever venture into the woods without him—especially not this soon. When they reached our back wall and saw the multitude of blackened trees, Kyle, who was fifteen at the time, chickened out. Freddy and Ronnie were furious at him for this, since they'd gone to the trouble of bringing him along at his insistence. Freddy adamantly told him there was no way in hell they were going home, at least not until Freddy and Ronnie were goddamned ready to do so!

"Kyle began to whimper and hyper-ventilate, and as the older boys were afraid he'd start bawling and either wake us or the Palmers up, they tried to calm him down. That didn't happen until Freddy told Kyle he could wait for them near our property, and then also promised him that he'd be given full access to Freddy's Sony Playstation mature-level games for a week. Freddy and Ronnie helped him climb over the Palmer's wall, since it was lower than ours. Kyle crouched low in a corner next to our property to avoid detection by the Palmers, while Freddy and Ronnie began their trek to the clearing through the woods behind our home.

"I doubt if either of them had ever ventured into these woods before, and it's hard to say how much of Vydora's handiwork they actually saw in the darkness. Before long they were moving down the other side of the hill, on their way to the old bridge that crossed the Tombigbee River. Roughly thirty minutes later they stood in the midst of the clearing.

"By now, the night was older and the sky was still clear. As the moon had traveled toward the northwest corner of the sky, the multitude of stars was now more visible. The clearing benefited from the moon's illumination, which was still pretty bright, making it easy to see the old fort ruins.

"Freddy and Ronnie moved over to the ruins, excited to verify the scene from Jeremy's run-in with the strange critter from the previous afternoon. They were in the process of examining the building closest to them when they noticed a blue glow emanating from the top of the rock formation, which as I mentioned before sat near the clearing's western edge.

"Jeremy's buddies were a lot like him in that their foolhardiness usually ranged from moderate to outright insanity. Needless to say, they were attracted to the strange blue light like mayflies to a bug zapper. They ran over to the rock formation and quickly climbed to the top. I can easily imagine their surprise once they discovered the source of the blue glow was actually a fiery mass throbbing fervently from the depths of the bubbling pool itself.

"They nearly fell off the ledge when they scrambled to reach the bottom. No sooner than they touched the ground, they heard a murmur and thrashing sound coming from above them. They looked up, but didn't see anything other than a mist hovering just above the top. Not wanting to stick around and find out if a critter like the one that went after Jeremy was coming after them, they took off running. The bugs and nocturnal animals swarmed and scurried around them as they ran. Then, suddenly, every living thing around them froze, and the clearing became deathly quiet.

"Freddy and Ronnie became aware of a low thud-like sound coming from the depths of the pool. The sound grew steadily louder, and the mist hovering above the rock formation began to thicken and lengthen. Before long, the mist became a volatile cloud that continued to climb high into the air above the hot spring, growing larger and denser as it did so. It soon altered its color as well, changing from pale gray to pitch black.

"The cloud towered more than a hundred feet in the air, and bolts of lightning were thrown from its midst into the surrounding area below. It finished lifting itself up out from the pool and rock formation. As it did so, I imagine the bubbling water probably grew quiet, as the true source of its heat had now abdicated from its depths. The dark cloud headed east, in pursuit of Jeremy's buddies, who were looking over their shoulders from the eastern edge of the clearing before racing into the woods. Plants wilted and trees fell aside, and the air was filled with the popping sound of fireflies and other insects that ventured too close to the cloud.

"Freddy and Ronnie followed the same overgrown path we had traveled along, stumbling here and there as the cloud followed close behind them. Like a depraved stalker, it mimicked their exact footsteps, angling back and forth as it pursued them. It continued this bizarre behavior until they neared the river's edge, where they dove for cover behind a thick blackberry bush. The cloud crept toward them, but then stopped once it reached the foot of the bridge.

"The cloud remained there for a moment, as if contemplating its next move. Then it drifted down to the water's edge, just a few feet away from Freddy and Ronnie's present hideout. It began to spin rapidly by the Tombigbee's bank, and soon took on the funnel-like appearance of a cyclone, whipping the water in front of it with tremendous force. The river's instability increased, churning powerfully with huge waves slamming against the fragile bridge and shoreline. When the Tombigbee seemed pushed to its final limit, the water suddenly shot upward, climbing high into the air and leaving a sizable passageway in the middle of the riverbed.

"Like the story of *Exodus*, where the Dead Sea parted for Moses, the spinning cloud crossed the riverbed and returned to its original form once it reached the eastern shoreline. The unfortunate fish, snakes, and snapping turtles in its wake were torn apart, while the grass and plant life on the eastern bank withered and died as soon as the cloud's swirling edges touched them.

"The twin walls of water remained high in the air until the cloud safely cleared the river. Each wall somehow absorbed the Tombigbee's powerful southern thrust toward the Gulf of Mexico. Once the cloud reached the eastern bank, hovering above Black Warrior Road, the walls of water crashed back down upon the earth below. The crushing force from this completely destroyed the bridge, and the river overflowed its banks in either direction for several minutes.

"Meanwhile, Freddy and Ronnie scrambled up the bank in terror. The water's force threw them both to the ground, but they managed to climb away before it could pull them down into the raging current. They turned and watched the towering cloud move swiftly toward the hill. It ascended the path along the hillside, scorching many of the flagstones with lightning strikes along the way to the top. While the river steadily began to grow calm once more, the cloud moved into the charred remains of the woods behind our home.

"Freddy and Ronnie were relieved the cloud was no longer interested in them. But when they realized where it was headed next, they panicked because there wasn't time for them to warn Kyle or any of us in our house that it was on its way. Since the bridge was gone and the water's current too swift, they had no choice but to travel at least a mile through the densest woods in the region to reach Bailey's Bend Road. Taking them nearly two hours to reach our house, they arrived only after it was all over.

"Once the cloud emerged from the woods, it headed for our house, wilting away the tall grass and weeds in the field that separated our property from the woods. It threw an old weathered signpost from the field against our back wall that flipped over into the Palmer's backyard. Kyle was terribly afraid but peered over the wall anyway.

"I imagine he was overwhelmed by a mixture of fascination and terror. The towering cloud that slowly swirled before him seemed to shimmer in the moonlight as it hovered at the border of our property. Even as naïve and frightened as he was, Kyle knew right away the cloud's glow wasn't caused entirely by the light of the moon. It was as if the thing had actual emotions, like it was alive. All Kyle could feel was what emanated from the twisting mass...hatred.

"Kyle heard Banjo whimper on the other side of the wall, just a few feet away. As was Banjo's custom, he usually slept in the northern corner of our backyard, since it normally was the coolest spot available. Kyle climbed up the side of the wall to gain a better vantage point to check on him. A barrage of lightning bolts suddenly flew from the cloud to the ground near Banjo. Kyle watched him cower deeper into the overgrown grass and weeds, trembling in terror as a trail of smoke rose from the strike.

"None of us in our farmhouse had stirred yet, but that was about to change. A portion of the cloud crossed over the wall and began to spread out into the backyard until it touched the sphere. Immediately, the cloud recoiled itself and withdrew to the other side of the wall, like a child touching the red-hot burners on an oven. Kyle said it then pulsed with even more malice, and then swirled faster and faster until it'd regained its tornado-like appearance. The wind from this sudden change whipped across the backyard, sending violent gusts toward our house. The oaks' solid branches were severely bent and began to break.

"Kyle noticed the kitchen light suddenly came on, indicating someone in our house was now awake. The menacing cloud spun even faster just outside the gate. Kyle watched it move to the right as it picked a new spot to cross into our yard. But before it crossed over the wall, the sphere rolled in front of it. The cloud then moved over to the left side of the gate and found the sphere waiting for it once again.

"The cloud began moving quickly from side to side to elude the sphere. Yet, the sphere continued to stay with the cloud, matching its moves perfectly like this was some kind of surreal chess match. The contest continued, but remained a stalemate. Then, just when the cloud seemed to tire of the whole affair, it suddenly juked weakly with its thicker top portion going one way and its lower funnel-shaped portion going in another direction. The sphere followed the top portion of the cloud, and a split second later its pointed lower section jumped over the wall into the backyard. The cloud landed next to the sphere and before it could respond the cloud brought its upper portion over the wall, which had formed a mouth-like opening in its midsection. A rapid series of lightning bolts flew out from this opening and landed directly on top of the sphere, exploding it into hundreds of fiery, meteor-like fragments that flew in every direction.

"Kyle immediately ducked down, although none of the fragments came over the wall into the Palmer's yard. When he looked back over the wall, he saw that most of the fragments had reached the backside of our house, where they burrowed through the thick masonry walls and crashed through the windows on both floors. The tornado wasted little time in closing in on us, tearing the massive oak out of the ground and hurling it toward the Johnson's farmhouse nearly half a mile away. Incredibly, the tree flew like a missile toward its target and scored a direct hit. The building buckled and collapsed on impact, and a moment later exploded as the main gas line to the house ruptured. The explosion sent fiery timbers and debris into the barn next door. Within minutes a fiery inferno engulfed the remains of both buildings, obliterating any evidence of Vydora's earlier visit there, as you know.

"According to Kyle, the cloud shimmered brightly, as if delighted by its masterful throw. Next, it picked up the old truck remains and other junk and hurled them at our farmhouse. The truck crushed the back porch, with the bulk of it carrying on into the kitchen, while the appliances were sent flying into Jeremy's and my bedrooms upstairs. There was a loud explosion in the kitchen and flames soon poured out of the broken windows on both floors. Kyle said he could tell we were frantically scurrying about inside, and as we did so, the tornado descended upon our house.

"Grandpa was jolted awake by a loud thump coming from the back porch. He'd fallen asleep in his recliner while starting to read what was the latest James Patterson novel. His reading lamp was still on and his favorite pipe was lying on the floor next to his chair. The television was on, too, although the volume was turned down to its lowest level, and Jeremy was huddled asleep on the couch. Grandpa stood up and grabbed his shotgun, and then went through the dining room on his way to the kitchen, turning on the lights in each room as he made his way to the back porch door. Once he reached it, he peered out through the door's window.

"The powerful swirling wind in the backyard was lifting small to medium pieces of wood and other debris into the air. He noticed what was left of the oak tree's branches being pushed and pulled in extreme angles to where he knew they'd break at any moment. But, it was the train whistle noise and the rusted pail and washboard impaled through the porch railings that commanded his attention, along with the sudden explosion of the security light on the other side of the oak tree. A tornado was somewhere close by and he needed to waken Jeremy and me to get us all safely to shelter before it hit the house, which he realized could be at any moment.

"'*Jeremy!!! Jack!!! Wake up!!!*' he called out frantically as he ran from the kitchen toward the front of the house. '*A tornado's coming!!! Goddamn it... GET UP!!!*'

Jeremy staggered out into the foyer from the living room to meet him, his long hair billowing wildly around his face as he struggled to get his shoes on. Just then, a barrage of molten rock fragments from the exploding sphere came crashing through the rear of the house. Grandpa and Jeremy dove for cover at the base of the staircase, a pair of basketball-sized fragments whizzing by their feet, barely missing them. The continuous sounds of wood splitting and glass shattering on both floors made it obvious we couldn't stay in the house much longer, and that any place of refuge would have to be found somewhere in front of our besieged home.

"'*Jack!!! Are you all right??*' shouted Grandpa. He motioned for Jeremy to take cover and sit tight near the bottom two stairs while he ventured up to the second level to look for me. He hadn't made it very far up the stairs when I suddenly appeared at the top with my own hair disheveled, and clad only in a pair of blue jeans.

"'*Get down here, son!!!*' Grandpa shouted at me.

"Another fairly large fragment came flying through the upstairs back wall and hit the floor not far from me. It flipped up into the air before landing again, and then rolled on over to the stairway and on down the stairs. It finally settled on a step in the middle of the staircase where its molten flames ignited the carpet runner. Within seconds, the fire quickly spread across the stairway as it threatened to join the myriad of other small fires that'd sprung up throughout our home.

"I scrambled down the stairs where I soon joined my grandfather and brother. Yelling over the noise, we tried to figure out what to do next. Meanwhile, the old truck and appliance remains crashed into the house, sending even more splintered wood fragments and glass shards into the house, and shaking it to its very foundation. We were nearly out of time as the train-like whistle grew louder...closer.

"Grandpa cursed under his breath that there wasn't any safe place to hide, either inside or outside the house, and that he'd left the Jeep's keys sitting on the kitchen counter. As soon as Jeremy understood what Grandpa was upset about, he checked both of his jeans' pockets and found he'd kept his truck keys inside the left one. He quickly pulled them out, dangling them excitedly in Grandpa's face to let him know we had a means of escape. Jeremy threw open the front door and we all sprinted to his truck, which sat in the driveway next to the house.

"The truck was a black beauty, equipped with a chrome spoiler and headers to go with the custom-made wheels for the oversized tires and wheelbase he'd paid dearly for. The interior of the truck's cab was just as fancy, with plush upholstery and a state-of-the-art sound system, among other extras. The best part for Jeremy, though, was the extra power the expanded engine gave him, and we prayed that fast engine would save us now.

"We climbed into the truck and shut the doors just as the tornado converged on the house. For the first time, we could see the spiraling cloud in its fantastic magnificence. It was as densely black as coal, but the light afforded by the moon and the frequent lightning strikes emitted by the cloud allowed us to see its details quite clearly. It loomed ominously high above us while it easily dismantled the weakened structure of our house.

"Jeremy immediately put the key in the ignition and tried to start the truck. The engine wouldn't turn over.

"'*My God!*' Grandpa said reverently, his voice nearly a whisper. '*I've never...I've never seen anything quite like that before! Not any tornados, anyway—Jeremy!!!*' he shouted as he suddenly interrupted himself. '*Let's get the hell out of here, son!!! What's taking you so damned long to get this thing started, anyway??*'

"'*I don't fucking know!!!*' My brother shouted back. '*I can't get the goddamn mother to start for some reason!!! Wait! There it goes!!*'

"The slumbering engine rumbled to life just as the cloud finished obliterating what was left of our house. Grandpa grimaced at losing the place that'd been his home for most of his life. But our immediate survival was the only important issue right then. Jeremy threw the truck in reverse and we sped out of the driveway toward Lelan's Road, the tires squealing as the tornado quickly bore down upon us.

"Just as we pulled onto the road and Jeremy straightened the truck, the tornado uprooted the pair of maples standing in the front yard. It threw them both in the direction of our fleeing vehicle. Jeremy glanced back incredulously after the first one barely missed us. '*Holy shit, y'all!!!*' he exclaimed in disbelief. '*I think that mother fucker's actually aiming for our ass—I really do!!!*'

"He deftly eluded the second tree, although it shook the road mightily as it crashed down right next to us. Grandpa and I turned to look behind us while Jeremy kept an eye on his rear-view mirror. All of us murmured '*Oh Shit!*' when we saw the cloud suddenly turn and follow us down Lelan's Road. I was certain then Genovene had something to do with this, and I was pretty sure Jeremy and Grandpa thought the same thing.

"Jeremy pushed the accelerator to the floor in an effort to try and distance us from the fast approaching twister. It briefly appeared to work, as the swirling cloud grew smaller in the rearview mirror. But within the next ten to fifteen seconds, it picked up a lot more speed and closed the gap to less than a hundred feet.

"Suddenly, the truck began to slow down. Horrified, Jeremy looked down at the speedometer and tachometer. We were losing speed, but the rpms remained high. The tornado was directly behind us, its train-whistle sound becoming an almost deafening roar in our ears. Jeremy floored the accelerator again, pushing the rpms to the danger level. Yet the truck continued to slow down, and an overwhelming feeling of dread swept over all of us.

"We murmured in terror amongst ourselves, silently berating ourselves about the fact we didn't leave sooner. All at once the truck lifted up off the road. It drifted above the ground for only a brief instant and then began twirling in midair, spinning faster and faster around a central point in the cloud while continuing to rise higher and higher into the air above Lelan's Road. We were frightened beyond anything we could've ever imagined—especially from the maddening horror of not knowing what was to come next. All we knew was Genovene's malevolent nature, and that she probably wanted us dead.

"Faster and faster we spun around, and all three of us screamed in terror. When I thought we might all faint from fear and our exhaustive panic, the truck was sent flying through the air until it landed violently in the field that sits to the right of Lelan's Road. Fortunately for us, the vehicle landed upright and remained on its wheels, although the tires ruptured on impact and the truck's axles were cracked and bowed inward. Despite this, Jeremy made a remarkable attempt to steer the truck. He did this even though the initial jolt severely injured his shoulder and neck, just as it'd also hurt Grandpa and myself. But in the end, his very best effort failed to regain enough control of the truck as it careened and skidded through the bumpy field.

"We flipped over a tree stump, just before crashing head on into an irrigation ditch near the field's north-eastern corner. The truck bounced up and finally stopped, resting with its back end inside the ditch and its crumpled front end sticking out over the ditch's bank. My head throbbed mercilessly and my vision was blurred. On my left, my brother moaned in extreme pain. To my right, there was no sound. Grandpa wasn't moving.

"The moonlight illuminated the truck's cab, and I saw the wet splatter of blood from all three of us upon the smashed windshield and the dashboard. I looked over at Jeremy, and saw that he was covered with blood on his right side, though at least he was moving. As I tried to turn and look over at Grandpa, a dark shadow suddenly distracted me. It was the cloud.

"It hovered above our broken vehicle left stranded in the ditch. The cloud had quieted its spinning, and it seemed to draw ever closer to us. I instinctively tried to push myself back against my seat, but this sent immediate waves of pain through my head. I noticed the back of my shirt was soaked, and knew it was my own blood.

"Consciousness had begun to leave me and I found it hard to concentrate. I was awake long enough to see a shining image from within the cloud. It was Genovene, guised in all of her voluptuous beauty once more. She smiled curiously at me for a moment, but then stopped smiling altogether, studying me in sullen seriousness. Finally, she shrugged her shoulders, winked, and blew me a luscious kiss.

"Blood was pooling on top of my head. It began to spill down upon my face in warm crimson droplets. As it did so, she threw back her head in amused laughter. I could clearly hear it, though fortunately for me her cackles soon faded. While blood continued to pour down my face, I tried to look away from her in order to check once more on my grandfather. I never made it," Jack added with sadness, looking at Agent McNamee.

Jack pushed his chair back from the table and stood up suddenly, stretching his back. "As we discussed already, I didn't regain consciousness for nearly three weeks," he continued. "So, I missed out on Genovene's final assault on our property, as well as her probable relocation to your family's neck of the woods in Mississippi."

He turned away from Agent McNamee and began pacing near the center of the room. For the moment, he seemed completely absorbed in his thoughts. Peter allowed Jack his space for the moment, not wanting to interrupt the flow of information passing through Jack's lips. He waited patiently for him to continue, and a few minutes later he was rewarded.

"We've already discussed that our yard was left completely barren of everything that'd been there before this unfortunate event, except for the tool shed," said Jack. "But, other than the Palmers, did anyone ever tell y'all what became of the twister that night, after it finished its second pass on our place?"

"It's always been hard to determine what happened exactly," Peter replied, turning in his chair to watch Jack continue his nervous stroll across the floor. "But to answer your question, I believe the prevailing thought back then was that it dissipated back into the atmosphere."

"Well, there's more to it than that, I assure you," said Jack, stopping to directly face him. "I believe Genovene's main objective after getting her revenge on us was to find a new home. Obliterating the rest of our property on her way out of Carlsdale was just an added bonus. Keep in mind there's an eyewitness to this, other than the Palmers. Kyle Stinson was still hiding in the far-left corner of their backyard, shaking helplessly, yet surprisingly unharmed. But he was still curious enough to watch everything going on nearby.

"Interestingly, he never saw the Palmers while all this shit was going on. It baffles me how both their stories are similar in ways, although I think you'll see Kyle's account is a bit more complete.

"According to what he told Jeremy, he was huddled next to the wall and promising Jesus he'd change his life if only he lived long enough to do it, when he suddenly heard the train whistle sound returning. Despite his obvious terror, he bravely peered over the wall again after he also heard Banjo bleating in similar fear. Kyle tried to get him to move closer to the wall, but Banjo refused to budge. He just stood where he was, trembling and crying hysterically as this goddamned twister closed in on the back portion of our ruined property.

"The tornado-cloud zigzagged across the yard, bouncing violently off the tool shed as it raced toward Banjo's corner of the yard. Kyle panicked and ducked back down into the corner of the Palmer's yard, hoping the tornado didn't crash through the wall. All the while, Banjo's awful cries pierced the twister's whistle.

"Kyle braced himself for the worst, but suddenly, the cloud's sound changed. He looked up and was greatly relieved to find it'd lifted off the ground. It climbed high into the sky with its funnel end leading its charge forward as it sped to the west. In a matter of seconds, it vacated the area, leaving a death-like stillness in its wake.

"His curiosity got the better of him, and he lifted himself back above the wall to witness the final result of the cloud's wrath. Under the moon's revealing glow, his view was the same as it remains today, and without any trace of our beloved pet."

Jack slowly returned to the table and sat down. He eyed Peter thoughtfully and then spoke again. "After what you shared with me earlier about your nephew, I'm convinced now more than ever the cloud headed for Mississippi. Knowing how reclusive this bunch is, they would've sought a place offering them lots of potential victims while remaining off the beaten path, so to speak. There were too many witnesses to stay in Carlsdale."

"Bienville National Forest." Peter said softly.

"Yeah, that's exactly what I'm thinking," said Jack. "Even though you were able to tie yours and my experiences together long before today, believe it or not, I figured that's where Genovene and her kin ended up immediately after reading about your nephew's disappearance in a couple of tabloids," Jack explained. "I remember Bobby's story. But to be honest, I forgot his first name long ago. I mean, eight years is a long time when you consider I was only a kid back then. I never forgot the other details that made national headlines, and each tabloid's report gave me enough clues to piece together what'd happened.

"Not to purposely touch on your pain, and I realize you've already put some pieces together from the information I've revealed so far. But, if you'd like me to share my own ideas on what happened to your family as it relates to Genovene, then I certainly can do that."

Peter tapped the end of his pen against his bottom lip while he carefully considered Jack's proposal. "Go ahead," he finally told him.

"All right," said Jack. "One thing in particular that made me immediately think of Genovene was how your sister, Mrs. Northrop, stated she felt like she was being watched by some unknown voyeur hiding in the woods behind her beautiful home. According to the news story I read, and that you touched upon earlier, she'd felt like this for a few weeks before her son's disappearance. I guess her husband and others thought she was overreacting a bit and didn't give this notion any serious consideration until it was too late."

Jack hesitated before going on, studying Peter's face to accurately gauge how to proceed with this delicate subject. He could barely recall *The Star*'s images of Eileen Northrop in his mind. He only remembered she was truly beautiful, which Peter confirmed when he showed her picture to him earlier. What a contrast it was to the tabloid photos taken of her later, just a month after her beloved son's abduction, depicting an emotionally worn and haggard woman, with only traces of her beauty left.

Peter returned Jack's steady gaze, this time effectively hiding his true feelings from his counterpart across the table. Instinctively, Jack recognized this was his normal demeanor, and the outburst that happened near the beginning of this interview was a rare event for him. He smiled ever so slightly. "Go on, Jack...please," he said.

"Very well," said Jack. "That was only one clue, though. There were others, like the hot spring and rock formation, which were discovered in the forest while the authorities searched for the little guy. Although this was mentioned in passing, its significance wasn't lost on me, which I'll explain further in a moment. Also, the other story I read told of the zoologist you mentioned earlier, who identified the reptilian footprints alongside Bobby's scent. The fact this scientist said he'd never seen anything like them grabbed my attention. I now had enough information to figure what likely took place in Mississippi. If I'd known then about that golden haze you mentioned earlier, it would've removed any doubts I had at the time.

"By the time the cloud reached the forest, I imagine it took on a more peaceful appearance so it didn't draw any unwanted attention to itself. Perhaps it drifted softly through the trees as a mist. I figure it moved through the forest until it reached the very edge, where Genovene surely noticed your loved ones' neighborhood. Once she and her kin found their newest hunting ground, they would've retreated deep into the forest. As soon as they found a small brook or spring, I believe they burrowed deep into the ground beneath the water source. In fact, I'd be willing to bet my life the individual rocks that make up the rock formation in the forest came from directly beneath the forest's floor. From the looks of it, the *National Enquirer*'s photograph of the formation, the mist or cloud might've returned to its cyclone form and drilled itself into the earth's crust. That's what I think, anyway... So, what do you think about my thoughts on this, Agent McNamee?"

"Well, for one thing, I wish you'd just call me 'Peter'," the agent chuckled, perhaps surprised at how painless Jack's musings actually were. "Did you ever share your thoughts back then with Jeremy?"

"Yeah, I did," Jack replied, smiling weakly. "As you can imagine, he thought it was a stupid notion at best. He changed his tune considerably once we took a trip to the old bridge site and the clearing."

"So, there's more *still*?"

"Yeah, there is. But we're nearing the very end of what I've got to say. By now I'm sure you're glad I'm almost finished."

"That's hardly the case, Jack," Peter assured him. "Please go on."

"All right," said Jack. "As you know, I was in a coma for nearly three weeks and my grandfather was in one for almost as long. Grandpa spent another three months in intensive care to recover from his fractured hip and thighbone, not to mention the ruptured spleen and lacerated kidney that had nearly killed him. His head injuries were almost as bad as mine, too, although the fact he was able to heal so quickly at his age borders on miraculous. By the end of the year, he was pretty much fully recovered.

"I've still got a long scar across the top of my head, but considering what might've been, I'd say I'm damn lucky to be alive. We all were. Jeremy recovered the quickest, but the torn ligaments in his left knee eliminated his dreams of playing football again. His shoulder and neck healed within two weeks of the accident, which was fairly amazing in itself considering how much pain he endured during his first few days in the hospital.

"It was a strange feeling waking up to find I'd missed three weeks of my life. Jeremy was there along with my aunt and uncle. Grandpa had woken up a couple of days earlier, but was in no condition to leave his room. It was good to have some family there to welcome me back to the world of the living, and by the next morning I was able to visit Grandpa in his room. A few days after that, we were able to go to our new home in Tuscaloosa, which was my aunt and uncle's guesthouse located in the rear of their property.

"By this time, a few things had changed in our world, other than the fact we no longer lived in Carlsdale. Wanting to focus on something I enjoyed, I checked on my favorite sports teams. The Braves were still winning, and you could tell even then that the Falcons were going to suck. That especially bothered me, being they were my dad's team and they'd made it to the Super Bowl the previous January. One upsetting thing my family had to tell me about, though, was the fact Carl Peterson and Sheriff McCracken were both dead.

"It didn't help matters that all five of us, including Uncle Monty and Aunt Martha, could hardly go anywhere without being followed. I mean, your buddies at the bureau would always be nearby, all spiffed up in their goddamn suits and sunglasses!" Jack laughed at this and Peter smiled, aware this jab was not toward him personally.

"Shortly after school started that year, Grandpa, Jeremy, and I decided to revisit our old home in Carlsdale," Jack continued. "Jeremy and I wanted to return as soon as I was healed up enough to do so. But Grandpa steadfastly refused to let us do it. When he finally relented, it was with the strict understanding we'd visit only what remained of our property. Reluctantly, Jeremy and I agreed to these terms. We made the trip the second weekend in September, and Uncle Monty and Aunt Martha decided to join us.

"One of the sedans I mentioned earlier followed us all the way from Tuscaloosa down to Carlsdale, tailing us by a couple hundred feet on Highway Forty-three. As soon as we exited onto Baileys Bend Road, it didn't follow us further. Perhaps, whoever was in the car knew where we were headed and didn't need to physically confirm this. Once we turned onto Lelan's Road, my uncle whistled under his breath, while my aunt whispered *'Great God Almighty!'*. Grandpa, Jeremy, and I sat in solemn silence as my uncle's Navigator crept up the road to our former home.

"The field we almost died in sat to our left. A large fir was impaled upside down into the earth near the very spot where Jeremy's truck came to rest in the ditch. I realize tornados can leave behind some pretty bizarre reminders from their visitations, like an occasional piece of straw drilled into a telephone pole and shit like that. But, I'll bet very few of them leave behind a token as disturbing as what we were looking at right then. It made me shudder to think just how close we'd come to getting killed.

"Uncle Monty almost stopped the truck, but Grandpa urged him to keep moving so we could get on with the reason for our visit. As soon as we reached the Palmer's place everyone gasped at the barrenness of the land where our beloved farmhouse once stood. We all got out of the car to investigate everything, catching a glimpse now and then of someone peeking through the curtains at the Palmer's—those fucking nosey assholes! It really bothers me that nothing, I mean *absolutely* nothing was harmed on their property, not even a goddamned daisy!"

"That's one of the things Agent Mark Jenkins said about the scene at your former home," Peter said. "He's been with us eighteen years now, and over the last few years he and I've gotten to be great friends, Jack. He's another guy acutely interested in your family's history."

"Then I guess he must've been as amazed as we were at the condition of the tool shed," said Jack. "I mean, aside from not receiving a scratch from the twister, I noticed for the first time its paint was free of nicks and any signs of wear—which one would expect, as old and vulnerable as the damn thing is. Grandpa swears to this day that he's never painted it.

"When we finally decided we'd seen enough, we drove back home to Tuscaloosa. That was the second to last time I visited our old home. Grandpa soon sold it to a wealthy Australian named Malcolm Donohue. Mr. Donohue, as I'm sure you know, purchased the Johnson's farm and eventually the Palmer's place, too."

"Most of Carlsdale, actually, Jack," Peter told him. "He purchased the woods and clearing you mentioned as well. He's building an amusement park incorporating several ancient Mississippian Indian ruins recently uncovered near your old home. At least that's what the original permit lists as his proposed development plan. From what I understand, he has completed the first few phases, while the remainder of the project is on hold. An NCAI petition to insure the protection of the ruins is currently under review before the Alabama Supreme Court, so we'll have to wait and see what happens with that."

"Really? Well that explains what Jeremy and I discovered around Thanksgiving that year," said Jack. "Do I have time to share it, or will your recorder run out of space?"

"It's still got about half an hour left," Peter advised. "Regardless, I want to hear what you've got to say."

"I'll try to make this quick," said Jack. "Grandpa was strictly against any of us returning to Carlsdale, since he felt we'd already seen everything of importance there. To him, it was better to remember our old place as it once was.

"Jeremy and I managed to live with this mandate for a month or so. But, we really missed our friends. Grandpa remained strong in his resolve to keep us from going back, until Thanksgiving break. He finally relented because our old buddies were out of school that Friday, as were we.

"Grandpa's orders were for us to stay away from the woods and the river. We promised to obey his wishes; fully knowing we'd visit those very places before the day was over. If he'd felt up to it, I'm sure he would've insisted on joining us, just to make sure we stayed out of trouble.

"Me and Jeremy were excited. My brother had purchased a brand new truck just two days earlier with the insurance money he received for his previous one. He could hardly wait to show Freddy and Ronnie, and I was looking forward to having him show it off to my buddy Lee as well.

"Though it wasn't as awesome as his other truck, the Dodge Ram he'd purchased was still a beauty. Metallic dark purple in color, it shimmered in the sunlight out on our uncle and aunt's main driveway. This one came equipped with a shiny chrome spoiler and headers. The tires were oversized, too, just like his last truck, and the chrome wheels were the most expensive ones he could find in Tuscaloosa. Everything else was top of the line as well. For my first few trips riding in it, I was pretty fearful I might scuff up the interior or spill something. That'd been pretty bad for sure!

"We arrived at Freddy's home in Demopolis late that morning, and went out for lunch with him and Ronnie. Then we left them to visit Lee. It felt strange driving along Lelan's Road in a truck with Jeremy again. It was much weirder than when we went there with the rest of our family back in September.

"Lee, as I believe I told you, lived right across the street from the field we wrecked in. He and his family have since moved to Birmingham. I imagine Mr. Donohue had a hand in that, too, especially since the Hornes lived just a few houses away from us. That afternoon, Lee and his family were fixing to head over to Mobile for the rest of the weekend, so we didn't visit long with him either. We now had plenty of time to visit our old home again, and everywhere else we planned to go.

"We didn't spend much time that day at our former residence, as the only thing we desired to see was the old tool shed again. Jeremy and I still couldn't get over the fact it'd remained unscathed by the tornado's furious assault. It was here that I discussed Bobby's disappearance with my brother. He recalled hearing something about it on the news one night, though he hadn't paid enough attention at the time. I shared what I'd learned about Bobby's abduction in Mississippi, including the stuff about the reptilian tracks and the newly discovered hot spring in Bienville National Forest.

"He asked me where I'd obtained my information, since he was unaware of most of what I told him. I confessed that for the most part it'd come from *The Star* and the *National Enquirer*. My brother looked at me as if trying to decide whether he should burst out laughing or scold me instead.

"'You've got to be fucking kidding!' he told me. 'You got your facts straight from a couple of grocery store tabloids?' He threw his head back and laughed heartily, he was so tickled at this.

"'Jack, they're goddamn gossip papers for Christ's sake!' he scoffed, looking at me incredulously. 'You've got to be careful what you read into that shit, man! I mean, come on, was the article you read plastered right smack between the story about the baby with three heads and another stating Elvis is alive and well amongst the Aborigines?' He placed his hands on his hips in an effort to keep from doubling over in his amusement, his face wearing the smirk I'd learned to loathe so dearly.

"I was infuriated, but I couldn't think of anything to refute his point. I decided right then to show him some hard evidence instead. I was pretty sure that for whatever happened in Mississippi to occur, something significant would've had to happen first in our area. I knew

I'd find some evidence in the clearing.

"Jeremy agreed to let me try and prove my theory, still chuckling to himself as we got back in his truck. Unbeknownst to us at the time, that'd be the last time we ever visited our old property. I'm glad I got one last good look at it as we drove away. I believe the image of our decimated yard will remain with me forever.

"'Jack, even if that stuff you told me about had been in the '*Constitution*' or the '*Herald*', or even in *USA Today*, you've still got to be careful,' Jeremy told me as we turned onto Baileys Bend Road, his brotherly admonishment not yet finished. 'I'd take all that pseudo-journalistic crap with a grain of salt if I were you.'

"'All right,' I said. 'But, do you think you can wait and see what we find out before you lecture me some more?'

"He eyed me like our grandfather so often eyed him, as if wondering whether my remark was smart enough to warrant a solid backhand across my mouth. When he looked away and back to the road, I could tell he was still debating the issue. He continued to do that as we turned onto Black Warrior Road. But as soon as we reached the spot where the old bridge once stood, he completely forgot my remarks, as did I.

"In place of the rickety wooden structure stood a brand new one, and what a new one at that! It was colorful and fancy, and looked like something straight out of Disneyworld. It was wide enough to allow for two vehicles to travel along its length side by side, and it had a chain barrier across its opening with a sign advising all trespassers to keep out. Of course, at the time, we had no idea Malcolm Donohue owned most of the area by then.

"'The barrier was enough to keep us from driving the truck across the river, though it didn't deter us from crossing by foot. After parking the truck near the same spot we left Grandpa's Jeep four months earlier, we set out across the bridge and reached the clearing a short while later, where even more surprises awaited us.

"Just as the tornado flattened our property, the landscape here was likewise altered. But, rather than by nature or a supernatural force, it was done by other people. Two bulldozers and a backhoe were parked near the middle of the clearing, and the fort remains and rock formation had been reduced to two piles of rubble. The entire area was barren, as the land was recently graded. Only the Indian burial mounds and the surrounding woods that bordered the clearing were spared.

"I walked toward what was left of the rock formation, with Jeremy limping after me once he realized where I was headed. His knee still bothered him quite a bit back then, as it ended up taking a good year for him to be able to walk pain free. '"What's up, Jackie?' he asked, slightly winded once he caught up with me.

"'I've got a hunch, based on the so-called 'pseudo-journalism' I told you about a short while ago,' I told him, and then hurried over to the pile of dirt and rock fragments that sat where the hot spring and rock formation once sat. It took me a moment to locate what I was searching for, which was the remains of the two pools from the hot spring. Both were full of dirt and debris. Only the slight gurgle of the ancient tiny brook that'd fed the hot spring remained, leaving a small puddle in the center of the main pool.

"'*Well??*' he demanded, when he caught up to me again.

"'It all fits, Jeremy. It all makes perfect sense now,' I said. I pointed to the puddle and then briefly explained what it had to do with the tabloid stories. It was obvious the machinery surrounding us couldn't have shut down the hot spring, despite the damage it'd definitely wrought upon the rock formation itself. Whatever had provided the thermal energy for the pools had definitely left the area, and I was determined to prove to him that it'd moved on to Mississippi.

"'I'll grant you it's not a good idea to rely on tabloid shit for your news coverage, but it brought me here. Right?' I remember telling him. 'What about all of *this*, man? Where do you think the hot spring went? Don't you think it's possible it could've gone someplace else? And one just happened to be discovered last month where it didn't exist before?

"'I'd bet Grandpa would think the same thing as me,' I continued. 'I'll even bet the folks who've gone to the trouble of tearing this place up know something about this, too. I mean, why would they go and do all of this work to the area now, in the middle of nowhere, after it's been neglected for so long? Don't you see the strange connection in all of this? You should at least be open to what I'm thinking after all we've been through this year.'

"I turned away for a moment, allowing my gaze to wander throughout the area. It always fascinated me how sparse the wooded areas in southern Alabama would look in late fall and throughout the winter, as compared to spring and on throughout the summer months. I could see for quite a distance in any direction. But I clearly recalled this very place in summer, when visibility beyond a few feet into the dense foliage was a virtual impossibility. 'I think you do believe it, too, Jeremy,' I told him as I turned back to face him. 'I'd bet money on it that you do.'

"Jeremy just snickered and shook his head. 'Well, we might never know for sure on that, Jackie boy.'

"'Why not?'

"'Well for one thing, I rarely kiss and tell,' he told me, smiling wryly. 'But for another, we've got company.' He pointed to a figure in a flannel shirt and hunters cap carrying a rifle with a scope mounted on it, climbing over the Indian burial mounds located just south of the clearing. Once the man reached the bottom of the last mound, he ran toward us.

"'We better get the hell out of here!' urged my brother, limping even more noticeably as we raced out of the clearing. From behind us, we heard a loud report from the rifle the man carried, though we didn't hear a bullet whistle by. I figure he shot a warning toward the sky. But he didn't need to worry, for we weren't planning to stay or even go back there anytime soon. We didn't slow down until we reached Jeremy's truck on the other side of the river.

"We sped out of there and didn't slow down until we were on Baileys Bend Road again, all the while checking our rearview mirrors to see if anyone followed us. We struggled to catch our breath as our run had been damn near a mile, and streams of sweat ran down our faces.

"'*Whew-w-w!!! That* was close!' I said, relieved the danger was safely behind us.

"'I wonder what that fucker was up to back there, anyway?' said Jeremy. 'Hunting Season's over now, isn't it?'

"'I believe it ended last week,' I replied.

"'Perhaps that stuff sitting in the clearing was his, or at least his to guard,' said Jeremy. 'I couldn't see his face too well, but from where we were standing, he looked pretty pissed.'

"'We better let Grandpa know about this.'

"'Why? It'll just upset him because he'll know we were there. I think that's a bad idea.'

"'I think we should tell him regardless, Jeremy,' I countered, turning toward him to better emphasize my point. 'He'd be mad just a little, since I'm sure he'd appreciate the information we'd be sharing with him.'

"'We'll see,' he sighed. 'I still think it's a bad idea, but let's think on it until we get home. Okay?'

"I agreed to wait, and before long we were heading north on Highway Forty-three. For the next half hour, we rode together in silence. I let my mind drift back to the first time I met Genovene near the river's edge. If I'd only known then what I know now. The whole mess could've been avoided.

"'You're thinking about all of this shit, too, huh?' Jeremy suddenly asked me, as he watched me stare absently through the passenger-side window.

"'Uh-huh. I'm just trying to make sense of it all,' I told him.

"'Well, don't kill yourself trying to do that, Jackie,' he said. 'I think we may never know what the fuck's going on with all the bullshit happening around here.'

"'I guess you're right about that,' I said. 'So, you don't think things will ever change, huh? I mean, do you believe we'll ever get back to having a normal life like everybody else?' I turned to see his reaction to what I just said. He smiled weakly. The look on his face was one of curious admiration, like he was truly growing to like me despite every effort on his part to see me like he once did. But things had changed significantly since then, as life had changed. More importantly, *I'd* changed, and had a more detached outlook on life.

"'I seriously doubt it, Jackie,' he said. 'Sorry I can't offer you a rainbow and sunshine in regard to our future, but that's just the way I see it.'

"'Yeah, I figured as much,' I sighed in disappointment. 'I just hope you're wrong.'

"'Me, too, Jackie—*Goddamn it!! Here they come again!!*' Jeremy grimaced into the rearview mirror and stepped harder on the gas. I looked into the passenger-side mirror and craned my neck to confirm the dark sedan that'd snuck onto the highway behind us.

"No matter how fast or slow we traveled, the mysterious sedan kept pace with us, several car lengths behind us. Jeremy launched into one of his worst profanity-laced tirades. He pushed the throttle even harder, and the truck roared along the highway. Even so, the sedan closed the gap between us to less than a hundred feet. It was as if the car's occupants wanted to reaffirm to us that we couldn't escape their surveillance. They stayed with us until we were just a few miles from our uncle and aunt's home. Then, it steadily fell back until it disappeared from our view.

"We did end up telling Grandpa about our little adventure, but not until Christmas that year. Since we weren't planning on ever going back to Carlsdale, he was pretty understanding about it all, readily forgiving us for our broken promises to him.

"The continual surveillance lasted for the next few years, even after Grandpa purchased a new home for us in Tuscaloosa. It was a lot smaller than our beloved farmhouse, but Grandpa seemed okay with the three-bedroom bungalow located near the southern outskirts of the city. The house itself was another old one, built in the late nineteenth century, and he said it reminded him of the home he and our grandma first purchased in Carlsdale shortly after they got married.

"I was fortunate to do well in both athletics and my schoolwork at St. Andrews, and elected to attend the University of Alabama on a full-ride baseball scholarship. Meanwhile, Grandpa and I were just as proud of Jeremy for straightening out his life and for his newfound ambitions. I damn near had to pinch myself when he raced through Alabama's undergraduate program in three years, maintaining a near perfect 4.0 GPA. And, now he's doing the same thing while finishing work on his master's degree in ancient studies at the University's graduate program.

"I guess that pretty much brings us up to date, Agen—I mean, Peter, " said Jack. He settled back in his chair again, only this time he felt relieved. He felt a little euphoric as well. The revelation of so many secrets to a complete stranger seemed to lift a burden from his soul.

"Wow, absolutely incredible story, Jack!" Peter enthused. He stood up and walked over to the coffee machine and threw his empty coffee cup into the nearly full wastebasket next to it. He then came back to the table, where he leaned down and turned the recorder off. "I'll be right back. I've gotta go again," he advised, motioning his head toward the restroom. "When I return, we'll wrap things up and get out of here. If that's all right with you."

"Yeah, that's fine," said Jack. He watched the agent disappear into the restroom, feeling confident he and Jeremy would return home to Tuscaloosa by the next day at the latest. But he worried about Jeremy's reaction to the fact he'd broken the vow of silence they shared with their grandfather.

Soon Peter returned to his seat at the table, armed with a fresh cup of coffee. "Do you want anything more to drink, Jack?" he asked.

"Nah, I'm fine."

"Are you sure?"

"Yeah. But, I'm just about ready for dinner."

"Me, too, brother. Me too." Peter smiled and stirred a small packet of cream into his steaming cup, breaking his routine by adding something to his usual black coffee. "I must say you've been very helpful, especially to me personally, Jack. I'm very grateful for the information you've provided me," he said, removing the recorder from the table and placing it back inside the duffel bag. He then folded his hands in front of himself on the table. "As I told you earlier, it's my turn to provide you with some meaningful information."

"Does that mean I get to check out those two books now?" asked Jack.

"Well, to be honest with you, I'd rather you wait to check them out while we're driving you guys to the airport," he said, frowning slightly as he glanced at his wristwatch. "Actually, I'd really like for you and Jeremy to accompany me to Richmond tonight, and then fly home from there tomorrow. In fact, I'd *truly* appreciate it if you'd do this, because I'd like to introduce you to my boss, Stu Johnson. He might even grant you access to some of the more interesting items locked away in our archives. At least it would give you more time to review these books."

"This isn't the same 'Stu Johnson' my grandfather referred to in his story, is it?" Jack's face immediately became clouded with suspicion while Peter was taken back by the implications in his question. The agent looked as if he never even considered this thought before now, and after a moment spent silently debating this idea he laughed nervously to himself. His radiant smile soon returned, and he eyed Jack in much the same way a loving parent would eye their young child who claimed to have found a boogey man lying in wait under the bed.

"No, Jack. I'm positive they're not the same person," he assured him. "For one thing, it takes a long time to move up in the ranks of any federal agency, and if we do the math involved here, the 'Stu Johnson' your grandpa knew would have had to be with us for at least a decade before he encountered him, say what...twenty years ago? Yeah, that would be right, because the report on the sphere was published in 1987.

"The 'Stu Johnson' I work for has been with us for just twenty-two years, and would've been a kid practically fresh out of college if he was in fact the FBI agent who set your grandpa off so badly back then. It's just not possible. Besides, I'd be willing to bet we've had many guys with that name who've worked for our agency over the years." Peter straightened himself in his chair, keeping his hands folded together just beyond his cup of coffee, in affect corralling it with his arms. If it weren't for the sincerity that exuded powerfully from him, Jack would've lumped him right then with the life insurance salesmen who used to call on his grandfather in recent years.

"You'd like the man I work for, I guarantee it," Peter continued. "He's a great guy, and is one of the most compassionate men I've ever been around. He took me under his wing when I began my career, after my father introduced him to me down in New Orleans. Then, after he was promoted to our Richmond office, he recruited me specifically to assist him with the 'unusual' cases we have that deal with the paranormal. He has the same level of passion for this kind of thing I have, and was the one who told me you and your brother were here. In fact, he arranged for this very interview. I'm sure you'll find him to be a powerful ally for you and your family."

Jack wasn't sure what to think of this information on Stu Johnson. On the one hand, he trusted Peter's sincerity, knowing the agent believed in what he was telling him. But on the other hand, he wasn't so sure the 'Stu Johnson' who kept his grandfather prisoner in his own house for three months nearly twenty years ago was in fact a different man. Peter's argument that his boss would've been too young for such an assignment didn't convince Jack in the least. The strongest evidence for this was sitting across the table in the person of Peter himself. Jack knew the man was at most a few years older than he, and had been handed a fairly high-profile investigation. Even the senior agents present earlier deferred to the much younger agent from their Richmond office the very instant he entered the interrogation room.

Jack's stomach began to rumble loudly, so he decided the issue wasn't worth worrying about. "Perhaps you're right," he said. "As far as the trip to Richmond is concerned, I'd like to do that. I'll need to check with Jeremy first to make sure it's okay with him."

"That's fine. I certainly understand," said Peter. "I'll get the ball rolling to get you both out of here shortly, after I share a few things with you." He leaned in closer, just enough to show that what he was about to tell him was quite important. "I'll start with a curious item or two, and then I'll wrap it up with some current events I want you to keep in mind as you return home. First, I've got another interesting tidbit concerning the tool shed. Since you haven't been back to Carlsdale lately, I doubt you know about this.

"Malcolm Donohue apparently felt it was an eyesore, though surely he knew something of its strange history when he bought your place. My guess is he didn't know near as much as we do, since he tried to move it. The structure is anchored in bedrock, Jack, which you might not be aware of. After considerable effort and expense, Mr. Donohue obtained the means to remove it from the property. No sooner than his people dug it up, loaded it onto a flatbed truck, and then hauled it away, the mysterious structure somehow made it back to the exact spot where it had rested before."

"You're kidding?" Jack felt envious of anyone who got to see this happen.

"No, it's true," said Peter. "Mr. Donohue had guards stationed on the property, perhaps related to the gunman you and Jeremy encountered. They followed the truck as it turned onto Lelan's Road, and before they made it back to their post, they saw the tool shed or whatever this structure really is sitting in its original spot. It's still there today. Mr. Donohue decided to leave it where it is, covering it with a facade in the 'Honey Bear' children's section of his amusement park."

"That's fucking amazing," Jack whispered, shaking his head as he pictured this. "Actually, it's damned near unbelievable!"

"Yeah, it is," agreed Peter. "I thought you'd get a kick out of that." He suddenly grew silent and frowned slightly, and eyed Jack seriously before speaking again. "Since the moment I found out you were here, I've debated whether or not to tell you what I have on my mind. It could potentially piss off some of my colleagues, I suppose. But it's something you really should be aware of. Who knows? Perhaps the bureau will see it from my perspective, that letting you in on some events headed our way may actually help us figure out how to effectively deal with them."

"What are you talking about?" asked Jack.

"Do you remember hearing about the luxury cruise ship, *The Escapade*, that went down near the West African coastline early last week?"

"Yeah, I do," replied Jack, wondering what this had to do with their present discussion. "Only thirty-one people survived. I believe that was what the news report said."

"Thirty-two, actually," Peter confirmed, clearing his throat before continuing. "The official report stated that part of the ship's structure came apart, and as a result, the vessel sunk within a minute. Six of the survivors, the only ones on deck at the time, reported to the Moroccan authorities who handled the original investigation that a massive structure which gleamed in the moonlight rammed through the middle of *The Escapade*, effectively cutting it into two pieces. As these terrified passengers frantically scurried for their lives, they watched this tower of gold clear the ship's debris. It soon faded and vanished within seconds, perhaps disappearing down into the depths of the Atlantic Ocean, the sinking halves of the ship being the only other proof for its existence."

"I take it this tower was like the one I told you about tonight," observed Jack, fearing the obvious answer.

"Yes, but there's much more," the agent advised, smiling grimly. "Throughout the world there have been other sightings like this. The majority of these instances have taken place in rather remote areas with either poor news reporting facilities or minimal casualties, except for the cruise ship. All in all, at this time we feel we have accurately identified eight of these magnificent towers on the move around the globe."

"There are *eight* of them??"

"Yes." Peter sighed and picked up his other journal, paging to a section where several pages were paper-clipped together. He removed the clip and separated the pages, holding them loosely in his hand. "Perhaps the best way to explain all of this is to tell you a little about each individual tower. I just told you about the one that sliced through *The Escapade*, which was last sighted to the west of the Canary Islands off the coast of Morocco. We have reason to believe this one originated in Egypt near the Sphinx in the Sahara Desert. The other sightings of it have been described as a 'towering golden windstorm in the sand' as it crossed the African continent through Libya and Algeria before crossing Morocco on its way to the Atlantic Ocean.

"The next one's also from Africa, although much further south. It apparently originated near the Congo River in Zaire, traveling to the west coast of the continent before adjusting its course toward the north. It reached the Atlantic Ocean along Africa's western coastline, but re-entered the mainland as it cut a destructive path through the Ivory Coast and Guinea as a 'shimmering golden hurricane'. It moved northwest from that point before disappearing into the Gulf of Guinea.

"We've confirmed there are two more of these things moving toward the west from the Middle East as well, although at first we thought there was only one from this region. The first originated in western Jordan near Jerusalem, crossing quickly through Israel and on into the Mediterranean Sea. We believe the second one originated in Iraq near the city of Karbala, which is southwest of Baghdad. It traveled through Syria as it also headed to the Mediterranean Sea. We have unconfirmed reports that this one's travel path was witnessed by thousands of Iraqis, but the new Iraqi government quickly moved in to eliminate any evidence confirming its existence. With the tense religious climate throughout that area these days, I'm sure they feared something this amazing would cause a major uproar, both politically and culturally. In addition to this information, we've just confirmed another report that says this particular tower demolished a Turkish destroyer, killing nearly six hundred sailors before it disappeared into the Mediterranean.

"Both of these structures re-emerged side by side as they passed through the shallower waters of the Straits of Gibraltar on their way to the Atlantic Ocean. These things move quickly, then disappear completely once reaching the ocean. Because of this, proof is hard to come by." Peter stopped for a moment, looking warily toward the wall to his left. When he turned back to Jack, he leaned in even closer. "I need to speed this up, I'm afraid," he said. "We've identified four other towers as well. One is traveling north from Peru and had already moved through Columbia about a week ago before it submerged itself within the depths of the Atlantic. Despite briefly losing track of it, we received recent confirmation from our intelligence sources that its present location is now somewhere near the western coastline of Cuba, and it should reach the Gulf of Mexico in the next day or so.

"Two other towers are presently in the Pacific Ocean. The first originated from either India or Burma. Our intelligence reports haven't been able to pinpoint the exact starting point for this one yet. Last week it was witnessed on several occasions from the water as it moved through the South China Sea on its way past the Philippine Islands.

"As far as the other structure is concerned, the seventh obelisk, we feel certain it's presently moving through the Pacific Ocean toward Mexico after it first originated in China, with the most educated guess being central Mongolia. We almost missed out entirely on any information concerning this tower as the Chinese government managed to keep news of its existence a complete secret until it passed Peking on its way into Korea. Once it hit the water, it was spotted by a number of Shanghai fishermen in the East China Sea just south of Japan. Apparently, some of them followed it from a safe distance until it disappeared into the Pacific. Interestingly, this one's path is slightly off course from the others. Unless it's rendezvous point is intended to be with the others moving across the Atlantic"

Peter paused and helped himself to a hearty drink from his cup of coffee that had cooled substantially since he first poured it a short while ago. Again, he glanced warily at the wall and seemed reluctant to reveal anything further to Jack.

"That makes seven. Where's the eighth one coming from?" Jack finally asked. When Peter didn't immediately address his question, he pushed further. "The last one's in Mississippi, isn't it?"

"Yes," said Peter, obviously pleased he didn't have to spell it out for him.

"So, is it safe to assume all of them are headed, at some point, for the States, and that they're likely going to meet up in Mississippi?"

"Not bad, Jack. Not bad, at all!" Peter congratulated him, smiling again, though still apprehensive. "You're close. But there's one other thing involved here. The tower in Mississippi, which is surely the same one we've discussed this evening, is also on the move."

"Really? Where's it headed?"

"Oh, I suppose it's picked an old familiar place to meet up with the others." Peter smiled wryly, as if Jack should be able to easily figure this out on his own. Once Jack realized this expectation, the answer became glaringly obvious.

"*Alabama?*" Jack blurted out suddenly. "They're all headed *there?*"

"Yes," Peter replied evenly. "That's the apparent destination, as far as our best analysts can tell."

Jack didn't know how to respond to this news, shaking his head in disbelief as the agent continued.

"Obviously, we've got one hell of a problem on our hands," said Peter. "We're pretty goddamned nervous about the whole affair, and wondering who or what in the hell is directing these giant monoliths toward us. It's tough to comprehend a phenomenon like this when there's been nothing like it in modern times.

"To make matters worse, governments throughout the world—including the Middle Eastern powers we're frequently at odds with and our tenuous allies—have been monitoring the path of the towers outside of the United States. Islamic extremists are already celebrating what they believe is Allah's wrath and final judgment upon the United States, since they feel these structures have been sent by God to punish us for our imperialistic meddling in their business."

Peter stood up and walked around the table to where Jack sat. He looked down at Jack, who in turn silently studied the agent. The smile on Peter's face suddenly faded. Some unaddressed issue simmered just below the surface of his carefree facade, which now barely camouflaged the debate he had waged within himself since even before their interview began several hours ago.

"I'm going to cut to the chase and tell you why you and your brother were brought here in the first place," Peter sighed softly. " While it definitely has everything to do with Dr. Oscar Mensch, it has nothing to do with his death. We know you didn't kill him, and we know Jeremy wasn't involved with the professor's death either." He moved away from the table and leaned up against the wall, staring down at the floor while he gathered his thoughts.

"Roughly within the same time frame that these sightings began, we have proof Dr. Mensch received a package from one of his longtime acquaintances in Pakistan," he said. "I know you and your brother were very close to this man, but I can tell you he's got some stuff in his past that would shock you. I've already given you far more information than my superiors would've liked, so I'm going to honor their wishes and not detail any of the shit he has dabbled in over the years. Suffice it to say, he was on the lam internationally when he re-emerged as a professor at the University of Alabama—please, don't ask me to explain any of this right now, Jack—."

"I'm not, Peter," Jack interrupted him. "I just want to know what was sent to him. I mean, was it some deadly virus or chemicals, or the ingredients to a bomb?"

Peter returned to his chair as he studied Jack, a deeply perplexed look upon his face. "You have no idea, do you?" he finally asked him. "Surely you know it wouldn't have to be a weapon to get him in trouble with the law, being that anything coming into our country from Pakistan is considered suspicious in nature. We don't believe it was a weapon, at least not in the conventional sense. But, a strong case can be made for a weapon if it turns out these towers are on a hostile mission to our country. After all, they did all suddenly appear and start moving toward us within days of Dr. Mensch receiving the mysterious package. If we only knew where to look for it, or better yet *what* to look for, we might finally get a handle on this."

"I wish I could help you," offered Jack, extremely puzzled by this information. "I honestly didn't see any package when I found him bleeding in his living room, and he never mentioned anything like it to me in the hospital either. Do you know when he would've received it?"

"We're fairly certain he got it two to three days prior to the beating he received in his home," said Peter.

Jack didn't have a single clue as to where the mysterious item or items could be. He was having a hard enough time picturing Dr. Mensch as a villain who may have intentionally set a terrible chain of events in motion. It would've been easier to believe the legendary Mother Theresa once lived her life as an international terrorist in disguise.

Aside from that, Genovene was on her way back to Alabama. Was she coming in response to Dr. Mensch's invitation as well? The answer sat just outside the reach of his awareness, and he was far too distracted at the moment to retrieve it. In frustration he abruptly stood up. "This is all *so* fucked up!" he fumed, and began pacing back and forth behind his chair.

"I'm truly sorry to be the bearer of bad news in regard to your friend," said Peter. "But hopefully you'll thank me later, especially if you happen to think of anything that can help us. You will do that for me, won't you, Jack?"

He stopped pacing long enough to nod he would.

"We believe the assassins responsible for Dr. Mensch's torture and death were also looking for this package and its mysterious contents."

Jack stopped and glared at Peter. "So, you know who killed him?" he asked accusingly.

"Yes," the agent replied softly. "But, as it's difficult to prove, I'm not at liberty to divulge the group's identity. Let's just say these folks have a vested religious and political interest in making sure whatever was taken from Pakistan is safely returned to that country. If we'd been able to capture and detain these individuals, we wouldn't have bothered to bring you and Jeremy out here. Although, as I said earlier, I'm grateful for the information you've shared with me. Maybe I'll have a real chance to heal and find the happiness I long for, Jack."

Peter's words rang true to Jack, and after considering all that had taken place since he came to his rescue earlier that evening, Jack returned to his seat, smiling wanly at the agent across from him.

"Why don't we stop here and go get a bite to eat?"

"I'd say that's an excellent idea."

"All right then. I'll get yours and Jeremy's clearance taken care of," Peter advised. He finished packing his duffel bag and attaché case, and then stood up, extending his hand for Jack to shake. This time, Jack readily grasped his hand, responding to the agent's strong grip with his own. "It has been a pleasure to visit with you these past few hours, Jack," said Peter. "I'm sure you'll enjoy coming to Richmond with me if your brother consents."

"I hope he does, Peter,' said Jack. "I honestly mean that."

The agent smiled warmly and Jack flashed his own handsome smile in return.

"It shouldn't take us more than twenty minutes to get out of here, once the necessary paperwork is completed and signed," Peter told him. He headed for the door with his duffel bag and attaché case. Just as he opened the door to leave, he turned to face Jack one last time. "The ride to Richmond takes a couple of hours, so you should get a good opportunity to look over the books on the way down there. If Jeremy is anxious to get home tonight instead, you'll still have roughly an hour or so to view them on the way to the airport in Washington. Thanks again for your cooperation this evening." Peter McNamee saluted him, and Jack nodded in return. A moment later, the heavy security door slammed shut with a resounding thud, and Jack Kenney had the entire interrogation room to himself.

PART VIII

The Aftermath

Jack wandered aimlessly around the room while waiting for Agent McNamee's return. At one point he was tempted to get a better look at the wall Peter frequently glanced at, but then thought better of it. The mental image of being scrutinized by some unseen voyeur deterred him.

Once he figured twenty minutes had passed, he returned to the table and turned his chair toward the door. He sat down and absently drummed his fingers upon the tabletop. God, how he missed his watch! Irritated, he wondered what was taking the agent so long. Irritation gave way to worry until suddenly the door swung open. The screech from the door's weight made him jump up out of his chair.

Agent Ben Casey strolled into the room carrying a pair of handcuffs by his side. The cuffs clanked together softly as he walked over to Jack, his face expressionless and his eyes as cold as they were earlier that day. Filled with unease by Agent Casey's nonchalance and Peter's absence, Jack stepped back from the approaching agent.

"You're cleared to leave, Mr. Kenney," Agent Casey informed him, the meanness of his look transferring easily into his acidic tone of voice. "You'll need to put these on again until we're safely removed from the premises. Standard protocol."

Jack nodded warily and moved over to the agent, who motioned for him to stop where he was.

"Where's Peter?" asked Jack.

"You'll be joining him shortly," advised the agent. "He'll be waiting for you at our destination."

"And, Jeremy?"

"He's waiting in your car, now."

Jack stuck his arms out in front of him, indicating he was ready to be cuffed.

"Uh-uh-uh," chided Agent Casey. "Turn around with your arms outstretched behind your back." Warily, Jack did as he was instructed. He felt the coldness of the steel around his wrists and then heard the click as they fastened. "Now, face me and we'll be on our way."

Jack turned to face him. The agent grabbed him roughly by his right arm and led him out of the interrogation room. From there, the two walked down a long corridor with armed guards posted at various points along the corridor's length. As they passed these guards, each one exchanged nods with the agent, but stared straight ahead as Jack passed by. He wondered if the same silent communication took place when he first arrived at this building, since he was blindfolded without any sense of the guards' presence.

At the end of the corridor was a flight of stairs that led up to the building's main level. Even though the guards posted here seemed to know Agent Casey fairly well, they still verified his I.D. badge before stepping aside for him. The agent led Jack up the stairs and over to the building's exit, where the last four guards awaited them. They stood solemnly at attention while Agent Casey placed his badge into the security slot next to the door.

Unlike the previous access points, this one also contained a retinal scanner. A thin green beam of light flashed into Agent Casey's right eye, and once his physical identity was confirmed, the door slid open. He nodded to the guards, who again acknowledged his presence while ignoring Jack. The two then stepped out of the building and into a small parking area.

Except for a single lamp above their heads, the area was shrouded in darkness. If it weren't for the taillights and soft engine purr from the pair of sedans parked just in front of them, Jack wouldn't have been able to tell either car's location. It seemed to him that the center's location must be somewhere remote. Yet, it still had to be accessible to a metropolitan area for Peter to have mentioned Richmond's close proximity.

The front passenger door from the closest sedan swung open and Agent Steve Iverson stepped out of the vehicle. Jack immediately felt a lump form in his throat that grew even larger as the dome light illuminated the car's other occupants. Agent Frank Reynolds' massive frame was squeezed into the driver's seat, and Jeremy was seated directly behind him. The sullen anger on his brother's face let Jack know he had an urgent bone to pick with him.

"It's so good to see you again, Jack! Did you miss me?" taunted Agent Iverson. "I believe your brother's *really* missed you, because he sure seems anxious to talk with you!" He moved over to the sedan's rear door and opened it, motioning for Jack to join Jeremy in the back seat. "Bring him over, Ben, so we can get moving!"

Agent Casey shoved Jack toward the open door, and as soon as he was close enough, Agent Iverson grabbed Jack by the shirt and threw him into the back seat. Before he could sit up straight, both agents moved in and secured his seat belt tight enough to completely restrict his arms.

Confused by the rough treatment, Jack glanced at his brother hoping he could provide an explanation. He was shocked to see Jeremy's upper lip was bleeding and a pair of welts just below his eyes.

"Ben, you're riding with Bo Cochran," said Agent Iverson. "We'll follow you over there."

"So, Bo's coming along for this after all?" Agent Casey sounded amused as he stepped away from the car. In the soft glow provided by the dome light, Jack could see the perplexed look on his face.

"He needs to be there—just like the rest of us!" Agent Iverson eyed Agent Casey sternly until he nodded obediently and walked over to the other sedan. The rear passenger door slammed shut and Steve Iverson climbed into the front passenger seat. Once he closed his door, the dome light slowly dimmed to darkness.

Agents Reynolds and Iverson turned to face the brothers. Jack immediately looked down. He felt vulnerable and ill prepared to face the hostile glare from either man. He chanced another look at his brother and was surprised to find Jeremy glared at him as well.

"You told them, didn't you?" Jeremy sneered disgustedly.

"Told them *what*?" replied Jack.

"Your story, Jack. Your *goddamn* story!"

"I...I didn't tell them everything, Jeremy. *Honest!*" he said. "I only talked to Agent McNamee—I swear, man!"

"Ah, but you knew we were listening in, didn't you?" said Agent Reynolds, smiling in amusement at the potential fight brewing between the brothers. "That was quite a tale, I might add. Though, definitely worth keeping to one's self."

Jeremy looked away from Jack and studied Reynold's face in the sparse illumination provided by the car's dashboard.

"Yeah, I'd have to agree with both your brother and Frank here," Agent Iverson added, snickering as he turned to face the other sedan, which had begun to creep along a dim driveway. "I'd say you're pretty much fucked, now!"

"*What??* Where's Peter? I want to speak with him *right now!!*" demanded Jack.

Frank Reynolds turned to face the driveway and soon followed the other vehicle's lead.

"Why'd you do it?" Jeremy lamented, his voice barely above a whisper. His anger had changed to bewilderment. "Why in the hell did you tell this Agent McNamee anything at all, Jackie?"

"Jeremy, we can trust him—I'm sure of it!" implored Jack. "It's these other guys I'm not sure abou—."

"*Damn it, Jackie, stop!!*" Jeremy interrupted him. "You're so fucking naïve, man! I mean, he's one of *them*, just like these fine gentlemen sitting here with us!" He motioned with his head to the front seat where the two agents glared at him.

Meanwhile, the sedans reached the end of the driveway, where it forked into two roads. The sign on the left said 'Manassas Municipal Airport, 13 miles'. The one on the right said 'Manassas Park, 3 miles'. In between these roads sat a guard station.

A retractable barrier fence blocked both roads, and an armed guard stood on either side of the station. The lead sedan pulled up to the small building, and a large black man stuck his head out through the driver side window. In the bright glow provided by the station's lights, Jack saw Agent Casey sitting in the passenger side of the vehicle. Since no one else was in the sedan, the driver could only be the agent the others referred to as Bo Cochran.

The guard speaking with Agent Cochran motioned for him to continue to the right, as the barrier began to slide open. As soon as the lead sedan moved through the open gateway, the guard motioned for the other sedan to follow. Both automobiles turned onto a deserted dirt road located a short distance away.

"Don't you get it, Jackie?" Jeremy continued. "I mean, for one thing, they don't seem too worried about what we can see. Granted, it's nighttime. Nevertheless, you and I know a lot more about the place we were taken to now than when we first got here. Right?"

Jack nodded. They both were blindfolded when they left Alabama two days before. 'Standard protocol' was the phrase Agent Casey used then as well.

"How do you think I got these 'beauty marks'?" asked Jeremy, tilting his face toward Jack so he could get a closer look at the matching pair of welts under his eyes and his split upper lip. "I bet they figured I was free for the taking once you started talking, roughly four hours ago by my estimation. And here's the kicker, little brother. You can bet every penny your worth that there's a pair of bullets nearby with yours and my name on them."

Jack stared at Jeremy in disbelief. He had expected a pleasant ride, either to the airport in D.C., or down to Richmond with Agent McNamee. His mind was filled with eager anticipation at the mere thought of being allowed to review the books in Peter's possession. To be so cruelly duped by the agent seemed incomprehensible to him. He slumped in silence while Jeremy mumbled softly to himself.

Suddenly, the car started shaking as both sedans pulled onto another road. This one was deeply rutted, and the group traveled for nearly a minute like this in the country darkness until both vehicles came to an abrupt halt.

A cloud of dust splashed up against the car's windows. When it cleared, Jack could see the lead sedan in the headlight's beams. Both Agent Cochran and Agent Casey had stepped out of their car and were on the way over to them. Cochran carried a semi-automatic pistol equipped with a long silencer.

"Well, I guess this is the end of the line for you boys," Reynolds advised, unlatching his seat belt. He drew a 9mm pistol from his jacket and released the safety. An instant later, Iverson did the same thing, eyeing Jack in such a way that sent an icy shiver down his spine. The man liked to hurt people, and if he could somehow create an excruciatingly painful demise for him and Jeremy, he would surely do just that.

Jack straightened up and looked over at his brother again. For the first time in years he sensed fear building within Jeremy. But, he still held out hope that Peter would resolve this if only he could speak with him. "Before you do something you're sure to regret, *please* let me talk to Peter!" he pleaded with Agent Reynolds, looking past the smirk of Iverson.

The senior agent chuckled and glanced over at his partner, who laughed lightly to himself. "What do you think, Steve?" he asked. "Should we take him over to Peter and see if he'd be willing to listen to him?"

"I don't know that Pete would care to, actually," Iverson replied, feigning an air of seriousness. "Especially after all the trouble this asshole caused him."

Cochran tapped his silencer's tip against the driver's side window, letting Reynolds know he and Casey were ready for them.

"Ah, hell, why don't we take these boys to see good ole Pete—we're coming, Bo!" said Reynolds. He and Iverson stepped out of the sedan, slamming their doors shut in unison.

"This may be it, Jackie," Jeremy sighed. "I seriously doubt they're going to wait on what your buddy has to say." He looked over at his younger brother for what he thought was the last time. Jack was immediately overwhelmed by the sadness and compassion in Jeremy's eyes. "I'm not holding anything against you," Jeremy went on. "This shit was bound to happen sooner or later."

The rear passenger doors clicked and swung open. Jeremy struggled to smile and Jack bit his bottom lip to keep from crying.

"I love you, Jeremy," said Jack.

"I know," said Jeremy. "'Same to you, bro."

Before they could say anything else, they were both yanked forcefully from the car. The immediate area around the sedan grew very dark once the vehicle's dome light dimmed and Reynolds turned off the headlights with his remote access key. The only illumination at this point came from a flashlight held by Casey.

"Bo and Ben...these boys want to have a word with Peter before we bid them 'adieu'. It shouldn't take long, I imagine," said Agent Reynolds. "Why don't you bring that light over here for a moment, Ben."

The agents prodded the brothers toward the rear of the car. Reynolds directed Casey to point the beam from his flashlight just above the trunk, which was slightly ajar. He raised the trunk's lid slowly, grinning maliciously.

Once the trunk was fully exposed, all Jack and Jeremy could do was stare at its contents in horror. Sprawled out before them, amid a tire jack, shovel, and three twenty-pound bags of lime, lay the stiffening corpse of Peter McNamee. With his face frozen in a silent scream, a small river of blood had already congealed just below the bullet wound in his left eye socket.

Jack gazed helplessly upon the dead body of the only remaining hope he and Jeremy had for escaping their present predicament alive. He saw that Agent McNamee died without a struggle, for his designer suit, shirt, and tie were unruffled, nearly as neat and pressed as they had been when he first arrived that evening.

"Go ahead, Jack, ask away!" encouraged Reynolds. "Ask to your heart's content, but don't take too long. Save a moment for your last words to your creator."

"We're so *fucked!*" Jeremy whispered, unable to remove his eyes from the gruesome sight before him.

Casey moved closer to the trunk, when suddenly the light flickered out. Immediately, everything was cast into thick darkness where none of the men could see one another. An instant later, the flashlight flickered back on and its beam returned to full strength.

"I thought you said that goddamned thing was brand new, Ben!" Reynolds scolded him, visibly irritated by what just happened.

"It is, Frank," Casey replied, grimacing from his boss's rebuke. "Maybe it's a lemon. Let's hope to God it's not!"

"Well, *shit!* That changes our plans a little," said Reynolds, reaching into the trunk to pull out the shovel and one of the bags of lime. "It may take us longer to take care of our business here this evening, but I'm going to make sure there are absolutely no fuck-ups with this. That means we'll dispose of these boys one at a time. Is everyone with me so far?"

The other agents told him they were.

"Good. We'll start with Jeremy," he continued. "Bo, grab Jack and throw him into the trunk for now. Then, you and Steve grab Jeremy and take him to the site."

Bo Cochran was an enormous man with incredible strength. He moved over to Jack and effortlessly lifted him off the ground, and then stuffed him inside the trunk next to Peter's body. Jack wondered why they just didn't let this behemoth twist his and Jeremy's heads off their shoulders and be on their merry way.

"Go ahead and close the trunk, Bo," Reynolds instructed. "Ben, we're going to leave you here just in case anybody stumbles upon us out here…"

The rest of the agent's words were reduced to a muffle for Jack, as the trunk's lid suddenly slammed shut. Almost immediately, the buildup of heat and lingering exhaust fumes engulfed him, along with the familiar scent of Peter McNamee's expensive cologne. Aside from the tire jack and remaining bags of lime, it was just the two of them lying side by side in the trunk: one sweating profusely from terror and the trunk's cramped oppressiveness, while the other lay rigid from the mortification process that began shortly after the bullet shredded Peter's brain.

Jack soon discerned an acrid smell among the other noxious odors permeating the trunk. He grimaced at the thought that Peter should've relieved himself one last time of the many cups of coffee he consumed during their interview. Since he couldn't move away from the agent's leaking corpse, it made the experience even worse.

He tried to distract himself by listening for noises outside the sedan. Suddenly, he heard the faint sound of gunfire. This was followed by two more evenly spaced shots, and then finally, one last report came to him. A death-like silence soon enveloped the entire area surrounding the car.

Jack squeezed his eyes tightly shut as burning tears of sorrow and fear welled and trickled down his cheek. He also felt an odd sense of pride that Jeremy didn't go down easy since there were so many shots. Then there was quiet. The unnerving stillness lasted for only a few minutes, but seemed like an eternity. At one point, he thought he heard Ben Casey call out to his comrades. Then, all grew quiet again. The wait for whatever was to come next grew unbearable.

A slight glow began to seep through the rear taillight reflector nearest to his head. Casey shouted something indiscernible just before a heavy object landed on the ground next to the sedan's rear-end. A moment later, a key jiggled inside the trunk's latch and the lid flew open, allowing a rush of fresh air and near-blinding light to fall upon Jack's face.

"Let's get the hell out of here, Jackie!" It was Jeremy, though Jack couldn't see him yet. Jeremy reached into the trunk and pulled him out. As he did, he lowered the flashlight enough for Jack to see him clearly. His handcuffs were gone and he now held the pistol with the silencer in his left had. "Stand up and turn around!"

Jack did as he was told and Jeremy quickly removed his handcuffs, tossing the keys into a nearby bush when finished. Jack noticed his brother's shirt was soaked with blood, and the wetness glistened grotesquely in the flashlight's glow.

"*What* happened? Are you all right??" asked Jack, worried by the amount of blood covering Jeremy's clothes.

"I'm fine, but there's no time to discuss anything right now," he replied. "Do you need any shit from in here?" He motioned to the open trunk, shifting the flashlight's beam to Peter's lifeless body.

Jack immediately thought of the agent's duffel bag and attaché case, probing for them with his hands around the corpse.

Jeremy only allowed him a moment to do this before nudging him on the shoulder. "Whatever it is you're looking for, you need to forget about it," he advised. "I'm serious, Jackie, we need to get the fuck out of here!"

The bag and case weren't in the trunk and Jack soon confirmed they weren't anywhere else inside the sedan either. He moved back to the rear of the sedan just as Jeremy closed the trunk. That's when he noticed Agent Casey's body lying face up on the ground.

"We're taking the other car," Jeremy advised, quickly moving to the other sedan parked a short distance away. The flashlight's beam lingered long enough on the agent to reveal several dark streams trickling down the side of the man's face.

"*Did you do that?*" Jack asked him in shock, pointing back at the lifeless form that soon was engulfed by darkness.

"Yep." said Jeremy, as he reached the other car. "Now, get your ass over here before anyone else decides to join our little 'going away' party." He moved up to the driver's side while motioning for Jack to get ready to enter the sedan on the passenger side of the vehicle. He then unlocked the door and pulled it open, but hesitated before climbing into the front seat.

"Are the others dead, too?" asked Jack.

Jeremy nodded 'yes', but then pressed the silencer's tip to his lips. "You'll have to hold your questions for now, man," he whispered. "At least until we don't need this set of wheels any longer. Get in!"

Jack wasn't sure if he could control his curiosity or not, but climbed into the car with his brother. In the brightness afforded by this sedan's dome light, he studied Jeremy more closely, noting the large amount of blood greased upon his shirt and pants. If it weren't for Jeremy's acute alertness, Jack would've never believed he escaped serious injury, based on his appearance.

Once they closed their doors, Jeremy motioned again for Jack to remain silent and then started the car, pulling the sedan back onto the bumpy dirt road that brought them to this desolate place near Manassas Park. Before long, they reached the main dirt road that would either take them back to the agency's interrogation center, or on into the park if they turned right. Jeremy rolled down his window and cut the lights off for a moment, as he listened to the air around them. Once he was satisfied there was no one from the center immediately on their way to get them, he turned right onto the road and headed toward the park.

The road soon merged with another one that was paved, and Jeremy continued to leave his window down until they were nearly a mile inside the actual park. He relaxed and looked over at Jack, smiling weakly. Jack stared back solemnly.

The sedan's dashboard was equipped with an agency communication and computer system. Jack finally looked away from his brother to study the various components attached to the dashboard. Although the system stirred his curiosity, he knew that dabbling with it might give away their location. A digital clock in the dashboard presently read 11:04 pm. He prayed the remaining hours of darkness would give them a significant head start on whoever pursued them.

Jeremy suddenly veered into an unlighted picnic area with a large restroom. He stopped the car and cut the lights. After placing the pistol underneath his seat, he motioned for Jack to get out of the car and follow him. The area seemed deserted, and Jack was grateful for Ben Casey's flashlight to illuminate their way to the restroom. They moved quickly over to the men's portion of the building and stepped inside.

"Keep a look out for me, Jackie," whispered Jeremy, once he discovered the restroom contained a shower stall. "I'm going to try to get cleaned up a little bit." He moved over to a trashcan, tearing his blood-soaked polo shirt off and throwing it inside the container on his way to the stall. Jack was getting increasingly frustrated with his brother, but followed him anyway.

"Just leave the flashlight on the ground. Here, take these and see if you can get most of the blood out." Jeremy handed his jeans to Jack, who eyed them in horror, gingerly holding them as he moved over to a nearby sink.

"What in the hell happened back there, Jeremy!" Jack demanded disgustedly, looking over his shoulder as he laid his brother's trousers in the sink.

"*Sh-sh-sh!!!* Keep your voice down, Jack!" Jeremy whispered harshly. The water pipes murmured as he turned on the shower.

"*Well??*" hissed Jack.

Jeremy's only response was a hearty serving of his most crude vernacular, tempered by his determination to keep his voice at a whisper. For the moment, the shower's cold water commanded his complete attention.

"*Goddamn it, talk to me, Jeremy!!!*"

Still no answer, other than the sound of Jeremy working quickly to rid himself of the foulness that had soaked through to his skin. As Jack's throat now ached from his whispered rebuke, he reluctantly turned his attention to the task of cleansing Jeremy's jeans.

Blood oozed into the sink's basin the very instant the water from the faucet touched the jeans. Jack scrubbed furiously to clean them, hoping to not prolong this experience longer than necessary. In the sparse light available where he stood, he was disgusted and horrified at how quickly the water in the basin turned dark. After repeatedly rinsing and wringing out Jeremy's pants, and after refilling and draining the sink several times, the pants' bloody residue finally decreased to where only slight traces were visible.

Jeremy turned the shower off, and Jack hurriedly wrung out the remaining water from the jeans, turning away from the sink as he held the damp trousers out in front of him. Suddenly, the flashlight flickered out just as Jeremy stepped around the corner from the shower stall. "*Goddamn it anyway!!*" he hissed. "*Jackie, where exactly are you?*"

"I'm right here, maybe four or five feet in front of you," Jack replied.

"All right" acknowledged Jeremy. "Walk over here slowly and bring my pants to me, and for God's sake don't trip and fall while you're doing it!"

Jack moved slowly toward Jeremy's voice, still holding the pair of jeans out in front of him as he did so. He couldn't believe how black it was in here. For all he could tell, the restroom's interior had completely disappeared, leaving him and his brother in a deep and empty void. This initial impression soon gave way to reality, as he scraped the side of his right arm against a steel paper towel holder attached to the wall that separated the row of sinks from the shower stall.

"Are you all right?" Jeremy asked while he grabbed Jack's left arm.

"Yeah, I'll live," Jack replied, grimacing slightly. "At least for now, anyway."

Jeremy let go as he grabbed his jeans, struggling in the dark to pull them back on. After a shrill whistle and a few more choice words to describe how much he enjoyed the damp coldness against his skin, Jeremy zipped up his pants.

"Help me find my shoes, Jackie, and we'll get the hell out of here."

"Where'd you leave them, Jeremy?"

"Well, I believe over here. *Oh shit—!*" He kicked the flashlight that lay hidden in his path. It skidded across the floor several feet before it flipped over. The flashlight flickered again until it was able to maintain a solid beam of light once more.

"*Hallelujah, thank you, Jesus!!*" Jeremy exalted sarcastically. "I'd say it's about time we get rid of this thing. That's the third time in the past hour this has happened. What's the saying, Mr. Baseball? Three strikes and you're out. Right? Although, the second time it happened is the reason we're still among the living." Several streams of water dripped upon his muscular shoulders from his hair. Naked from the waist up, Jeremy's build was still the envy of Jack, who was built fairly well himself. A colorful tattoo of a buxom female posed seductively on a Harley just below his left shoulder was the only vestige from Jeremy's younger and wilder days. The dark flowing locks were long gone, but the mature version of Jack's brother, who lacked just one full semester to complete his second master's degree in archaeology, often still carried the glint of fiery excitement in his piercing green eyes. Like right then. "My shoes are right behind you, Jackie,' he advised. "Scoot them over to me and let's leave."

"First, why don't you tell me what happened back there?" said Jack, moving the shoes toward his brother. "I'm dying of curiosity, man. If you were me and I pulled this shit on you, we wouldn't be going anywhere till you were satisfied with my answers. Right?"

"Oh, I'm sure I'd beat it out of you if I had to," he agreed, chuckling. "But, that's not the point. The point is we've been in here longer than I believe is prudent. We'll be the center of attention for a lot of folks soon if we're not already. Trust me, bro. I'll fill you in completely once we're far enough away from here."

Jeremy picked up the flashlight and Jack followed him out of the restroom. The cool night air was a welcome relief to Jack's nostrils after their most recent assault from the restroom's cramped foulness, though Jeremy certainly didn't appreciate the coolness as much. They moved quickly back to the sedan, which remained the lone vehicle parked in the area.

"Are you going to be all right like that, without a shirt?" asked Jack.

"For now, I'll be fine. Remember, Jackie, 'mums the word' once we reach the car," Jeremy advised, his voice falling to a soft whisper once more. "You know how surveillance happy these assholes are."

"'Got it," whispered Jack, motioning that his lips were sealed.

They opened the sedan's doors and quietly slipped inside. Jeremy started the engine and they slowly moved back onto the main road, heading northeast toward the park's exit.

The dashboard's clock read 11:29 pm, and Jeremy's misgivings from the restroom were soon confirmed when another car crept up behind them. Though the vehicle was barely visible behind its bright headlights, he and Jack detected the faint outline of a row of lights along the top of it. At the moment, these lights were dormant.

"*Shit!*" Jeremy hissed. He slowly reached under his seat to confirm the pistol was still there, and after he did so, he slowly withdrew the weapon and placed it in his lap. The two automobiles traveled like this for several miles until they reached Highway 28, at which point Jeremy turned right while the police car turned left. The brothers now headed due north on the highway.

"Oh God. Thank God," Jack let out raggedly. He felt as if he might throw up, but the feeling subsided. This immediately brought a reproachful look from Jeremy, who pressed his index finger to his lips again.

"Not yet," he whispered.

Before long, the road they were on merged with Highway 7, near Broad Run Farms. It was here that Jeremy pulled the sedan off the highway and down a deserted road. They drove down this road for more than a mile, passing a handful of darkened houses. Once they passed the last house in this group by a safe distance, Jeremy pulled the car over to the side of the road. He silently told Jack that he intended to replace their present vehicle with another one from this neighborhood. Leaving Jack with the keys to the sedan, he backtracked on foot to the area they had just passed through.

The dashboard's clock now read 12:14 am, and every minute Jeremy was away heightened Jack's anxiety. To pass the time, he rummaged through the area around his seat; locating two boxes of cartridges for the semi-automatic pistols the agents had armed themselves with. Finally, at 12:31 am Jeremy returned, driving an old Ford pickup truck.

The truck idled roughly, and at first Jack was reluctant to leave the comfort of the sedan. But once Jeremy explained this was the best he could provide them with at present, and that they were pressing their luck by driving the sedan any further, Jack helped him hide it in a nearby wooded ravine.

"I sure as hell would've preferred we waited on this, but after what just happened, I didn't think we should risk it," said Jeremy, once they finished moving the sedan. "Perhaps that cop back there was following us on account of the park's curfew—most places have them, you know. I thought for sure we'd get stopped. When we didn't, I reckon he believed we were a pair of agents out there on some sort of surveillance, or some shit like that."

"Were you going to shoot that cop, Jeremy?" Jack asked him.

"Only if necessary, Jackie," he replied. "If it was going to be 'us' or 'him'. Or her, if it was a female." He moved to the rear of the sedan, grabbing a pair of rifles and ammunition from the trunk, while Jack made sure he picked up the two small boxes of ammunition he recently discovered as well. Jeremy threw the car's keys deep into the woods, and the two quickly moved back to the truck.

The old Ford was definitely not the optimum choice in transportation. For one thing, it was loud. Plus, its engine was a definite gas-guzzler. Originally built in the late-1960's, it was significantly older than either Jack or Jeremy. The odometer showed just forty-two thousand miles, but surely it had clicked over more than once.

The truck's cab was torn up pretty badly. The dashboard was bare and primitive, equipped only with an AM radio. Since this was all they had to work with for the moment, Jack tried to ignore the rusted-out holes in the floorboard and the steel coils poking through the bench seat. "How are we going to buy gas for this thing?" he asked once they closed the doors and Jeremy sat both rifles behind the seat.

"You don't need to keep whispering, Jackie," Jeremy replied, smiling smugly as his usual self once again. For the moment, he kept the pistol beside him as he turned the truck around to head back to the highway. "We've got three quarters of a tank, so I figure that should easily get us to the state line. We're on our way north, in case you're wondering. We'll decide exactly how far north once we leave Virginia."

"That's fine. But, are you relying on your looks to get us there? I mean, how are we—Hey! Where'd you get that shirt from?" He just now noticed Jeremy was wearing a white T-shirt, stretched tightly with an orange 'ten' stenciled in large numerals on the front and back of it. Jeremy snickered in amusement, but waited to answer him until they were back on Highway 7.

"Well, I suppose you could say the kind folks who provided this wonderful piece of shit-on-wheels for our use were even kinder to leave this shirt for me," he explained. "Seriously, man, it was folded up right where you're sitting now, with a Peterbilt baseball cap resting on top of it. The shirt's clean, too!"

"No shit, huh?"

"No shit, *indeed!*" Jeremy enthused. "As for how we're going to pay for gas, food, and some brand new clothes for both of us... I guess they took your wallet, too, for you to be asking that."

"Yeah. They took it when they confiscated my watch and pocket knife," said Jack. "I guess we're really fucked once we run out of gas!"

"I lost my watch to those bastards, too," said Jeremy. "So, as far as keeping track of time, we're probably fucked for now. But, I've got more than seven hundred dollars in cash on me, courtesy of those very same bastards. Here, Jackie—I've got Bo Cochran's wallet with me. Never mind that I managed to keep it from you until now. Most of the money's his, though there's contributions from the others as well." Jeremy withdrew the damp, bulging leather wallet from his front right pocket and handed it to Jack. It had indeed belonged to Agent Cochran. Jack frowned as he studied the man's driver's license and the pictures of his wife and kids.

"Don't let that fool you," Jeremy told him without taking his eyes from the road before them. "I'm sorry for their loss, but I'd bet my very life he's the son-of-a-bitch who murdered your buddy. God knows he was leaning on me pretty hard during my interrogation. Let's not forget he was about to put a bullet through my head."

Jack closed the wallet and handed it back to his brother, who stuffed it back into his jeans' pocket. The truck shook noticeably as Jeremy pushed the accelerator to sixty-five miles per hour. "God, I hope this thing stays together until we're at least off this road!" he said. "I've counted just six other cars along here with us so far. That might be a good thing if this baby holds up. Jackie, I believe I saw a map in the glove compartment when I first broke into the truck. Would you mind grabbing it for me? I'd like to make sure we're heading in the right direction."

"After that will you finally tell me what happened back there?" asked Jack, just as he opened the glove box. Lying underneath a crescent wrench and flashlight was a small Rand-McNally road atlas. He removed the map along with the flashlight, grinning slightly once he tested the light and found it worked much better than the last one they had. "Hey, how about this!" he chuckled, and then shut the glove box door. "One other thing, too, and I'll be happy to verify where we're headed. Since when did you start breaking into automobiles and stealing them for a hobby?"

Jeremy turned and eyed him suspiciously. "During the reckless days of my youth," he told him, and then turned to face the road once more. "Actually, Freddy was the one breaking into cars back then. I simply helped drive them. Of course, I learned a thing or two along the way. But if you ever mention *any* of this to Grandpa..."

"I won't," Jack assured him. "I was just curious, that's all. Highway 7 should take us to Winchester, and from there if you want to still head north, you'll need to take Highway 11—which could be 81. Otherwise, you and I will be heading due west, like we are now."

"What do you mean by 'could be 81'?"

"Well, both numbers are shown along that route. This thing was printed back in 1990, for Christ's sake! I guess that's the last time anyone took this truck anywhere."

"That's probably true," agreed Jeremy. "We should reach Winchester within an hour. A sign we passed a little while ago indicated it was less than forty-five miles away. Although I must admit I wasn't paying attention to what it specifically said. Anyway, I know you're dying to hear about the events that kept us among the living, so here goes.

"Right after big Bo closed the trunk on you, he and that fucker Iverson each grabbed onto one of my arms and escorted me to their designated execution area, which turned out to be an old woodshed at the edge of the park. I guess it was roughly two hundred yards or so from where we left you, and Agent Reynolds led the way there with that flashlight he was bitching about. Apparently, he and Iverson forgot to bring theirs. I know they were cussing a storm about it. You didn't hear any of that?"

Jack shook his head 'no'.

"Well, that left you and Agent Casey in total darkness, but I'll get to the importance of that shortly," said Jeremy. "As soon as we reached our destination, Agents Cochran and Iverson forced me down on my knees. Big Bo used one of his monster-sized paws on my shoulder to keep me still, while the other asshole joined Agent Reynolds, who stood directly in front of me with the flashlight's beam shining directly in my face.

"'Well, this should prove to be the highlight of my day,' Agent Reynolds told me. 'Actually, I believe all three of us will deeply enjoy watching you die, Mr. Kenney. The only thing that could make this any sweeter is to see you squirm and plead for your life.' He laughed and then the other two joined in, whooping and hollering with their insults concerning my manhood and the legitimacy of my birth. Mind you, all the while I couldn't see any of them on account of that goddamned light shining in my eyes.

"I guess they noticed the tremendous amount of contempt I felt toward them, which you know almost always brings a smile to my face. It pissed them off even more. I'd bet if they'd had more time allotted for our demise, they would've beaten the shit out of me right then. As it was, big bad Bo dug his steel-like fingers in behind my collarbone.

"I can't even describe how much that hurt, Jackie, but I wasn't about to give in. Especially, since I was about to die anyway. Agent Reynolds asked me if I had any final words before they administered my death sentence. I leered into that annoying light as meanly as I possibly could and told him, very matter-of-factly, to go thoroughly fuck himself until his heart's content. As I'm sure you can imagine, my comments produced an immediate response. I felt the cold tip of this silencer laying here now against the back of my head, and heard Agent Cochran release the pistol's safety. In the next few moments I'm sure my life would've ended. But in the instant that preceded the bullet marked with my name, a God-honest miracle took place. The flashlight went out again."

"So, that's what you were referring to earlier," said Jack.

"Yep," said Jeremy. "But it gets better. Since we were all thrown into complete darkness, I now had a sliver of a chance to still save your ass and mine. I had to move quickly, though. Thank God for all of the coon hunting trips Grandpa used to take us on as kids—that, and the tae-kwon-do lessons he let me take back in high school. Otherwise, I don't believe we'd be discussing any of this now. The window of opportunity would only last so long.

"Big Bo loosened his grip for just a second, but that was enough for me to roll out of his grasp. I then squeezed my butt, legs, and feet through my arms to bring my cuffed hands in front of me, and quietly stood up. By now, my eyes had adjusted somewhat to the darkness, and I could tell their eyes hadn't.

"Agent Cochran alerted the other two that I'd escaped his grasp, but he couldn't tell where I was. He frantically reached around himself, grasping nothing but air. Meanwhile, I could see the others had pulled their weapons and were pointing them in the area I'd just vacated, near where big Bo was standing.

"I wasn't sure how long I had before their eyes adjusted and they could finally see me. So, I dove at Agent Cochran's feet, which I'm sure most folks would think pretty foolish, given his enormous size and all. But my idea worked. He cried out in surprise and fell over me. The other two began firing in the darkness, thinking, I'm sure, they'd hit me. They didn't, though they nailed big Bo at least four times. His worst injury came to his throat, and I'm sure it was serious enough to have killed him. That's where most of the blood on my clothes came from.

"I grabbed his weapon with my bound hands and started shooting at the pair of silhouettes closing in on Bo and me, for I was partially pinned beneath his enormous frame. Luckily, I hit pay dirt both times as the pair of assholes crumpled to the ground. Once I freed myself from Bo's body, I heard some keys moving around in his pants' pocket. I fished them out, which was difficult to do since my hands were still tightly handcuffed together. Believe it or not, it was a helluva lot easier to shoot the fucking gun than get those damned keys!

"I found Bo's car keys with another smaller ring attached to them. The five keys on this ring were small enough to fit my cuffs, and after the first four failed, I was greatly relieved when the last one opened the lock. I threw the handcuffs aside and stuffed all of the keys into my pocket. Next, I moved over to Agents Reynolds and Iverson. Both were groaning from their wounds and unable to move much.

"I got to thinking about Agent Casey, as I certainly didn't want him alerting any more of these shitheads as to what was going on. I attempted to create a consistent theme. Since I'm sure he'd heard the earlier gunfire, I decided to finish off these assholes using their weapons. I'm sure I would've been up a creek if Agent Cochran hadn't brought the silencer, for Agent Casey was unaware of the shots I'd just fired.

"I removed Agent Reynolds' gun from his hand and shot him in the head with it. I'm pretty sure he was nearly dead already from my previous shot, because he seemed barely aware of what was happening. Next, I moved over to that pussy Iverson. Now, he was definitely aware, as my earlier shot had merely wounded him in the stomach. Unfortunately for him, his weapon had flown out of his hand when he fell to the ground.

"You should've seen him grovel for his life, Jackie—crying like a baby. If he wasn't such a sorry son-of-a-bitch, I might've been tempted to spare him. But, after all the mean-spirited comments he said about our family and all... The only mercy doled out was for my ears, since his whimpering ended once I plugged him between his eyes.

"With that done, I knew I needed to get back to you before my luck changed. That's when I heard big Bo moaning on the ground. I couldn't believe he was still alive! He, too, begged for mercy, but by then I was totally sick of that shit! So, I put a bullet in his head as well. With that taken care of, I retrieved the flashlight. Amazingly, it started working again the very instant the last of those fuckers were carried off to hell.

"I wouldn't have thought to take anyone's money, but the flashlight's beam shined directly on Agent Cochran's enormous waist, and I noticed his wallet partially hung out of his pants' back pocket. Temptation got the better of me and I picked it up. Once I found out he had nearly five hundred dollars cash in it, and remembering he'd been present when Agent Reynolds confiscated my money, I didn't mind so much taking his. As a matter of fact, I felt pretty goddamned good about it! So good, in fact, that I decided his dead buddies should also pitch in! When all was said and done, I pocketed big Bo's wallet and roughly seven hundred and thirty dollars in cash!!

"I quietly moved back to where their cars were parked, turning off the flashlight so Agent Casey wouldn't see me coming. By the time I reached him, he was looking out anxiously toward the area to where I'd been taken. For a moment, I even thought he could see me. Once I circled around him and he didn't follow my movements, I realized the motherfucker was as night-blind as he was stupid. I snuck in behind him and whispered, 'Boo!'. He nearly jumped out of his skin as he whirled around. I flicked on the flashlight and shot him twice in the face, making sure my second one blasted his left eye like his buddy Bo Cochran had done to the agent in the trunk with you. Even then, Agent Casey just stood there, like he was determined to die standing straight up. I pushed him over and he landed hard on his back.

"Since he was already dead, I immediately checked his pockets for the keys to the car you were in, praying to God Almighty I didn't have to go back to where the other three agents were to find the damned things. Luckily, they were in his pants' pocket.

"The rest you already know. Once I opened the trunk and shone the flashlight into your pretty-boy face, that is." Jeremy smiled at Jack before turning his attention back to the road ahead of them. Jack smiled as well, for he was proud of his brother's courage. He even thought about telling him this, but knew Jeremy would scorn such blubbering.

They drove along in silence and soon reached the quiet town of Winchester, Virginia. A Shell station with a food mart that was open all night sat near the outskirts of town. Since the truck was nearly out of gas, they decided to stop and fill it up. At Jeremy's insistence, Jack wore the Peterbilt ball cap and took enough money to pay for the gas and buy some snacks and drinks for the road. After paying for everything, he also purchased a cheap kid's watch on display at the checkout counter. The cashier, a girl who didn't look old enough to work overnight, cheerfully told him the correct time was 2:06 am He smiled politely and thanked her, thinking sometime later that day she might regret having been so nice to a federal fugitive.

Once back in the truck, the brothers headed north, taking Highway 81 out of Virginia and on through West Virginia. The old Ford truck moved too slow and needed too much gas for them to make serious headway, and they were forced to stop for fuel again near Hagerstown, Maryland. It was here that Jeremy agreed with Jack that they should contact their grandfather to tell him what had happened before traveling much further north. Jack wanted to be the one to make the call, but Jeremy insisted on doing it instead.

"It'd be better if you let me handle this, Jackie," he told him.

"Grandpa and I developed a language for just this type of emergency years ago. Trust me on this."

They stopped at a small market just south of Hagerstown's city limits. The store was dark and probably wouldn't open for business again for at least a couple more hours, they figured, since the little watch Jack had just purchased currently read 3:23 am A payphone was located at the northern corner of the store's parking lot beneath the lone streetlight in the area.

Jeremy pulled up to the phone and parked the truck. After taking the ball cap from Jack and placing it snugly on his own head, he jumped out of the vehicle and walked over to the payphone. With his back turned toward his brother, he used Bo Cochran's calling card to call their grandfather.

While Jeremy was on the phone, Jack kept an eye out for any potential trouble coming up behind them. To gain a better vantage point, he turned around on the bench seat, inadvertently kicking his foot against the door in the process. Instantly, he felt a sharp stabbing pain in the side of his foot and let out a slight yelp in response.

"Are you all right in there?" Jeremy called back to him.

"Yeah, I'm fine," said Jack, to which Jeremy nodded and resumed his conversation with their grandfather.

Meanwhile, Jack reached down and removed his loafer from his aching foot. When he reached inside the shoe to find the source for his pain, he discovered the sharp point of a skeleton key sticking out through a tear in the small zippered coin compartment in the side of the shoe. He had purchased the shoes only two months before, largely on account of the coin compartments hidden inside each loafer. Having always been fond of gadgets and such, he couldn't resist the idea of owning a pair. Especially since each compartment was large enough to conceal other items as well, such as the key that had torn through this one's side.

The irony for him was he completely forgot about the key's presence in his shoe. That, along with two other keys as well: a large house key in the damaged loafer, and a smaller house key in the other shoe. Jack removed the keys from his shoes. They glistened in his hand under the streetlight's illumination. He suddenly recalled where they came from, marveling at how he completely forgot about their existence until now. Perhaps the events of the past two weeks were much more traumatic than he realized.

The keys were an odd mixture. The skeleton key was definitely the oldest, belonging to some antique piece of furniture. The other two keys were made for standard door locks, with the larger key being the most obvious as to what it was. All three were made of steel, and each of them once belonged to Dr. Oscar Mensch.

The first time Jack ever saw them was when he discovered the professor lying unconscious on his living room floor. When he checked for vital signs to see if Dr. Mensch had survived his terrible assault, the keys slipped out of a small pocket in the professor's sweater. At the time, the keys were joined together on a small brass ring.

Jack had picked them up and deposited them into his pants' pocket with the intent of giving them back to the professor just as soon as he regained consciousness. For some reason, he decided to withhold them from the police department's knowledge that night. In retrospect, he believed now it was a good thing he did that.

On the night when Dr. Sutherland called him to let him know Dr. Mensch had finally regained consciousness, Jack made sure he brought the keys with him. He hoped this would serve to brighten the professor's outlook on the tragedy that befell him. Jack now clearly recalled everything about that evening, especially what he and Dr. Mensch discussed together.

When he peered into Dr. Mensch's private room at the hospital, he found the professor propped up in his bed while he finished his dinner. His face was covered with bandages and the only way he could feed himself was through a straw.

"Should I come back later?" Jack asked him as he stood in the doorway.

"No, Jack. I sent for you specifically," he replied. "Didn't Jeremy tell you? He dropped by to visit awhile earlier."

"No, he didn't," Jack told him. "Dr. Sutherland called me and told me you were awake. I hurried down here just as soon as I could."

"Very good. Well...are you going to visit from the doorway, or would you rather come in?" Dr. Mensch's voice was weak, but the powerful warmth of his personality came through nonetheless. He motioned for Jack to pull a nearby chair up to his bedside, since the weakness in his voice made it hard to decipher his English through his thick German accent.

"How are you feeling, Doc?" He sat down next to the professor's dinner tray.

"About as good as can reasonably be expected," Dr. Mensch told him, chuckling painfully as he repositioned himself to gain a better view of his guest. "And how are you, my young friend?"

"I'm fine, just worried about you."

"Don't be," said Dr. Mensch. "Sometimes these things happen. It's part of life, though I certainly hope you are spared anything quite like this." He slowly raised his hands and pointed to the bandages on his face, which were steadily turning pink as they absorbed blood from his wounds.

"But, enough of that already," he continued. "I didn't send for you to draw your pity. I have much more important things to discuss with you." Dr. Mensch stopped and stared at him, a look of child-like innocence and excitement shining in his eyes. "Do you believe in premonitions, Jack?"

"You mean, like gut feelings and visions, and other stuff like that?"

"Yes I do. How about dreams? Do you believe they sometimes can be the same thing?"

"Yeah, I guess so, anyway," Jack replied, ever fearful the many nightmares he suffered over the years might someday come true.

"That bothers you, eh?" Dr. Mensch asked him, concerned by his reaction.

"No. Not really," said Jack, pushing his previous thoughts aside. An uncomfortable silence followed. He needed an effective distraction to keep things from turning awkward, and decided to use this opportunity to give the professor his keys back, pulling the brass key ring out of his pocket. "I've been saving these for you," he said, handing the key ring to him. "They fell out of your sweater when I found you lying on your living room floor."

Dr. Mensch reached out slowly to take them, and then studied them as if he had never seen them before.

"I'm truly grateful you saved my life the other night," he said, finally, and then held the keys out in front of him, motioning for Jack to take them back. "I'd prefer that you keep these for now, but in a safe place."

Jack took the keys back as the professor requested, just as the nurse Peter McNamee later identified as Nurse Rison entered the room. She moved directly in front of Jack as she approached Dr. Mensch's right side.

"Looks like you didn't eat all of your dinner, Doctor," she chided, casting a suspicious glance toward Jack that made him believe she blamed him for this.

"I ate most of it, didn't I?" Dr. Mensch replied, feigning contriteness in a playful way. "Perhaps I can finish it later—or better yet, how about some dessert? I've always wondered what apple pie or chocolate cake would taste like through a straw."

"You're terrible!" she teased back, and playfully winked at him. "Tell you what, Doc. Let me check on you a bit later after your company's gone."

"That sounds like an excellent idea!" he beamed, and he and Jack watched her saunter from the room to check on her many other patients. As soon as she was far enough away from the room to where Dr. Mensch was certain she wouldn't be coming back any time soon, he grew serious and reduced his voice to a mere whisper. "Where did you put the keys?"

"In my pocket," Jack told him, pointing to his pants' pocket.

"No! *Don't* leave them there, Jack!" the professor scolded him. "Do you not have a less obvious place to carry them? Surely the brother of Jeremy Kenney, a master in craftiness, can think of a better alternative, eh?"

Nothing like a comparison with the one person on the planet he felt inferior to for Jack to think quickly in a way that would impress his mentor. Almost immediately, he remembered the hidden coin compartments in his shoes.

"How about in here?" he asked, removing his loafers to show the professor the hidden zipper pouches in each one. "I'd have to take the keys off this ring in order to get them to fit inside, but they'd definitely be concealed."

"*Yes*! I believe that will work," said Dr. Mensch, the light returning to his eyes once more. "Good job, Jack! Now, before you actually place the keys inside your shoes, let me advise you of a few important things to remember. Number one, remember this address: 1016 South Queens Court. It's just a few blocks from the University. Have you got that?"

"1016 South Queens Court," Jack replied softly.

"Excellent! Next, I need you to keep in mind that each of these keys is important in its own right. The largest one goes to the front door of the house on 1016 South Queens Court. The smaller house key goes to the basement door. The oldest one, the skeleton key, goes to an immense desk down inside the basement. Will you remember all of this?"

"Yes. I won't forget any of it."

"I believe you won't," Dr. Mensch agreed, grimacing slightly. Jack knew this wasn't entirely due to his physical condition. An overwhelming sense of sadness emanated from the professor. "Now, put the keys inside your shoes and get them back on your feet before anyone notices," he instructed Jack. "Then, I'd like to discuss my latest dreams. Would you mind?"

"No. That's fine if that's what you'd like to discuss," Jack told him, carefully placing the keys inside the loafers' compartments before slipping them back on his feet.

"It is, indeed," said the professor, drawing a deep breath before continuing. "They are all the same, these dreams. In each one, I'm lying on my back in a field full of wonderfully beautiful flowers. The sky is as beautiful as I've ever seen it, with soft clouds billowing above where I'm resting. There are birds everywhere, and their wonderful songs make me want to get up from where I'm laying and go investigate. Once I think this, immediately I'm walking through this wonderful field, which I soon realize is a sprawling meadow.

"Suddenly, I'm transported at incredible speed to an immense courtyard of gleaming gold, that is filled with fountains, ponds, and waterfalls of such splendor I've never seen anywhere in my travels throughout the world. Just as I think nothing can improve upon this magical vision, an amazingly beautiful woman, dressed in a lavender gown of exquisite silk, with flowing hair as white as snow and eyes as pure blue as any sapphire I've ever seen, steps up to me.

"'Welcome, Oscar!' she tells me. 'Welcome to the place that will soon be your home!'

"Well, I don't know what to say to this gorgeous woman in response to such an unusual greeting. But it doesn't matter to her. At least that's what she tells me. 'What matters most,' she says, is that I'm about to be 'rewarded for a work well done.'

"I'm quite confused, so I ask her what she means by this. She refuses to let me in on her secret. Instead, she tells me that I need only to trust her and do her bidding before my life on earth is over. I tell her I'm not ready to die, and I offer arguments as to how this can't be true, that I still have much left to do on earth. She smiles and waves me off. In fact, in *every* dream she then tells me the very same thing: I must deliver a message to a dear friend of hers on earth. If I simply do this, she will see to it that I prosper in her world in such a way that will make all my earthly accomplishments seem mundane..."

Dr. Mensch paused and looked at Jack intently, his eyes glowing with excitement. This only heightened the fear and horror building within Jack. He didn't want to hear what he knew instinctively the professor was about to say. It simply wasn't possible.

Dr. Mensch smiled and nodded as if reading his thoughts. "This beautiful girl told me to tell the young gentleman for whom her message was expressly intended, that she misses him terribly...that she needs him," he said. "She will do *anything* that's necessary to once again play a major role in his life. Surely you already know this message is for *you*, Jack!"

A bead of sweat began to form along Jack's hairline, and as his heart raced and his palms grew clammy, he thought for sure he would pass out and join the professor as a patient in the very same hospital.

"So, she *is* real! I see it written all over your face. This 'Genovene' is *real* after all!" Dr. Mensch eyed Jack intently again as he waited for him to officially confirm this statement. Jack felt a sudden urge to do just that, to do it in such a way that would warn the professor about the deceitful nature of Genovene. But when he tried to speak, he couldn't. The mere shock of what he had just been told left his tongue thick and heavy, while his throat closed to where he could only cough nervously.

"Do you need a drink of something?" the professor offered. "I certainly didn't wish to upset you with this information. I suppose you've enjoyed an intimate relationship of some sort with her, based upon your reaction. She's definitely—how do you say down here in the south? Ah, yes. She's definitely quite a *peach*, eh?"

Jack continued to cough and struggle to catch his breath, and he allowed the professor to give him a drink from a glass of water sitting on his nightstand.

"Perhaps you are upset at the news I may not be here among the living much longer. Is that it?"

As this was partly correct, Jack nodded a positive response while he worked to regain control of himself.

"I've lived a good life, which for the most part is without regrets. Whatever I would've looked forward to exploring during my final years on earth would likely be prevented anyway. Can you imagine what those who did this to me would do if they were presented another opportunity?" He lifted his trembling hands to point them to his face once more. "But why fret? Genovene has promised to make it worth my while to leave early. She has even gone so far as to assure me that my research will not be lost or forgotten. And, now you have the necessary keys, just as she told me you did. Jack, *you* are the one who will finish my work."

The professor paused again, casting a wary glance behind Jack, which made him look over his shoulder as well. As far as he could tell, no one else was listening nearby. In fact, the only distraction he could detect was the on-duty nurses' footsteps echoing in the hallway as they made their evening rounds several doors away from Dr. Mensch's room.

"It's time for you to go, my young friend," said the professor. "Remember what I've told you and don't forget the address, '1016 South Queens Court'."

"I won't forget. I promise," said Jack, looking back over his shoulder to the empty doorway. What did Dr. Mensch sense that he couldn't? It made him uneasy, but he didn't want to further upset this man whom he admired so much. "Get some rest, Doc. I'll be by to see you again real soon—maybe tomorrow." He stood up to leave, smiling down at the professor who raised his hand to wave goodbye.

"1016 South Queens Court," Dr. Mensch reminded him.

"Don't worry, Doc, I've got it," said Jack. He delivered a grin and wink he thought would even make his grandfather proud, and then turned to leave the room. "1016 South Queens Court," he whispered to himself as he walked through the doorway and on down the hallway past the nurse's station, on his way to the elevator...

Jack shook himself from the trance he was under. He looked down at his left hand and was shocked to find he was bleeding. He had gripped the keys so tightly that the skeleton key's sharp point had pierced the skin on his palm. He searched throughout the truck's cab for something suitable to treat the wound with, settling for an old handkerchief when the only alternatives were the map or his T-shirt. Jack wrapped his hand and was tying the ends of the handkerchief when Jeremy opened the driver's side door and climbed back into the truck. Jeremy immediately noticed the makeshift bandage on Jack's wounded hand.

"What in the hell happened to you?" Jeremy asked lightheartedly, but with a look that let Jack know he was concerned about the injury. He started the engine and then pulled out of the parking lot. "Man, I tell you, little brother. I can't leave you alone for long, can I? You've got a knack for finding your way into mischief, one way of another—that's for goddamn sure!" He smiled and gave Jack a hearty slap on the shoulder before turning his attention to the road. A moment later, they resumed their journey north on I-81.

"It'll be all right," said Jack. "Is Grandpa okay? What did he have to say about our situation?"

"Well, he's fine. He's been worried sick about us, not knowing where we disappeared to and all. As far as our abduction's concerned, I told him pretty much everything that's happened so far. And, I told him to keep a good perspective on things when the shit hits the fan later this morning. I figure all we can bank on at this point is that we've got a significant head start."

"Where are you planning to take us, Jeremy?"

"Canada," he replied, and Jack knew he was dead serious about this. He probably knew their destination the very instant he escaped Agent Cochran's grasp. "Grandpa and I developed a special code for an occasion such as this long ago," he continued. "So, I told him you and I were going to chill out with a couple of bottles of Cuervo Gold before we decided what to do next. That told him we were on our way north to Canada without tipping off anybody who might be listening in on his line, and you've got to believe the wiretaps are active at his place these days. It's the opposite of what they'd expect, since Cuervo Gold comes from Mexico. If I'd told him we were planning on sipping a few bottles of Moosehead, he'd have known that Mexico was our destination, instead of Canada. I'd say it's pretty cool that after five years we finally got to use this idea. Thank God he hadn't forgotten about it!"

Jeremy glanced briefly at his younger brother and then returned his attention to the road before them. "So, what do you think, Jackie? I realize we'll have some major challenges getting through the guard patrols along the Canadian border, but we'll figure out a plan to deal with that shit, I'm sure. Are you ready to hole-up for a while in the real land of 'sky-blue waters'? Not to mention, I'll bet we'll run across some lovely French-speaking darlings as well, if we make it far enough north. How about it, bro?"

Jack didn't immediately answer him. Instead, he focused his attention on his throbbing left palm and the three keys in his right hand. Jeremy looked over at him and Jack felt the weight of his brother's stare grow heavy upon him. He finally turned to face him.

"Well?"

"I think it's a bad idea, Jeremy, going to Canada. A *very* bad idea," said Jack. "We need to go home. We need to go back to Tuscaloosa, and we need to do that *now!*"

"*What? Are you on crack??*" Jeremy pulled the truck over to the shoulder of the highway and immediately slammed on the brakes. A cloud of dust quickly surrounded the vehicle in the pre-dawn light. "What in the hell are you *thinking??*" he demanded furiously.

Jack was certain the response and the look of puzzled horror to go along with it wouldn't have been any different had he told his brother that he underwent a recent sex change operation, and then pulled his pants down to prove it. Rather than being drawn further into an all-out argument, he simply showed him the keys in his right hand.

"So?" said Jeremy. "What the fuck do *those* have to do with anything?"

"They belonged to Oscar."

"*What??* Where in the hell did you get them from?"

"From him," Jack explained. "He gave them to me the night he died. Actually, that's not exactly true, as I originally got them when I found him lying on his living room floor. When I tried to give them back to him the last time I saw him alive, in the hospital, he made me keep them. They go to an address near school, and he told me I needed to finish something he was working on."

"Why '*you*' of all people?" Jeremy mused aloud, more from puzzlement over all that had recently happened, and not as an insult directed at his younger brother.

"I don't know for sure," Jack replied, unable to entirely mask the wound he just received from Jeremy. "I believe it has something to do with Genovene. He told me she came to him in a dream and foretold his death. Did you ever tell him anything about her?"

"No. Never," said Jeremy, the angry look on his face melting quickly into one of somber bewilderment. Jack went on to explain all that Dr. Mensch told him. Then, he went on to tell his brother everything Agent McNamee had shared with him as well, including the mysterious package the professor supposedly received from overseas and the unusual events recently taking place around the world.

Once he finished explaining everything, they both sat in silence: Jeremy trying to decide on what they should do next, while Jack waited patiently for that decision to be made known to him. Jeremy looked out toward the open road before them, as if picturing what it would be like if they were to reach the other side of the Canadian border safely. A moment later, he turned toward his brother with a sly smile on his face.

"You know, Jackie, to go back home to Tuscaloosa would be nuts," he told him. "Actually, I believe the word 'asinine' is a better way to put it. But for some goddamned reason, I'm thinking we should do it anyway. Perhaps it's because of how much Oscar meant to me. He was like a father to me...the father I never knew. Or, it could be the intrigue I've always felt about Genovene and her unique place in history—at least our *family's* history. Hell, it could be both of these reasons, to be honest. Regardless, have you ever known me to turn down an invitation to a good party, or back down from a necessary fight?"

"No, I can't say I have," said Jack, chuckling. Jeremy chuckled along with him, and Jack could tell by his ardent eyes it was no longer a question as to whether or not they were going home. It was strictly a question of how quickly could they do it.

"All right, Jackie. We'll go back home," Jeremy told him. "You're going to have to trust me on how we do it, though. Okay? I mean, can you bite your tongue at least until we reach Alabama?"

"Yeah. I believe I can do that."

"Good. Make sure you do, because if I'm spared any unnecessary distractions, I might be able to get us home by tonight. What time have you got there, anyway?"

"It's five minutes past four," said Jack, showing him the watch's glowing digital display.

"I think our chances of making my prediction come true are pretty damn good." Jeremy pulled the truck back onto the highway, heading north. Jack started to say something, as he wondered why they didn't just turn around right then and head south. Jeremy immediately gave him a look that said 'Just trust me, damn it!'.

Jack closed his mouth and settled back against the bench seat. Before long, they reached the residential areas of Hagerstown and were coming up on a large apartment community called 'Brook Meadows'. As it wasn't gated, Jeremy pulled into the apartment complex and drove the truck around to its eastern section, parking the vehicle near a large trash bin.

"Wait here," he told Jack as he cut the engine. An avalanche of ideas poured through Jack's mind as to what his brother was up to, but he realized it was pointless to fret about anything at this point. After Jeremy left the truck, he didn't return for nearly twenty minutes. When he did, he was driving a 2004 model Toyota Camry.

He motioned for Jack to help him quickly unload their necessary supplies from the truck's cab, which consisted only of the weapons, flashlight, and map, and bring them to the Camry. Less than five minutes later, they were back on I-81. Only this time, they headed south.

The burgundy sedan was quite plush, with all of the modern comforts the brothers were normally accustomed to. At least for the time being, their journey would be quicker and much more pleasurable, as their present mode of transportation wasn't likely to shake and convulse at speeds over sixty-five miles per hour. The digital clock in the Camry's dashboard currently read 4:41 am

When they reached the I-40 overpass, Jeremy exited onto it, heading east toward Frederich, Maryland. Once again, Jack could only wonder why his brother did this. Yet, he succeeded in keeping his mouth shut, allowing Jeremy's plan to cleanly unfold.

Jeremy must have figured Jack's thoughts were full of questions as to where in the hell he was taking them, for he suddenly decided to tell him. "We're heading east, as obviously you've noticed by now. It may seem a bit risky, but we're on our way back to D.C. via I-270. 'Back into the hornet's nest', I'll bet you're thinking. There's a definite method to this madness, and I'm betting we're at least a step ahead of whoever's looking for us.

"I'm thinking once we get through D.C., we'll get onto I-95 and take it south through Richmond. After that we should be able to get onto I-85. At least, that's what I gathered we could do when I looked at the map earlier. You can confirm it if you'd like."

Jack took the tiny atlas and opened it to the state map of Virginia. "Yeah, it does, Jeremy," he confirmed. "It looks like we'll reach I-85 near the city of Petersburg."

"All right then," Jeremy continued. "Once we're on I-85, it should be a straight shot through North and South Carolina, all the way down to Atlanta. From there, we'll take I-20 into Alabama and straight home to Tuscaloosa."

"'Sounds like a good plan to me," Jack told him. He closed the atlas and laid it down between their seats. "I just hope it works out to where we get home in one piece."

"Me too, Jackie. Me too."

They pulled onto I-270 south around 5:30am, just as an array of brilliant pink, blue, and orange colors spread across the sky above them from the east. Within the hour, they passed through the nation's capital and were well on their way to Richmond. Jack was finally able to relax once they safely cleared the city limits.

They raced through Richmond and decided to pull over for breakfast once they neared Petersburg. Jeremy found a Denny's just off the highway and sent Jack inside to grab a couple of breakfasts to go. He first gave him the Peterbilt ball cap to wear again, pulling down the cap's bill to partially conceal Jack's eyes. Then, he gave him enough cash to pay for their food.

It was just past 7:30 am when Jack entered the crowded restaurant. The first thing he noticed was the television set above the cashier booth. The local news was on with a special national report that had interrupted whatever program was previously in progress. He approached the hostess stand and was in the process of placing his order, when the female reporter on the television began giving details of a brutal multiple homicide involving five federal agents near Arlington, Virginia. Everyone in the immediate area of the television set turned their attention toward the reporter, as the striking young woman delivered the details of the crime.

According to the report, the police revealed that four of the five agents had been shot more than once, with all five receiving fatal wounds to the head. Most disturbing, said the pretty woman, was the fact one of the slain agents had been stuffed into the trunk of his own sedan, which was later abandoned by the two suspects some thirty miles north of the original crime scene.

"Those *bastards*," Jack whispered to himself, scarcely believing the FBI or police had gone to the trouble of making sure he and his brother seemed like the most vicious rogues possible. Why else would they transfer Agent McNamee's corpse to the other sedan he and Jeremy had taken and later abandoned? Unless, of course, they figured someone might learn the actual truth of what happened and blow a whistle on the government's covert operation near Manassas Park.

The reporter went on to identify the assailants as 'twenty-five-year-old Jeremy Kenney and his twenty-one-year-old brother, Jack Kenney'. Cold sweat formed between Jack's shoulder blades and soon trickled down his back. He tried to focus his attention like everyone else around him on the television set in order to remain unnoticed."Your order should be ready in just a few minutes, sir," the hostess advised, tugging on his arm to distract his attention from the driver's license photos of he and his brother plastered right then across the television screen. Jack didn't immediately hear her, but when he realized she was talking to him, he allowed her to direct him over to a nearby wooden bench.

Just as he sat down, he heard the reporter state the authorities investigating this terrible crime believed the Kenney brothers were heading north to Canada. Jack felt somewhat relieved at this news, until the woman also advised the FBI had already posted a 'one hundred and fifty thousand dollar reward for any information leading to the capture of these dangerous fugitives'.

At that moment, it seemed like all eyes in the restaurant were upon him. He instinctively looked down and focused his gaze upon his feet. Once he drew enough courage to carefully look up from under the bill of his cap, he found that only one or two patrons were actually looking in his direction, perhaps not even noticing the young man seated near the restrooms.

"...In other news, the death toll from the F-5 tornado that struck near Meridian, Mississippi last night has risen to 85 confirmed, with another 210 people still unaccounted for. Authorities from that area are now stating the earlier reports, which depicted the deadly twister as an odd anomaly that seemed to have a golden glow and that one witness described as a 'golden twisting tower of destruction!', were extremely exaggerated. Regardless, the staggering amount of victims already confirmed from the tornado's path make it the worst natural tragedy to hit the area since the early 1900's. It is the second major weather disaster to hit the state of Mississippi since Hurricane Katrina decimated Gulfport and Biloxi less than two years ago..."

Jack stared dumbly at the television set, though he no longer could hear anything the reporter was saying. His mind was stuck like a broken record on the phrase 'gleaming golden tower of destruction'. It repeated over and over in his terrified mind, with the steady drone of his own pulse throbbing noisily in his head as he fought to remain calm. In desperation, he closed his eyes and took several slow deep breaths, praying that this effort to soothe his nerves wouldn't make him stand out.

"Here you go, sir!" the hostess called to him, abruptly grabbing his attention. He had been so involved with his breathing exercise that he failed to notice the television station had returned to its original programming, which for the moment featured a local bass fishing show.

Although it took less than twenty minutes for the cooks to prepare two hefty orders of bacon, eggs, and pancakes (along with juice and coffee, which was obtained by the friendly hostess herself), it seemed more like an hour to him. After paying for the food, he gathered the pair of large bags that contained everything and smiled at the hostess. She returned his smile, but something in her eyes made him certain his nervousness didn't go unnoticed by her, as she had ample opportunity to study him.

After leaving the restaurant, he quickly made his way back to the car, where he immediately started telling Jeremy about the news report and his suspicion the hostess may have recognized him. He did this before he was safely inside the protected privacy of the Camry, much to his brother's irritation.

"Calm down, Jackie!" Jeremy chided him. "Now is not the time or place to lose your composure! Here, you hold onto this shit and let me get us out of this place before you alert anybody else to our presence."

Jack told Jeremy about the news reports, and Jeremy seemed to take all of the information in stride, never giving an indication as to how it affected him. But, the mere fact he wasted little time in getting them back on the highway said all that was needed, even though he did so smoothly and deliberately so as to avoid any further unwanted attention.

The brothers ate their breakfast while heading south, and soon were on I-85. By 9:00 am they had left Virginia and were well on their way to Greensboro, North Carolina. They stopped briefly in Durham to fill up the Toyota with gas, and to purchase two pairs of sunglasses to go along with another baseball cap.

After passing through Greensboro around 11:00 am, they made it down to Charlotte by 12:30 pm. They took their lunch at a local Wendy's drive-thru restaurant, and were back on the highway in under ten minutes. By now, Jeremy was running out of steam, since neither of them had slept at all in over twenty-four hours. He felt he had just enough resources to last another hour or two, so he let Jack sleep while he drove them to Greenville, South Carolina.

Once they neared the outskirts of Greenville, Jeremy decided it was time to replace the rest of their wardrobe. He pulled off the highway and drove until he found a discount department store, settling on

Target since it was the first one he found. Again, Jack was elected to go inside the store to purchase their supplies. Disguised in the new ball cap and sunglasses, Jack quickly grabbed two pairs of jeans and a couple of dark T-shirts apiece for him and Jeremy, along with two packs of underwear briefs and socks. He made excellent time doing this until he neared the audio/entertainment department of the store.

Unable to resist the temptation, he slipped in amongst a row of television sets on display. Moving quickly while trying to remain nonchalant, he turned one of the sets to CNN Headline News. Since it was three o'clock that afternoon, he felt fairly confident he would be in time to catch the latest developments in the search for him and his brother. His hunch proved correct. But the updated report indicated serious trouble for them. Local agencies and other authorities had since joined the intensified manhunt, and the worse bit of news was the fact the search had shifted to the southeastern section of the country.

Upon learning this, he immediately worked his way over to the checkout counters, anxious to escape any suspicious stares from the multitude of shoppers around him. After he paid for the clothes, he fought the urge to simply run out of the store, forcing himself to maintain a steady pace all the way to the car. He nonchalantly climbed into the front seat, where he then explained the latest developments to Jeremy.

"*Damn it!*" Jeremy hissed and slapped his open palm against the steering wheel. The disappointing news immediately revived him. Once they exited Target's parking lot, Jeremy made a beeline for the highway. He remained focused like this until they were safely in Georgia, at which point Jack heard him whisper a prayer of thanksgiving under his breath that no roadblocks were set up yet.

"I believe it's time to make another switch, Jackie, as far as our mode of transportation is concerned," he said. "And, we need to do this before we reach Atlanta. We'll have a better chance of avoiding detection with local plates on our vehicle. I'm certain of that much."

Jeremy made his move near Braselton, Georgia, this time securing a Jeep Grand Cherokee from the year 2000 near the far end of a local supermarket. Though it was a few years older than the Camry, he was surprised anyone would leave a nice vehicle parked so far away from watchful eyes. He wasn't about to look a gift horse in the mouth, especially when it felt like time was starting to run out on them.

For the third time, they gathered their gear and moved into a new vehicle, carelessly leaving the Toyota nearby. At first Jack worried about this, since it seemed like leaving an open invitation to their pursuers. But once they made it through Atlanta and were on I-20 with a full tank of gas in the Jeep, he felt better about their situation. The only things he did worry about were the roadblocks he overheard an older couple discussing at the Shell station they had just left, and the sheer exhaustion threatening to overtake him and Jeremy. Hopefully, the abundance of coffee and Max Alerts would sustain them at least to Birmingham.

As they approached the border of Alabama and the likely prospect of being stopped, Jeremy suddenly headed south on Highway 100 near Jake, Georgia. Jack was far too tired to even question this sudden change of plans, finding it difficult to care about anything other than a good night's rest or a decent meal, now that his stomach began rumbling again.

The Jeep's clock read 6:40 pm when Jeremy actually set out on this road. They stayed on it for nearly twenty minutes until it flirted with the Alabama state line. At that point, Jeremy switched over to Highway 48, leaving the state of Georgia behind near the Alabama town of Graham. He followed the highway until they reached another small town, called Wedowee, where they exited onto Highway 431 north, taking this historic thoroughfare until it brought them back to I-20 again.

Jeremy got them safely into Alabama without the confrontation Jack fully expected to take place at the state line. He let out a joyful whoop as they now sped toward Birmingham, the last stop before they would reach Tuscaloosa. Despite the prospect of a smooth ride home, Jack wasn't able to join his brother's celebration. He couldn't stop thinking about everything that had happened during the past few days. He felt drained and saddened by it all, which reminded him again of the horror he experienced with Genovene so long ago.

Much had changed since he was a carefree thirteen-year-old kid in Carlsdale. Granted, things change for most folks as they grow up. But, the continual impact on his life from that adventure seemed like it would never end. Jeremy and Grandpa's lives had changed nearly as much, and for all three of them, there was no turning back to reach that simpler time. Yet, what loomed on the horizon was assuredly more ominous. The rendezvous he and Jeremy were irresistibly drawn to might shape the course of history in ways most human beings could scarcely imagine.

A beautiful sunset, that was far more magnificent than the wonderful sunrise they witnessed earlier, spread steadily across the western sky. It was the type of natural, yet simple, event that inspires one to hope and give thanks for being alive. Jack smiled wearily. He hoped there would be many more spectacular sunsets to see. But it all depended on what awaited them at 1016 South Queens Court.

Whatever it was, he knew it would affect more then just Jeremy or himself. After what they had been through and seen, he knew it had to be much larger then he could even imagine. As the Jeep's engine droned on, he looked over at his brother and offered a silent prayer. That somehow we would all survive.

About the Author

J. Stefan Jackson began writing stories in the summer of 1997, after spending fifteen years pursuing a career as a songwriter. Many of his songs dealt with the mysteries of the supernatural, where he explored the angst and personal struggles that often result from broken human relationships.

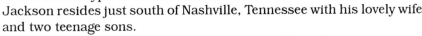

It was a natural progression for him to leave this mode of expression and venture into the world of a different type of wordsmith: the novelist. Mr. Jackson resides just south of Nashville, Tennessee with his lovely wife and two teenage sons.

J. Stefan Jackson's website is at www.jstefanjackson.com

Printed in the United States
62928LVS00003B/109-123